# Sebastian

# Sebastian

## The Life of Sebastian and Hanna Greene

### Elizabeth Johnson

*Dearest Brenda,*

*Thanks for the support.*

*Best wishes*

*Elizabeth Johnson*

Strategic Book Publishing and Rights Co.

*March 2015.*

Copyright © 2013 Elizabeth Johnson. All rights reserved.

No part of this book may be reproduced or transmitted in any form or by any means, graphic, electronic, or mechanical, including photocopying, recording, taping, or by any information storage retrieval system, without the permission, in writing, of the publisher.

Strategic Book Publishing and Rights Co.
12620 FM 1960, Suite A4-507
Houston TX 77065
www.sbpra.com

ISBN: 978-1-62212-068-0

# Dedication

I will love to dedicate this book to God Almighty for His love and inspirations. Then to my wonderful husband Andrew, for his patience and support. Also to my three beautiful baby boys Josiah, Jesse and Jaden. Not forgetting my mother who is my number one fan. I love you all and I thank you for your endless support.

Dearest Hanna,

If you should ever find this journal, it would only mean one thing: that I no longer exist in your world, and I have found a way to undo that which you did.

I know you may never forgive me for what I did, and I understand completely. If it's any consolation, I never forgave myself. I wronged you, and I know now that there is no redemption for what I did. I was untrue to you because I loved you. I love you still, and I know, even in death—if it's even possible—I will always love you.

I would have waited for you forever if I thought you would have changed your mind about us, but I can see now, very clearly, my love, that we were doomed from the start.

This journal is the story of my life as I remember it and how you changed my life completely: my thoughts, my feelings, and the extraordinary memories I shared with you.

I hope that this journal may finally help you understand that with all my flaws, you were the reason I was created.

So long, my friend, my lover, my heart—

Forever yours,<br>Sebastian

# Chapter 1

December 14, 1803
London

## Sebastian Francis

I turned round and felt her strong grip on my shoulder. She spun me away from her, before I could catch a glimpse of her face, and tightened her hold on me. Then she bent my head to the side, exposing my neck. I tried to wriggle free, but her strength overpowered me. In my attempt to break free, I waved my hands around fitfully and grabbed a bunch of her hair. *How could this be happening to me today of all days? Who have I wronged?* I thought. I treated everyone with kindness. Why would anyone want me dead?

I could feel the swell of her breast pressed against my back. Her body felt like steel as her cold breath greeted my neck. Then I felt a piercing sting as her teeth sank into me, and a sharp ghastly pain shot through my whole body. I knew then that death had come knocking.

I looked down at my father and found it sad and very ironic that I'd been dealt the same hand as he on this very night. I wondered what he was thinking. I bet he would be grinning if he could see me so close to the end of my life on the day I turned eighteen. I thought I had turned into a man this morning, and this wasn't exactly how I had planned my freedom from him.

It's a shame I'll never get the chance to prove them all wrong—all those who said I would turn out like him, who reckoned we'd been cursed. Perhaps they were right. I did all I could to get out from underneath him and all the hatred that consumed us both. I guess some things do not change however much it is willed.

I felt my blood dripping down my neck and felt very light. I wondered why I ever thought it was a good idea to find him. He wasn't worth it—definitely not worth losing my life for. It is true what they say: Your whole life flashes before you when you know death is inevitable. I found myself suddenly thinking of the events of my life that had led me to this horrible night.

I remember putting on my torn coat and stepping out into the frosty, foggy night. I tried to steady myself against the gusting wind—it felt like a tornado was in town. Everyone was rushing home and getting their children inside, while I was heading out against my better judgment. The ground was wet and filled with black ice, as it had snowed heavily two days earlier. And if that wasn't enough, the clouds opened up and rain started to pour down. All the elements seemed to be against my coming out tonight, but staying in was not an option until he was found.

I walked quickly along, being careful so I wouldn't slip on the ice. I secretly wished I was at home in front of a warm fire, sipping hot tea, and feeling it slide down my throat. No one in his right mind should be out on this night, but leave it to my father to always put me in situations like this.

I pulled up my collar to keep the rain from slipping down my neck and wrapped my coat around me once more to keep warm. It was impossible, because I was drenched, and the nips and tears on my coat made it even worse. I was cold and shivering down to my spine. I dragged my hat down to cover my ears and rubbed my hands together to stop them from freezing. Even though I was wearing gloves, the bitter cold was turning my hands numb.

For a thousand times, I wonder why I am subjecting myself to these harsh conditions for his sake. It's not like I care for him. And if I don't, why can't I just let him pass the night wherever he sees fit? I have talked myself out of looking for him so many times just to find myself doing the exact thing I hate to do. It's because no one else will, I tell myself; nobody cares what happens to him, as nobody around here cares what happens to me, either. We have no living relatives in England, so I couldn't pass the buck to someone else if I wanted. Not that any sane person would stick around for him. The only other relative we have is my mother's wealthy brother who lives in America.

These are the times I miss her most. No matter how bad things got, she always found a way to fix them. I would like to think that if she were still around, things never would have gotten this bad. I miss her, and I miss the oblivion to the pain and suffering life constantly dealt out when she was alive.

Thinking about my life took me away from death for a second. She released her hold on me, and I felt my body slump as I hit the ground hard. Her hair, which I had pulled in my attempt to break free, was in my hand. I felt her knees beside me, but I couldn't move. I wanted to scream for help and tried to open my mouth, but a big cough came up my throat, and I spurted out blood instead. I gasped for air as my blood choked me. I didn't deserve to die like this. I wanted to ask her why.

She stood over me, hovered above me, and examined me. She smelt different—*expensive* I would say—not like anyone I have come across around here. I looked straight at her, but couldn't make out her face. I couldn't tell if that was due to the fog or just the fact that I was dying and in pain, which made it difficult for me to process anything. It pained me even more that I couldn't picture her face. I should at least know who was killing me and why. I reckon most people know who their killers are; why has mine taken that from me? The pain was getting to uncomfortable heights. Why was it taking so long, and why was she making me suffer?

Three hours ago, I had been standing in front of the ship headed for America and watched as the captain called the last passengers. I had my ticket in one hand and my bag in the other, but I stood and watched as it sailed away. I should have taken my uncle's offer and hopped on that ship. I should have gone far from here and never looked back. That's what mother would have wanted. I had my chance and let it slip out my fingers—for him.

I imagined him laughing uncontrollably, saying what a fool I had been—and this time he wouldn't have been wrong. I *was* a fool to have stayed back. His voice in my head was the last thing I wanted to hear, but all I could think about was the number of times he'd said, *I told you that you would never be better than me, that you would never amount to anything.* I tried to block his voice out of my head, which brought me back to the pain that was consuming me. I thought of my mother instead, the only person who'd ever loved me. I wanted her with me now, I wanted to hold her hand, I wanted her to tell me not to be afraid, and that we would be together soon. I tried to picture her face, but like always, I couldn't remember what she looked like.

*Sebastian*

I wondered why I didn't die the minute I hit the ground. If she meant to kill me, why was she taking her time? A glimmer of hope lit up in my head: Perhaps I should hang on as much as I could bear; someone could pass through and save me from the clutches of death.

I found it difficult to breathe. The air around me felt so hot, and my body rejected each breath I took. I could feel my lungs shutting down. It was now a big struggle to stay alive. Every single second was a battle, but I held on to the hope that I may yet be rescued.

I never believed in bad luck or curses just because I had been tagged with it since my mother's passing. I always felt that if I didn't believe in it, then when I was old enough, I could turn it all around. I hoped for a life away from here. I had dreamed of finding a girl to love and be loved back. I hoped that one day, if I were lucky enough to father a child, I would adore and give him all the love in the world. It seemed, even though I never believed in it, it found me still.

My mother, Elizabeth Hanna Francis, died when I was eight years old. We were very close. She was the centre of my universe, and I was hers. I loved her very much, and she doted on me until the day she died on her way home, I was told, from the market. My father said she was attacked by an animal and bled to death. My father wept like I had never seen him weep. He had been a mess, and then he quickly buried her the next day. He did not waste any time getting rid of all her possessions. He was angry that she had left him so soon, and he smashed up everything in the house in that anger. You would think she had left him to be with another man or that she had asked to be killed. Everything that reminded him of her he gave away or chucked out. I begged him not to give away the keyboard my mother taught me music on. We had sat by the fire every night, and she played to me. She taught me to understand music and how it affects life. He sold it without considering my feelings. I had no say and watched with sadness as it was hauled away. I had no right, according to him, to keep anything that belonged to her. Soon enough, with everything of hers gone, it was as if she had never existed.

For me, my mother's death was a shock. I never got my head round it. To make matters worse, he didn't allow me to come to her burial. He left me with a neighbour when he went to bury her. I never got to say goodbye. I hate him because of this. I hate everything about him, but mostly I hate the fact that people always say I look like him. I am nothing like my father. However, the sad truth is that each time I look at my reflection, I see the green eyes, the dark locks, and the build and height of a man I detest.

We may look alike, but we are nothing alike. Each time I am faced with a decision, I ask myself *What would my father do?* and then I do the opposite—a decision that has brought me to this horrible night.

Ten years on and it still seems like a bad dream to me. There are times I think I will wake up to find it all has been one horrible nightmare and my mother is still here. I remember nights waking up yelling for my mother, and sometimes it didn't seem like a dream when I heard her voice in my ears whispering to me or singing. It felt so real, but as soon as I was fully awake, the reality soon hit me.

My father hated it when I called for her. He would yank me up from my bed and throw me across the room. He didn't understand what I was going through. He couldn't help me grieve, and I couldn't help him in his pain, although he had his bottles to help pacify him.

*Sebastian*

One night when I dreamt of her, I could feel her touch on my skin. I opened my eyes and called for her. He got really mad and slapped me across the face and said, "Never ask for her again! Never call her name! She is gone and never coming back! Do you understand, you twat? Next time you do this, I will throw you out!" I could tell he meant every word, because his eyes were dead—there was no compassion in them. I never asked for her again. I was too scared of him, and the nightmares never stopped.

It's a funny thing how life changes on you without notice. One minute you're in heaven and the next minute you feel as if you are living and dining with the devil himself. He hated competing for my mother's love, and she always chose me over him. At least back then he was not a drunk, and he never hit me. We just didn't bond like a father and son should. He never tried, and I never gave him the chance. So it's no surprise that he decided to ignore me after she passed. Her death made way for his darker side. He beat me at the slightest chance and fed me like I was his dog and locked me up for days while he went out to do his shenanigans.

*Not long now*, I thought. The glimmer of hope I had has faded. There was no chance of living now. Perhaps I should accept my fate and stop fighting. Maybe if I stopped fighting, this pain would cease, and I could be at peace. Then I felt her cold hands on my forehead, wiping the sweat pouring down my face. I felt like I was on fire, even though the weather was freezing. I knew I should give in now. I was getting tired of fighting. I needed the pain to stop so I could rest. It would be the easiest thing to do, but I couldn't allow myself to just give in. It felt wrong accepting that my life would be over in a few minutes.

I have struggled to survive all my life, begged for food and clothes, and run all kinds of errands to survive, because my father didn't care if I lived or died. Between his gambling, whoring, and drinking, he hardly knew nor cared where I got my daily meal. Some of my mother's old friends pretended not to know who I was and ordered their children away from me like I was a plague. If I could survive all that, then surely I could hold on to a few more minutes of agony.

From the corner of my eye, I looked at my father and wondered if he had gone through the same pain as I am.

I stumbled upon a human pile on the floor of a lonely alley as I searched around for him. On a closer inspection, he had not disappointed me. He was lying there, drink still in hand. I wasn't surprised at all—I had picked him up from the street a number of times when he had passed out from drinking.

But something was different; I could feel it as I stood over him. I gently kicked him on his side, and he didn't stir. His eyes were looking right at me, and in my heart, I knew he was gone, but I needed to be sure. So I took off my gloves and placed my left hand on his neck to check for a pulse: There was nothing. I must admit, I was a little shaken. What one does immediately after discovering one's father's dead body was unknown to me. Everything and everywhere was quiet. I felt like the whole world was waiting for me to decide how I was going to feel. One thing was certain: I was never going to cry for him. I wondered if anyone would cry for him, judging by his track record.

His face looked white and grey, the colours that signify life had left him—not that he had much left with his way of living. I wondered how long he had been lying down here lifeless. I squatted next to his body. Somehow, I felt relieved of a burden and didn't feel ashamed of my thoughts. I dug my hands into my pocket and pulled out the ticket that should have seen me well away from here hours ago. In a way, at that moment in time, I was glad I stayed—at least now that he's dead, if I go away, I won't have to wonder how he is. For once in his life, he finally did me a good turn, and I could now make that trip to America.

As I was about to pick him up, I heard a sound behind me and could feel someone standing very close. For some reason, the hair on the back of my neck stood up, and suddenly I was very afraid. Slowly I turned around to see who it was, and, before I could blink, she grabbed me. The next thing I knew, her teeth were sinking into me.

I was tired and had no fight left in me. I wanted peace now at any cost. I wanted to be free of the pain consuming me.

"Let go, you will be fine," she whispered to me. I thought to myself, *there is no reason to struggle to live anymore, no one to stay alive for, no one to miss me, and no reason to suffer this much.* So I die the same day and the same night he died and on the day I turn eighteen. What does it matter now that I can't do a thing about it?

The pain climaxed again, and I knew this time that I couldn't hold out any longer. She wiped my forehead again. I wondered why she was doing that. I didn't want her touching me. She is the reason I am dying after all. My body was shutting down, and it was time to rest. I knew that now was the time to let go, time to set myself truly free. Like she could read my mind, she held my hand as if to reassure me once more. It didn't matter anyway. I was tired of fighting a losing battle. I let out a little air in relief and could feel my body flop as the lights went out.

# Chapter 2

## THREE DAYS LATER

I opened my eyes and found myself alone in a strange room. I wasn't really sure where I was, but I was alive and not dead. I tapped myself just to be sure this was real. It seemed strange that I was not dead. Not that I am not thankful, I was just pondering how I had survived such an ordeal. Someone must have come for me.

    I was happy in a way. It meant that I mattered to somebody. My body felt different though: whole. I never felt more alive than I did just then. All that pain from before seemed like a dream now. I took in my surroundings: The room was very large, but empty. There was nothing in it apart from the bed I was lying on. There was a big window right in front of me, and the sky looked bright—it looked like it was noon. I knew then what I must do immediately while the sun was still shining: I wanted to get out now, thank whoever brought me here, and start my life afresh away from here. I got up from the bed and walked toward the window. I wanted to feel the fresh breeze on my face and remind myself again how lucky I was to still be alive. My feet felt heavy at first, but with each step I took, they became lighter.

    But to my disappointment, upon closer inspection, I discovered there was no window. It was just a painting, but it looked so real. I began to panic. I suddenly felt enclosed and trapped. I looked round for an exit and noticed two doors on opposite sides of the room: one made of wood and the other looked like steel to me. I ran to the wooden door, which was closest to me, and tried to open it, but it was locked from the outside. Something didn't feel right. Why have I been locked in I wondered. "Hello!" I shouted. "Can anybody hear me? Hello!" I continued to shout, but there was no response, and no one came. "Hello! I am awake now! Is somebody out there? Hello! I need to get out of here now! Can you hear me? Please open the door," I shouted again.

Then the strangest thing started to happen. I could hear people talking around me as though they were in the room with me. It was as though the voices were in my head. It scared me, and for a minute, I wondered if I had got it wrong. Did I die? Perhaps no one had come for me, or was it all a bad dream. I stopped for a while to consider which of them might be true. I turned away from the door and slowly walked half way across the room when my gaze fell on the steel door. I continued walking until I was standing in front of it, all the while still hearing people chattering about in my head.

I ran my hand over the surface of the door and pushed on it a little. I could feel the strength of the steel underneath my palm. I wondered why anyone would go through the trouble of putting such a thing in place to keep me trapped.

Just then, an aroma filtering through the steel door greeted my nostrils with something delicious. An aroma like no other, and I was suddenly feeling famished. I forced myself on the door, pushing with my whole body. At the back of my mind, I knew it was physically impossible for me to shift the door, but somewhere, even deeper within me, was this desperation to eat that somehow overtook my senses, and all I was able to do was repeatedly throw myself at this door to get it to budge. I realised now that the more I took in this heavenly aroma, the dryer my throat felt. I was thirsty and hungry and could feel my body beginning to shake in anticipation.

Then I turned towards the wooden door again, which was not the same as the steel one, and I was sure that if I pushed hard enough, I would be able to break free. I began to move towards it, and as I got halfway across the room, I started to lose the aroma that had consumed me earlier—I couldn't have that! I stopped and turned my head back in the direction of the steel door and took in a deep breath. The scent returned sparingly, but I wanted more, so I took a couple more steps back towards the steel door. I was soon bathing in the glory of the mouth-watering scents again. As I hurried back toward the steel door, my feet became even lighter on the ground. Even so, I was impatient and, before I could blink, I moved with such an unbelievable speed and found myself right in front of the steel door.

It was incredible how fast I was. It didn't feel right that I should be able to do that, but I couldn't think now—I needed food like my life depended on it. So why was I back here and not breaking out like I had planned earlier? I knew the answer to my question: The scent—the aroma—had taken control of me, and I didn't want to part from it.

I threw myself at the door numerous times, trying to force it open, and still I couldn't hack it. I was tired, and the voices in my head didn't let up. I stopped for a minute to think, however impossible it felt, and something clicked in my head: The voices were tied to the aroma controlling my senses. Each voice I heard carried a different scent. I found myself following each trail of scent until it faded and another began. It was driving me mad this hunger, this want, these scents. *What kind of food could these people have on them*, I wondered, or is it me? Am I mad now? Did I die? And is this some place people go after they die? If that's true, it would explain all this confusion. I wondered if my father was in a place like this as well.

I could still hear voices in my head. I sat at the foot of the door and considered what to do next. Then I started to hear the click of shoe heels as they passed and the heartbeat of each person who passed. "Help me!" I shouted in desperation. "Somebody help me! Hello? Can anyone hear me? I am in here! I have been locked in here! Help me please!" They all carried on like no one had heard me, but I could hear them: their heartbeats and the food each one had. I felt cheated, locked away in hunger, and I was angry. It was strange how I could not see them, yet I could somehow sense where they were. So many things were happening to me for which I had no explanation. I must be dreaming. I shut my eyes tight and hoped I would wake up soon. Even so, I couldn't concentrate on anything– my hunger, the smell of food was driving me crazy.

Angered more than ever, I repeatedly hurled myself at the door, screaming. Then I heard someone say, "Calm down. They can't hear you, Sebastian." I spun round immediately to see who it was. I hadn't heard anyone come in. A woman stood just in front of the wooden door, which was slightly open. I thought about running, but she must have read my mind because she shut it immediately. There was something oddly familiar about her. Then I sniffed the air and recognised the smell. I will never forget that scent, the very last one I smelt before I thought I was dying.

"You! You attacked me! Why? What did I do to you, and what am I doing here?" I asked her a hundred questions at once. But then that face, the face I never thought I would see again, the face that I had mourned every day for ten years. I could not believe who I was looking at. She had not changed one bit. She was still as I remembered her from when I was a boy. I had grown into a man, and she hadn't changed a bit.

Confused, I let myself recall the event that supposedly led me here. I remember standing over my father's dead body and being attacked by a woman, but I could not make out her face. "I don't understand. Why did you attack me? You—this can't be real. I have gone mad! Now I am seeing ghosts. Why does nothing make sense? This all must be in my mind. I am sure none of this is real. Tell me I am right, that it's not you standing there." There was no response from her. "What am I doing here? Why can't I open this door? And if you are real, why are you standing there saying nothing?" I yelled. Still she said nothing, but looked from me to the steel door and began to move closer to me. I didn't want her near me, not after what she had done to me. I moved away, creating more space between us. The whiff of the scents hit me again and the hunger for food took over. I began to desperately bang on the door with my fists.

"Stop, Sebastian, you will only get weaker. That door is never going to open unless I want it to."

I stopped and turned round and faced her. *I wouldn't be here now if not for her*, I thought. I couldn't fathom the fact that she was alive, and if she was alive, then I must be, too. *I didn't die that night after all*, I thought. "You died, didn't you?" I asked, just so she could tell me she hadn't. "You died! I was told that you had died. But you faked it? You faked it, didn't you? Why? Was it because of him? Why have you come back after all these years?"

She just stared blankly. She didn't look remorseful for what she'd done to me, and I resented her for it. So I continued, "Look, I don't care why you came back. Just let me out. I'm hungry and need to eat, okay. Let me out!" I shouted. She looked on with no emotion, without the slightest change to her facial expression. I noticed something odd with the way I spoke: My voice was unnecessarily loud. Funny thing is, every day since I thought she died, I wondered what I would do or say to her if by some miracle she wasn't dead and it was all a bad dream. None of those emotions I thought I would feel surfaced. To be honest, I believed I would be able to think better after I had eaten. I resumed my quest for food, murmuring curses about her under my breath.

"I know you're angry with me, and you have all the right to be. But you have to stop—"

"Don't tell me what to do! You don't get to tell me what to do!" I roared, and it rang deep in my head. "What is wrong with me? Why do I sound different?"

"In time, Sebastian, I will explain it all to you, but now you must come with me. You must feed to gain your strength or you will die, believe me." Die! What does she mean by that? My mind went back to that night again, and I could feel the pain all over me. I remember feeling vulnerable and thinking it was better to give up. But I didn't die. I am here. Aren't I? Or am I just imagining all this? I slapped myself across the face to make sure. I looked at myself, and for the first time, it registered that I was dressed differently. I looked at her perplexed. I was dressed in a long-sleeve white blouse and a pair of tight black pants. I wondered how I had got into them—I didn't remember wearing them.

"My clothes! What happened to them? What have you done with them?"

"I took them off you and changed you into these."

"You had no right," I said bitterly. She looked away, still no emotions. "You took my clothes off! This just gets better! Is this how you greet people after you disappear from where you were? First you attack me, then you trap me here like a common prisoner, then you take my clothes away, and now you tell me I can't go out! Who are you to tell me what to do?" I was beginning to get used to the sound of my voice and its resonating power, and, for some reason, the more I heard myself, the more confident I became. "Pray tell, how long have I been here?"

"I will tell you all you need to know soon, Sebastian. All that anger you have is going to drain you of energy fast. Come with me."

"I am not going anywhere with you!" I took a deep breath to regain my strength. She was right, the more I shouted, the weaker I began to feel, not to mention the hunger pang I was feeling already. I decided to stop letting my anger take over, but it was hard. "You didn't answer my question, how long have I been here?" I asked a bit quieter, but I didn't lose the bitterness. I watched her eyes closely and told myself that if she didn't answer straight away, I would force it out of her if that's what it took. It was as if she knew what I was about to do.

She responded swiftly, "Three days."

"What? Three—You mean I have been here for three days? Doing what?" She was quiet again. I felt famished, and the hungrier I became, the more uneasy I felt. I turned round to the door where the whiff of food was coming from, distracted by the scent all over again. I needed answers, but eating was more important now. "Listen, save your answers for later, right now I need to eat. Can you please open up so

I can go out and eat whatever that—that food is? The aroma is driving me crazy. Just let me out. Now I know why I am so hungry: I've been here for three days!"

Somehow she had refused to cover the distance between us and remained at the other end of the room. I guess she was afraid of what I might do to her, and rightly so. Then she spoke, gently, but firmly, like she had when I was a child and she mattered to me. "Come with me, Sebastian, and I will help you feel better. There is nothing out there for you. You belong here now. Here, with me." I started to laugh aloud. I wanted to go to her and shake her for abandoning me and pretending she was dead. I wanted to hurt her for having the audacity to say those words *You belong here with me*. I always had thought she was the better one of my parents; the only one who cared for me, but they were both the same selfish, self-seeking people. It's no wonder they had found each other—they had married themselves. She is even worse than him. At least he didn't run away or pretend he was dead so he could have a chance at another life. I wanted to ask her why she had come back and what she wanted and expected of me now. I hope she didn't now think I would take her back and act like she hadn't just disappeared for ten years. As far as I was concerned, my mother had died.

I looked over at her. She still had the same nonchalant look about her. Irritated, I took a step forward towards her and, in a flash, I was beside her. *This speed thing is getting out of control*, I thought. She immediately moved away in the opposite direction.

"What just happened? How come I can move so fast?" I wanted explanations. "What have you done to me? What is happening to me?" I yelled at her.

"Calm down, I have a lot of explaining to do, but it will all be clarified in due course. First, you must eat. You are hungry. Come with me please."

"You will answer my questions first or, as God is my witness—" I said defiantly.

"There is a lot to talk about, and I will explain everything to you, but now is not the time. Come with me."

"Something tells me you know I am not going to do as you say. You either start talking or you open that door and let me out of here."

"Like I said, Sebastian, I will tell you in—"

Impatient, I leaped forward and attempted to grab her, but she shoved me to the other side of the wall with one push. "I'm sorry," she said. "I never wanted to do that, but you have to learn to listen. I know right now you are confused and angry, as you should be. Your hunger is making you irrational, but you must calm down. Come with me and eat, and you will feel better. Then we can talk. There is a lot I have to tell you and teach you. You have to learn how to control that hunger and the anger brewing inside you. I am your mother, and I know you are angry. I wasn't around when you needed me, but I am back now; I am back because of you. Now get up and follow me. You have to get something into you. You must eat or starve to death, and I am not going to let you die however much you want it."

As she spoke, I became so livid. What right did she think she had to call herself my mother? With a blind rage building inside me, I got up and swung myself at her again, but she dodged me, and I hit my head on the steel door but, amazingly, I was on my feet instantly. I tried again, aiming my fist towards her jaw. I wanted her to hurt; I wanted her to feel a fraction of how much hurt she had caused me over the years when she abandoned me. This time she didn't move away, but caught my fist and locked it in her hand. She forced me to my knees. I tried my hardest to break free, but I was groaning in pain. The more I tried, the more my strength failed me. Then I tried to bite her hands to gain some freedom, but before I could clasp my teeth, she used her free hand to hold me by my throat, choking me, and locked me to the ground. I couldn't move at this point.

"You are angry," she said. "I would be, too, in your position. I would love to sit you down now and explain everything to you, but I can't—at least not now. You must calm down, Sebastian. You are my son, and I am not going to hurt you, but if you carry on fighting me, we are never going to get anywhere."

For the first time, I caught a glimpse of real emotion, like she truly cared, but I was too cross to let it register. I knew now that something was definitely wrong with me. How else could I explain the speed, the confidence, and my imposing voice? She was also different. She was very powerful. I remembered how she grabbed me that night and how defenceless I had been. I was feeling exactly as I had felt that night.

"Listen, this is not how I pictured our reunion, Sebastian. Stop fighting me. It will not do you any good. Now I know you have all these questions that you want answers to, and I will provide them, but not now. Do you understand?" I kept quiet. "Tell me you understand," she said. I then nodded, and she let go of me.

*I have to calm down*, I told myself. She has all the answers that I want, and she has made it clear she won't tell me until she is ready. I knew I did not want to die. I had suffered enough in my short existence to just allow my life to end now.

I reluctantly followed her. She opened the wooden door, and I walked behind her into the adjoining room. We walked through a short passage before entering a spacious living room. It was sparsely but tastefully decorated. I sniffed around me in disgust, because something smelt horrible and its odour filled the room. I put my hand to my nose to stop myself from puking. I looked around to see where the smell was oozing from and noticed three seats and a round table sitting on a large Persian rug. A big piano sat at the end of the room facing a pretend window—a theme around the house I suppose. She gestured to a seat, and I shook my head and remained standing. On the table was a transparent jar that had some kind of crimson liquid inside and a couple of glasses were next to it. I could sense where the odour was coming from now and wondered what was in the jar. She wasn't covering her nose like I was, and I wondered if she had lost her sense of smell. I watched as she reached for the jar, poured the contents into a glass, and then presented me with this shocking-looking, awful-smelling liquid.

"What is this?" I questioned, puzzled that she was presenting me with the very thing I identified as smelling awful. I covered my nose again to stop myself from inhaling the stomach-retching liquid. It was nothing like the aroma from the other room, it was completely opposite.

"It's your food, animal blood, drink it. You will feel better," She replied, expressionless once again. I looked at her completely lost for words. Did she really expect me to drink blood? Why would she be offering me blood? I am hungry and she gives me this thing she is calling blood and expects that I drink it.

"I am hungry, and you're offering me blood! Why would you do that? Have you no nose, or have you lost your senses?

It stinks! I don't want it! I need food. Proper food, like I smelt in that room we just came from."

"Sorry, Sebastian, but this is all there is."

"Well, then let me go out and help myself to something better."

"That's not an option," she said. There will be no going out. Not now, not yet. Please, let's not fight. Believe me, it will make things easier for the two of us. Let me take care of you, it's my job. I've missed taking care of you."

"Take care of me! You talk like you've been away for a couple of weeks and now you're back to fix everything! I've gone without you for years! I don't need you now. And one thing I definitely don't need is you trying to mother me. Nobody needs a mother like you. I will be fine by myself, thank you. I'm glad we've cleared that up. Now, can you open the doors and let me out?" I closed my eyes and tried to remember the aroma from the other room. I wish I were stronger. I would be free to eat what I like. She smiled.

"What was that I smelt in there? It smelt so good. I can already taste it on my tongue. *Mmmm*. Get me some of that if you want us to get along." I collected the glass of blood from her and threw the contents in her face in anger.

"I told you, Sebastian, this is not the time to pick fights with me. You must learn to control your anger and to keep a leash on that craving." She simply took another cup, filled it up again, and handed it to me. "Drink up. This is good for you. This is all you will be surviving on, nothing more. The more you drink, the better you will feel, and the better you will be able to control your cravings. As for the smell and taste, with time your body will adapt. You just need control and focus and you will be fine. Now, drink up, because you will not be stepping out of this place until I am sure you can control your anger and be in charge of your cravings. If I were you, I would get started," she said.

"Why? What if I don't want to? Tell me, what will you do? Will you throw me out? Why don't you just throw me out and do us both a favour. I have told you I don't need you. You never wanted me so you faked your own death. Tell me what it was that finally made you run. Was it me or him? Because if it was him, I'll say good on you for cutting yourself off before he took a bad turn. What I don't get is why you left me with him, why you didn't take me with you. Was I such a terrible child, so difficult to love? We could have both faked our deaths. Why did you leave me? Why did you leave me with him? I had nowhere to run, no one to run to, and no one to love me. I—I don't want to be near you. I don't want you in my life, and I do not want this . . . common blood! Are you out of your mind? Why would you even give me this? Ever since your sudden re-emergence, you seem to be keeping a lot of things from me. And strange things keep happening to me. Tell me what you did to me!" I yelled.

"Not again, Sebastian. I thought we established there would be no more fighting."

"Yes, and since your reappearance, you've been hounding me. You've not answered any question I've asked you. Earlier you said that I had been here for three days. Tell me how come I didn't know I had been here for three days? Was I sleeping for three days?"

"In principle, yes," she said, "but you were transiting all that time."

"Transiting? Into what?"

She closed her eyes and took a deep breath. "Vampire," she said beneath her breath.

I clearly heard her, but I pretended I didn't. "What?"

"When I bit you that night, it wasn't to hurt you. I was making you like me."

"Like you?" I questioned, somehow understanding why she was so strong now.

"You are now a vampire, Sebastian."

"Is this a joke? Do such things even exist? Why would you do that to me?" I asked, examining myself.

"You look the same, but now you are different. You are stronger and faster, and you will gain more strength and be even stronger once you start feeding. You will never age, but I guess you know that already. You heard stories when you were young, and you considered them myths. Well, most of them are untrue, but this one is very true. I waited until you were old enough to turn you, so we could be together. I know you are hurting and you blame me for not being there. Believe me, son, if I could, I never would have left you. I never stopped loving you. You suffered a lot. I witnessed most of it and felt all your pain, but it made you a better human. Right now you are blinded by your anger, but deep down you are good, my son. I know this very well, and that is why I made you into a vampire, so that we can be together forever. You will be a good vampire. You just don't know it yet." She was quiet for a minute, and I didn't say anything, either. It was all too much for me to comprehend.

"So now, you must learn the rules, like the ways and mannerisms of a gentleman," she said. "You need to be well-groomed before facing the world. Don't be angry. This is a gift, not a curse. We get to spend the rest of forever together. There is only one rule for our kind, but for you there are two rules: First, you must never alert a human of our existence, and second and most important, you must never kill a human." I looked up at her with sadness etched on my face.

From what I had understood, vampires could only survive by feeding on human blood.

"How am I to survive then?"

"For us it will be different. We will feed on the blood of animals. It's not necessary that human blood be shed each time we thirst. That's just pure greed and evil on the part of our kind. We will not be taking part in such habits. What you've been sensing since you awoke is the smell of human blood. You must prepare yourself to ignore it. Together we will tackle your wildness and your lust for human blood. Erase the thought from your mind. Now drink up and let's begin."

I found it very hard to believe what I had become. I had heard such stories, but never really believed such creatures existed. Only now, I am one—eternally doomed. It's not that I know what human blood tastes like, but I can't shake the feeling of wanting what I crave. At the same time, I know to do that I will have to take a life. Deep down it disturbs me that I will always have this monster living inside of me.

For two days, I refused to drink the blood she gave me. I focused my mind on getting out. I tried every way to escape, but she wouldn't let me go. I became frail and exhausted, but I couldn't imagine putting that garbage into my mouth. Every day she left me to go hunting and locked me in so I couldn't escape, and before she came back, I looked for ways to escape. I wanted to get out, and as much as I didn't like what I had become, I knew the first thing I would do once I escaped. I had been tormented with the scents so much that I knew it would be very easy for me to kill the first human I saw.

I stopped talking to her. I sat in a corner coiled up and observed her. I watched as she poured away the old blood and poured another for me. She sat on the chair knitting or playing the keyboard, like she used to do when she was human. She was making it all look normal, and I found it unbelievable. I was beyond famished and could barely walk—I had tired out my body. I knew I couldn't continue like this unless I truly wanted to die. I picked up the jar of blood and started to gulp it down, forgetting the stench. None of it mattered, because I had to live. I finished drinking the blood and then started to lick the bottom of the jar. She filled it up the following day, and I quickly and greedily quaffed it down and even asked for more, but she never gives me seconds, just enough to get me by for the day.

Soon my body became used to the ration I was given each day. As soon as she realised I had stopped asking for seconds, she began to reduce my daily ration. I hated her for treating me like a beggar. Just when I thought it couldn't get any worse, she reduced my feeding to just three times a week. At first, it was just a day that I would go without a feeding, and I found it hard. I was mad and angry and fought her daily over food. Then when my body had readjusted, she took out another day.

"You may think I am being wicked, but this is what you call tough love. To live amongst humans, you must teach your body to crave less, to ignore its needs. You must learn to survive on little rations and still be in control of yourself."

Like she said, day by day, month by month, until years later, I found the smell less and less disgusting, so much so that I started looking forward to it. I could go a week without blood, and I would be fine. It never stopped me from yearning for human blood, but I never hungered for it. That doesn't mean that if I were left alone with a human, I could resist the temptation of not wanting to have a taste.

For years, I was not allowed out until she was satisfied that I was able to manage my craving for human blood. When I was eventually allowed to start mingling with humans, she remained at my side, always tightening her leash on me. I found young girls and women clustered around me, while I tried hard to ignore the blood flowing through their veins. They thrust themselves at me brazenly, gracing me with the swell of their breasts, lifting their heads high and their necks bare. If only they knew what I was and what I could do to them. All that was left was for me to sink my teeth into them and finally fulfil my greatest desire, but each time I tried, my mother was always close enough to stop me. She was tempting me and then restricting me, and I found it infuriating. I knew I had to put a stop to it once we got home.

"If you love these humans so much," I said, "why put their lives in danger? You know I could easily kill them."

"Yes, I know, but you haven't yet. Can't you see that you have more control in you than you give yourself credit for? You are surrounded by humans daily, yet you haven't killed or bitten any yet. I am proud of you, Sebastian."

"Don't be proud, Mother. It's taken every bit of strength I have to stop myself from digging in. I beg you, let's stop this mingling nonsense now before I do something you will regret. If you insist, I will not be responsible for what happens."

"Stop talking nonsense. You'll be fine," she said. "You're stronger than you know."

"I can already taste it, Mother. My throat yearns for their blood. Every day I am filled to the brim with the whiff that exudes from them, and I know I cannot control myself any longer. I am sorry, Mother, but I don't think I can do this humanity thing. I can't keep your stupid rule. It's killing me inside living like this. I can't survive like this, and I am not going to lose out on something great just to make you proud."

"How would you know it's great when you haven't experienced it?" she asked.

"But I can smell it," I replied, "and it calls to me. Each time I drink that garbage you insist I live on, all I can think of is what it would feel like to have a drop of human blood."

"Forget it, Sebastian. Not while I am alive. These people are your friends and neighbours. You mustn't see them as your food. Moreover, it's not like you are dying and your life depends on it. It's just greed, and you must learn to stave it off. You mustn't let it rule you. If it does, it turns you into a monster."

I laughed aloud. "You have to stop this pretence of yours, acting like you're normal, like you're still human, because you're not. I am a monster—you made sure of it, and there is nothing you can do to change it. No matter how much or how long you want me to pretend that I am human, one day I will get to live like I am truly supposed to." She didn't say anything; she went and sat by the window, ignoring what I had just said.

"I don't understand what you see in them. Why are you so obsessed with their safety? They are so flawed, so cruel, it's beyond my imagination. Stop protecting them, it's useless, it's a lost cause. I should thank you, Mother. I've been so angry at you for changing me, but I've had time to think, and I am glad you did. I am glad I am not that weak. Think about it, Mother, no one cared about me when you died, so why do you care? Why should I care about them? They said I was cursed. At least now they are right, but I am also stronger, faster, and, even without a beating heart, not as evil and devious as they. It's life, Mother. There is always going to be prey for the predators, otherwise there would be no cycle."

"I know what they are capable of, Sebastian, but I would not do the same, knowing I am adept at hurting them more. Yes you are a vampire, and I understand we crave human blood. I crave it, too. It's a natural and easy thing to do, but only the weak-minded go that route. I am teaching you to be strong, Sebastian, to turn your weakness into your greatest strength, to be kind and gentle like I taught you when you were a boy. You suffered a lot, and no little boy should have to live through what you went through. I am sorry I wasn't there to protect you, but I am here now. We are together again. Don't let a stupid thing like the eagerness to feed on humans bother us now. Don't let your thirst determine who you are. You are better than that. I know you are, and that's why I made you. You are stronger than you know. Moreover, once you taste human blood, it will be hard to come back from it—you won't want anything else."

"And why would I want to come back from it, Mother? Who in their right mind choses to make life difficult for themselves? You said so yourself: It's the natural thing for our kind to do. That is what vampires do—we feed on humans."

"You don't understand now, but you will. I know it's much easier to let loose, but to be able to preserve whatever humanity is left in you is worth more than one drop of human blood. We must fit into the community, not wipe them out. We cannot turn ourselves into beasts, as others of our kind do."

"That's easy for you to say, since you've tasted it before. You've had your fill of human blood and now you forbid me to try it. Let me decide for myself which I prefer. Okay,

Mother? Let me have one human. I promise I will do whatever you say after that."

"You won't be able to come back after one. You will always want more, Sebastian, and it will change you. Is that what you want? You want to turn into a killer? You want to kill families just so you can satisfy your hunger?"

I laughed out loud again. "But you did it, Mother. Don't you think you are a hypocrite asking me not to do what you did? If you can do it, so can I."

"I didn't have a choice. My maker fed me human blood, but my love for you helped me. I loved you when I was a human, but after I was turned—you can imagine how much more you meant to me. I was constantly coming back to check on you, and I knew it would only be a matter of time before I killed you if I did not do something about my cravings for human blood. It was hard, the hardest thing for a young vampire, but the love I had for you helped me. I did not ask for this, Sebastian. And as much as I loved you, you were just another meal to me, and I had to do something before I ended your life. I am better because of you, but believe me now when I say this, I made you, but I will end your life before I let you turn into a monster."

"You choose them over me."

"No, Sebastian, I choose your humanity over what you could become. Once you go down that road, it's hard to come back from it. It would only take something or someone you care for more than yourself to come back from such destruction. It would be the most difficult thing you would ever have to do. Once you switch off your humanity, it's hard to find it again."

I was going to have another argument, but I was tired of fighting. I understood why she wanted us to be together, and, beneath all the anger that had taken me over, I still loved her. For now, I will continue to do as she says until I find a reason good enough to do otherwise.

\*\*\*

February 1834

My uncle, my mother's brother, died and willed everything he had to me, because he had no children of his own. He is obviously not aware of what I have become and since no one else knows that I died and became a vampire, I became the sole owner of his entire empire upon his death. I visited him over the years when I could, but after a while, it became difficult to continue visiting him. There were things that were becoming apparent. For one thing, I was not ageing, plus the temptation to kill him was becoming too great. My mother insisted that I go and see him because he was the only family she had left. She tried to make me look older. That worked all right at first when I was twenty eight in human years, but still looked eighteen, because I could get away with not ageing so much. Years later, my mother started making me up to get me to look the right age, and I could only visit my uncle at night when the sun had gone down.

He started to question my long absences and strange habits. I could never eat around him or get too close to him in order to avoid accidents, not that it mattered where he stood—his blood was always enticing me. It was becoming a little obvious that I was hiding something from him so I stopped visiting. He wrote to me to come, but I would reply and make up reasons why I couldn't visit him at that time.

When he finally died, it was a relief for me, because it meant the last family we had was gone and we had no more obligations to anyone. I then sold most of the assets, apart from a few properties in England, and banked the money. Every thirty to forty years, I opened another account for both my mother and me and transferred the money into the newest account to keep away any suspicion.

For a century, we moved from place to place, country to country, depending on the season and the weather and where we were most likely to find animals to feed on. Most of the time we hung out in England, especially during the winter period since it gets dark earlier in the day. The weather makes it easy to mingle and be friends with people in our community during the day, but the drawback to living in England is that there is no variety of big game to hunt. So we always had to leave for better hunting grounds.

All the while our bank balance kept increasing with interest. I bought more properties in London and around the world. I owned several houses in the most prized areas all over the world. Mother and I enjoyed comforts, and we knew if we were looking to live forever, then we needed to make sure our money never ran out.

# Chapter 3

October 23, 1973

We moved to a little village called Harrogate in North Yorkshire three years ago, with the plan to stay for another seven to ten years before having to relocate again to avoid suspicions.

My mother, as usual, fitted in well with the neighbours. They loved her. She was always resourceful and always knew the right thing to say. I kept to myself most of the time and only mingled at mother's command, which I reluctantly obeyed. I have learnt to stop fighting her, since she always gets her way in the end. Mother accepts invitations and drags me along, although I would prefer she left me out of this crazy idea she has that we can socialize with humans when each time we are offered human food, we have to make up an excuse why we can't eat it. I don't especially feel comfortable at these outings. Sometimes,, I feel like my mother takes me along to show off her son. I have been doing these things for more than one century, and they just bore me now.

I am surrounded by women at these events who introduce me to their teenage daughters looking for courtship. Some just shamelessly want me to have my way with them even when they are spoken for or clearly have husbands. I don't understand what mother thinks she will accomplish putting me in these painful situations. None of these women interest me. Nothing clever ever comes out of their mouths. It's really frustrating, because they are all the same. They want to be told they are beautiful, they want to gossip about their so-called friends they just kissed seconds ago, they want to know if I value their friendship, and who I like most. To me they're a constant torment. I can't feed on them, and I can't play with them, either. Sometimes, I want to rip out their veins to shut them up, but I know I can't, because, no matter how irritated I get, I've been taught to never lose control. From one generation to the next and from place to place the only differences, I dare say, are their faces. I've seen it all now and, to be honest, if this is all forever brings, then I'm quite bored now and would gladly soon have it over with.

Things were all right for a while and then three years after we settled in Harrogate, people started to go missing. We did not know what to think. We were out one evening and found a young girl lying in her own blood: She had been bitten and left for dead. We knew vampires were involved, but it had nothing to do with us. We knew of an older vampire who lived not too far from us. He'd lived there for quite a while, but he would never do anything as ridiculous as leave his victims in plain sight or hunt in the same village in which he lived. A few vampires passed through sometimes, but it is a known code to never create a mess where others of their kind abode.

We discussed moving away. Bodies were being found everywhere, and the last thing we wanted was to be caught in this mess. Mother was a little reluctant at first, because she had made some human friends that she wasn't in a hurry to leave behind. But she soon changed her mind when we had a visit from Margret Hayes, a friend of hers. She came to tell us that we must leave town immediately. Somehow someone hinted to the humans that we may be responsible for the recent events. Vampires have no heart, but they have a very strong attachment to their makers.

My mother's maker was Lyon Cuthbert. She had to leave him when she decided she would turn me into a vampire. To do that, she had to give up the human blood on which Cuthbert had raised her. I was angry at her for years for doing this to me, but now I understand that she had to do what she did. You can't control the love you feel for another and rather than watch me grow old and die, she decided to give us another chance to be together. Lyon Cuthbert had been against it. He had asked her not to make me into a vampire. He had made her because he was lonely and wanted a companion for himself. My mother had kept coming back for me and never wanted to leave the town I was in. There had been nothing Cuthbert could do to convince her that part of her life was now over, so he decided to move on. They have different views on humans: He saw them as food and my mother didn't. He felt she wasn't fun to be with any longer—not the type of companion he wanted.

It was inevitable that they would part ways—they weren't like-minded. It was a surprise when, without warning, he dropped by a couple of weeks before the recent killings. He said he had business in a town nearby and wouldn't be staying long. He had to see my mother before he left. He stayed in his town house a few miles from us. Mother visited him there once even though I told her I didn't think it was a good idea, but I couldn't stop her. He is after all her maker, her father, and she cared for him still.

So, when Margret came with the news that humans had killed him at his house in broad daylight, my mother was deeply hurt. She kind of knew something was wrong. She spoke of him all day, something she rarely did in all the one hundred and seventy-one years we had spent together. I did not like him, but I detested the way he died. There was no way he could have saved himself. The sun was at its highest point and they knew his power would be limited by the sun—it was the best chance they had, and they succeeded. He was set ablaze and then drawn into the open before he was staked. His death humbled me. Until then I had never heard of a vampire dying. Although I have been to many funerals of humans, I just assumed we vampires could never wither away or die of diseases or silly little accidents as humans do. Now I know we are not immortal after all. We just live longer than humans, but death finds us all one way or another. He'd lived for five hundred years; I guess it was time he found some peace. That is, if ever there is a thing called peace for vampires when they pass.

Margret insisted we immediately flee the village. We also had been made somehow. None of us were safe. If Lyon Cuthbert could be killed, what hope had the rest of us? We had to go and start life somewhere else.

No sooner had Margret left than we began preparations to leave town. As always, I had to feed before embarking on a long journey. We were going to leave before midnight, so I quickly went into the woods to hunt. There was no big game, but it didn't matter—I just needed something to keep me from twitching. I found some rabbits, squirrels, and a couple of foxes. When I was on my last drink, I felt strange, as though someone had ripped my heart out. I'd never felt such pain before. All I could think about was my mother. I hurried home, running faster than usual, and sensed a bunch of humans running away from our house. It was dark, so I didn't think my mother could be in danger from the humans, but something still felt odd, and I still didn't feel good, so I ran even faster. *She is all right* I told myself; nothing that bad could have happened, not tonight when we can't be touched. *They wouldn't dare* I assured myself.

Something was burning, but it wasn't coming from the house. I ran straight inside to check that my mother was fine, but she wasn't there. Our entire luggage was packed and ready; her purse was on the table. I could still smell her there; she must have been sitting here waiting for me. I ran back outside and headed directly to where the fire was burning. To my horror, my mother was lying in the fire, a stake in her heart. I rushed to her and dropped to my knees, and I pulled her out of the fire. "Mother!" I yelled and pulled the stake out of her and flung it away. Her eyes were open looking at me. Her body was dry and flaky, and she looked like dirt. All her beauty had disappeared. I knew she was gone, but I still couldn't believe it. I just saw her about an hour ago. How could this have happened? I knew I was to blame. If I hadn't needed to have my little drink, then we could have fought together.

"No, no, Mother, please don't leave me!" I yelled. I could feel my body trembling with anger. She was gone. She had left me alone again. "Why didn't you fight, Mother," I said quietly as I held her. I felt the life drain from me. Everything that was good about me was gone, and I knew it. "Why didn't you fight for me?" I let out a loud groan and held her closer to me. How did this happen? Why didn't she fight back? Why did she let herself get killed? I sat with her body and held her closer to me. What was I going to do now, where am I going to go? How was I to live without her, when all I had known is her? I regretted all the troubles I caused her and wished I had told her how much she meant to me. "I'm sorry, Mother," I whispered into her ear. "I'm sorry," I said repeatedly. I was beyond hurt. I couldn't contain my anger, and I knew then what I was going to do. They would all have to pay for her death.

I picked up her body and carried it inside. I would bury her first, but as soon as she was in the ground, all their loved ones would follow. I went to the garden and dug her grave. As I filled the grave with dirt, my body shook in fury. In almost two hundred years, I had never told her to her face that I was glad she had come back for me. I had never told her that I appreciated her or loved her, even though it was always on the tip of my tongue. I had been robbed once again, and everyone in this town would feel my pain. I was no longer in a hurry to go anywhere. They had declared war when they took her life. They had killed the so-called humanity in me and now I was afraid for them—afraid of what they had created in me.

I will torment them so much they will be afraid to close their eyes at night fearing they might see me in their dreams. Their men will hide cowardly in their homes forgetting about work and feeding their children. Their women will not part with their young ones, terrified of what will happen to them.

I dusted myself down and immediately started to track down each scent I had sensed earlier. One after the other, night after night, I visited their homes and lured them out into the open. I killed wives in front of husbands before ending the husbands' lives, too. As for the ones still living with their parents, I killed one parent after the other, and made each watch, knowing it would soon be their turn. I enjoyed watching them tremble and shake in their boots. I saw grown men piss their pants knowing I had come to take their life. I relished every single drop of blood. I knew then there was no going back from this. They deserved the heavy weight of my vengeance. With their own hands, they had unleashed the monster in me, and I rained evil on them night after night, until I was satisfied that I had given my mother the justice she deserved.

I felt different, untouchable. It was a new experience, and I felt reborn. I could not believe how pleasurable human blood was. I especially got satisfaction when the humans were so afraid for their lives, which I took anyway because I could. I had become that which my mother feared I would become, and I was enjoying it. No vampire should ever have to live like I had lived for almost two centuries. I had suffered and denied myself for the humans' sake, and they repaid me with evil. Even after killing those responsible and their families, I went out every night and hunted more.

Most times, I was not hungry, but somehow the feeling I got after taking a life gave me a high, so I went out to recreate the feeling. It was like a drug, and I was now an addict. I was on top of the world. I loved the satisfaction I got when I knew their hearts had beat for the last time. I loved the smell and the taste of each kill, which took me right back to that day when I was driving myself mad wondering what could smell so delicious. Now I knew what I had been missing, and I was going to drink so much to suffice for all the years I had been cheated and stopped from feeding like a true vampire. The best thing about it all was that no one had a clue that I was the cause of all the misery in town. I wiped out all those with knowledge of what I am, and the rest were there for the picking.

I was starting to enjoy those functions my mother used to drag me to. I enjoyed the attention I got from the women, knowing what I would do to them later. I yearned for the looks I got from the jealous husbands. Like a predator, I tracked them down on their way home and killed them. Every night, without mercy, I snuffed out lives. I became greedy and did not have an ounce of guilt for them, just as they did not feel any for my mother. I wanted them to mourn for their mothers, their fathers, their brothers, and their sisters as I mourned for my mother.

\*\*\*

November 1974

It has been a year since I started killing for pleasure and, as much as I enjoy my new diet, it all has begun to get to me. I don't understand why. I still don't feel guilty about killing. The buzz and pleasure I originally felt gradually faded until it was all gone. I no longer was on a high, so to correct this, I killed more in hopes that it would return. To make matters worse, I was beginning to see the faces of my victims, and it bothered me. They disturbed my peace. I was not supposed to feel remorseful. I couldn't let humanity crawl its way back into me. If I allowed myself to see them as anything but food, how was I going to get my body to readjust to drinking nasty animal blood again? Each time these thoughts flooded my mind, I went out and killed just to prove it wrong. They had to die. The humans have to pay for taking my mother's life. She never harmed anyone, not while I had been with her anyway, which is one of the hardest things to do—control your thirst and preserve every bit of humanity as a vampire, when all you really want to do is rip their veins out and suck every drop of blood until the life is gone out of their bodies.

So many humans were reported missing—those were the ones I bothered to hide; the others I just killed and set their houses on fire. The police were trying to convince the remaining residents that they had everything under control. Those with half a brain had already fled town. I watched as they accused and arrested the wrong people. The general theory was that the town was cursed. I attended meetings with them and discussed how to better keep the children safe. I shared their fears and pretended like I was a victim also. They all assumed the same fate had befallen my mother. What they didn't know was that they all suffered because my mother was wrongly killed.

I should go somewhere else and start afresh, but each time I make the decision to leave, I end up staying. I am not able to move on. Something is keeping me around, and I don't know what it is. It could be that I am reluctant to leave because my mother is buried here. Whatever it is, it's not good news for them, because as long as I remain here, I will continue to kill until I feel that I have exerted enough justice on them for her sake.

***

## November 23, 1974

It was especially quiet on this night; you could hear a needle drop on the street if you listened hard enough. People hardly leave their houses anymore. Everything is closed by four or five, and you rarely see anyone by six—you would think it was midnight. They've come to the understanding that most of these crimes take place at night. The only humans out there these days are the police. I keep my hands off them, because

I know better than to draw unnecessary attention to myself. It's not fun anymore. There are no more parties to attend. The whole town is in constant mourning.

I wasn't thirsty, but, as usual, I was out to take a human life. After hovering around undetected for some time, I decided to go back when I sensed a human. She had just passed by the officers and had two bags on her. They stopped her and questioned her—I assumed they were reminding her how dangerous it was to be out at this time. I loved this. Killing her before their noses would be fun. I was no longer going home. I hid away ready to pounce at the first chance. Two officers escorted her to the train station, and when they were sure she was safely within the walls of the station, they left her, but not before telling her to be very cautious. She bid them goodbye and thanked them. There was something urgent in her voice, like she had something to hide. I knew where to wait for her, so I was not detected. One bag was hanging on her shoulder and the other she carried delicately. The contents of her bags didn't interest me; it was the thrill of taking her life that took me over. One of the officers turned back to look at her. She waved at him, and he nodded in reply and then turned back around.

I then made my move. I immediately grabbed her, put my hand over her mouth, took her into the alley just by the station, and, without a moment's hesitation, quickly went for the kill, and drained her until she was white. I felt her body slump and immediately felt guilty and very remorseful. Was something wrong? It was meant to be fun. I was supposed to feel on top of the world, and here I was wishing I had not left my house that evening.

Just as I was about to hide her body, I heard a gurgle and then a baby's cry. My attention was drawn to one of the bags.

I unzipped it quickly and found the baby. I was in shock for a minute. I knew what I must do, but as I stared at this creature, I hated myself for even thinking I could harm her. I wondered why I hadn't sensed her before now. She was just a human baby, and I should have felt her presence. I couldn't leave her here, so I picked up the bag and took it along with me.

I have been told by older vampires that a baby's blood is a special delicacy. It is, however, frowned upon by many to kill children—after all, vampires *are* descendants of humans even though we are superior. It was thought that children were to be preserved because of their innocence. Yet, it is this same innocence that makes their blood so appealing. In my quest for vengeance, I resisted taking children's lives, although I had fed on a few teenage girls, but no one below sixteen years of age.

Now here I was with a baby no one would miss. I figured I was untouchable. I could add this conquest to my resume, but each time I thought in that direction, I felt sick to my stomach for even thinking I could do such a thing. I took the bag home with me and brought out the baby. It was a girl who couldn't have been more than a few days old. She had big, beautiful blue eyes that looked at me with expectation. I was transfixed and couldn't bring myself to hurt her. There was something about the way she looked at me that got to me. I wanted to protect her from the likes of me. I hated myself for ever thinking of hurting her. Something was obviously wrong. Since taking her mother's life, I haven't been myself. I'm not supposed to feel anything towards humans, and, yet, I know I would kill anyone in a heartbeat if they touched a strand of her hair.

# Chapter 4

## Hanna Greene

I took the baby with me to the village of Froxfield in Hampshire where I have a house. I didn't want to be apart from her, which was strange, but to keep her, I knew I would have to stop killing and become better. I had to find someone to raise her. I thought about getting her a nanny, but then realized I probably would kill every single one I hired. That wasn't going to help me become better, and I couldn't be feeding on humans if I wanted to remain in her life. So I came up with the idea that it would be better if I found her another mother, a family. That night after she slept, I went out in search of a family for her. I went from house to house, listening to families' conversations to see if there was anyone in need of a child. I suppose it was a terrible idea, but it was the only one I could think of that might work, even if it meant compelling whomever I found to raise her. After a long night and no success, I came home to a screaming baby. I searched through her bag for food for her—there was just a little left. I put her on my lap and fed her and then rocked her until she fell asleep. I was beginning to worry. I couldn't keep her for too long, because it would deprive me of my day sleep, and I was beginning to run low on supplies.

The next day, I went to the store to buy more of the things that had been in her bag. Once again, I fed her and rocked her to sleep before stepping out to look for a family for her.

For a week, I kept going out to find a family for her, as it was becoming particularly difficult to keep her with me, and it was becoming difficult for me to be up both day and night without rest. I had to find someone soon or consider leaving her at a hospital or a police station. Both options I found unthinkable. I could not just disappear from her life. I needed her to help me become better. Since she came to me, I had not spilled human blood and had not missed it. Every day my feelings for her grew, I had fallen in love with her and found it exciting that there was another person on this earth whom I was capable of loving. I will be her father and love her like a daughter.

I nearly gave up finding a family for her. I was almost revisiting my idea of nannies, when one night, I heard a woman wailing. She was crying for a child she had just lost. I listened and heard her husband trying effortlessly to console her. She had given birth prematurely to a stillborn. I knew right there and then that I had found what I had been looking for. This was where I would bring her, and I hoped they would appreciate the gift I was giving them.

I ran home and quickly wrapped her up and put her back in the bag I had found her in, wrote a cheque for a hundred thousand pounds, and put it in the bag with her. I put all the things I had bought for her in another bag, and then I gazed at her for what seemed like a lifetime. A big part of me regretted the idea already, and I truly wished I could raise her myself. I wondered what my mother would think if she were still here. And then it occurred to me that the baby girl did not have a name, at least none that I knew of. I set her down and wrote a note to the family I would be giving her to.

The baby started to cry as I rattled around my head for a name for her, but nothing came to me; nothing stood out. I tried out various names like Tara, Julia, and Leah, but I didn't like any one of them for her. Then I wondered what my mother would have called her. The baby's cries became louder, so I went to her to console her. I picked her up and gently rocked her from side to side. The more I rocked her, the quieter she became until she stopped crying. I tilted my head to the side and admired her beautiful, big blue eyes, and then it came to me what she would be called. I pulled her close and whispered into her ear, "You, my dear, will be called Hanna, my beautiful Hanna, after my mother. You must forgive me for what I am about to do." I wrote her name on the back of the letter I had written to her new family and then set her back carefully into the bag. I put the letter in the bag with her and made my way out.

I went back to the couple's house, set her on the doorstep, and knocked on their door several times before disappearing into the bushes. I waited until the man came out and found her. He put her back down where he had found her and started looking around for who had dumped her in his doorway. After a couple of minutes, he went back, picked up the bags, and went inside.

I stayed hidden, but close enough all through the night to hear what was going on inside, listening to them making up their mind about keeping her. I had thought the woman would jump at the slightest opportunity to replace her dead child with a living one, but she was the exact opposite. She wouldn't even look at the baby, let alone touch her. I felt pained at the thought of Hanna being rejected. Then I heard the man argue on Hanna's behalf. He was trying to convince his wife to keep the baby.

"Joan, look at her," he said. "She can't be more than a few weeks old. Nobody will even know our baby died. She is a blessing for us. We have a second chance here. Let's not waste it. Can't you see that God doesn't want us to suffer, Joan?"

"No, Joseph. She is not mine. I can't possibly see her as a blessing when I just lost my child. He didn't even get a chance to fight for his life. So don't bring that baby close to me. I don't want anything to do with her, do you hear me? Take her away from me. Take her somewhere else, anywhere but here for goodness' sake. I—I just want my baby, can't you see that? I only want my baby!"

She was weeping, but I could not understand why she did not see my Hanna as a gift. Why didn't she appreciate what I had just done for her? The rage in me grew, and I felt like going into the house to silence her talking about Hanna with so much contempt. Then I thought about my Hanna, and I knew I couldn't do it. I could not find it in me to hurt them. No one had mentioned the money yet. Perhaps they had not found it. I waited patiently, controlling my anger to kill the ungrateful woman. For Hanna's sake they will live tonight.

"No, Joan," I heard the man say again. "We've been waiting for a child for so long. Someone abandoned this poor soul in that freezing cold. I would not do the same. Can't you see, my love, that this is a miracle? We lost a child and someone has gifted us with another on the same night. Nobody has to know, Joan. She can be ours if you want, darling."

"Joseph, I only want what's mine, our child. I want him back."

"I know, love, I know, but we can't get him back. You know we can't. This baby girl needs us. We can call socials if you want, or we can pretend we never lost our child," he said.

The woman was quiet. I waited. They were both quiet. Then I heard footsteps going up the stairs and back, and still no one said a word. I could hear Hanna's heartbeat, and she seemed fine. It didn't sound like they could make a decision just yet, so I gave them more time. I hoped she wouldn't convince him to give up the baby before sunset the next day. I left to go hunt and then get some much needed rest.

The next day, as soon as I could make it out safely, I was back at their house. I needed to know what they had decided to do. I had been restless all day, wondering if they had already turned her over to the police or called the social service. That would be a dumb thing to do, and, for their sakes, I hoped they chose wisely.

No sooner had I got there than I heard Hanna crying. I was so happy and thankful to hear her voice. They still had her, which was good news for me. I wanted to see her. It was as if she was calling out to me, like she knew I was there. I could hear the couple downstairs talking about the cheque I had written them. I knew I had to enter their house, but I needed permission, an invitation. I racked my head for something, anything, that would give me access into their house. After a short while, I came up with an idea and decided to test it immediately.

I could still hear them arguing about the money and what it meant. I knocked on the door, and Joseph came. "How can I help you?" he asked, a little distracted.

I tried not to look at him directly before responding. "Hello. Sorry to disturb you, it's just that my car broke down not too far from here, and I was wondering if I could use your phone to get help?"

He was quiet for a while and then said, "Sure, yeah. Come inside."

I was relieved. I had been invited in, which meant that I could see her whenever I wanted. I deliberately stood in the hallway, not wanting to be asked any questions. Joseph came back with the phone and asked to be excused. I nodded gracefully and pretended like I was calling for help. After a few minutes, I hung up, thanked him for his help, and made my way out.

Without wasting any more time, I leapt into her room through the window and was at her side at once. Strangely enough, she stopped crying. I felt content seeing her. She smiled at me. I gently reached forward with my hands and caressed her tender cheek. She grabbed my finger and held it tight. Her beautiful, big, blue, dreamy eyes beamed as she happily kicked her legs in the air. I felt enveloped by this little human and trembled with fear at the thought of ever losing her. I couldn't believe I had become so attached to her already.

I could hear the couple downstairs still arguing about Hanna and didn't understand why the wife needed so much convincing. I guess humans don't really appreciate what they have until it's taken away from them. Just as they didn't know what killing my mother would cost them.

"I know you are hurting. I am not trying to be inconsiderate, darling. You can't see what I see because of how you feel now, but I know we can do this, and I know you will feel differently later. We can raise her and give her all the love we have together. Have you forgotten how long we have been waiting for a baby, how long we have been trying? She needs us, darling, and we need her even more."

Then she spoke, "But she is not ours, Joseph. Our baby died. That baby upstairs is not mine."

"I know, darling," Joseph said. "I know our baby died and there is nothing we can do about it. I am not saying we can just forget what happened. We can't, nobody can. I am just saying we can also find a place in our hearts for this little one. She can be ours if we choose. You haven't even allowed yourself to look at her, Joan. She is adorable." She was quiet, so he continued. "I lost a child, too. It may not look like it to you, but I am also in pain about losing another child. He was mine, too, and if I could bring him back, Joan, if I could bring him back into our lives, I would, but I can't. I wish I could, but I can't, love. But that baby upstairs, she needs us, she needs you. She needs a mother. I see it when I look at her, and I know we are capable of giving her all the love she wants. I know you can love her too darling, because I know you, and you've got so much love to give. That heart of yours is so big, you just have to let her into it, and you will find space for her."

"What about the money? Joan asked"

"What about it?" Joseph replied.

"I mean, whoever gave her up, if they have so much money in the first place, why abandon her? Don't you think if we take her in and give her all our love that her real parents will just come by one day and demand her back?"

"I didn't think about that, but I can't allow myself to think that way. If and when that situation arises—and I pray it does not—we will deal with it. Right now, let's just worry about taking care of her. She is ours now, and you can finally be a mother to her if you want."

Joan was silent for a moment before saying, "Okay, but you will have to give me some time. I still have to mourn our son."

"Aw, Joan, you don't know how relieved I am to hear you say this. You can have all the time in the world as long as we get to keep her." They were both quiet, and then Joseph spoke again, "So what do I do with the money?"

"We keep it," Joan said, "and raise her with it. That's what it was given for, but it's a lot of money, Joseph."

"Yes, that's true, maybe to clear their guilty consciences, but we are not doing this for the money. With or without the money, I still want us to keep her."

"Didn't you say she is blond? How are we going to explain the fact that she doesn't look like either of us, Joseph, when we are both red heads."

"Another thing I didn't think of. Well, it doesn't matter. She is ours now, our little bundle of joy. Wait here a minute, and I'll go bring her down just so you can look at her." I reluctantly left the room before he came in. He picked her up and took her downstairs to his wife. I could hear him talking to Hanna as he made his way back. I was happy I had made the decision to bring her to them. She should be happy here, and I could always come and check on her.

"Here, Joan, take her," said Joseph. "Look how beautiful she is." I did not hear her reply. I wish I could have seen her face to know whether she agreed with what her husband had said. "It's okay. You can hold her, darling. She won't bite," he said calmly.

I could hear Joan breathing heavily, and her heart was drumming so fast at the thought of touching her. "I don't know, Joseph. I am not ready yet. I am not ready to say goodbye to our son just yet. If I hold her now, it will be just like he never existed. I can't, not now, please give me some time. I promise when I am good and ready, I will be able to do it." She was clearly still in pain and I understood.

I know what pain is, so I didn't begrudge her for not wanting to let go. I do not believe what is happening to me. A year ago, I wanted them all dead, each one who crossed my path. To my shock, I have not been able to kill a human since I met Hanna, and I know that for her sake, I have to give up human blood and embrace my old habit. Mother was right—it takes someone you love more than yourself to attempt a return from such a dark place.

I left knowing she was in good hands. She had her own family now and would always be loved. I had to leave them alone to be a family together. I had to go fight my own demons. I have destroyed that which took me a century to perfect, and I know I am going to need years to be better. I won't be seeing Hanna again until I am better and worthy to be in her presence.

# Chapter 5

January 1979

I haven't seen Hanna for five years now, and I have to battle with myself every day to keep it that way. I left England to make it harder for me to return to her life. I tell myself that she is okay now, that she doesn't need me, but I have found it difficult. I close my eyes and her little face clouds my memory, and I wonder why I am so wired to her. I never knew it was possible for me to like a human, let alone love one, and I fell in love with this little human the moment I clapped eyes on her.

As time went on, the urge to see Hanna increased. I couldn't stop myself any longer; I had to see how she was doing. As soon as I made that decision, I could barely keep up with my excitement. I had to know that she was all right, that she has been treated well. Sometimes,, I feel guilty, like I never should have left her, but I also know that I couldn't have remained in her life when all I wanted was human blood. I tell myself I did what was best for her, for us both. Although she doesn't know me or how much I care and love her, I know what meeting her as done for me. In five years, I have not killed a human. I slipped twice in the first year of my rehabilitation when I went to visit Isobel, an old friend, and her mother, Margret, and drank some human blood, but I never took a life. I soon left them because I knew they were not good for my newfound life. I was determined and, as hard as I found it, I stuck to drinking animal blood. There have been times when I have been so close to killing a human, when the smell of their blood has overpowered me, but in the last minute, I thought of Hanna and saw her lovely, deep-blue eyes and snapped out of it. No one has ever had such a strong hold on me, not even my mother, and I am glad I found her.

I have been writing checks of a hundred thousand pound sterling to Hanna's parents every year, and they have been cashing them, no questions asked. Each time a check is cashed, I tell myself they still have her and she is doing fine. I want to give more, but I have to know they are using the money the way I hoped they would.

I arrived and stayed in my house for three months. I couldn't quite bring myself to go over to their house. Each time I thought of how close I was to her, even though I had not been able to go physically, my body pumped with adrenaline, and I tried to talk myself out of going. I got scared, I didn't know what to expect. Should I just watch from afar or try to initiate some contact? It saddens me that Hanna may never know what she means to me or that I exist. She is the reason I have been able to conquer the monster in me.

It has been four months since I came back. I have not yet summoned the courage to see her. Most nights, I set out to go, but turn around half way there and go back home for fear that when I see her, I may not be able to leave. By the end of the fourth month, I finally decided to see her. I can't be this close and not know how she is doing or see her even once.

I went round to their house, but there was no one home. I could tell because I couldn't sense anyone in there. The bathroom window was open so I entered the house. It's a good thing I had permission already. I went downstairs and started looking around to see if I could spot a picture, anything with her in it. The house looked fresh and clean and well decorated throughout. By one window was a white grand piano and several framed pictures. I could see her from where I stood. She may have grown a little bit, but nothing has changed. Her eyes were looking straight at me as if she were there in person. I knew then that I would find it hard to leave. I went over and picked up the picture, ignoring the other frames of other people. I stood there just staring at it and then realised they might soon be home. I started to look through the drawers to find bank information for them. I needed to stop sending checks and do a bank transfer instead. I found some statements for each of them and one with both of their names. I jotted down the account numbers and all the information I would need to enable me to put money into their accounts.

I went back upstairs to search her room. It was nicely decorated in pink, purple, and white. There was a dollhouse, a castle, a white dressing-table with a little oval mirror, different dolls, and lots of toys sitting nicely around the room. Her bed was properly made. I looked around once more and took in a deep breath and filled my lungs with her scent. I still had the picture in my hand and traced her face with the tip of my fingers. I tried to memorise her face again. She was different now. Her eyes are as beautiful and dreamy as ever, but she has grown. It is amazing how humans can change with time while I remain the same. There were no signs of another child in the house. *It's a good thing they decided to keep her*, I thought.

Now, more than ever, I wanted to see her in person, to watch her as she lives her life. I wanted to be there to share her happiness when she smiled, to console her when she cried, and protect her from harm. To watch her when she sleeps, to wonder why she is angry or whether she has secrets. To watch her eat and talk and learn about everything that she cares about, the meaning of everything she does, and be able to teach her the little I know of life.

To my shock, I heard the door close behind me. It was careless of me to still be here. I wasn't aware of my surroundings. Why I didn't sense them as they approached the house baffled me, I should have. I tucked the picture into my coat before turning around and there they were, those big, beautiful, blue eyes staring straight at me. I was startled, she had sneaked up on me. Why didn't I hear her coming? If not her, her parents when they entered the house? I couldn't move. I was staring back in shock and disbelief. To my surprise, she did not look scared that I was in her room. She looked even more adorable and beautiful in person. I felt like scooping her up in my arms. I knew I couldn't—I was no more than a stranger to her. I am no more than an intruder, and she would probably scream for help. *Perhaps it is for the best,* I thought. I can't be any good to her when I am responsible for the death of her mother. Perhaps I am just seeking redemption for all the wrongs I have done. But there can be no redemption for me, because I have been too evil to be gifted with her. That's why my life will remain meaningless without her, and I cannot be with her when I am just another stranger to her.

"How are you?" she asked in a very sweet, innocent voice. I couldn't speak; I was frozen and just stared back at her.

"Are you all right, mister? Can't you speak?" I found my voice. I swallowed a lump and before I could say *Hanna*, I heard her mother call her. She turned round to answer back, but before she turned back round, I left through her window and heard her reply, "Yes, Mummy?"

"Who are you talking to up there, Hanna?" Joan asked.

"No one, Mum," she lied. *Why did she lie*, I asked myself. To her I am just a stranger. Why would she protect me? She can't possibly remember me; I was barely with her for a week. It bothered me that she felt safe around me. I could have been anyone, and she would have kept it from her parents.

"Come downstairs, darling. Your food is ready. Hurry up before it gets cold," Joan said.

"Okay, Mummy," Hanna answered.

I still had her picture with me. I wanted to keep it, but then they would know someone had come in, so I had to return and then leave town. It felt good to know that Joan was on board now. Numerous times I had worried about Joan and how she might be treating my Hanna. I could leave now with the understanding that Hanna would be fine, because she was in a good place.

Later that night, I came back while they were asleep to return the picture. I entered the house through Hanna's bedroom window and saw she was sleeping. I wanted to touch her hair, brush it back from her face, but I could not risk waking her up. I went downstairs to replace the frame and went right back to Hanna's room. I had done what I had come for and should leave, but I couldn't. I just stood on the side of Hanna's bed and watched her as she slept. *How can I leave now*, I wondered, *when all I want to do is to remain by her side?* I couldn't possibly stay. I had promised myself one visit only, and I would leave, but I wanted more.

There was something about her. I had not quite figured it out, and it drew me to her. I was different around her, like I was someone else, someone who wasn't eternally ruined and

*Sebastian*

had everything to live for. I looked at my watch and saw that I had about forty minutes to get home. I watched as Hanna shifted and turned on her side. I wanted to lean over and kiss her goodbye on her forehead. I was sad. I had to leave. What I was doing was wrong. If I didn't leave England, I would always find an excuse to come here every night. This was no way for her to live. I took one last look before leaving, and I knew then it would be a long while before I came back.

## Chapter 6

Year 1992

In my journeys round the world to avoid being in England, for obvious reasons, I visited friends of mine and my mother's for a while. I needed to be in the company of others to preoccupy my thoughts. Since my mother's passing, it had been Margret's wish that I come over and stay with them. She and her daughter, Isobel, were like family to us. Margret is the closest thing to a sister my mother ever had. Margret and Isobel have been around for over five centuries. Margret made Isobel a vampire, and they have been together ever since. Isobel was the only daughter of a farmer and lived alone with her father–her birth mother had died while giving birth to her.

Isobel had been struck by a mysterious illness that she was not going to live through. Her father did all he could to save her, but no one knew what ailed her. Margret said she heard him weeping at Isobel's bedside while she hunted. She took pity on him and told him she could save her, but he would never be able to see her again, and he agreed. He wanted her alive at any cost. After Margret made her, Isobel made her way back home and killed her father. I asked her why once. I found it hard to believe she would do that to someone who had loved her. She never responded. I wish I had had a father like hers who cared what happened to me. Margret once said she thought Isobel did it to cut all ties with the human world. I think that was too precious a tie to cut. I love her like a sister, but she is too unpredictable, and that doesn't set right with me.

I couldn't stay with them too long. I was battling a demon, amongst other reasons, and their lifestyle fuelled the evil in me. Isobel and her mother never understood my mother's view on humans, and she wasn't alone there. I haven't yet come across a vampire who didn't laugh in our faces. Before Hanna and my mother's death, I believed the same as they did, even though I never practised my beliefs. But now everything is different. I hate the monster I became. I am ashamed of all the humans I have killed. Something is different now. I can't undo the evil I did, but I am willing to try my hardest to be the vampire my mother hoped I would become and be worthy in Hanna's eyes.

Everyone expected me to revel in my freedom now that my mother, my maker, was gone. Each time they fed, they invited me to participate. I slipped twice, and both times, I felt like I was betraying who I was. I didn't enjoy it. The addiction and satisfaction I celebrated previously were no longer there, just the greed of feeding on humans. I wanted no part of it anymore, and they didn't understand. In their minds, that was the first time I had tried human blood, as I have kept my shameful ways a secret. Perhaps if I didn't talk about it, I could pretend I had never been that person. For this reason, I decided to move on. I did not want to be around temptation, and I knew that I would only be lying to myself if I pretended that I could watch them feed on humans and not let my greed take me over.

Before the Hayes met my mother, they killed their victims, but their friendship with my mother changed them and stopped them from being brutal. They were never going to give up the blood no matter how much they loved my mother. My mother knew this as well, but it didn't stop her from trying to convert them. Now at least they just take what they need and send the humans home. Mother may have failed in her attempt to change their diet, but she also saved several lives, which was more important to her. In the eyes of any human, feeding on their blood is considered cruel, but feeding and sparing the life of one's victim is the most difficult act of mercy a vampire can possess, apart from abstinence.

For over a hundred years after I had mastered the art of control, I never understood why most vampires had no control—why they couldn't just have their fill and send their prey home. It's easily done; it just takes dedication and control. That said, I also understand the greed that comes with consuming human blood, although my greed was born out of vengeance. The greed makes you ravenous and insatiable, but this theory is quite understandable to the extent that, when a vampire is starved for days, he needs every drop of blood he can get to survive and regain strength. At the same time, that lust for blood powers a vampire to kill his prey. To have their fill, but continue to drain the human until there is nothing left, to me is greed.

There is a thin line between greedy vampires and monstrous ones. They both end with their victims dying, but a greedy vampire has no control over his appetite and is constantly hungry because of lack of training, which always results in the loss of a human life. Whereas a monstrous vampire does not only kill to survive, but also has to kill because he enjoys the fear and power he has over the humans. They love the thrill, it seduces them, and the dominion they feel they have over humans makes them feel untouchable. In my opinion, once a vampire lets the blood control them, it is quite difficult to be anything but a killer.

My mother and Margret tried endlessly to make Isobel and me into more than just friends so that we could unify our friendship into a proper family. I knew Isobel wanted the same—she made it clear. She told be in no uncertain terms that she was in love with me, but I wasn't attracted to her. I love her, and I know I would do anything to protect her, but I can't be with her like she wants, because I am not in love with her. "What does that matter," My mother once argued. My being with Isobel was the only other crusade my mother had going. She wanted Isobel and me together. It puts me in an awkward position to have someone I like declare her love for me when I cannot reciprocate the same. Isobel is a year older than I am in human years, which means she was made when she was nineteen, and three and half centuries older than I am in vampire years.

Isobel is beautiful and very pleasing to the eye, and I often wonder why I am not attracted to her. She is always the life and soul of any party and never fails to get men drooling all over her. Most of the time when we party together, I notice how eager other men and vampires alike want her. I use this to my advantage and try to encourage her to be with someone else, but she never takes the bait. I don't particularly enjoy being around her anymore, because I know she hurts because of me, and I am unable to soothe her need.

Mother never understood why I couldn't be with her. She argued that the kind of love I talk about doesn't really exist. She wanted me to be with Isobel so I wouldn't end up alone, should something happen to her. She might have been right, not that I have been searching for love, but in over a hundred years, I have never really come across anyone worthy of my love. I was never going to be with Isobel to pacify my mother. Isobel deserves better than me. She needs to find someone who can give her all the love she needs. I knew I had to make Isobel understand where I was coming from. She could do better than me if she only gave others a chance. I sat her down several years ago and explained to her how I felt about our situation, and to my surprise, she took it well and has never bothered me about being together in that way since.

It's been a while since I last saw Margret and Isobel, although Isobel wrote to me frequently, worried about me and wishing for my presence. As much as I needed her to know that I was all right, I also knew that going back to them was not the place for me. I wasn't strong enough, and it would only lead me back to my demon. Moreover, they lived too close to England. I last saw them about seventeen years ago. I kept busy always travelling around the world. I never stopped in one place for too long. I had to keep moving. The more I moved about, the more I was able to occupy my thoughts and pretend that Hanna didn't exist. But when you've seen it all before, eventually boredom begins to surface, together with whatever you are running away from.

It's been over twelve years since the night I was in Hanna's room. I left as soon as I got back home that day—it felt like the right thing to do at the time, because if I were away, I wouldn't be able to go to her house, and she could get on with living and not have to remember that she had monster me in her life. Each day away was a struggle. At first I locked myself away from the world. I felt that if I stayed away from the world then I wouldn't be faced with temptation, but that didn't help; it just made it too difficult whenever I encountered a human. So I decided to go back to my mother's routine. I started the same way she had started with me: rationing my feed and gaining back control by forcing myself to go out amongst the human population.

I started lending my time to the vulnerable, working with the poor, and joining causes to help me regain my humanity. I empathised with the less able humans, and they helped me greatly. I formed relationships, got to know each person I worked with, and each day I was more ashamed of what I had done in the past. I knew then why it was important to my mother to live in a community and form relationships. There was always temptation, but knowing the people in my community helped me conquer my demons. I am still a vampire, capable of terrible things, and I know not to allow myself alone with any one of them. I have my control back, and I feel better, because I understand now what mother was teaching me.

At the back of my mind as I roamed the world was Hanna's little face, and even though I was not near her, I knew it was because of her that I was becoming better. Nights were good for me, because I was helping out the humans. Nothing was too much for me to do, and it helped me to keep busy, because it kept me from longing to see her. Day times were stressful. I tortured myself with worry. I felt like a father who purposely had abandoned his child. And what made it worse was knowing that she may never know who I am and what she means to me. I increased the money I give to her parents to one million pound sterling a year so she never has to want for anything, and still I wish it were me she saw every day of her life.

I was in Africa when I made the decision to return to Hanna's life. A young girl I had known for a few years died tragically in an auto accident. It reminded me of how flimsy and weak humans are. It scared me. What if something had happened to Hanna? What if she was sick? Humans get sick all the time. The fear of what could happen or what may have happened already to her put things in perspective for me. I packed up at once, before I could convince myself otherwise, and started towards England. I owed Margret and Isobel a visit in Italy, too, and I was going to pass through quickly before getting to England. For some reason, I couldn't contain my joy; I was happy I was heading back home. The joy I felt at the prospect of seeing her again was indescribable.

Margret and Isobel were not happy when I told them I was only staying for a day. For me that was too long when I could be headed to England already, but I tried to hide my excitement. Isobel pleaded with me to stay longer, but my heart—if I had one—was elsewhere. I could not imagine staying away for one more day. Somehow it felt right to be returning, if only to be able to see Hanna from afar. I pretended to be interested in the things Margret and Isobel were talking about. They were happy I was visiting, and I was glad, but I really wished I were in England. I could tell that Isobel suspected that something was wrong when she asked me a question and I didn't reply.

I was annoyed at myself for arousing Isobel's suspicions. She is the last person I want on my case. I know she has accepted that we can't be together, but she will never understand what Hanna means to me and why I can't wait to see her. Isobel can be a beast when she is jealous, and there was no need for me to feed the beast.

## Sebastian

There were three other vampires staying with them when I arrived. "They are Isobel's new-found friends," Margret said. Although I had heard rumours of them and their merciless, monstrous way of life, this was the first time I had ever met them. They looked very cosy with Isobel, like they all had been friends for a long time. The four of them looked like they were planning something together, but each time I came close they stopped talking or spoke languages I didn't understand. It's not like I cared. I would never get in bed with them anyway, and, judging by their reputation, whatever they were cooking up would be bad for business. I wondered what it was Isobel had going on with them and knew I had to warn her to stay away.

These three vampires were notorious for the evil they evoked in their wake. They call themselves brothers and have roamed the world together for centuries causing unnecessary bloodshed. Anton Doyle became a vampire at the age of sixteen. After he was made, he killed his family, and then he and his maker wiped out an entire village. He later killed his own master with the help of a witch—something that is rarely done—and was on his own for almost a century before making a companion for himself. He found Hector Sayers, who was only seventeen, and turned him. Together they found Zacchary Peterson, also seventeen at the time.

The three of them have since caused all sorts of misfortune to the human population. They fight other vampires for territories that don't belong to them and cause all sorts of disasters wherever they settle. Their beauty knows no end, which makes it very easy for young girls, their age in human years, to easily fall prey to them.

I do not know much about them. All I know is what I have heard from other vampires who have spoken of them.

I have been told that Hector is the kindest of the three, the only one who sometimes has mercy on his victims, and that Anton, their leader, and Zacchary are the most vicious. They are quietly feared—even some vampires fear ever wronging them. Each has lived for more than six hundred years. Having seen them in person, they look like they couldn't harm a fly. They are very courteous, classy, and refined in appearance. They are tastefully dressed and very graceful when they talk and move about.

Anton is the youngest in human years, since he was made when he was just sixteen. He has a boyish smile that complements his age, and he can be very charming with it. His dark eyes and eyebrows make him look arrogant, but I guess he can get away with anything with that winning smile.

Zacchary, the tallest of the three, has long, flowing, blonde locks falling down his back. His face is narrowly shaped, with high cheekbones and full, symmetrical lips. He is as vicious as Anton and loves to kill girls who fall in love with him. He woos them, and when they are smitten, he kills them.

Hector is considered the most handsome of the three. I imagine that both girls and women drool over him. He has a slim face with high cheekbones and a prominent, lower jaw and chin. His hair is dark, his eyes are blue and kind, and he has a well-proportioned and pleasing appearance. It's no surprise that the majority of their victims are females who fall hopelessly at their feet and die without mercy.

For the life of me, I wonder what they want with Isobel and why she has invited them over to stay. I noticed that Margret was avoiding them—she never sat in the same room with them, but remained courteous throughout. She is never one to pick a fight or stir up trouble, which is why she and my mother got on so well, and I wished her daughter were the same.

I debated talking to Isobel about her friends before I left. I didn't like that she is friends with them, and, although it is none of my business who she befriends, I still felt like I should say something to her. I walked into the room where they all sat. Anton and Hector had just finished feeding from a female human. I watched as her naked body dropped to the floor. I looked over at Isobel, who avoided my eyes, and I was disappointed in her. I thought she had stopped doing this, but it seems she has gone back to her old ways. I wondered if I was to blame for this. Maybe I had stayed away too much and she became greedy. Although I didn't see her participating, I could see she was enjoying the show. The others were clearly having fun. Another girl was sitting with Zaccary, and I knew she was going to die, too.

The three brothers turned in my direction and I nodded in acknowledgment. "Can I have a word with you?" I said quietly, looking at Isobel.

"Excuse me, guys," she said, getting up and following me out into the field. We took a long walk through the fields into the woods. I wanted to make sure nobody else could hear us. I have many disadvantages compared to other vampires I have come across. One is that I am young compared to these three, and I am not looking for a fight. Moreover, fighting them can be suicidal. Another is that they feed on human blood every day, which makes them even stronger. So I have to be careful and not provoke them.

When I was satisfied that we were safe from any form of interruption, I stopped, but before I could say a word, she said, "If you are here to judge me, Sebastian, don't."

"Judge you?" I questioned. "I just wanted to have a word with you, that's all."

"You want to have a word, and you bring me this far just to talk?"

"Listen, I know I have been selfish. I stayed away and shut you guys out of my life, and I am sorry. I was grieving, and I needed space. I grieve still, but I am much better now. Look, I—I just want to make sure you are fine, really."

"Well, I'm fine. You shouldn't worry about me."

"You know what I mean."

"I don't understand. I already told you I'm fine."

"You are very intuitive, Isobel, but I will get to the point. I was just wondering about your new friends. That's all. You know as much as I do that they are bad news. What are they doing here?"

She hissed, "It's none of your business who I am friends with. Do I question you on the things you do or the friends you keep?" I did not want to offend her, and I could see she was beginning to lose her temper. If there is one thing sure about her, it is that she can be very unpredictable with her moods.

"Don't get offended, Isobel. I am just trying to make sure you are not in any kind of trouble, that's all. Of course it's none of my business whom you choose to be friends with. As your friend, as your—brother."

"Don't do that," she said.

"Do what?" I asked.

"Say you're my brother," she snapped. I was quiet for a while before speaking. I wanted her to calm down a little.

"Okay, *as your friend*, I feel like it's my duty to make sure you know what you're doing."

"Oh, *now* you want to be friends. Where were you in the last, say, seventeen years when I needed you? Listen, you're not the only good-looking vampire around with a shoulder to cry on. Stop with the petty jealousy. It's touching but unnecessary. They are good, trust me, and I have my reasons."

"Good looking? You're funny. You think this is all a joke, don't you. You know I am not jealous of anyone. I care about you. I have always cared about you, and you know it." I noticed she started to let her guard down.

"So you do care about me after all? I was beginning to think you were no longer interested in me. Wait, you did say once that you would consider being with me after you've lived as long as I have. I still want you."

"I don't remember saying such a thing," I said.

"I took you for a gentleman. I have no reason to lie," she said.

"Even if I did I say that, would you possibly wait that long for a man? Anyone who would make you wait that long does not deserve you. I don't deserve you."

"I know, but here I am, still willing to wait, even if it means forever."

I had to divert her attention to the reason I brought her here. "So these reasons you have for being friends with them, do you mind telling me or is it a secret?"

"Are we still talking about them? I thought we were going to discuss how we feel about each other."

"Don't take this the wrong way, but you know what I am talking about. You are my friend, my sister, and I will do anything for you, but you know when I say I care about you, I don't mean it like that."

"I see you haven't changed your mind then," she said. "So tell me, what is so wrong with me that you find it so hard to love me? Am I so repulsive, that you can't bear the thought of being with me, wanting me?"

"Isobel, don't start. You can't guilt me into being with you. You know what—forget it, do what you like, you've always done what you like, so just do whatever."

"Why do you hate me so much?" she asked.

"Hate you? Come on, you know I don't hate you!"

"Then what is so wrong with me? Tell me, and I'll fix it. I'll do anything to be with you. Please, Sebastian, I can't keep pretending that I don't love you. I can't pretend that I don't want you."

"I am sorry you still feel that way. I love you, Isobel, but I am not *in love* with you. I just don't see you like that. There is nothing wrong with you. You are perfect and very beautiful, but you are and always will be like a sister to me. You are the only true friend I have. You and Margret are my family. It would be unjust of me to be anything less than you expect of me if I pretend that I want you as a lover."

"I would not see it as unjust, my love, if it means sharing eternity with you. You would come round to loving me if only you would try to spend more time with me. Believe me, I know these things. I have been around long enough to know it is you I want to spend forever with. How can I love you so and you don't love me? Do you know how painful it is for me to have these feelings for you that won't go away and to also know you will never reciprocate it while I still live in desperate hope that one day you will change your mind? Please, Sebastian, if you really care for me, tell me you will try. Promise me you will at least give us a chance."

I was quiet, I couldn't promise her that and raise her hopes up when I knew I could never do what she was asking. I watched as tears rolled down her cheeks. I wanted to wipe them for her, but how could I make her feel better when I am the reason she is distraught?

"I see," she said. "Okay then. At least let me come with you. Take me to England with you. I know I can make you happy, just give me a chance to show you. Look at your eyes, those gorgeous green eyes. They were once so full of life a lifetime ago. Now all I see is loneliness and sadness."

I looked at her and it saddened me to know how desperate she wanted to be with me. Yes, a while ago, when I lost my mother, my eyes were sad, but not anymore—not since Hanna. I wished I could help Isobel feel better. Her eyes were the ones with sadness, and it troubled me that I couldn't do anything, short of deceiving her to make her happy. The disturbing truth was that she would know I was pretending, yet she would be happy to go along with it for the rest of forever. And by so doing, I would forgo my happiness. I would have to forget Hanna completely. The very thought of it was unbearable.

"Please let me come with you," she said. Her hands were on my face, moving gradually to the back of my neck, her lips inches from mine. I did not like being put into this situation.

I moved her hands away from my face and placed them at her sides as gently as I could. "I am sorry, Isobel. I know this must be hard for you. It's hard for me, too, to watch you suffer as you do. If I could flick a switch inside of me so that I could have those kinds of feelings for you, I would have done it by now. We can't be together like that, and I am sure I will not feel any differently in the next century. I am not attracted to you in that way, and if I don't feel that way now, I don't think it's a matter of how long we spend together. Please, let's not spoil what we have. Pretend that our friendship is enough."

She didn't say anything at first. She walked away from me and then turned around and walked back towards me.

She stood very close to me so that I was forced to take a step back; she followed. "Tell me, Sebastian," she said, "is there someone else? Is there someone you care for above me?"

I was quiet again. I didn't want to talk in case I gave her a cause to keep hunting for answers. *This has gone on too long*, I thought. I had to get out now before it gets out of hand.

"There *is* someone, isn't there? Tell me, Sebastian. Admit it. I can see it in your eyes. You are thinking of her right now, aren't you? Your eyes glisten when you think of her. Who is this person whom you cherish more than me?" she asked. Her eyes were like fire. She pushed on my chest with her palm.

She was right, but I was not about to tell her the truth. I was not going to put Hanna in any more danger than she already is with me, so I lied. I held Isobel's face with both of my hands and spoke as sincerely as I could muster. "Calm down, will you? I wish it were true that there was someone capable of making me beam from ear to ear, but you're wrong. There is no such person, alive or dead. You are beautiful, Isobel, and if you just allow yourself, you will find someone out there who will make you happy. I am your friend, and I always will be there for you. I came to visit you, to check that you're all right. I am sorry if by so doing I made you hopeful about us. That was not my intention. You've told me you are fine, and I believe you are. I'm sorry, I will have to cut this visit short."

"Please take me with you, Sebastian. I'm sorry. Listen, I accept now that we can only be friends. Just take me with you so we can spend time together. Please let me come. I have not seen you in seventeen years, and you're going again. Who knows when I will see you next? Let me come with you."

"And if I say yes, what will become of your guests?"

"They will keep Margret company for some time. She won't mind. She loves you and knows what being with you means to me. Please let me come with you."

She continued to plead with me. If I were going anywhere else other than to see Hanna, I might have considered it, but as it was, there was nothing that would make me take a human, blood-sucking vampire to the town she lives in, let alone a jealous one like Isobel.

"I am sorry. Some other time maybe, but I have to go alone. I will visit soon, if that would make you happy. I will not wait this long again, I promise you. You must tell Margret for me that I will visit again. Goodbye, Isobel." I kissed her on the forehead to placate her before taking my leave.

## Chapter 7

Taking the next available flight, I got to England that same night and immediately went to Hanna's house. I could not wait another night to see her. But to my horror, when I got there, I couldn't sense her or her parents. They had moved and a different family was living in their house. I was annoyed with myself. Why had it never occurred to me that they might move? I just assumed they would never leave. I mean, with all the money I sent, I should have known they would probably want a better life.

I went back home disappointed. I opened the door and let myself in. Everything was as I had left it, thanks to my caretaker—not that I cared right now. I had taken my eyes off the ball, and now I didn't have any idea where on earth Hanna might be.

I was not mad at them for moving; I was mad at myself for not being one step ahead. Now I had to find her, and I didn't know how long I would have to wait before seeing her again. I tried to think of places where they might move, but it was no use, because I didn't know them well enough to guess where they could have gone. Now, armed with more money, the world was their oyster.

I immediately set to work and rang an old vampire friend I had met in South America long before my mother was killed. I had saved Mason Benedict's life once when I was out hunting years ago, and it was time I called for a favour. I had been in the rainforest searching for food when I heard a faint cry for help. As I looked for the source of the cry, I came upon a large rock sitting alone in the middle of the forest. I placed my ear close to it and heard the cry again. I moved the rock and found an entrance to a dungeon. Mason had been left in a prison more than fifty feet below the surface of the ground in the thick of the rainforest.

A set of small, steep stairs led to a dark, mouldy, cobwebbed, and stale earth-festering tunnel. At the end of the narrow tunnel was a thick blockade made of rocks. Behind the rocks was a larger rock, which was very heavy, and it took all of my strength to move it away. The whole place was very dark. It would have been impossible for a human to see anything without the use of a torch, but I could just about manage—one of the perks of being a vampire. The dungeon smelt like death and had dry brittle bones of rats and other unknown animals scattered everywhere I looked. A frail-looking vampire was lying on the floor. He didn't look as though he could still be alive. And although his mouth wasn't moving, I could hear him more clearly now asking for help. He looked like death itself, motionless but alive. He had on a dirty, black, regal-looking cloak that looked like it had decomposed with time. I tried to move him to his side, and the cloak started to break away as I touched him. His body felt stiff. The skin on his face was dry and flaky. Dirt had moulded into his thinned-out grey hair. I wondered how long he had been here. I put my hand to his mouth to check whether he was breathing—not that it mattered, since there was no air this far below the ground.

I wondered who could have done this to him and what he had done to deserve such a punishment. Why wasn't he just killed? He must have wronged someone who felt that death was too easy a punishment for him. I wondered whether I should leave him here or carry him out. I sat beside him to debate what to do. I wanted to help him, but wasn't sure if I would be doing the world any good by setting him free.

When I got up to go, I sighted a gold ring on the floor next to him. It had a symbol on it with words engraved in a foreign language. It must have fallen from his long, bony fingers. I picked it up and pocketed it. I could still hear him. He was begging me not to leave him. I wondered how he had known what I was about to do. I took another look at him and changed my mind. I picked him up and placed him on my shoulders and made my way out into the open. Once we were above the ground, I wrapped my coat around him and carried him to my car and then drove to my house.

My mother was in shock when she saw him. We fed him blood constantly. Mother opened his scrunched-up mouth, and we forced some animal blood down his throat. We did this every day for about a week before his body slowly began to respond. His body loosened up and life began to return. After the first three weeks, his recovery was pretty fast. He regained his strength, and his beauty returned. It's so amazing the transformation from a dry-looking skeletal-form to this magnificent, handsome vampire. As he recovered, his grey hair gradually began to change back to its original dark colour, which hung down his back. His skin plumped back up. He didn't look older than thirty-six in human years, about the same age as my mother. He and she became very fond of each other. Mother liked to braid his hair into a single plait, and he seemed to enjoy her doing it. She loosened it daily and redid it all over again. If I didn't know better, I would think they had a thing for each other. Although I didn't see her falling for a vampire that I definitely know drinks human blood. Even though he was being civil for her sake, I knew he would soon resume his normal diet, and I knew she knew that, too. Although he liked her, he was already taken, judging by that ring I found. He never asked me if I saw his ring, but I noticed he constantly robbed the finger on which it should have been.

One day, a couple of months after I had found him, I placed the ring on the table in front of him without saying anything. He looked up at me, said *thanks*, and immediately put it on. I noticed that my mother's eyes stayed on his hands for a while, but I guess she already knew he was not available. I stood there observing him. He must have known that I wanted to ask him questions about the ring, but I could tell he wasn't going to say anything to me, so I decided to leave it alone—everyone deserves to have their secret as long as it doesn't affect me. I somewhat felt like he owed me an explanation about how he ended up where I found him though, but he didn't say a word about it, and I was not going to push it. Mother asked that we not get involved, so I stayed out of it.

I once overheard him and mother talking about politics and the world in general, and he said, "Take it from me, Betty, I am over a thousand years young, and nothing is new to me—nothing surprises me anymore. I have seen all the world has to offer, and it's all just about repackaging to keep me interested." It depressed me to think that after a while I might start to think like him. *When you've seen it all, what else do you live for* I wondered? And it got me to thinking about my life. Apart from my mother, I really didn't have anything to live for, and I wondered what the purpose of eternity was.

Until then, I had never been around someone that old. If he has been around this long, it means whoever put him in that dungeon must be more powerful.

My mother did her best to try to convert him. She thought that if he could go that long without human blood, he could change his diet. But I knew she was wasting her time. A vampire that old cannot be easily changed. He knows what he wants, and being away from human blood means he's missed it even more. Also, I didn't think she should concern herself with controlling his diet. While he was with us, he was doing exactly what she wanted, and I had never met a more graceful vampire. He had good poise and dressed elegantly. He delicately touched everything he came in contact with, as though he was afraid if he held on too tightly he might destroy it. He was never in a hurry to do anything, and nothing seemed to ruffle him. He told my mother stories and loved to listen to her stories as well. He made her happy. It seemed she had found a new friend. He stuck by our rules and never hunted a human. There was nothing to dislike about him, but I wasn't sure I could trust him—he had too many secrets. He stayed with us for about three months before deciding to leave. As he was leaving, he left us details on how to contact him. He begged us to stay in touch and to call if we ever needed his help. He made me promise that I would be in contact, but I never needed him until now.

It felt like a long shot, but I remember how shocked Margret had been when my mother mentioned that she knew Mason Benedict. "It's good to have friends in high places, and you, my friend, have the very one person every vampire wishes was on their side," she had said to my mother. I didn't make much of it then.

The phone only rang three times, and I instantly recognized Mason's voice, as though it had only been yesterday that I last spoke to him.

"Hello, Mason."

"Who is this?" he asked.

"Er—I don't know if you remember me, but it's me, Sebastian."

"Sebastian? Yes, Sebastian! How can I forget? You saved my life."

"Well, someone had to do it," I joked.

"Why has it taken you this long to contact me?" he asked.

"Because I didn't need to until now," I said.

He was quiet for a while. "Well, I am glad you finally need me. What do you want from me? Name it, and it's yours."

"I need a favour, and, if it's not within your powers, I hope you know someone who can help?"

"Speak up and see it done, Sebastian."

"Okay, I need to find someone who is of great importance to me, and I wondered if you knew of anyone who can help." He was quiet again for about thirty seconds. "Hello?" I knew he was there, but he said nothing. "Mason? Are you still there?"

"I'm still here, son," he said. "I was just thinking. I know the right person for the job. You mind telling me who it is you are trying to find? I don't mean to be intrusive, but it may just help speed up things."

I was silent for a second. "Is it all right, if I keep the identity to myself. It's not that I don't trust you, but it's just that this is very personal to me. So if you don't mind, I would like to keep it that way."

"But of course. We all have our secrets, don't we? Consider it done. Before I forget, please accept my condolences on your mother's departure from amongst us."

"Thank you. I didn't know that you knew."

"Oh, but of course I knew. I make it my business to know everything that happens around me, especially about those I consider family. You do know that is what you are to me?"

"Family?" I half laughed, being careful not to offend him. "So how is it you never called after she died?" I said, almost in anger.

"You must forgive me if I didn't do the right thing by you, but you were angry and vengeful. I thought it best at the time to let you grieve in your own way as you needed time to heal. I also lost someone once that I loved dearly, and I know of the ache and pain that follows and still plagues me to this day. I didn't think anything I could have said to you would change things or make you feel any better. But I was really saddened and bitter when news of her demise reached me. I am sorry. Please forgive me if my actions, or lack of any, was unsympathetic to you."

"It's okay. It had nothing to do with you. I am sorry. I shouldn't take it out on you. You should forgive me for my behaviour." I was angry with myself. I needed to let it go and move on. I felt mortified for even thinking it, but I knew it was time I accepted that she was never coming back.

"There is nothing to forgive, Sebastian. I understand. Keep in touch if you can. I know we only knew each other for a short time, but I wish we had spent more time together. And I meant it when I said I consider you family. If you ever need my help again, you know I will always be willing to give it. Bye for now, son, and take good care of yourself."

"Thank you, Mason. Goodbye." I was glad I called him. I knew now that I was a step closer to finding Hanna. It felt good talking to Mason, knowing he would have my back if the need ever arose.

## Sebastian

I waited impatiently for whomever he was going to send. I was not sure if he would send someone to me or if it would just be a phone conversation. Meanwhile, I knew I was one step closer to finding Hanna and felt relieved and happy at the prospect of seeing her again. I wondered if I would stick around this time or leave like I had before. I knew I couldn't make that decision until I saw her again. I got up from my sofa and went to sit by the window. I looked up at the sky and all the many stars that lined up its walls and wondered what she was doing right now.

Then my phone rang. A man named Patrick told me that Mason had asked him to call. I couldn't believe how quickly it was all happening. He asked me for names and previous addresses. I gave him Joan and Joseph's address, with no mention of Hanna. I asked him how long it would take to find them, and he said he would call me as soon as he found anything. I hung up and went to have a shower. I was getting dressed to go hunting when the phone rang again. Patrick gave me an address and hung up. I was impressed. The joy within me couldn't be measured. I went hunting happily. I was finally closer to seeing Hanna.

## Chapter 8

I must have thought about my reaction to when I would eventually meet Hanna over a thousand times. I even got in front of the mirror and practised introducing myself to her should I get the courage to do so. In the end, whether I meet her or not, it's seeing her and knowing that she is fine, well looked after, and loved, that truly matters to me.

The next day, before heading out, I looked at the address I had jotted down. Hanna's family was now living in a village called Grosmont, somewhere in Yorkshire. I got in my car and sank into the luxurious, cream, leather seat, rolled up the dark-tinted window to keep the sun off me, and started the four-hour drive to Yorkshire. After about three hours of driving, I parked on the side, brought out my map, and then followed the route to her house. I pulled to a stop just opposite the house.

I wanted to jump out of the car immediately. I could no longer stomach the thought of waiting another minute, but I had no choice. It's not like I could just go and knock on the door and introduce myself. In fact, I had no plan as to what I was going to do once I got here. I took a couple of deep breaths to calm myself and then glued myself to my seat. I kept telling myself that I only came here to see her and nothing more. Over and over I said out loud, just to convince myself, "Once I see her and know she is fine, I will be gone."

I looked over at the detached, stone-built house on the edge of a small forest. It had four, big, wooden windows and a double-door entry. It was very pretty to look at. There were trees in a row along the drive leading towards the house. From where I sat I could make out a willow tree sitting alone in the front garden on the right side. The house looked like it was sitting on about two acres of land. I was impressed with it and happy they were spending the money the way I wanted it spent. I liked that there were trees around—it meant I could come round and stay hidden without anyone being any the wiser. There were two cars parked outside on the drive, and I wondered if she were home.

I closed my eyes and told myself again, "Once I see her and know she is fine, I will be gone." I had to keep convincing myself of that. I wished that she needed me and that she knew me. I wished that she missed me and would beg me never to leave again. I wished, most of all, that she loved me. Irritated at myself for wanting and wishing for things that would never happen, I reached into my glove compartment and took out my dark glasses and put them on—I had to remain anonymous in case I was spotted by anyone.

Then I heard a silky laughter coming from behind me, and then . . . nothing. I closed my eyes and concentrated on where exactly the laughter was coming from. Another outburst of laughter rang into my ears. I sniffed a familiar scent, but it was diluted with this weird, awful, wretched dog scent. Immediately I turned my attention to where the scent came from, and there she was: this slender girl. The wind was blowing her hair away from the sides of her face. She was standing a few feet from my car with her side to me. Everything in me froze for a few minutes. I couldn't believe my eyes. I was looking at her. I knew it was her, because I could never mistake her scent for another, not in a million years. It seemed as though everything went by slowly as I watched her. My stomach dropped, and I was suddenly nervous. She had grown into an extremely beautiful creature of about five-feet, seven-inches tall. Her light blonde hair glowed as it blew in the wind away from her pale skin as though she were basking in the full glory of the sun. She smiled and gestured at someone. I followed her elegant hands with my eyes until I noticed the boy with her. I returned my gaze to her, still amazed by her beauty. She smiled at him, and he must have said something to her, but I didn't hear it; I wasn't listening. I just couldn't take my eyes off her. I watched as her cheeks flushed scarlet, and her red, luscious lips parted to say something to him—for the first time, I was jealous.

Then she turned in my direction for a second with a curious look as if she knew I was watching her, but I knew she did not see me because of the tinted window. There was something odd about her expression. Her eyes seemed to pierce through me. I did not take my eyes off her—I could not have even if I had wanted to. I could feel myself drowning in those big, beautiful, piercing blue eyes. She looked even more beautiful than I thought when she had her side to me. She turned away and resumed talking to the boy beside her. I had forgotten about him until then. He said something to her again. Then she giggled at him again, and it annoyed me that she enjoyed his company. I was irritated because he was capable of making her smile while I remained a stranger. It upset me even more because there was nothing I could do about it and it looked like she liked him. I wondered how she felt about him and what he meant to her. I couldn't stand him being so close to her. I looked at the boy I was jealous of. He had thick, dark hair and olive skin. He was wearing a T-shirt and cargo shorts. He was about a foot taller than Hanna. I could see why she would be attracted to him: He looked like the kind of boy most girls her age would love to be with. I disliked him immediately.

"You've seen her now, and she is fine. Now it's time to—" I couldn't bring myself to finish the sentence. I couldn't imagine leaving, not now. I wanted her to know me. I wanted her to like me. I listened in on their conversation. It seemed harmless enough, and there was nothing to indicate they were involved with each other emotionally, although I could pick up a few signals from him that told me he was into her and would want more from her if given the chance, that is if they were not an item already.

There was something also very wrong about him. He did not smell nice to me, not like humans do. His scent was different. I haven't come across such an appalling stench in all of my existence, yet he appears human. It bothered me, even more because of Hanna. Something wasn't right about him. I looked at her again, and she was leaning on him, trust written all over her face. I knew now that I couldn't leave. I had work to do. Like Mason had said, *we all have our secrets*, and I would love to find out what his secrets are.

*She needs me now more than ever to protect her from him*, I told myself. I wondered if I was making up an excuse to stay, and then I sniffed his scent again and convinced myself I was staying to protect her. I watched as they said goodbye. They hugged and gave each other a kiss on the cheek. I looked down for a moment, and by the time I looked back up, he had gotten on his bike and rode off. Hanna stood for a while staring at my car and then turned around and walked down the drive until she got in front of her house. She turned towards the car and looked directly at me, as if to let me know that she knew I was watching her, and then, with a smile, she went inside.

I must admit I was a little rattled by her behaviour. But then again, she probably was wondering what I was doing parked in front of her house. Reluctantly, I drove away and followed the boy unobserved. I had to find out where he lived. He left the main road and scurried into the woods. I parked my car and followed him on foot. He was gone by the time I made my way to the woods, so I started to track his horrendous scent until I found him entering a house. It wasn't exactly a house: it was a big castle that looked like it belonged in the sixteenth century. It was so big, you could fit a hundred people in it and still have space for twenty more. I wondered if he lived there, so I stayed hidden until I could find answers to my questions. Then I heard him speaking to people he referred to as Mum and Dad. They spoke of his sisters who were not back from school. A man came out of the house—I assumed it was Dad—and got into a car and drove away. The funny thing is that he had almost the same disgusting scent. I was happy I followed him. Now all I needed to do was uncover his secret. I looked at the sky; it was late. I checked my watch to confirm the time and ran back to where I had packed my car and then drove to the nearest hotel.

After checking in, I went out to hunt. When I returned, it was one in the morning. I had a quick shower to wash off the woodland before setting out for her house. This time around, I would be walking. I knew that I should wait until the next day, but I did not have the strength to stay away—not with her being so close.

I stood outside her house under the willow tree and just watched. I tried to listen to her breathing. I could hear all three of them sleeping. Joseph was snoring loudly, and Joan woke him up to stop him from snoring. I listened closely and intensely, but I couldn't hear her as loudly as I could hear her parents. I couldn't believe I was standing right outside of where she lived. I closed my eyes and tried to remember what she looked like this evening. I pictured her golden hair blowing in the wind, kissed by the sun, and her beautiful face and supple pale skin. I wondered if I could have raised her myself. I've ask myself that every day since being away from her, and I tell myself I did right by her. I gave her a chance at a normal life, and by the looks of things, I don't think I could have done a better job. I wondered why she had been looking at my car. It had felt like she could see me, even though I knew she couldn't have. Throughout the night, I just stayed outside of her house. It was comforting to be this close to her. It was a shame the sun would soon rise, or I could have remained there all day.

When I got back to my hotel, I drew the curtains shut, put a *do not disturb* sign outside my door, and then called reception to make sure no one came inside my room while I rested. I found it hard to rest, though. I kept contemplating my next move. I questioned why I was so jealous earlier. I had never felt like that before. I was so confused at the feelings coursing through me. I couldn't help it. I saw her face in my head nonstop. I always knew I loved her, but, to me, it was never the way a man loves a woman. Not that I am experienced enough to know the difference, since I have never felt this way before.

I still do not know why I felt so much contempt for that young boy, just because she smiled or giggled at his moronic joke. I shouldn't be mad at him because he made her smile. Thinking about it made me even more jealous. *I have no right to feel that way about her*, I told myself, and I shouldn't expect her to love me. She deserves better than me. I am not worthy of her love, just because I knew her as a baby, and not forgetting that I am the same monster who took her mother's life.

I wanted so much to meet her, even when I knew I shouldn't. My head knew better, but my whole being wanted to be in her life. I shut my eyes and started to think of ways to introduce myself to her, where I would meet her, and what I would say to her. *What if I can't speak once I meet her? What if I melt or freeze? What if she doesn't like me at all?* I tried to stop myself from thinking about her. The whole idea of her was draining me of strength, and I needed to rest. I shut my eyes and tried to think of my mother the last time I had seen her alive, and before I knew it, I found peace.

## Chapter 9

As soon as I was sure it was safe to come out, I was out on the street, heading straight to see a house that I had spoken about with an agent earlier in the day.

I have a habit of being on time, seeing that most work places close by five thirty. The sky was dark already, and it was only four thirty, exactly how I like my day to begin. It had rained earlier and, by the looks of things, it was still going to rain some more. I was early on purpose—I wanted to see the place for myself before the agent arrived.

The house was on the outskirts of town and very remote—I liked that about it. When I arrived, I took the time to quickly go round the house. It did not look like anyone had lived in it for a while, but it was well presented: Nothing structural needed doing from what I could see. I couldn't enter, but I could see inside through the windows. The decor was not to my taste—it was old and depressing. It looked as though it had sat for centuries. The walls were covered in old, mouldy, wallpaper, most of which was hanging off the walls. I could smell the moist from inside and knew if I decide to buy this, it would have to be boned and brought up to modern time. I have very delicate but expensive taste, especially when it comes to my living space. Having had a terrible childhood contributed to my desire for always wanting the best in everything. I was at the back garden when I heard the agent's car pulling in, and I quickly went round to the front of the house.

"Oh, hello. How are you?" His voice was strangely high, not like it sounded when I spoke to him over the phone, and his eyes expressed a little confusion. I could tell he wanted to know if I was the one planning to buy this house. I stood upright with my right hand in my pocket and the other behind me just so I could avoid shaking his hand. It was a gesture I had perfected over the years to avoid unnecessary body contact with humans. "Sorry I kept you waiting. My name is Michael. I take it we will be waiting for your father? It was he I spoke with earlier today, wasn't it?"

"Oh, yes it was," I said. "But I'm afraid you will be dealing with me from now on. He's only gone and left it all in my hands." I smiled.

"Oh, I see. In that case then, what do you think of the house itself from the outside?"

"I quite like it," I said.

"Oh, okay, that's good to hear. As you can see, this house dates back to the fifteenth century, and it's a gorgeous house that needs some tender loving care. A lot of work has been done to it over the years, but unfortunately, the last owner was not able to give it the love it deserves. I must warn you before we go inside, it will need a lot of cosmetic work, and if your father decides this is what he wants and puts in the work, it can finally return to its former glory. Anyway—enough said. Shall we go in now so I can show you the rest of the house?"

"Er—that won't be necessary. We'll take it." I had seen enough to know that I wanted it. Also as he doesn't own the house, he does not have the power to permit me entrance. So until the house becomes mine officially, I shall not be doing any entering.

"What? Are—are you sure? You've not even seen the inside. And how can you be sure it's what your father wants?"

"I have seen enough, and I like it already. Trust me on this. And don't worry about my father. As long as I like it, I'm very sure he will love it, too." I wanted this over with quickly. Every minute I spent here was time I could have spent watching Hanna, or coming up with a plan.

"Oh, but you don't even know what the asking price is," he said.

"Oh, that. Whatever it is, I am sure we can cover it. We'll take it."

"This is a first for me," he said, "but I tell you what—you will put my mind at rest if you could just take a look inside. I don't want you to rush into something you might regret later. If you remember, earlier I said it needed a lot of work doing to it," he insisted. I wish I had the time to take a tour around the house pretending I was interested in his sales technique, but I didn't. I will just have to stop him from nagging me.

"Er—sorry, may I call you Michael?" He nodded. "Okay, Michael. This house is for sale, and I like it. Now, all you need to do is tell me the asking price, and it will get paid as long as the vendor is still willing to sell. To me that sounds like a good deal, don't you think so?"

"Yes, but I will be happy if your father sees it as well," Michael said.

"And what good will that do either of us? C'mon, Michael, you want to sell the house, and I am willing to buy it. Let's not complicate things. I'm already sold, so you just name the price and tell me where to sign."

"Well, if you say so, but I must warn you, it's rather expensive. It comes with twenty-eight acres of land all around it and four stables. If you have a bit of time, I will walk you round the land."

"That won't be necessary," I said.

"Wow, this is definitely a first for me. I hope your father has deep pockets. I still think you should consult with him on this one before we commit ourselves."

"Michael, you are doing it again." I gave him that *you-have-to-do-as-you-are-told* look. I normally don't like to compel humans to have my way, but I can tell he wouldn't do a thing I wanted because he thought I'm too young to commit to buying a house this size. He was starting to annoy me. I tried to restrain myself from making him do as I wished. I could tell the stare I gave him was already working; why compel him also.

"Or—or not—er—as you wish. Um—This house is on the market for nine hundred and fifty thousand pounds, but you might also want to consider another one not too far from here if that is too high a price tag. I was going to show you and your father another house. I am very sure it should be in the range of your budget, if you tell me how much you are willing to spend."

I looked from him to the house and ignored his comment about another house. "Did you just say the asking price is nine hundred and fifty thousand? That is almost a million."

He looked at me as if to say *I told you so*, like it was too expensive for me to make such a decision without even taking a proper look at the house. "So are you sure you don't want us to wait for your father, or at least take a look," he asked smugly.

I wondered what his problem was. I thought agents died for this type of sale. In the days when I still fed on human blood, I would have gladly wiped that smug look off his face, but I am different now. I took a breath of air to calm myself down before I did something stupid. I walked away from him and considered what to do about him after this deal was done.

"Michael, if this house is on sale, then I am buying this one. Call the vendor and put in an offer for the asking price." He looked at me in shock, and his jaw dropped to the ground.

I walked over to him and handed him contact details for my hotel, careful not to let our hands touch. "You just do your part and see that the house is off the market. You would do well to drop all the documents I will need to sign at reception, and I will make sure that the money is paid to the vendor. I will need the keys to this house soon. So please don't let the process take too long." He just looked at me open-mouthed. I understood he didn't want me to spend money on a house I hadn't seen, but it's my money and my decision. His face still looked confused, but I had to go; I had no time to help him understand why he had just made so much money.

"Shouldn't you be celebrating? I mean, what's the most commission you get paid on a sale like this?" I smiled and left him there still staring at me. I was angry that I had wasted so much time convincing the real estate agent to sell me a house I could afford a thousand and more times over, instead of using the time to find out more about that boy from yesterday. I could have just compelled him from the start and have it over with like most vampires do, but I wanted to have a proper conversation, and he just proved to me that sometimes it is okay to control humans.

Eventually, after the completion of the sale, I will have to make Michael forget he ever saw me. That is the only solution to curious-minded humans, apart from killing them.

I went straight to the house of the boy from yesterday and waited patiently for about two hours, but he was nowhere to be found. Then it occurred to me that he probably was not home, but with Hanna. Quickly, as fast as I could, I ran to Hanna's house. I was right; he was just leaving her house. He was waving to her as she shut her door. It annoyed me that I had just spent the last two hours standing around waiting for him while he had been here all that time with her. I decided to let him go this time. I had all the time in the world to sort him out later. First I had to know if she liked him more than I thought she should.

Again, her parents were home, and I began to wonder if they ever left the house. I hid in my usual spot behind the willow tree. It was dinnertime—I could tell by the stench oozing from their house, and to think a lifetime ago I called it food. It's not like I am doing any better now, but what I survive on is far better than what humans call food. At first it was quiet—a lot of chewing but no talking. I wondered what it was they were eating that required so much silence. Then just when I thought the silent treatment was never going to end, Joan spoke, and thank heaven she did, because I was getting exasperated listening to their jaws moving up and down.

"Hanna, you and Huritt Denali seem to be getting very close these days. You are hardly apart. What I am trying to say is, you are not little kids anymore."

"So?"

"It's just an observation. I'm not saying there is anything wrong with that, which brings me to my next question."

"Mum, can I just eat in peace? I think I already know how this is going to end."

Now I know his name is Huritt; that will save me from calling him *the boy from yesterday* each time he comes to mind.

"Don't get lippy with me, young girl. What I am getting at is this. You do like him a lot, don't you?"

"Off course I like him, Mum. Is there a purpose to these questions?"

I wonder how much she likes him. Just when I thought I would not get an answer to that question, Joan helped me out again. It was as if she could read my mind.

"I know I shouldn't be asking you this, but you do realise that he likes you more than a friend, don't you? I mean, anyone with eyes can see the way he looks at you and follows you about. He adores you. I would even say he might be in love with you."

"Mum! Don't say that. You don't know that. Huritt and I are just friends and nothing more. It doesn't matter that he follows me about. Stop seeing things that don't exist."

"That's my point exactly, Hanna. You see him as just a friend. Perhaps it's time for you to start appreciating him more. He's good looking and comes from a very good family, and we've all known each other for many years. What's not to love about him?"

"What are you trying to say, Mum?"

"I'm saying that you should give him a chance. Who knows where it might lead?"

"For heaven sakes, Mum, I am seventeen. I don't want a serious relationship, and I definitely don't want one with my best friend. Dad! A little help here please."

Joan continued ignoring her cry for help. "And you're becoming a woman. You're going to be eighteen soon, and its time you started taking things like this a little more seriously. You're an extremely beautiful girl who's never dated a boy before. I mean, no boy that I know of, unless you're hiding things from us. I just think Huritt would be a very good start for you."

Yes, I thought it was time Joseph helped a little here. What is Joan thinking: *he comes from a good family*? A family that reeks of dog more like. For a moment I thought we were on the same side here, and then Joseph spoke.

"I am sorry, Hanna, you know your mother. Once she gets an agenda into her head, there is no talking her out of it. You don't have to do anything you don't want to do, dear. If he's just your friend, then that's what he is. Ignore her, darling."

*Spoken like a real man* I thought, but then Joan was not finished.

"Yes, Joseph, keep encouraging her to ignore me. I am only looking out for her. She doesn't have a boyfriend. Our daughter has never dated a boy. Maybe she hates boys, I don't know. Maybe she plays for the other team, a lesbian. And if she is not, she should be dating now. When I was her age, I was on my third boyfriend before you came along."

"Too much information, Mum. Keep it to yourself, thank you. I don't need advice on whom I should be dating, let alone about Huritt. And I know I should just ignore what you said earlier, but just to put you straight, I don't play for the other team. I just haven't found that special person yet. Come to think of it, nobody in this town attracts me. Perhaps I am just not interested in giving my heart to someone else. Mum, just let me be. I promise I'll let you know when my circumstances change."

"Real love takes time to build, darling. You need to nurture it. Maybe yours has been Huritt all along, but you just can't see it. We have all come to love him. I mean, what harm can there be in giving it a try, not to mention the fact that it wouldn't hurt our family to be united with his family. Talk to her, Joseph. She listens better to you. We don't want to lose him now that he is besotted by her. Who knows what can happen if he meets someone else and loses interest in her?"

Joseph sighed. Not only was I frustrated with Joan, but so was her husband. I wondered why she was so determined to see Hanna and Huritt united. If she only saw them like I did.

"Mum, you do realise I am still here, don't you? Why don't you just cart me away now? Didn't you understand a word of what I just said? I am not dating Huritt Denali. And I am not going to date someone just so you are happy. You don't think I want to have a boyfriend? I do. It's just a pity we live in such a small town. All the boys are taken. Every girl my age is in love with a boy or breaking up with one. Some just love to have sex with a boy they met five minutes ago; maybe that's what I will do, too. I don't know. My point is this: I have not found that person yet. I can also tell you that if I do, it is not going to be Huritt. Gosh, he is like a brother to me, Mum. I cannot even bear to think of him as anything beyond that. And just so you know, Mum, I am not blind. I know he wants more from me, but I have also been careful not to get his hopes up, because I don't feel that way about him. I don't see myself with him like that."

"Hanna, you are young and naïve," Joan continued.

"Drop it, Joan," Joseph said quietly.

She ignored him and continued, "I am sorry. You may think am going on about this, but the best marriages are the ones you have with your best friend—"

"Marriage! Mum, what are you on about? I can't believe I am actually hearing this. Sorry, Dad, you have to excuse me.

I cannot do these serious marriage talks. If you need me, I will be in my room." I could hear her climbing up the stairs and mumbling something under her breath.

I was relieved to find out that there was nothing romantic between Hanna and the Huritt boy. That aside, I have never found anyone as annoying as Joan. Tonight she was like a dog with a bone. Joan and Joseph started to argue between themselves after Hanna left the table, and I wasn't surprised, not after the debate over Huritt.

"Joan, you are unbelievable sometimes. She is still just a child. Let her breathe, Joan, and stop this Huritt campaign. What is it that you want from that family anyway that you don't have already?"

"Stop it! I am just looking out for her future, like you should be doing. That's what good parents do. They secure their children's future."

He laughed aloud. "You are even crazier than I thought you were. You call this securing her future? You know what you are doing? You are driving her away from you with this stupid matchmaking that you are so obsessed with."

"Call it whatever you want to label it, Joseph, but I know I am right and what I am doing, I am doing for her. You are not the only one who loves her, you know. I am her mother. I raised her, and I think that gives me the right to try and secure her future."

"I am not questioning your love for our daughter, woman, but there are other ways to look out for her without pawning her out to that family because they have lots of money. We are doing fine. Since she came into our lives we have never lacked for a thing and that should speak volumes to you." Then he lowered his voice. My guess is that he did not want Hanna to hear what he had to say next. "Think, darling. If someone out there cares so much and generously gives a million a year to make sure she doesn't lack a thing, how many more lengths do you think he or she would go to make sure her future is secure? I say you drop these shenanigans now and let her be. No more matchmaking talks. She befriends and dates whomever she chooses when she is ready. You should be more concerned about other matters like, God forbid, should this person ever return to claim her. What would we do then? She is all we have."

"I never thought of it like that before," Joan replied.

"Well, you should. I am going down to the pub. Apologise to your daughter. I can't believe you're talking about marriage to a teenager."

"Joseph, wait. There is something we should talk about."

"What is it now, Joan? Paul is waiting for me down at the pub."

"I know, and I'm sorry, it's just—I know we've spoken about this lot of times before now, but it's just that now you've raised the topic of this person, I've got this nagging concern at the back of my mind."

"What about it, Joan? We've gone over this numerous times."

"I know, but don't you think it's time we stopped taking the money? It feels wrong all these years."

"Joan, we've talked about this. We take the money because, if we stop now after seventeen years, we don't know what the result might be. We could lose her altogether. She is more important to me than any amount of money, and I can't imagine not having her in our life or her ever finding out. I say we continue and take whatever we are given, not because we always need it, but because we didn't say no in the past. We watched as each year our bank account filled, and we've been living a good life with Hanna. If we stop, and whoever is responsible comes knocking, how are we going to defend ourselves to the world? It doesn't hurt our Hanna, and sure hasn't hurt you, so let's not rock the boat."

"Okay, whatever you say, Joseph."

"For the last time, leave it alone, Joan, and, please, can you make sure you don't ever raise this again, not with her in the house?"

"I'm sorry," Joan said.

I heard him slam the door as he went out and got into his car. Moments later, I heard Hanna coming down the stairs. "I am going out, Mum."

"And where do you think you are going at this time of the night?" Joan questioned her.

"I am going to Emily's house. I will be back soon," Hanna replied.

"Well, I don't think so, young lady. It's dark outside. Why don't you go see her tomorrow? I hate worrying about you."

"Mum, she only lives down the road. It's not like I am going clubbing. And I bet that's what I should be doing. You do still remember what it feels like to be a teenager, don't you?" Hanna mouthed off to Joan.

"You will watch your tone with me, young lady. I am not stopping you from living your life. I am only looking out for you, because I love you. I hope you realise that, Hanna. I may seem difficult to you, but everything I do for you is so you're happy and safe. You are my only child, after all," Joan said.

"I am sorry, Mum. I didn't mean to raise my voice. You know I love you, Mum. It's just that you go a little crazy on me sometimes. So can I still go? I won't be long, I promise."

"Not that again, Hanna. Its nearly nine o clock. I thought I already said—"

"C'mon, Mum. I will soon be eighteen. Kids as young as fourteen—what am I saying—even younger than that—do what they like these days. I am just going round the corner, and I will be back before you know it."

"I know kids younger than you do what they like these days, and I am glad that's not you. I raised you better than that, Hanna. I don't know what's so important that you and Emily can't wait until tomorrow to deal with, but since it means a lot to you, this once—*just this once*—I will allow you to go, and don't stay out late."

"Oh thanks, Mum! You're the best! I promise I will be back soon."

"You had better be," Joan warned. Then I heard the front door open and close.

I secretly followed Hanna until she got to her friend's house. I observed her as she rang the bell. She looked back nervously like she knew someone was watching her. I froze for a minute until someone opened the door for her. I wondered why she was so nervous. She couldn't have spotted me. I could hear her and her friend giggling and talking about a boy in Emily's life. I tried not to listen to what they were discussing. I was prepared to hang around for a while but, to my surprise, they were saying goodbye already. I wondered why she didn't just give Emily a call and save herself all that argument with her mum. I walked discreetly behind her until she was safe inside her house again.

Now that I knew she didn't love the boy, Huritt, I noticed the rage of jealousy I had for him disappeared. I had nothing to fear now. I knew she didn't belong to him, and I could now just focus on finding out what his secrets were.

I was glad that I could count on Joseph and his wisdom to always do right by Hanna. Listening to Joan and Hanna earlier, and the bond they have, made me happy I had left her with them. No one could have done a better job of raising her than those two. Joan is a little strict and a bit pushy with her, but I don't think it's a bad thing. She is a good woman and a good mother. I can't believe the child she didn't want to touch years ago has grown on her this much. Mothers can be controlling sometimes, so was my mother, and I can't fault her for looking out for her future. My mother did the same by turning me into a vampire. She also tried to match me with Isobel. Joseph, on the other hand, you could read like a book: what you see is what you get. He would make a very good vampire I should think, not that I am planning on making him one.

I went back to my hotel earlier than I had planned. There was no need of torturing myself by being this close to her. I had to keep a little distance for sanity's sake until I was able to come up with a good excuse to bring us together. She seemed a little rattled. I must not allow her the chance to spot me before I get a chance to properly introduce myself to her. I still don't understand why she gets twitchy and nervous when I am around. If I don't do something fast, she might actually spot me one day, and that would be it; she would brand me her stalker, and there would be no redeeming that.

## Chapter 10

For another two weeks, I kept going over to her house every night, waiting until dawn, just to be close to her. A couple of times, I saw her walking home with her friend, Emily. I thought about seizing the opportunity to somehow find a way to introduce myself, but nothing I came up with felt right, so I decided to wait until I found a proper reason.

One day as they ate their dinner, I heard Hanna tell her parents that she was going to be restarting a piano class in the evening after college. I knew this was the chance I had been waiting for, but I wasn't sure how soon she was going to be starting this lesson or where it would be taking place. Then, days later, she confirmed her enrolment as they sat together watching television one evening. I heard Joan asking her about the days she would be attending and the time the lesson finished. At last I had all the information I needed to make our meeting look genuine.

Excitedly, I quickly went to search out the place and enrolled for lessons, too. I also found out that this place isn't only for piano lessons, it also was an art and music centre where most of the kids in town spend much of their time in the evening. All sorts of lessons were taking place from dance classes, to acting classes, book clubs, you name it. It was great, because it meant I could fit in the crowd and plan my move perfectly and, if for some reason I was too cowardly to go through with it, I could just blend back into the crowd.

It's not like I needed any training when it came to the keyboard—I like to think myself a maestro. That's one of the plus sides of living very long and having all the time in the world at your disposal: you can try to learn something over and over again, if you are willing, until you can do it with both eyes closed. However, if pretending to be an amateur was going to give me the chance to at least say hello to Hanna, then I would grab it with both hands.

A day before the lessons were to start, I found out how well Hanna played the keyboard. It made me wonder why she thought she needed lessons. She was playing for her parents. I lay on a branch and shut my eyes as I listened to her fingers flow over the keys. I felt so proud of her. I bet she was only taking these lessons to escape her parents. Then another idea popped into my head: I could pretend I was really struggling with my lessons. Maybe, if I were lucky, she would offer to teach me. As terrible as I felt about lying to her, I also knew telling her the truth would never help me here. I was desperate and ready to lie a million times over, if it gave me a chance to get to meet with her.

I arrived at the music centre before it was time to start. I just wanted to familiarize myself with the humans I was going to be surrounding myself with so as not to do anything irrational, like going too close to smell a human because I couldn't resist its scent. I sat in the lobby in the far corner so as not to be in any human's way, waiting for Hanna to appear and going through what I would say to her if I were lucky enough to have her look my way.

I was struggling as I waited—my nostrils were being bombarded with many different scents and flavours. It was crazy, and I was losing the plot. Something wasn't right. I was always in control of myself. I wasn't a newborn, so why was my body reacting like I had just turned? This was supposed to be my opportunity, and already I could feel it slipping away. I tried to calm down, but my nerves were getting the best of me. It's because of her. The anticipation of being really close to her has somehow messed with my whole system. Now I was seconds away from ripping a human open for blood, even though I had been *celibate* for a while. The tension of it all was too much for me. I couldn't be like this around her. Perhaps this had been a bad idea; I should never have come.

I got up swiftly to leave before I relapsed there, of all places. I was playing with danger. I wasn't ready for this, not now. In my effort to make a quick getaway, I pushed the door hard and swung it open. Unbeknownst to me there was a human on the other side reaching for the door. It was too late. By the time I realized there was someone there, the door had hit her in the face already. She lost her balance and headed for the ground.

I quickly grabbed her before she hit the ground. I am usually very careful, and I didn't understand why I was suddenly such a wreck. I hate it when I am not in control, and it seemed everything was out of my hands. Nothing was happening the way I had expected. I had not fed properly for almost a month; the squirrels and rabbits clearly were not enough. I should have gone out to hunt big game. I always knew I needed something more substantial, but my obsession with being with Hanna had made me ignore my needs.

Carefully, I brought the girl back on her feet. I tried not to hold her too close to me—it was bad enough that I had smashed her face. I didn't want to do more damage by squashing her body also. But then I sniffed in her scent and smelled a scent that has been part of me since she was a baby, the same scent I had bathed in since I arrived.

I could tell even without looking that I was holding Hanna. To think I had hurt her when all I wanted to do was protect her. I had just swung the door in her face. Her hands were on her forehead, and she was bleeding. I closed my eyes and tried to ignore the blood dripping down the side of her face, which I found very hard to do. I couldn't believe what was happening. It was as if the world was testing me, and I knew I was going to fail. I told myself to just shut my eyes and not look at her and pretend she was someone else. But it *wasn't* anyone else; it was my Hanna, the very one I swore to protect, and I was losing control. Her blood was too strong to ignore. I wanted to touch it and taste it just a little. I lifted my free hand towards her forehead and wiped off some of her blood and stared at it in amazement. Then I heard myself say her name at the back of my mind. *Why her, why now?* I thought. Why does it have to be today that my body wants to relapse? The universe must be against me. Of all the humans who were around, why did it choose her to test me?

The blood was beginning to overpower me as I looked at it trickling down, wasting away. It felt wrong, but it was Hanna's blood. I held my breath and shut my eyes, so I wouldn't smell it or see it. Even so, I could still see it in my head and taste it at the back of my throat. It had taken over my senses. Every part of me was quivering and longing for it. *Just a taste will do*, I told myself.

"Are you all right?" Hanna said. "You look like you are going to be sick."

I opened my eyes. She had spoken to me. This is what I wanted, what I had come here for. This is what I had been looking forward to all these years, and here was I, battling my lust for her blood. That was not how I wanted her to see me or talk to me, not in such terrible circumstances. I was fighting myself to control the urge to drink her blood publicly. With all the blood pouring down the side of her face, she still looked like an angel. She looked at me like she knew I was struggling and fighting a battle inside to not attack her.

"Don't worry, you'll live. I'm the one who got a cut to the head. You can let go of me now and thanks for not letting me fall," she said quietly with a smile that melted my heart—if I had one. I did not understand how she could be so gracious about it. I had just battered her, yet it was she who spoke the pacifying words.

Something had happened the moment she began to speak. I don't understand it, but I began to lose my appetite, and the power the blood had over me was gone, like it had meant nothing. All I could see now was her face. She was glowing, just like she did the day I arrived. Was it only me who noticed, or were there other humans who could see this as well. I looked over my shoulder at the humans now rushing up to help, but no one seemed to notice anything. And before I knew it, they had taken her away from me and were carefully leading her to a seat. I stood and watched as everyone gathered around her to see if she was all right. There were so many people around her now that I could barely see her face.

I felt terrible having caused her pain. I tried looking at her through the crowd surrounding her. I caught a glimpse of her face, and, to my surprise, she was looking at me with a smile plastered on her face, as if to tell me it was okay. It was as though she knew I was dying inside for what I had done and *was about to do* to her. Confused by her reaction and annoyed with myself, I decided to leave the scene. There was nothing I could do for her now. I had let myself down. After all those years of abstaining from human blood just so I wouldn't put her in danger, and the moment I get close to her, I almost bite her.

If I had left weeks ago, right after I saw her as originally planned, none of this would have happened. I knew that to make sure she was never in danger or suffered any harm from me again I had to leave town immediately and let her continue her life without my interference. As much as I knew that it was the right thing to do, I didn't know if I had the strength or power to actually carry it through.

There were no words to describe how disappointed I felt. I had let myself down, and I had let her down as well. I always knew it was impossible to seek any form of relationship with her, which is why I had given her away in the first place. Nothing had changed except time. She is still human, and I am what I am. I was stupid to allow such an unrealistic idea to overpower me. *Love, what do I know about love?* I questioned myself. If this was love, then I didn't want it. It had made me careless and unpredictable.

I went to my hotel to pack my things. There was a message for me. I already knew what it was: the documents and keys to the house I had just bought. It was the third time Michael had left a message for me. He first called to tell me the vendor had accepted my offer. The second time he required my signature and gave me an account into which to put the money. This message says I own the house. I should be happy now, but I was not. I was dying inside and saddened with the turnout of events. I had built up Hanna in my head, and the realisation of it all was bitter. Why couldn't I just forget about her and let her carry on with her life. Why am

I so weak? Here I thought humans were the weak ones, yet I crumble all the time before her.

I knew then why it was so wrong for vampires to have any kind of affection towards humans. They are too fragile to be with and, even if by some miracle they survive you, they will die eventually and leave you broken hearted. I threw my clothes into my bag in annoyance. Most relationships between humans and vampires that I have heard of do not end well. Eventually, the human accidentally becomes the food. Why did I think this would be any different? I was not going to let her suffer the same fate, especially because we were in a town where proper food is limited.

I had finished packing my bags when I saw the keys and documents to the house I had just bought. What do I do with it? If I keep it, it will just be another excuse to come back into her life. I sat for a while and muddled over what to do with it. My head told me to put it straight back on the market, but I refused to entertain the idea. It was foolish to just sell it, when Joan and Joseph could have it. Like everything else I had given them, they had taken without question, so I doubted they would question this latest addition.

I thought about sending them the documents by post, but a part of me wanted to deliver it myself—for obvious reasons. I didn't try to talk myself out of it once I had made the decision. I picked up my stuff, threw it on the backseat of my car, and drove towards their house. On my way there, I saw Hanna's friend Huritt and a friend of his on their bikes. I remembered I had not even found out what he was, but, then again, he did not look like he would endanger her, and I did not want any excuse to make me stay. I knew if I told myself I was only staying to find out what I could about him, that I would be drawn all over again into wanting to be with Hanna.

Little did I know that things were about to change in ways that even I hadn't expected. By the time I was within one mile of Hanna's house, I was hit by the scent of vampires. I had been here for a while now and had not yet come across any vampires, so to sense the presence of vampires this close to Hanna's house troubled me. I began to imagine the worst. I knew I was bad for her, but I couldn't leave her at the mercy of other vampires

The scent was so potent, I could tell vampires were still around or had just left. I immediately parked the car around the corner, got out, and ran straight to Hanna's house. I needed to make sure everyone and everything were as they should be. I couldn't feel her presence, which was a good thing. She was probably still at the art and music centre. I started to track the scent back to where I had first sensed it and followed it until I got to the middle of the road, where it seemed to just disappear. This could mean something or nothing at all, and it worried me. The vampires could be passing through, or they could have business here in this town, which meant that everyone, including Hanna, were in danger. There was something peculiar about the scent. I am not the best tracker, but I knew I had met these vampires before, only I couldn't put names to the scents. There was no storming off for me anymore, not when something big could be happening anytime soon. This was the time for me to protect Hanna like I always promised I would. *Perhaps that was all I am good for,* I thought, *to help fight other monsters like me.*

I stayed in my usual hiding spot and watched as Hanna drove back home. She looked all right, but I still couldn't forgive myself for bringing her harm and for what I could have done. I was exactly like the monsters I was trying to protect her from. There was no point in pretending to be any better. I felt even worse, because in my deluded mind I thought I had changed for her sake, and it pains me to think I am still that monster my mother warned me about.

I stayed until almost dawn before going back to the hotel. I made the decision to wait around until I was sure she was out of harm's way. I needed to figure out why we had visitors in town, which made me feel useful, even though Hanna didn't know me or what I was doing for her sake. It was important to me that she stayed safe. I knew sacrificing my time wouldn't pay for the disaster from my last encounter with her. Nonetheless, I was happy to be doing something for her, even if it meant that was all I would do for the rest of her life.

Two weeks later, and I still had not seen nor perceived any vampires since that one day. I was hungry and needed to go hunting. I knew I should never allow myself to become desperately hungry, but I lived with the constant fear that something might happen to Hanna while I was away from her. For that reason, I resorted to raiding a nearby farm. I left the dead animals in such a way as to make it look like a fox or bunch of wild dogs had attacked them.

I had always known it wasn't wise to stay in a hotel. Generally speaking, I struggle every day with ignoring the desire to feed on humans, even though I had been off the diet for years. But living amongst humans is the best way to gain control for someone like me. It is a dangerous decision, but my mother trained me by using humans as bait. This time around, I knew I could no longer continue to live among them, because I get hungry a lot. So I made the decision to move into my newly bought house until I was sure Hanna was safe.

The floor creaked as I walked inside. The door made a loud screeching noise as I shut it behind me. Dust and spider webs were everywhere, and my nose could just about tolerate the smell of mould. I reached for the light switch and flicked it on. Lit up, the house looked like one Dracula would love to live in. Everything was falling off the walls and the ceiling looked like it was about to cave in. I understood then why Michael was insistent that I see the inside. I had seen a little through the window that day, but I never thought it was this rotten. I wondered how long it had been since anyone had lived here. I went to the windows and closed the dirty drapes. I was tired and emotionally drained, and I needed to rest so I could think things through. Although the house was awful, it didn't bother me that much, because I knew I could fix it. What did bother me was the situation with Hanna and the mess that could be visiting this town soon. That I *didn't* know how to fix, and it stressed me.

I glanced round the living room for somewhere to lie down. Old furniture and books were everywhere I looked. A pile of old newspapers were stacked on a long, filthy chase. I shoved the stack to the floor and lay on the chase, supporting my feet with a stool. I gave the room one last look before shutting down for a much-needed sleep.

I woke up earlier than usual. If I was going to live here, then work needed to be done. I called an interior decorator who arrived an hour later. I told her I wanted the whole house redone, including the creaky floors. I placed a special emphasis on dark curtains and a bright, airy feel all throughout the house. She understood what I wanted, and I had a good feeling that she could deliver. We were on the same page. She was a bit sceptical, however, and I knew she was wondering whether I had the money, or needed approval first, to do work of such magnitude. I took her aside and persuaded her to get started on the work. There was no need arguing with her. Sometimes, it's just easier to not have to explain things to people. She left soon afterwards with the keys, and I left the house immediately and checked back into the hotel until the work was finished.

# Chapter 11

Every night I went to Hanna's house and stayed until almost daybreak before returning to the hotel. That was all I seemed to do now, and, as boring as it may seem, I always looked forward to it. It made me feel important, like I mattered to her. I felt useful, alive, and needed. I must be honest though, it was hard for me to be so close, yet so far away, but I knew it was best to stay away.

A month after I hired the interior decorator, she had completed all the work and I moved into my newly-refurbished house. I started to enjoy living in the same town as Hanna, and thoughts of moving on, although paramount, were somehow pushed to the back of my mind. Since that one day, I had not sensed any vampire scent around, which probably meant they were just passing through, but I knew it would be foolish to rule out a return visit. Most vampires I know stake out a town they wish to settle in to see if the territory belongs to another vampire before settling in. This has caused many a great war amongst our kind. I don't know what these vampires want, but I will die before I let Hanna live in the same town as vampires.

I limited my feeding to once a week so I would not be away from Hanna for too long. Each time I went hunting, I never felt at peace. The farms around have suffered a little because of my inability to go far for food. I am constantly petrified about leaving Hanna. Sometimes, in my head, I hear her screaming for help, and then I run to her house only to find that she is fine. The lack of food is beginning to become a problem, and the farmers are beginning to guard their farms more. They have no idea what's killing their animals. Although I can get to the animals without their knowledge, I don't want to push it. If I am found, I would have to kill a human to cover up my identity. Because of this, I have to go farther to hunt, which means leaving Hanna alone a few hours into the night. As it is, I have already pushed myself to the limit. I was starving and there was no way around it for me, so I went out of town early to make it back on time.

By the time I arrived for my daily shift at Hanna's, they had gone to bed. I missed the sound of her voice and her gentle laugh. I have become addicted to listening to her every night; it's what kept me going. I walked around the house quietly just to make sure everything was as it should be. I could sense all three of them in the house, so I went to my usual spot, lay on the floor, and shut my eyes in relief. I was happy I had fed and that Hanna was fine, even though I hadn't been around. I was beginning to wonder if I had made up all this danger just to keep myself here. I shouldn't be here, because no vampires are coming. Did I even sense them, or did I just make them up in my head so I could be with her (if I can call what I am doing as being with her)? But I know what I sensed. Whether I chose to go or stay did not cancel out the fact that vampires had come here two months ago.

It was completely silent, not even the birds chirped, and that's how I like it. My ears were to the ground, and I knew if anything moved I would hear it. Everything within a mile of her house was now very recognizable to me. I tried to stop myself from thinking about her, but, as if to punish myself, all I can see each time I close my eyes is the look in her eyes that unfortunate day and the warmth showing on her face afterwards as she tried to reassure me that she was fine. I felt like I was back in front of her, vulnerable and insecure. Having lived for almost two centuries, I can honestly say I have never felt so helpless in the presence of anyone until I met her.

Then her scent hit me afresh. I opened my eyes to check where she was. To my surprise, it was as if I had conjured her, because she was standing right in front of me. Like lightening I was on my feet. I couldn't believe my eyes. I shut them and reopened them just to make sure my mind wasn't playing tricks on me. She was as real as the very tree I was lying under.

I should have heard or sensed her before she got this close to me. Once again, I had allowed my emotions to garble my concentration. If I hadn't been thinking about her, I probably would not have been caught by her. My head was rambling, and a million thoughts jumped around my mind. What would I say to her? How would I explain my presence here? Stunned, I just stared at her, confused. How did she know I was hiding here? And what was she doing out so late in this freezing cold? She had on a long, cream-coloured, nightdress with a dressing gown on top, which didn't look like it would protect her from the cold.

"Hello," she said and smiled at me. I was still stunned; I didn't know what to say to her. "What are you doing out here in the cold? You are going to catch your death out here, you know." She spoke to me like I was a friend she had known for a long time. I didn't know what to say to her, and my lips wouldn't part with words. Why is she not freaking out instead? I wondered why she was concerned about me, considering she doesn't know me, plus I was trespassing on her property. "Hey, wait a minute. I have seen you before, haven't I?" she asked, looking puzzled, but I was still too shocked by her presence to say anything.

"Ah! You are the one! I remember now. You're the guy from the centre, the one who bumped into me. You took off. Why did you leave? Is that why you're here now? Is that why you've come?" She had two of her left fingers on her cupid bow lips, each finger resting on each lip, parting them just a little. It was only then I saw that she was surprised by my presence here. I nodded in response, as partly it was true. And then she smiled again.

"Saying sorry would have done it, you know. You don't have to kill yourself in this cold. The weather is horrible, don't you think? And I wouldn't even have known why you died here," she said jokingly, and I was forced to smile. I liked her humour. If anyone had told me that I would be standing here this night talking with her, I wouldn't have believed it.

"The news would have read *A teenage boy was found frozen to death in a garden*, my garden, and I wouldn't even have known you died because of me," she teased again. This time I allowed myself a proper smile. A mild wind blew her hair across her face, and I watched as she gently brushed it back. She seemed at ease with me, and I liked that, but at the same time I was worried, because she didn't really know me. I was still just a stranger in her garden.

I couldn't stop myself from staring at her; I was taken by her beauty. She was undeniably beautiful. She didn't even need the sun to glow; there was radiance around her even in the dark. She didn't seem bothered that I was rudely staring at her. She looked as though she was thinking about something. My gaze fell upon her lips again, and I watched as she bit her lower lip absentmindedly. An unexplained feeling began to rise within me, and it felt like I loved her even more. I didn't think it was possible to love her more than I already did, but I guess I was wrong. This time around, it felt different, different from how I felt about her as a baby, different from how I had felt about her thirteen years ago. If I am truthful, I have felt it since I first saw her that day in my car. *Is it right that I should feel this way about her?* I questioned myself. She is like my daughter. I mean, I see myself as her guardian, yet I can't shake this feeling I am having for her. The more I look at her, the more I know I have fallen for her and would find it really hard not to be part of her life.

I tried to compose myself and averted my eyes from her lips. I gazed at her forehead where she had sustained a terrible cut because of me. But to my surprise, there was no evidence of a cut, not even a scratch. *How is that possible*, I wondered? She noticed I was looking at her forehead and touched the spot where the wound should have been and said, "I told you it wasn't worth killing yourself over."

At last, I found my tongue. "How—how—how is that possible?" I asked, fighting the urge to touch it myself. "I was there. I saw the damage I did to you and all that blood pouring out, but now—nothing. There's nothing there," I said in shock.

She looked at me and said, "Don't worry about it. I can't explain it myself. It's just gone. I do not want to freak you out, but you cannot tell anyone about it, not even my parents know about it." I nodded, but my mind went to work. I did not understand. So many things weren't adding up.

First I couldn't figure out how she was able to sneak up on me and now I find out that she heals fast as well. I don't get it. If I did not know any better, I would say that she was not human. But she is, because I killed her mother. She has to be human, but things are not looking right.

"I can tell I have freaked you out. You should see the look on your face," she teased, smiling like we had known each other a long time.

"It's nothing. You haven't freaked me out, believe me. I was just thinking that's all." I tried to compose myself.

"Well, then, I'm glad. But I'm sure you're curious. You're wondering if I'm human. I wonder about it myself. Oh well." Then she giggled, but I wasn't amused.

"What are you doing out here so late?" I couldn't help myself, I had to ask.

She giggled some more. "I should be asking *you* that question. You *are* in my garden after all. Then again, since I already know why you're here, you don't need to answer that question. It's a good thing I came out here then, or you would have frozen to death by the morning. On a serious note, I couldn't sleep. I wanted to take a walk and get some fresh air. I hoped it would help me sleep. When I came out, I was somehow drawn to this place and here I am."

"*Drawn*, you said?"

"Yes, once I was outside, I just kind of walked over here."

"I'm sorry, I shouldn't be here."

"No, you shouldn't, but here we are. Would it be weird if I said I am glad you're here? Because I think I kind of like you already," she said and then bit on her lower lip as she playfully tried to stand on one leg, leaning her left hand on the tree for support. I wondered why she wasn't shivering from the cold. There were a lot of things I had to learn about her. I intently watched every move she made and her nonchalant approach to life and secretly wished I had the innocence of her youth. "You should go home now before you catch your death. All is forgiven. Were you seriously going to sit here all night?" I nodded. She looked strangely at me with a hint of admiration and shook her head. "Next time, just say *sorry*."

"Yes, yes of course, sorry. I am so sorry for my clumsiness and carelessness."

"It's all right," she said and smiled. "Like I said, no permanent harm was done. I will see you tomorrow at the art and music centre, won't I? You are going to be coming for lessons now that you know I'm okay?" she asked.

I knew I shouldn't, but I wanted more time with her. "Yes, of course, I will be coming now that I know—you—are all right."

"You promise?" she asked, as though she knew I might change my mind.

"You have my word." For some reason, it made her happy that she might be seeing me again. I didn't understand why or what she saw in me that made her want to be friends with me. Nevertheless, I was ecstatic and over the moon. "I am happy now that I know you are well. I still cannot forgive myself for what I did, but I'm thankful to you for being very gracious about everything."

"Aw, you're so sweet. Please forgive yourself. We all make mistakes, and you didn't see me. Thinking about it now, I wasn't really concentrating on where I was going. I was distracted. I don't think you would have intentionally wanted to hurt me."

"It's really very kind and polite of you to excuse my behaviour this way. I truly appreciate it." She smiled and I responded with a nod. Then we stood for a minute or so without talking. She was probably waiting for me to go now, so I offered to leave. "Er—um—I should take my leave now, so you can go inside. I don't mean to be rude, but that thing you have on doesn't look very warm to me. You must be freezing. Please go inside, and I shall see you tomorrow then," I said and was about to make my fake departure when she stopped me.

"Wait! Where do you live? I hadn't seen you around before that day. There is something about you, like I know you, like I have seen you before somewhere in my head. It's weird, I know. It's just—you feel very familiar to me, like I've known you all my life. It's strange, but I just feel like I can trust you with anything, and I promise you, I am not usually like this with people."

"Well, thanks. I don't know what to say. I wish I could say the same, not that I don't think I can trust you. It's just that my mother always said that the people with the most trusting faces are the ones you should be leery of the most. Maybe one day I will be able to earn your trust, but right now, I am just an intruding stranger."

"Your mother is a wise woman," she said. I looked away trying my best to ignore the reference to my mother. It's not her fault that I brought her into the discussion. "Hey, you still haven't answered my question," she said.

"Question about?"

"I asked where you live."

"Ah, I live—I mean my father and I live on the outskirts of town. We just moved down here not too long ago." It was a lie I was becoming accustomed to telling.

"Hmm, how long ago?" she asked. I looked puzzled. "Sorry, forgive me for questioning you. It's just your face—I can't get it out of my head. Something keeps nagging at me, but I don't know what it is, and I can't quite put my finger on it."

Surprised at how her memory served her, I tried not to panic. "I—I don't think we've met before. I must just have one of those faces," I lied.

"Oh, never mind then. Look, I'm sorry. I'll see you tomorrow I guess."

"Okay. Sweet dreams, Hanna." She looked at me baffled, as if I had just done something wrong. "Sorry, did I say something wrong?"

"Yes," she responded.

"What?" I inquired.

"My name, that's what's wrong. I never told you my name. How do you know my name?" I knew I had been stupid calling her by her name, but thankfully there were so many ways to explain such a blunder.

"Oh, I asked around. I felt so guilty for what I had done and wanted to see if you were okay, which is how I knew where you live as well."

"Hmm, that explains things." She smiled. "Remember, next time just knock on the door and say *sorry*. I don't bite."

I chuckled at that one. "Yes, I guess so," I replied. I stood there not wanting to go, because I was enjoying every minute of my time with her, and I knew she was going to leave soon. Strangely enough, the more I observed her, the more it seemed like she had this incandescence around her that she didn't seem to be aware of. I rubbed my eyes just to be sure they weren't playing tricks on me. The happier she seemed the more she glowed, and it baffled me.

"I should go inside before my parents send a search party for me. Does your father even know where you are?" she asked.

That was my opportunity to tell her that he was away on a business trip. "No. He doesn't know where I am, because he's not going to be around for a while. He travels a lot on business. He's gone on one of his trips which leaves me to do as I please."

"Lucky you, alone by yourself," she said. "My parents would never let me be by myself. I'm an only child, you see. What about you? Do you have any siblings?"

"Um—no, I don't. I am an only child too." I smiled. That part was at least very true. And I felt happy to be able to tell her something that wasn't a lie.

"What about your mother? How come you're not with her when your father travels?"

My mother is still a touchy subject for me. I find it hard to talk about her without seeing her in that fire the night she was killed. "My mother—she—er—she died. Um—I am eighteen, which means I can live on my own and by myself should I chose to." I could see she noticed I was upset. Without realizing it, my fists were clenched, and I could feel my jaw tighten. She took a step forward towards me, and I immediately took a step back. Her eyes were very sorry for me, and it warmed me, but at the same time made me upset, because I felt the pain of losing her all over again. I knew it was time to leave. I was suddenly feeling vulnerable, which meant I could become unpredictable, and I didn't want to scare her away, not after fate has finally reunited us. I looked up at her and she looked worried for me.

"I am so sorry. I didn't mean to pry. I was just trying to get to know you by making friendly conversation," she said quietly. She hadn't done anything wrong, yet I acted like it was her fault.

"I know," I said. I'm sorry. It's nothing to do with you. I just get like this when I—er—think of her—would you excuse me, I should go now, and I will see you later."

"Oh, okay. Goodbye then," She said.

"Yeah, goodbye."

I went away torn between going home and staying to keep watch over her. Although I had not seen any vampires around for a while, I also knew I would never forgive myself if something happened to her because I had left.

## Chapter 12

I got back home just before dawn. I was caught between the excitement of meeting her again and the way I had left things with her. My body tingled all through the day. I could not rest. I could not get her out of my head or control how happy I was inside. I watched the clock, impatiently waiting for the time to fly by, but it crawled along. I silently wished I had the power to walk in the sun, just to see her reflection. Her face and her scent consumed me all day long. It felt like torture having to wait for the sun to go down. I knew I should rest, but it was impossible to do so. How could I sleep when I was already dreaming of her? I replayed our conversations repeatedly in my head, and my body melted at the thought of being with her again.

At last it was safe to go out. Looking my best, I drove to the art and music centre. I wanted to get there before she did, just to watch her arrive. I impatiently sat in my car and waited until she arrived. She pulled in driving her Toyota Corolla and got out of the car. I saw her looking around as if searching for someone. I wondered if she was looking for me. As usual, she looked breath-taking. I opened the car door to get out, and cautioned myself not to make any fast moves in my attempt to get to her. I looked up at her again to see where she was. Someone was with her. I could tell who it was by the awful smell that greeted my nostrils. I became annoyed at myself for not getting out of the car sooner and angry at him for being here. I was not aware that he took lessons here too, although I am not surprised, seeing as he follows her about like a pet dog.

I followed behind them, walking at a slower pace and listening to their conversation. He bored me with his silly talk, and I just wished he would go away so I could have a moment with her. Not knowing what to do with myself now that her attention was elsewhere, I quickly walked past them, pretending that I had not seen them. Disappointed that she did not notice me, I carefully opened the front door to go inside not wanting to repeat the disaster from before. Then she called out. "Hi!" she said.

I looked back to see who she was greeting, and saw her eyes on me. "Oh, it's you again." I pretended as though I was just seeing her for the first time today.

"Yes, it's me. Were you expecting someone else?" she joked.

I smiled; glad I had her attention at last. "No, not really," I said, and she smiled back. I tried not to look at the boy next to her. Although I could not overlook the stench oozing from him, I did not want to look at him unless I really had to.

"Oh, how silly of me. You two haven't met have you? This is my friend, Huritt Denali, and this is—" I did not take my eyes of her as she tried to introduce us. "Sorry, I don't even know your name," she said.

"Sebastian," I responded.

"Sebastian," she repeated slowly. I loved the way she said my name. "What a lovely name you have." She smiled. "Er–Huritt, meet Sebastian."

I looked in his direction just for a second and greeted him with a nod of the head out of courtesy to her. His hands were already stretched forward for a hand shake, but I ignored them. I could see the anger in his eyes, although I think he tried to control it for her sake. I refused to let him distract me and focused my attention on Hanna, who seemed as excited to see me as I was to see her.

"I looked around for you earlier," she said.

"Did you now?" I asked, secretly happy that it was me she was scanning around for earlier.

She smiled and turned to Huritt. "Huritt, I will see you around later, okay? I want to have a chat with Sebastian." I looked over at him just to see his reaction, because I knew he would be fuming inside, and I was right. His eyes were like thunder, and I enjoyed his little expression of detest or anger or whatever it was he was trying to express. It didn't bother me one bit. I still had not found out what he was, but I hoped for his own sake that he was not what I suspected him to be. Glad that he was gone, I now had Hanna's full attention. She was looking at me.

"I didn't think you would come," she said.

"Why not?" I asked.

"It's nothing, just that I got the feeling I upset you yesterday with something I said."

"And I told you that you didn't say anything out of place. I'm sorry for my behaviour yesterday. It was uncalled for. It's just—I get like that when the subject of my mother is raised."

"I promise not to talk about her again," she said. I smiled. It felt amazing standing here talking with her. I have never felt like this with anyone.

"Thank you. That's very polite of you." She brushed her hair away from her face—I like it when she does that.

"So, what do we talk about then?" she asked.

"Anything you like," I replied.

"Are you sure? You would let me know if there was something you aren't comfortable with? I mean, sometimes I just ramble on, you know, without thinking."

"Don't worry about it. I am a good listener, and I have all the time in the world to listen to you ramble." We both laughed.

"You see yourself as a gentleman, don't you? I mean, for a teenager like myself, you are quite something."

"I do my best to always be on my finest behaviour," I replied and quickly added, "but by all means, let me know if you prefer the bad-boy image. It may surprise you what I can become in a short space of time."

"No this will do just fine," she replied. I noticed her blushing, and I was glad that it had something to do with me. Then she said, "Why do I feel like there is something mysterious about you, like something you are not telling me. I don't know, I just get this feeling like—"

"Like what?" I asked.

She paused and looked at me. "I don't know what it is, but there is something about you, and I just—I just want to know you more. I kind of want to spend more time with you. I'm sorry, I am doing it again. We just met, and already I am asking you to be generous with your time. I have no right—"

"There is nothing to be sorry for," I said gently. "I like talking to you," I reassured her.

"But I'm scaring you off."

I looked at her and could tell she was genuinely worried. I wanted to put her little heart at peace and made light of her worry. "I'm still here. That should tell you something. Look, I don't know what's going on in that head of yours, but there is nothing I don't like about you. I promise you, it will take a lot for me to be scared off." I chuckled, and I could see in her eyes that she was feeling more at ease.

"I'm keeping you from your lesson, aren't I?"

"No, you are not," I replied, and she smiled shyly and bit her lower lip. That's another thing that is beginning to grow on me.

"What are you here for anyway?" she asked.

"Sorry?"

"What lessons did you enrol to take?"

"Oh. Piano lessons."

"Seriously, I shouldn't keep you. I'm very good with the keyboard. I am just here to pass time really. I hate being stuck at home doing nothing. You should go before you miss your class altogether."

"What if I want to stay here with you?" I asked.

"Why would you want to do that?"

"Why? Because I like you, and you're growing on me," I said.

"I kind of thought I heard you say that before," she said.

"No, I did not. Earlier I said that there is nothing I don't like about you."

"It's all the same. And I like that you like me. Isn't it too soon to tell that you like someone? I mean we just met not too long ago."

"Maybe. You said you liked me yesterday after only five minutes. I'm allowed to tell you I like you too aren't I? It doesn't really make any difference to me the length of time in between. I've liked you since I first set eyes on you," I said.

"Is that true?" she asked. "Even with blood oozing off my face?" I smiled and looked away. I didn't know what to say to that. I do not like to remember the day I swung the door on her face. "I have said something you don't like, haven't I?

I can tell. Although you are smiling, your eyes look pained." I wondered how she could read me so well just by looking at me.

"You're right. It's just that I still regret the circumstances in which we met." She stared at me and was looking into my eyes, as if she was searching for something.

"Yeah, but there's more isn't there? I can see you're trying very hard to hide something."

"Like what?" I was puzzled.

"Oh God, I am doing it again. Sorry. I don't know why I keep doing this. It's just that when I'm around you I get this—this feeling, as if I've known you—it's weird. You must excuse me. I'm ruining it all." She was about to go.

"No, don't go. I'm—I'm not offended. I meant it when I said I like you, and if it means you are going to act strangely sometimes, I—I don't mind at all, as long as I get to spend time with you."

"Really?" she asked shyly.

I nodded and replied, "Yeah, really."

Then she smiled and looked relieved. "It feels right you know," she said quietly.

"What feels right?" I asked.

"Being friends with you," she responded.

I don't think there is anything about her I can fault. In my mind, it feels like I am drunk, only it isn't anything like that. I am just so happy to be with her, and I have never felt like this in my life, both, either as a human or a vampire.

For the rest of the evening, we sat outside by her car talking, which she did most of, while I listened. She enjoyed talking, and I, in turn, loved listening to her. She spoke about her childhood. I would ask her a question about when she was younger, and she filled in the rest. I loved it, because she told me those things I missed while she was growing up. Every night she told me a different story. We skipped music classes almost every day that we met. She felt guilty all the time, because she thought she was depriving me of my lessons. I convinced her that I was old enough to make my own decisions.

After about two weeks of hanging out together every evening, I already knew most of the things about her that I had missed. Occasionally, she would ask me questions about my past, such as wanting to know the kind of childhood I had. I noticed she never mentioned my mother again, and as it was my fault. So I decided to tell her about her. I tried to answer her questions truthfully, telling her the little I remembered about my human life. I told her how I felt when my mother died, and how lonely, depressed, and angry I became. I told her my mother had been killed and was found on the side of the road. I told her that she died when I was just eight years old, which is still very true, considering I was only talking about my human life.

Then she said, "I wonder what I would do if my mother died. I can't see her dead, you know. I can't think of it. Thoughts of her dying scare me. If someone were to hurt her, I don't think I have it in me to forgive such a person." My mind immediately went to that night I had her birth mother in my hands, and I regretted killing her all over again. *This is one secret that can never come out*, I thought, *or I risk losing her forever*. I tried to get the thought out of my head, because she usually can tell when I am hiding something.

"I have not seen your friend, er—what is his name again?" I said quickly, changing the subject, not that I cared about him.

"Oh Huritt? Poor Huritt."

"Why poor Huritt?" I asked.

"It's nothing really," she said.

"No, please tell me. I want to know."

"Oh, okay. He kind of likes me, I think. Okay, a little more than I think he should, you know. But the thing is, he told me he doesn't like that I'm friends with you, because he and I don't spend any time together since I became friends with you."

"Oh, well," I said in reply.

"Is that all you're going to say?" she asked.

"What do you want to hear? That I prefer to be in his shoes? Because the answer is I don't. I love being with you, as long as my presence does not bother you. Does it?"

"No, it doesn't. I love being with you, too." She flashed me that smile that I have come to adore. I looked at her and was swelling inside, because of what she just said. She looked away shyly, and I dropped my gaze.

"I feel bad, though," she added. I looked at her.

"I just chose you over him and am happy about it. It's selfish of me, don't you think?"

"Sometimes, we need to do the thing that makes us happy. You can't please everyone without hurting yourself. Allow yourself to be happy."

"Wow, he has wisdom as well. You are really something," she said laughing, and I snickered.

I had to go hunting. This time around, I needed to go far to find bigger game to feed on if I was to be around her this much. I did not want any temptation. I wanted to start early so I could return before dawn. I had not told her yet that I would be leaving earlier than usual. I wish I didn't have to leave, but it was important that I feed for both our sakes.

"Hanna," I called. She turned and looked at me. "I will be leaving early today. I have to go somewhere important."

"Is it far? Can I come with you?" she asked.

"I wish you could, but you can't—er—I have to leave now before it gets too late. I'll see you sooner than you think, though," I said, annoyed at myself for having to leave her, but it was necessary that I feed. She looked sad that I was leaving.

"Cheer up," I said. "At least now you get to take those lessons that you tell your parent you come here for." She laughed, and I was glad she was feeling better.

"Okay. Will I see you tomorrow then?" she asked, still a little disappointed that I was leaving.

"Of course, where else would I be?" I raised my hand to touch her face, feel her warmth, and just reassure her that I would be seeing her soon, but I could not. I did not want to get too close. Reluctantly I pulled it back and put it in my pocket and just walked away.

# Chapter 13

That evening, I combed the little woodland for food—a rabbit or fox, something to stave off my cravings until I was able to find something bigger. I was only able to find a couple of rabbits. When I looked at the time, I saw that it was a little past eleven at night and thought about going out of town to feed. A couple more deer would keep me strong for at least a week until I had to top it up again.

However, after calculating how long it would take, I knew it would take too long before I could get back, and I did not want to risk not standing guard over Hanna's house for even one night, so I decided against it and left the hunt for the next night, which would mean I could not be around her tomorrow, or any human, until I was properly fed.

I kept thinking how disappointed she would be tomorrow when I didn't show up, and I desperately wished I could see her, but I would be putting her life in danger, and it was a chance I was not willing to take. I stayed at Hanna's until it was almost dawn, and then went home to rest. When I am weak and in short supply of blood, I usually sleep more to conserve my energy.

The next evening, I left home early and went hunting. It upset me to disappoint her so, because I knew she would be waiting for me. I tried not to think about it. My hunger isn't to be played with, and I should be responsible and not endanger her or any other human. After driving for hours, I finally got to where I knew I could find big game. I sat in my car and waited until every human that I could sense had gone, and then I got out of my car and went hunting. I pushed thoughts of Hanna out of my head and scanned around again to see if I could smell any human before centralizing my energy on the hunt. I had to be sure before I let the taste for blood take me over.

Luckily for me, I found two red deer to feed on and started to feel myself again. I went back to my car and drove home. By the time, I got back to town, it was already three in the morning. I wished it weren't so late. I parked my car a good mile away from Hanna's and started walking towards her house. As I approached, I was hit by that scent again, the one from before. It was now clear to me that the same vampire, or vampires, that I had sensed here before were back. They had not just been passing through. They must have business in town.

I ran to Hanna's as fast as I could and went around the house cautiously. I could smell vampires all around her house. It shocked me that they chose to come to this very house. I had to find out what had drawn them to this particular house, although now wasn't the time. First I had to know that Hanna was safe. I looked up and saw that all the windows were locked. There was no way I could get inside to see if everyone was all right without going through the front door. I started to fear that something may have happened to them, but then, if they were all inside when the vampires came, they should be all right, because the vampires would need to be invited through the front door if they wanted access to the house.

I wondered why the vampires came on the night that I was not around. And what did they want from Hanna's family? After going around the house a couple of times, I couldn't see any sign that the vampires had made it inside. I calmed myself and listened and could hear Joan, Joseph, and Hanna breathing. I was relieved that she was all right but still very worried. Things had to change if I wanted her protected. And as much as I wanted to defend her, I would be useless if I don't know who the enemies were, what they wanted, and how I could stop them.

This wasn't good. In fact, it was terrible. I couldn't fight three vampires by myself, and who knows how old they are? If they are younger than I am, then I am at an advantage, but they have the edge because of their numbers. I had never been in a fight with a vampire before, so it would be tricky killing one of these three, let alone all three. I wasn't feeling very optimistic at all. There were too many things against me. I didn't feed on human blood, which put me at a great disadvantage, in terms of strength. Not to mention that I am alone and there are three of them. And if they are older than me, then God help me, not that He listens to the likes of me. But this means only one thing: I am going to die trying to protect Hanna.

I waited until it was almost dawn before going home. But before I left, I had to make sure that Hanna was okay. I took a stone and threw it at the wall to make a sound loud enough to wake them up. Joan woke up, who, in turn, woke up Joseph. Still not satisfied, I needed to hear Hanna's voice. I threw another stone, and this time I heard Joan and Joseph talking, and then Joseph went to check to see if Hanna was all right. I waited a while, and then I heard all of them talking about the noise they had just heard. Hearing Hanna's voice made me feel better.

All through the night, I debated about what to do to make sure Hanna was safe. I thought about just taking her away, but

I couldn't do that without giving myself away. And I doubt she would want anything to do with me once she found out who I really was. I thought about sending the parents an anonymous warning, asking them to leave town. I also knew that could spiral into something else which could involve the police. In the end, I knew I had to deal with the situation without bringing them into it. I had to make another phone call and ask for another favour. I hated needing other people to bail me out, but it was essential that I reach out for help if I wanted Hanna and me alive after this whole shenanigan was over. I thought about calling Isobel, but I knew too well she wouldn't be able to see past her jealousy. I could just as well be asking for more trouble. It's a shame, really, because I could do with both Isobel and Margret helping to fight these vampires. They had both been in battles before and they are strong and old, but I knew Margret would not come without Isobel.

I had no choice. I had to call Mason Benedict for help. The thing about Mason was that he had too many secrets; therefore, I reckoned he would have many enemies. I never wanted to get involved in his life, because I knew one day he would ask a favour of me that I wouldn't have in me to do, but I would have to do it all the same because of all the favours he'd thrown my way. There was another thing I needed to do: I wanted Hanna and her parents somewhere far away. I had no idea when those vampires were returning, but if there was to be war, I preferred they were somewhere else

I booked a first class ticket for all of them on the first flight out of England to New York that weekend and reserved the best hotel for them for fourteen nights. I put the tickets and details of where they would be staying in a brown envelope and wrote *For yourselves and Hanna. Use immediately* on the back on the envelope. I waited until dawn before delivering it to them and pushed it through their door early that morning before heading home. There was no time to start doubting whether they would go or not. If they questioned it, then I would have to compel them to do as I wished. I would do anything necessary to keep Hanna out of harm's way.

I did not meet Hanna at the art and music centre as she would have expected. That was the third night since I had last seen her. Even though I missed her, I needed to put things in place for their protection, and being with her would hinder me from thinking right.

I had to know how Joan and Joseph were taking the mysterious envelope, which would help me decide what my next action would be. I stayed in my usual spot and listened in on their conversation and heard them argue about going on the holiday. Joan didn't want to go at first, but joseph talked her into it. "We are going. There must be a reason it says to use immediately," Joseph said.

"I can't just drop everything and hop on the next flight to New York, Joseph."

"You can, and that's what we're going to do."

"I think we should go to the police."

"And tell them what, Joan? Humour me. What would you like us to tell the police?"

"Everything. We tell them everything."

"And you're prepared to do so, knowing it will break your daughter's heart? We vowed never to tell anyone, Joan, and we are not going to break that vow now over one little holiday. Listen, I am not going to lose my daughter. It's only fourteen days, so go and start parking."

"You don't get it do you, Joseph? If this is who we think it is, then we are not safe. They've found us."

"So you want to run to the police instead?" He laughed sarcastically. "It's you who doesn't get it. If this person has found us, he or she doesn't want to hurt us. In fact, I think it's the opposite. That envelops says *use immediately*. Maybe something is going down. I don't know. All I know is we were foolish to think we could take all the money we've been getting regularly and just live out our lives like that person doesn't exist. Now I say you start packing."

"Okay, if you think it's best." Joan finally gave in.

"I know it's best." I could always count on Joseph to steer her in the right direction.

Now it was Hanna's turn to protest. I heard Joan call her from her room.

"You didn't come down for dinner. Is everything all right?" Joan asked.

"I'm fine. I just wasn't hungry," Hanna replied.

"Hmm, okay. You worry me, darling. You've not been yourself these past few days."

"I'm okay, Mum. It's nothing."

"Well, then, your dad and I need to speak to you."

"About what?"

"We're all going to New York this weekend," Joseph said.

"What!"

"You heard right," he said.

"Why?"

"It's a surprise holiday. It's only for two weeks, darling."

"Dad, I don't want to go! It's just too soon! I have things already planned with some of my friends. I cannot just abandon everything now. Please, can't we go some other time? Please, Daddy," she pleaded.

I heard Joseph sigh. "Of course we can, darling. It's just that we already have the tickets and the hotel booked. It's all just going to be a waste. And here I was thinking you love surprises. There are so many teenagers who would love to be in your shoes right now, Hanna. Please, for your old man's sake," he begged.

"I don't know, Dad. The timing is all wrong. I can't just up and leave now." I did not hear Joan say anything, especially since she was reluctant to go a while ago. I hoped she wouldn't change her mind and take sides with Hanna on this one.

"What's so important that you can't spend two weeks with your parents in New York?" Joseph asked.

She was quite for a while and then she spoke. "I met someone," she said gently.

"A boy?" he asked.

"Yes, Dad, a boy, and I think I like him—a lot."

"That's a first for you, and I am happy for you, but, sweetheart, he will still be here when we come back, especially if he's right for you, don't you think? Er—Joan, a little help here, please."

"What do you want me to say to her that you have not already told her?" she replied

He ignored her comment and continued trying to convince Hanna to go. "So, this boy we are talking about, does he like you in return? I mean, what family is he from. Who is he?"

"He's new in town, Dad. He and his father just moved here. His name is Sebastian, and I don't know, Dad—I do not know if he likes me like that. I have not seen him for a few days now, and that's why I can't just leave. Don't get me wrong, Dad, I want to come, but not now. It's too soon. I mean, you guys can go without me so you won't waste the ticket. Trust me, I'll be fine on my own."

*Sebastian*

"Nonsense. Absolute nonsense. I can't believe you are entertaining the idea of being left alone in this house, because that is never going to happen, dear. And enough of this silly debate, because we are all going on that holiday and that is final. I was raised with nothing, and you, my dear girl, have been fortunate enough not to want for anything, but sometimes, you do act spoilt. It's a family holiday. Your father is doing this for all of us, so let's be grateful for the life we have. We are all going, whether you like it or not," Joan interjected a little angrily, I must say. It seemed necessary, and for once, I was grateful to her for being firm.

Hanna wasn't done yet, however. "You can't force me to do what I don't want to do, Mum. I am not a child anymore. Why don't you trust me by myself? I feel like a prisoner with the way you choke me with your love and protection, dragging me everywhere you go like a—"

Before she could finish, Joseph cut her off. "Mind your tongue, young lady. You have no right speaking to your mother like that. Now I know you think you have things to do, but whatever it is can wait until we get back. It has been a while since we vacationed, so I beg of you do not spoil it for your mother and me. She was really looking forward to it. When you are eighteen and you no longer wish to be in our care and under this roof, you can leave and be by yourself, but for now, you will do as you're told. You have two days to inform your friends of your impending absence before we go. That is it for now. You may leave for your room if you want to."

"Dad, we were just in Barbados five months ago. And any other time, I would be up for it. I just don't want to go right now."

"Well, we are going, Hanna. I know you feel like this now, but you will soon forget about this boy once we are in New York. Think of all the shopping you will get to do. Girls your age love nothing more."

"But I am not girls-my-age, Dad, and I don't want any more shopping. I like what I already have."

"Well, then, add to it. Buy more things that you like. You are not wriggling your way out of this one, Hanna. I know you want to stay around for this boy, but, like I said, he will still be here when you get back."

I heard her run to her room. I knew how upset she was, and I felt for her. Any other time, I would have been championing her, but I couldn't this time around. It just wasn't safe. I knew I had to make an appearance at the art and music centre the next day and convince her to go.

It wasn't easy for me listening to her cry and not being able to do something about it. I had never heard Joseph speak to Hanna like that before. I heard him go to her room to apologise and soothe her, but still she wept, silently. Every single teardrop made me feel guilty, and it pained me that I was responsible for her tears. I wondered if there was more to it than the fact that she had to go on a holiday.

The next evening, I went to the art and music centre early and waited for Hanna to arrive. I immediately saw her car pull in. I got out of my car and went over to her straight away. I wanted to take her in my arms and just comfort her, but I knew I couldn't. She would wonder why my body was so hard and cold, so I restrained myself.

"Hanna!" I called. She spun around from her car to look at me, and I could tell from the emotions on her face that she was glad to see me, but mad at the same time.

"Where have you been?" she asked. Before I could respond, she was questioning me. "You've been gone for three days!" What kind of a friend does that make you? I don't even have your number to call you or know where you live."

"I'm sorry, Hanna." I didn't know I would be gone that long. It's just—something very important came up, and I had to attend to it."

"I waited here for you every night. I was so worried."

"I'm very sorry. I didn't realise you would miss me that much," I replied.

"Who says I missed you? I never said that. I just missed not talking to you, that's all."

I smiled. Even I knew that was untrue. I looked at her, but she looked away shyly. Carefully I turned her face back to mine with my gloved hands. "Hanna, those three days away from you were like torture. I thought of nothing else but you. I missed your smiles, your beautiful blue eyes, the sound of your laughter, your beautiful face, but most of all I missed being with you. So even though you say you didn't miss me, it doesn't matter, it matters what you believe in your heart." Her eyes were glistening, but her face glowed with happiness just for a second and then she looked unhappy again and I knew the reason why. "What's the matter now? I am here now aren't I?"

"Yes, you are. You are here, and I have to go away. I am going on holiday with my parents this weekend and will be gone for two weeks. I tried to get myself out of it, but they weren't having it."

I quickly cut in. "It's only for two weeks. You should be happy, shouldn't you? It's a holiday."

"I thought you would be on my side," she said.

"But I am."

"How is that exactly? Educate me."

"Hanna, it's a holiday. It's not like you're moving to another country. I don't want you to feel guilty or anything, but I would give my arm and leg to spend some time with my parents the way yours want to spend time with you. Go on and have some fun. I'll still be here," I said.

"Who says it's because of you that I don't want to go?" she asked, and I chuckled.

"Forgive me. I was only kidding about me being important to you. But you should go and have a nice time. Where are you guys going anyway?" I pretended like I didn't already know.

"Oh, somewhere in New York. I don't know. Can I have your number? I can't believe I don't already have it," she said.

"Well, you never asked for it. Give me your hand." I took her hand in mine and gently scribbled my phone number on her palm. I was careful not to hold her too tightly. Although I was wearing gloves, I could feel the warmth and suppleness of her hands, all the while feeling her eyes on me. There was a sudden tension between us. I let go of her hand and looked away to break the tension. We were both quiet for a while, and then she spoke.

"So, we are leaving on Saturday morning. I was thinking that you and I should do something together tomorrow. I am open to anything, just as long as I get to spend the whole day with you. We could go shopping or bowling, you know, whatever you want to do."

As happy as I was to hear her say she wanted to spend the whole day with me, I knew that was not possible and I had to find a way to let her down gently. I could do the evening, but not the day. "Er—tomorrow morning is a little busy for me, but I will be available in the evening, say from around five or six. By the way, don't you have to be in class tomorrow?"

"No, I'm free tomorrow. It's a shame. I wanted us to hang out more, but I guess the evening will do. So what do you want to do tomorrow?" she asked excitedly.

I smiled, because looking at her made me happy inside, and for a moment I was able to just forget the reason I needed her to be away from here, but just for a moment, because looking at her made it clear to me that I would do absolutely anything to keep her alive. "Anything you want. You decide."

"Oh, okay then. Um—er—don't take this the wrong way, but I would like you to meet my parents, if it's not too much trouble. I told them about you already, so they won't be surprised or anything. Then we could go out after. Maybe to your place and hang out, or not, whatever you want to do."

"Sounds fun. I am up for anything you want to do."

"Great! I am so excited!" she exclaimed.

I chuckled at how childish and innocent she was just then. "I am glad you are. I am looking forward to it, too. So what do we do today?"

"Today we stay here and talk until it's time to go home, unless you want to take that lesson today."

I pretended to think about missing my lessons. "Hmm—No—I um—I like it here. Talk, we shall. You may begin. I am all ears."

# Chapter 14

The day had come when I would be officially meeting Hanna's parents, and I wanted to impress them. It was essential that they believe I was good enough for her. Somehow her parents' approval of me was important, even though I had given her to them. It was important to me that they know, when she was with me, she would always be safe. I was hopelessly in love with her, and I should feel ashamed of my feelings, but it felt right to me. I was beginning to look at her as a boy looks at a girl. I wasn't convinced that I had a right to be feeling this way about her, but I become weak in my knees whenever I thought about or looked at her. I couldn't carry on pretending that I only loved her as a father loves his daughter. What I felt inside was more than most humans are capable of understanding, and I couldn't find the strength to deny what I knew to be true.

I was nervous. I had never been out on a date before and wondered what I would do if she decided she wanted to hold hands or lean on me. I mean, the little things that teenage girls like to do. What if she offered me something to eat or they decided to cook dinner for me. These thoughts made me so anxious, that the fun I was hoping to have started to slowly disappear.

I drove to her house where we had agreed to meet. I was hoping we wouldn't have to spend too much time with

Joan and Joseph. I parked in front of their driveway and sat in the car. I didn't know if I should go up and press the doorbell or just sit and wait until Hanna came out. After a few seconds of debating what to do, I got out of the car and was about to press the doorbell, when the door swung open. As usual, Hanna looked excited to see me, just as I was to see her.

"You took your time. You didn't get cold feet now did you? Come inside," she said. I smiled and followed her through the hallway to the living room where Joseph and Joan were waiting for me. Before I knew it, she was introducing me to them.

"Mum, Dad this is Sebastian," she said all smiles. "Sebastian, these are my loving parents."

I moved forward to shake hands with Joseph, who was standing, while Joan was sitting knitting. "Hello, Mr Greene, Mrs Greene. I am very pleased to meet you," I said, shaking hands with Joseph. I looked in Joan's direction and bowed my head in acknowledgment.

"Well, hello, Sebastian. It's nice to finally meet the new boy in town. Our Hanna here won't stop talking about you." I looked at Hanna, who was now drowning in embarrassment.

"Dad, stop. Don't say that," she said. I tried to hide my contentment, because she was blushing.

"Do you blame her, Joseph? I can see why she can't stop blabbing about him. He is a pretty boy, this one, and well mannered, too," Joan said.

I didn't know what to say. If I weren't so pale, I would have been blushing, too. "Well, thank you, ma'am," I replied.

"So, where are you from originally? Oh, excuse my manners please. Take a seat," Joseph said, gesturing to the sofa. I obliged, minding my movements as I walked around

Joan to sit on the other side of her. Joseph's eyes were still on me, and my guess was that he was waiting for an answer to his question.

"Er—here and there, really, as much as I can remember. We never settled anywhere for long," I said. I could see all of their faces looking at me, waiting for an explanation, so I continued. "My mother, God bless her, died when I was quite young. So my father and I pretty much lived anywhere his job took him."

"Oh, I see. I am very sorry for your loss. I didn't mean to pry, I was just trying to make conversation," Joseph said, feeling remorseful.

"Oh, poor you. It must be really hard not being able to settle in one place, but I suppose you had no choice, plus growing up without a mother must not have been easy for you," Joan added, and I sighed.

"I try to make the best of what I am given in life," I replied, looking over at Hanna, who was standing in the corner of the room.

"That's very brave of you, son, and by the look of things, I can tell you're doing fine. Your father must have done a great job raising you all by himself."

"Thank you," I added.

"Oh, we haven't even offered you anything. Would you like a cup of tea or anything? You must forgive us. We got carried away. Please put the kettle on, dear," Joan said turning to Hanna.

"Oh no, I'm fine, thank you very much."

"Are you sure? I mean, I know you kids are going out, but I would think you could do with something hot to keep you warm. That weather out there is a killer. If we weren't going on holiday tomorrow, I wouldn't advise you to go out at all this evening, but I know our Hanna here won't hear of it. She's been looking forward to your arrival all day," Joan said. I tried not to look at Hanna, who would be annoyed right now I knew, because she gets embarrassed easily.

"Thanks, Mum. While you're at it, why not tell him that I dream about him, too?" she said, and I could tell she was rolling her eyes.

"Oh, Hanna, come on. You know we're only joking. You should learn to take a joke," Joseph said.

"Yeah, right, whatever. Anyway, we have to get going. Clearly this was a bad idea," Hanna replied.

"Don't be like that, Hanna. He only just got here. You think I am going to just set you loose with a total stranger without questioning him?" Joseph looked in my direction and said, "No hard feelings. She's our only child, and we worry about her. Its only right that we do. I mean, your father must get like that with you, too, doesn't he?"

"All the time, sir. I totally understand," I said.

"Well, Dad, this is more like an interview," Hanna cut in.

He ignored her and questioned me further. "So tell me, er, Sebastian, right? Where did you and your father live before coming here? It's just that you're very pale."

I quickly thought of a very cold place off the top of my head, and Alaska and Montana in the States came to my head immediately. "Um, Montana, sir."

"Oh, that's one of the coldest places in the world. I mean this here must feel like summer to you, coming from a place like that," Joseph added.

"A little bit, sir," I lied and looked over at Hanna, who was now getting impatient. I flashed a smile to make her feel better. "Wow, Montana. That's one cold place. I tell you what, I couldn't live in any place colder than this. I have been trying to convince Joan to move to a sunnier place, but she likes it here. What she sees here I don't understand. The weather is as unpredictable as a woman," Joseph said, winking at his wife, and I chuckled.

"You're sure you don't want anything?" Joan asked again.

"Yes, ma'am, pretty sure," I replied.

"Our Hanna here seems to have taken to you, and I don't blame her, because you are just too perfect. Handsome and well mannered—that's one combination you don't find easily these days," Joan complimented.

"Well, thank you, ma'am." I said.

"So, where are you originally from? I mean where is your home town here?" Joseph probed again.

"Er, I was born in London and lived there until my mother passed and we had to move," I said, being as patient as I could. I understood that they would want to probe any stranger who wanted to be friends with their daughter, and rightly so.

"I see you're originally a city boy then," he joked, and I smiled in return.

"I guess so," I replied.

"Well, enough with the interview, guys. We have to get going before the day ends. I hope you think I'm safe with him now," Hanna intervened.

"Well, he seems nice enough from what I can see," Joan responded to Hanna, looking at her husband.

"Hmm, from the little we know of you, I feel we can trust you to take care of our Hanna. Bring her home safely and on time, Sebastian," Joseph added.

"Treat her well. She's never been on a date before," Joan added.

"Oh, Mum, thanks. This just gets better and better," Hanna replied.

"Well, it's true isn't it?" Joan asked.

Joseph smiled and shook his head. "You've done it now, babes. She's going to be stroppy all week now," he said.

"I can't believe this is happening. C'mon, S, let's get out of here before I literally dig a hole and bury myself here," Hanna said, fuming. She came over and dragged me to my feet, and I followed her, but not before bidding her parents goodbye.

"I'll see you later, Mr and Mrs Greene. It's been nice meeting you. I promise to take good care of Hanna and will bring her home safely and on time," I said in a rush, as Hanna pulled me away, and out the door we went.

"I'm counting on you, son!" I heard Joseph call out to me, as we were already outside the house.

I opened the passenger side of my car for Hanna. It was the first time since my mother's demise that I had allowed anyone else to sit next to me in my car. I got inside and looked over at her. Her eyes were closed, like she was deliberately trying not to look at me.

"It's all right, Hanna. They weren't that bad," I said.

"That's all right for you to say. They aren't your parents. Gosh, how embarrassing was that?" she said, still not looking my way.

"Take it easy. Take a deep breath. I actually like them. They are nice and funny, and it didn't bother me at all that they quizzed me. I mean, it's nice to know they care about you a lot," I said, taking her hands in mine.

She finally turned to look at me. "Seriously, you didn't think they were too nosy?"

"No, not at all. If they didn't care about who you were with, I would have wondered about them. They are all right. You should be proud of them."

"Mum is right, you know. You are perfect. I mean, the fact that you didn't find any of that annoying. Let me apologise. It's my fault. I shouldn't have taken you to see them. I am sorry," she said.

"Will you stop, Hanna? Seriously, they didn't offend me, and, believe me, I am far from perfect. I mean, I wish I *was* perfect, but I am not," I replied.

"Oh, but you are, S. I can see it in you. I don't know what it is, but there is something you are hiding. I feel like it's something wonderful—something you don't want anyone to know about. Trust me, it's never as bad as you think," she said.

I looked at her as though she knew what my secret was. "What are you talking about? First, I am Mr Perfect, and now I am keeping secrets," I said inquisitively, to see where she was going with this.

"Oh, forget I said anything. I didn't mean to. It's just that sometimes I feel like I can read you. Like if I listen close enough, I can almost hear your innermost thoughts." She shook her head, as my eyes narrowed on her.

*What's she talking about* I wondered. One minute she is annoyed with her parents and the next she is trying to read me. "I don't know what you're on about today, but we better get going before the day ends and we're still in this car."

"Yes, of course. Let's go," she said.

"Where to?" I asked.

"I don't know. Surprise me, S. Didn't you plan anything?"

"I tried to, but I am a bit out of practice. It's been a while since I took a girl on a date," I said looking at her. I knew that was a lie, as I have never taken any girl, human or vampire, out on a date before. "And what's with the S you are suddenly calling me?" I asked.

She smiled. "Don't you like it? I like it. I had a sleepless night last night thinking about what to call you. Don't get me wrong, it's not like I go around thinking about you or anything. It's just I like your name, but it feels too long, you know. I don't want to have to say *Sebastian* all the time."

"You prefer to just call me S then?"

"I don't know what I can shorten it to, except Seb, and I don't like the sound of that. But S sounds fun, and it feels right, don't you think?" I just looked at her and chuckled. "You don't mind, do you? I mean, if you rather I call you by your *full* name, I can do that, too," she said, with emphasis on the full.

"Call me anything you like, Hanna. I don't mind. S seems nice enough. I wonder why I never thought of it," I said to make her feel better about it.

"Oh, okay then. Let's get out of here now, or my parents will be wondering what we are doing out here still."

I started the car. "Yeah, well, about that, I still don't know where to take you. You just name a place, and we'll go there. I'm sorry I didn't plan this better. I'm still kind of newish here."

"Oh, what about your place? We could go to your place. I mean, I just want to spend time with you. It would be better than sitting out here, plus I'll get to see where you live," she said. I thought about it and the dangers associated with her knowing where I keep. She might come during the day when I'm resting or expect me to come out in the sun with her. I didn't like the idea, but I had no inkling of any other place we could go—not if we had to remain in town.

"Don't you have a favourite restaurant or a movie you want to watch?" I asked.

"S, what my mother said was true."

"Meaning?"

"That I have never been on a date before. I know it's embarrassing, but it's true. So let's just skip all of it and go to your place."

"Are you sure?"

"Yes, I am."

"Okay, then. My place it is. Come on, fasten your seat belt," I said and drove out of their driveway onto the road.

## Chapter 15

I pulled onto my driveway, got out, and opened the car door for her. "This is it. Welcome to my home," I said, gesturing towards the front door.

"Gosh, it's lovely," she said.

I smiled and unlocked the front door for us and stepped aside so she could enter first, while I followed closely behind. "Well, what do you think?" I asked.

"What do I think? It's gorgeous, S. Don't take it the wrong way, but I never imagined that you lived in a place like this. I mean, you guys are rich. Not like it matters either way, but you never showed it. All this time and you never even said your father was this rich. Wow! This place is just breathtaking," she said, looking round in amazement. I loved that she liked it so much. I could stay like this forever, watching her galloping around the house in excitement. It made me happy that she was so happy. She was literally starting to glow again.

"I'm glad you like it so much, Hanna," I said, following her around and being careful not to get too carried away with my movements.

"There is nothing to fault here. I want to live here. Everything is just very sophisticated and beautiful," she said in awe.

"It's not as beautiful as you," I said.

She turned around and looked at me for a second or so and then resumed admiring the house. "Your father has good taste, and I like a man with taste. I hope you're like him. I'm just joking. What must you think of me?" she said and smiled.

"I know, Hanna. I know what you're like. I know you more than you think, believe me," I replied. I wished I could tell her the truth about me, but I knew I could not. I hated lying to her every day. But I also knew the truth would push her away from me for the rest of her life, and I could not risk not having her in my life, not now, not ever.

"Don't tell me you stay here all by yourself. My parents would never let me. Don't you get lonely residing in this big house with your father away all the time?" she asked.

"Well, I am kind of used to it you know. I mean, I am a big boy now. I can look after myself," I said, and she smiled.

I led her into the living room. She sat down on the big sofa, making space for me to join her. I ignored her gesture and sat on the chair opposite instead. Purposefully, I avoided her stare. I wanted to sit next to her; there was nothing I wanted more than to have her in my arms, but I did not have explanations yet when she noticed that I was not like every boy she knew, what with my cold, hard body. She looked a little disappointed that I did not sit with her but soon got over it.

She looked at me and smiled. "Which way to the kitchen?" she asked. I was suddenly nervous. *What does she want* I wondered. I got up to show her the kitchen, and she followed closely and quickly went past me to the fridge. She opened it and looked at me in amazement. "Don't you eat? There is nothing in here. I mean, what do you feed on? Air?" she quizzed.

I didn't know how to answer and diverted my eyes from hers before she tried to read me again. "I eat out." I said. I mean, I wasn't exactly lying to her.

"All the time? What is that like? You don't even have anything to snack on," she said. Then it occurred to me that she might be hungry. She probably thought I was taking her out to eat like the humans do. I was annoyed with myself for not thinking about that. It's not like I initially planned to bring her here, but I should have been more proactive.

"I'm sorry. I didn't think. I told you I'm out of practice. What would you like to eat? I'll order some food for you. Something, anything?" I asked.

"Oh, okay," she said.

"So what are you in the mood for?" I asked

"Er, I am not that fussy. I mean, I'll have whatever you order. It's up to you," she replied.

*Up to me!* I thought. I had no idea what human food to order. I mean, I've been out of practice for almost two hundred years now. Who knows what food people eat these days. "Hanna," I said, "you really have to help me here. I don't have a clue what to order. You have to tell me what you want to eat. There must be something you are craving," I said.

"Okay then, S. You really are bad at this dating thing. I will have Chinese then. What about you, what are you having?" she asked.

"Oh me? I'm fine. I'm not having anything. Let's just take care of you for now," I said.

"But you might get hungry later. You never can tell. C'mon, have Chinese with me," she coaxed.

This was exactly the reason I had been nervous earlier today. "Seriously, I'm fine. Believe me, if I were hungry, I wouldn't stand around doing nothing about it, would I," I replied.

"Oh, okay then, if you say so."

I went back to the living room to go through a pile of leaflets, to see if I could find a Chinese take-away restaurant. Luckily enough, there was one amongst the pizzerias and Indian food, all advertised on one page. I called the advertised number, not knowing what to get, so ordered most of the different meals they had. I didn't want to ask her to choose, because I would have to start explaining my lack of knowledge in that field. While I was in the living room ordering her dinner, she kept busy by going around the house. When I finished, I went to find her. Cautiously, I walked towards her so I wouldn't startle her. She was standing outside one of the rooms with her back turned away from me. She must have heard me coming, because she said, "Do you know what is funny, but doesn't make any sense?" she asked, turning around to face me.

I stood just a few feet from her. "What's that?" I asked. She was quiet for a while and just looked at me blankly, her eyes narrowing like she was thinking. I just stared back, admiring her, and wondering what she was thinking about now. I hope she wouldn't say she remembered how she knew me. That would really be weird.

"Er—your father—he doesn't live with you does he?" she asked.

I swallowed hard and looked away from her. "Why do you say that?" I could feel her eyes piercing at me for answers.

"Because I went through all the rooms, and there's just one room that's lived in and I am guessing that's yours— the master bedroom. So it makes me think that your father wouldn't have given you the master. He doesn't really live with you, does he?" she asked.

I was quiet, wondering whether I should just tell her the truth. I did not want to ruin the day. And then she said, "How can he be this cruel, to just leave you by yourself? I mean, I know you're old enough to be on your own, but still, he thinks because he has money, he can just do as he likes? He has responsibilities to you. To think I give my parents grief for caring too much and your father doesn't care what you get up to. I haven't even met him, and already I don't think I would like him very much." She was working herself up, worrying about me staying here by myself, when she didn't need to.

"It's okay, Hanna. I don't mind being alone. To be honest, I'm kind of used to it."

"Oh, but you should mind, S. No one deserves to be alone. I think you're letting him get away from his responsibilities to you. It doesn't all just end with money you know. He can't just buy a house, put you in it, and then disappear. Or has he remarried? Is that why he's not living here?" She was so worked up, I had to tell her the truth—well, part of it, and hope she didn't get too angry and leave.

"Hanna, it's not what it looks like."

"S, it's not right. I know you're old enough, but you need to talk to him. He needs to spend more time with you."

"Hanna, I can't. It's not what it looks like. It's impossible to talk to him."

"But he's your father, and you're his only child. You must have some kind of relationship with him?"

"I don't."

"But why?"

"Because he's dead."

"What!"

"My father's is dead. I lied to you about him. I'm sorry." I could see that she was shocked by what I had just said. Her face showed her confusion, and now I wish I hadn't told her.

"But—but you said—" I watched as she dropped to the ground and sat down. This was difficult for me, and I knew she could just run out that door and never look back, but I had to tell her something about me that wasn't a total lie.

"I lied—I lied to you and I'm very sorry. There is no excuse for lying to you. You were getting worked up just now over nothing, and it's my fault, so I will tell you the truth. I don't want you to worry about me like that. You are right about one thing—he never bothered about me. After my mother's death, he just drank and drank and it was never enough. Anything that came from a bottle ended up down his throat. He reeked of alcohol always. I don't ever remember seeing him able to stand on his own two feet. He was always staggering in and out of brothels. He defiled my mother's memory by sleeping with prostitutes. He never took care of me. I am very sorry I lied to you. I think it's just because I still like to believe there is someone there, out there that is related to me, and someone that cares about me. I bought this house myself. Everything I have, I inherited from my uncle, my mother's brother. He had no children so everything came to me when he died." I looked at Hanna and saw her slumped shoulders. She wasn't looking at me. I knew I had disappointed her by lying. There was nothing I could say or do to make it better. Now it was up to her. I sat on the ground, giving her a bit of space.

"How did he die then?" she asked.

"Who?"

"Your father."

"I don't know. I mean, I'm not sure. I found him slumped on the ground one evening, drink in hand and lifeless. I don't know what killed him. His body finally had enough, I guess. I mean, that's all I can remember," I said, looking away from her, because that same day my human life was taken away from me by my mother.

"Poor you. You must be very lonely all by yourself. No wonder you think I should spend more time with my parents. Hmm, you never know what you have until it's gone," she said, staring into space.

I had never actually told anyone about this before, because, apart from my mother, no one has cared about me this much. No wonder it felt terrible lying to her. I had to be careful, though, because I seemed to love spilling my guts to her, and before I knew it, I could be telling her how my mother had turned me into a vampire. I got up and went over to her to pull her up. She looked at the gloves I was wearing.

"It's warm in here you know. You can take those off now."

"I know, but I prefer to have them on." She smiled and was making her way down the stairs when I called out, "Hanna, you cannot tell anyone about me. I don't want anyone knowing what I just told you. It's important to me that no one else knows."

"Oh, Sebastian, I would never do that. Don't worry. Your secret is safe with me, like mine is with you. Now stop worrying. The day is almost over and we haven't even started enjoying it."

"Thank you," I replied. Before we got down the stairs, the doorbell rang. I told her to wait in the living room while I went to the door to get her dinner.

Holding my breath, I watched as she ate. She seemed to be enjoying the food. I tried to look comfortable as she ate, but the stench was turning my stomach. I tried to divert my attention from the food by thinking of what I had to do once Hanna and her family left for their holiday tomorrow. When she finished, I took the leftovers to the kitchen and dumped them in the bin. By the time I turned around, she was already behind me. "How do you do that?" I asked.

"Do what?" she inquired.

"Sneak up on me like that. I didn't hear you coming."

She looked confused. "I didn't know I sneaked up on you. I just wanted to surprise you, that's all." I sighed, and she looked in the bin. "Why have you chucked all that food away? You could put it in the fridge. That's what the fridge is for. I didn't even touch most of it."

"Don't worry about it."

"What! Are you serious? You are so wasteful. If you get hungry at night and you need to eat, what will you do then? Take it out of the bin. Gosh, I don't know how you survive."

I did not know what to say to make her understand that I do not eat human food, without giving myself away. "Listen, I don't like Chinese food. I don't like most food. I am kind of a vegetarian—what's the other one called? Er—a vegan. I am both of those two and more. Stop worrying about me, because I can take care of myself," I said.

She looked at me, as if she did not understand what I had just said. "Vegetarian, vegan, and more? You should have told me. I've been trying to force you to eat. What do you eat then? Are you allergic to food, or do you just hate food that much? No wonder your fridge is empty, but you look so strong. Who knew eating so little could make one this beautiful," she said, looking puzzled.

"Are you saying I am beautiful?" I asked, knowing it would get a reaction out of her.

"Yes. Oh no, you know I didn't mean it like that. I mean you're not bad looking. I mean, for a guy, you are something. You are good—"

"Good looking?" I quickly cut in. I liked watching her when she got like this.

"Good looking! Yeah, one can say that. I think you're okay. More than okay, I mean, most girls would say you're pretty handsome."

"So *you* don't think I am handsome?"

"I—I—didn't mean it like that. Off course—you—you are—"

She was looking at me, and our eyes locked for a minute. I could feel a sudden heat take over my body. I broke my gaze from hers. I knew where this was going, and I didn't think it was right to take advantage although it's all I wanted, but I knew I had no right to feel the way I felt about her. "It's all right. Don't worry about it. I was only playing with you. Come on, let's get out of here." I led her out of the kitchen.

We returned to the sitting room and sat down: she back on the big sofa, legs curled under her body, and I back in my chair. She looked like she was thinking, like there was something bothering her—I could tell because her face told a thousand stories. I wondered if she was still thinking about that food business or about what just had happened between us. I waited for her to tell me what was on her mind, but she just kept quiet, so I asked to see if she was all right. "Are you all right, Hanna?" She smiled and nodded and there was silence again. I began to think perhaps she was uncomfortable with me now.

"Did I do something wrong? Did I do something or say something that has upset you?" She just continued to stare at me. "Do you want me to take you back home?" She did not reply, and I was beginning to get irritated with myself. I could not think of one thing I had done right today. I couldn't really tell which one of my screw-ups upset her the most, from the lies to the food business to what just had happened.

Then she said, "Stop beating yourself up. You haven't done anything wrong, not to me you haven't." She smiled. "It's just that I feel like you have a secret—a very big secret. The things you say don't make much sense to me. They should, but I can't help questioning. I know you came clean about your father, but there's more, isn't there? You're very cautious when you speak. It feels like you're watching what you say to me."

"I don't understand. How do you mean?" I asked,

"Of course you do. We all have our secrets, don't we? Even me. I keep things from my parents, things I don't understand, you see. But I feel like I can share them with you," she said.

"What are you talking about?" I pretended like I didn't understand.

She was quiet for a moment before responding. "Okay, I'll tell you mine, just so you know you can trust me. You know the time you accidentally hit me in the head with the door? That wasn't the first time I healed fast, and it's not the only thing I can do." I did not like remembering how I had hurt her, so I tried not to dwell on it. I knew she healed fast, but I didn't understand how. But, then again, I didn't think it was fair for her to tell me her secrets when I wasn't willing to share mine with her.

"Hanna, you don't have to tell me anything. I told you once before that it doesn't matter what you can do. I'll never think of you as a freak."

She smiled and said, "I know. Sebastian, but I want to. It doesn't mean you have to tell me yours, either. I'm just tired of keeping it to myself. I need to talk to someone, you see. Someone I can trust, and somehow I know I can trust you." Her eyes started to water. I didn't like it, but I knew there was no stopping her. I gave her the handkerchief I always carry, although I never use it.

"Listen, I know you feel you have to tell me, but if it makes you feel this way, don't tell me. How do you know you can trust me?" I asked.

She smiled sweetly. "Oh, but I know, S. You've had a dark past, you see. I can feel it. Though you only choose to tell me what you like, I can see it. I don't know how, but I see something wonderful and kind in you amidst all the chaos in you. The beauty of it all is that you have chosen right. It's been tough, but it's the right path. That's how I know I can trust you." She got my back up speaking in parables. She couldn't possibly know what I am, though everything that she said pointed in that direction.

"You've lost me. What was inside that food you ate?" I asked, trying to make a joke of what she was saying.

She laughed and shook her head. "Make jokes all you want, but it can never hide the truth."

At that point, I was sure she was onto something. In a way, I was glad she knew something wasn't right with me, but I also knew it meant trouble if she knew, because it might eventually come out that I've known her for a long time, and she could hate me for it. I was quiet for a while. My eyes narrowed as I began to think of what to do with the information she had just given me, but before I could say anything, she started speaking again.

"When I was nine, my dad bought me a puppy—a Labrador retriever—for my birthday. I was so happy and named him Stone—I used to call him Stony. He was so beautiful and my best friend. Then one day, four years later, I was looking for something in my dad's study—he normally hides my presents there, you see. I was impatient and just wanted to see what he got me. There was no one else at home. I decided to climb up the shelves to see if he was hiding anything there. The shelf wasn't attached to the wall, but I didn't know that. When I had climbed high up, the shelf gave way and I fell and the shelf fell on top of me and I fell on top of Stone. Somehow I dragged myself out and only had a few bruises here and there that just healed. But Stone was just lying there not moving. At first, I didn't see where he was hurt, until I moved him to his side. One of the broken vases from the shelf had pierced his neck. Quickly, I pulled out the fragment and the wound bled. Still, he did not move. The weight of the shelf and me must have been too much for Stone. It was entirely my fault. He lost his life because I wanted to find my stupid present. There was no one at home. The sitter my mum hired just popped out to get something. I pulled Stone towards me and began shaking him and yelling for help, but no one came. I couldn't leave him lying there, you see, so I sat down on the floor next to him and cried, holding him, stroking his fur, and waiting for someone to come home, wishing I hadn't climbed up that stupid shelf, when suddenly Stony jumped back to life." I could not believe my ears. Was she saying what I thought she was?

Hanna looked at me. "I know what you're thinking. Believe me, I've thought the same thing for years. But it's true. I tried it on some little insects, and it worked. I always thought it was my touch, but I just have to think it or wish it and it happens. Like when you said I had sneaked up on you—I just wanted to be with you, and there I was. I don't know what it is. I don't understand it. After that incident with Stone, I convinced my father I didn't want him anymore. He didn't understand why, because I loved that dog so much, but keeping Stone reminded me that I wasn't normal, and I just wanted to be normal." She was looking at me to see how I was reacting to her revelation.

I was still in shock. If it were anybody else, I probably wouldn't be as shocked, but it was my Hanna. I couldn't believe she could do these amazing things—and she wishes *she* were normal. Sometimes, I, too, wish I were normal, but I'm different. Hanna and I are nothing alike: she is like an angel, while I am a demon—the two do not go together. "And your parents don't know about your abilities?" I finally asked.

"No—no they do not. I know they love me, but if they thought I was a freak, they might stop loving me. You're the only one I feel I can tell. Sometimes—sometimes, I get the sense that they are not my parents. It's stupid, but sometimes I feel like I'm disconnected. They love me very much, and I love them. In fact, no one can rival their love for me. Everything they do is because of me, but I feel like they are overcompensating. It's just weird. I feel like I don't belong with them. If you look at it, I am blond, and they are both gingers. Both their families are brunettes and gingers, apart from the ones who have dyed their hair blond. Once I asked if I was adopted, and regretted ever raising that question because it offended them, especially my mum. Anyway, maybe it's just me trying to find fault in something that is perfect. Like you. You're perfect, and I keep insinuating that you have flaws and secrets. Forgive me."

I sighed. "There is nothing to forgive. No one is perfect. We all have our flaws, including me." I almost wished that she were not going on holiday tomorrow. I couldn't believe the amazing things she had just told me and how right she was about her parents not being her real parents. I looked at my wristwatch to check the time.

"It's getting late," I said. "I should take you home. Your parents might start to worry, and I *did* promise to bring you home on time." She smiled, but looked sad. I wanted to say something to cheer her up, especially after she mentioned that she didn't think her parents were her natural parents, but I didn't know what to say to that, especially because it was true.

She got up without a word and followed me to the car. We drove in silence back to her house. When I parked the car, we both just sat, not moving, and then I asked, "Why did you tell me all that? And don't say it's because you trust me. There is more, isn't there?"

She kept quiet for a while, and then turned to look at me. "There is more. I told you because—because I feel like you're the only one who can understand. I don't know why, but I trust that you will listen and not judge me. I know I've only known you a short while, which is a shame, because I wish I had known you all my life, even though it feels that I have. Funny isn't it, but, yeah, that's why I told you." She looked straight in my eye, and then at my gloved hands, and said, "In time, I hope you can find it in you to trust me." She smiled and got out of the car, and then shouted, "I will miss you, S."

I sat back for a while and watched as she went inside her house. My body seemed to have frozen in one spot. As amazing as it was that she is capable of the things she just told me, I still could not get my head round it. Is she even aware of how powerful she is, if everything she said is true? And I wondered if a mere human could be so gifted.

*Sebastian*

    I had been so sure she was a human before, but now I was not so certain. I had met her when she was just days old with a human mother, but now I was not so sure she had belonged to that woman. *Maybe I didn't kill her birth mother after all*, I thought. It just did not make sense that she could be human with this ability. I took a deep breath. I was beginning to worry about what I should not bother with. I was happy she was not ordinary, and I wondered what else she might be capable of. It was a shame that she wouldn't be around for the next couple of weeks, because it felt like forever—I was starting to miss her already.

# Chapter 16

I drove away from Hanna's house and headed for home. I parked my car in its usual place and started to walk back to the house to stand guard, like I always do. It was quiet as though the whole town had gone to sleep. A sound caught my ear, and I could hear voices. They weren't very clear at first. I tried to ignore the voices and concentrate on where I was going, when I heard Hanna's name mentioned. I stood still to see if I could pick out what was being said, but the voices stopped, as if they knew someone was listening.

I held my breath and tracked down where the sound was coming from. I moved through the trees cautiously to avoid walking on the ground. After a moment of silence, the conversation continued. I could see the people talking clearly now, as I was above them. There was a familiar stench amongst them. It was someone I had met before. I knew who it was immediately when the disgusting odour hit me. A woman was standing facing me, and a man was facing her, so I couldn't see what he looked like, but there was Huritt. I didn't know who the other two were and why they had mentioned Hanna, but I was curious to know why they were talking about her at this hour in the woods.

"You are beginning to lose her," the woman said.

"I am not, I promise you. I know what I am doing," Huritt replied.

"What is that then?" the man said through gritted teeth.

"Is it so hard to befriend her until you earn her trust? This situation has taken too long already. We need to act now, and you need to step up your game or we are all going to pay the price," he said angrily.

Huritt was quiet, and then the woman spoke. "No one asked you to fall in love with her. You have to snap out of it and concentrate on the task at hand, unless you think she is worth more than your family, than your life."

"I know what I have to do. It's just hard because she is my friend, and it's just so difficult to see her these days or get her alone by herself. She's always with this new guy. Even when I get to see her, all she ever does is talk about him," Huritt said annoyed. I could taste the anger in him.

"And that is why you have to act fast. Forget those silly feelings. There are other girls around. Concentrate on the task at hand and don't act jealous when you see her with this guy, or you might risk pushing her away. If you don't get her to come by on her own, willingly, on the set day, we may all just forget about being human. I don't need to repeat what is at stake here, but just so you remember what we are fighting for, the life we all know will be over by the next two full moons."

I did not understand what he meant by *their lives being over*, but I didn't care, either. In fact, I was contemplating whether to end their lives right now. They want something from Hanna, and whatever it was, from what I can gather, it didn't sound good.

My blood was boiling. I could feel my jaws tighten and my fists clench. It took everything for me to control myself from ripping their heads off and tearing them into pieces. As if I didn't have enough to deal with already, now wolves, too, were after her life. I had suspected Huritt was from the dog origin, I just had not been sure, but the mention of a full moon put it all into perspective for me. Then the woman spoke, "I know what we are asking you to do is hard, but it's the only way to lift this curse. I wish it didn't have to come to this, especially since she and her parents are our friends. But you must remember that we've waited a long time for her. She is the only solution we have, and that's the only reason we befriended her family in the first place. Like your father said, we don't have to remind you what the consequences will be if this fails," she said, touching his face.

"I understand. You guys have told me many times, but, Mum, what if it doesn't work? What if she doesn't have the power to change anything? I have been around her for so long, and she seems very normal. She is just a normal girl. There is nothing special about her. It doesn't seem right to do this to her," Huritt nervously tried to explain.

"You can't think like that. She is not normal—that I know for sure. Don't ask me how, but I do. Now you decide—is her life worth more than the rest of your family and the rest of the tribe? What do you think will happen if we fail? You will never be human again. If that is not enough to persuade you, you need to think of your sisters who you love so much, because you won't know them anymore, and they could become food to us. If they are fortunate to get away from us, the same fate we are facing still awaits them in the next few years, and they would have no one to explain things to them, unlike you. We were there to explain it to you. It will be different and more difficult for them. Do you want that for them? Think about all your friends in the tribe—"

"Stop, stop, stop, Dad!" Huritt interrupted. "I know! I heard you, okay? I understand. I know what's at stake. I will do it. We still have time, and there is still a full moon before the next. I will do it, whatever it takes, but once I do my part, you must be ready. I want it to be quick and painless, Dad. Promise me, Dad, painless," he said, starting to sob.

His mother held him close to her. "It's okay, Huritt. Nobody wants this. We didn't ask for this, remember, but it will all be worth it in the end."

The anger in me knew no boundaries, but I wanted to know more. The father had mentioned a tribe and a pack and sisters, which meant there were more of them out there. I needed to find out everything I could before taking them out. What did he mean by quick and painless? It couldn't be what I was thinking they meant, because I would die before I let these awful smelling dogs go near Hanna.

"What am I going to do about the new boy? He's always with her, and she always wants to spend time with him. There is something not right about him. He doesn't smell like a human. I've never come across anyone like him before."

"When it's time," his dad said, "find out from her when and where she will be meeting him and get to her before he arrives and invite her over. She will be eighteen on the full moon. She must never grow past that age or we will never be able to use her. She will become more powerful, if she doesn't already know. We don't want her realising or gaining any knowledge about who she is. Otherwise, it will mean trouble for us all. As for that boy, point him out to me the next time you see him, and I'll find out what I can about him. Anyway, I don't see him being a problem, and he is not our priority. Just focus on her, okay?"

"Okay, Dad. I will do it," he said, reassuring his father.

"I'm very proud of you, Huritt," his mother said, wrapping her arms around him in encouragement. Then the three of them walked towards the road that led to their home.

Reluctantly, I talked myself out of killing them right there. I would kill them eventually and the sooner the better because I would die before I allowed them to touch a strand of Hanna's hair. This whole thing sounded like a movie. I couldn't believe what I had just witnessed. It's a good thing I came when I did. I knew something wasn't right about Huritt. From the first day I saw him, I knew his friendship was flawed. I wondered how it was that she couldn't tell about him, if she could read me so well.

How could she have so many enemies—first the vampires and now these wolves? What is so special about her that they all want a piece of her? So she can heal fast and wake the dead, but is that ability enough for them to want to end her life? I continued to quiz myself as I walked to Hanna's house. I was beginning to suffer from information overload. Just as I was getting my head around the fact that she has this ability, I overhear that she is to be killed because of that same ability. These dogs want her life in exchange for theirs—how ridiculous. I was finding it hard to keep calm. I had to come up with a plan. I had to keep one step ahead of them. My quest for blood had been rekindled, and this time, I didn't feel guilty about it.

All through the night, my mind was unable to concentrate on anything but how to kill and wipe away that dog family and all their dog associates. I understand there are other creatures walking this earth, and they all have a right to exist. As long as they've been put on this earth, they have a right to fight for their future. And it wouldn't be any business of mine what they did if it didn't have to do with hurting or killing Hanna. But I will be dead before I let a human harm her, let alone a dog or a vampire.

Before dawn, when I was sure Hanna would be safe, I walked back home. I had a big fight ahead of me and needed to be strong for it. I thought about going to a hospital to raid human blood to prepare for the fight, but I soon discarded the thought, because it would be too hard to wean myself off it, especially now that Hanna knows where I live.

I ruled out going to the woodland to find deer, although their blood is better tasting than the farm animals, mostly due to their wildness. The next evening, I went to a farmer not too far from Hanna's house to talk about buying a few animals from him. I told him I was just starting out a little farming business, and he happily sold me two ox and two sheep. I was grateful to him and paid him a lot of money for each animal. It was better than just stealing them. I took home the animals, drained their blood, and stored the leftover in the fridge for later.

I went by Hanna's house to confirm that they were gone and was happy to see that there was no one around. I missed her so much, but I was relieved to know that she was away from danger.

# Chapter 17

I called Mason Benedict again to see if he was still on board. He wanted to know the story behind my troubles, and I filled him in on the situation on a need-to-know basis. I omitted Hanna's name and the fact that she was the reason I needed his help. I told him the vampires had been coming around me instead and that they were trying to run me out of town. I knew he would believe my story, as vampires constantly fight for territory. He advised me to get out of town instead. He didn't think it was right to start a war, especially because he knew I did not feed on humans. He didn't understand my hesitation to remain in a town that was of no use to me. But I convinced him that it wasn't right that I had to run each time another vampire felt he could claim a territory that belongs to me, just because I don't feed on humans. After a while, he called and told me that if I was sure I needed his help, he would send three vampires my way to stay with me for a while and help with my battle, if the need should arise.

    I knew he was powerful to an extent, but I wasn't aware that he had vampires at his disposal to do his bidding as well. That made me a little thoughtful, because, for him to have that kind of power over other vampires, he must be well revered and very dangerous. Nevertheless, I didn't have a choice. I needed his help, and he had offered it to me the best way he could.

*Sebastian*

Two days later, along came three male vampires. Nicholas was tall, dark, and rough looking, with long, dark hair pulled into a ponytail. He looked as though he had been around since forever. It was hard to put a time to his age, but, in human years, I would guess that he had been made in his late thirties. His face was stern and serious, as though he hadn't laughed in many years. He didn't look as though he had done anything with his appearance to try to fit into this century. The word *fashion* or *moving with the times* must have eluded him. He wore a long, black, eerie-looking jacket with a white blouse. He also wore tight, black pants that looked like breeches and knee-high boots. I must say, in a way he looked charming in them. I guess he was still living in the century in which he was made.

Henry was much younger than Nicholas—maybe a little older in human years than I was. He had short, blond hair nicely cut in one of the current styles. He looked very sweet and innocent. If I hadn't known better, I would have easily thought he belonged in a boy band. Anyone without a clue would certainly be fooled into believing his innocence. His dress sense was very current: clean and nice. He had on simple, but well-fitting blue jeans and a brown, leather jacket with a stripy scarf around his neck. I almost wanted to burst out with laughter at how ridiculously normal he looked, but I couldn't, because I knew too many innocent, teenage girls would have lost their lives to him. He looked harmless, but his eyes told another story—that he was not to be messed with. He seemed to like to keep to himself a lot and only joined the others when he was called upon. He had a somewhat serious and dangerous presence in spite of his innocent looks.

The last of the three, Thomas, appeared to be in control of the other two, who seemed to go along with whatever he said. He was neither friendly nor beautiful or innocent in any way—not that I think women would not find him alluring, but he has an air of mystery about him. One look at him and you instantly know he is not to be messed with. He looked to be the oldest of the three in vampire years. My guess about Thomas is that he is either second in command to Mason or the commander of his army of vampires. I could not categorize him no matter how I tried. He just sat in a corner and glared at me. I found it uncomfortable, and I wanted to know what he was thinking each time I caught him looking at me. Unlike the others, he had his dark hair down to his shoulders, and it looked untidy, but okay at the same time. His dress was a balance between the other two: nothing showy and nothing to grab your attention. He is the type you don't see coming because he easily blends into the crowd just as if he weren't there. He could stand next to you for hours and you might not be able to say what he looked like. He seemed young in human years. My guess is that he was made when he was about twenty-five. His face looks very rough, and I knew not to mess with him.

Mason warned me to prepare for their arrival if I wanted to keep the humans in my village safe. So I had human blood ready for them that I had collected from the blood bank in the hospital. I am ashamed to say that I compelled the human in charge to give me enough blood to last the three vampires for at least three weeks. In return, I rewarded him with enough cash to fall back on in case he lost his job because of me. I also made sure to compel him into forgetting that we had ever met. That was a lot of blood to go missing from the hospital, but getting that blood was a lot better than what would happen in this town if I did not have the blood in place for these three.

They were not very fond of having to warm up their food because they were used to getting it directly from the source. Nevertheless, they indulged me by not complaining. My guess is that Mason informed them of my way of living and told them to go along with it. I'm happy they chose to listen to him.

Immediately after they arrived, they took turns training me to fight, in case the need for it arose. I enjoyed the training very much, although I took a lot of beating from each of them. I was flung from one place to another. My bones broke and healed many times. I could not believe how ridiculously rubbish at fighting I was. I always thought it would be second nature—maybe it is with humans, because they are so weak. With these three experienced vampire fighters, I was just like a baby. I took all their beatings, but I never gave up. I kept getting up to get more beatings and learned to defend myself. I learned ways to attack and kill a vampire if need be. I watched every move they made, how they dodged and slipped away so fast to avoid being hit. Thomas kept telling me to gauge the range between me and whoever I was fighting. "It's in the eyes," he kept saying. They took turns and fought each other, advising that I watch and learn how to defend and attack.

"Look at his eyes and you can anticipate what he's going to do next. It's all in your reflexes," Thomas said. By the end of the first week I was confident in my abilities, should I ever need to use them, but I did not stop training. Relentlessly I gave myself to the challenge. I was defeated almost every time, but I never gave up. Thomas told me that with three, strong, powerful vampires attacking me at once, the only way out would be to be faster than they. The only way I could win would be to catch them unaware, which seemed impossible, but I reckoned he had done it a few times before.

A week seems a short time to suddenly become a good fighter, but I did not have a choice really. I slipped out at night to see if the vampires I had sensed previously were at Hanna's house. I told Nicholas, Henry, and Thomas that I was going out to hunt for animals. I had finished the blood I had stored up for myself because of the training, which took most of my strength. Most nights I went hunting because I had to keep my blood level high enough to be in good shape for the fighting. I knew with my diet, I would not be strong enough to fight vampires, but I had been told it's not just about strength. It is also about being faster and skilled and knowing where to aim to weaken them before staking them in the heart. I was hoping these vampires were not good fighters or all the training would mean nothing, and I would be in the same position I was in before they arrived.

As much as I tried to concentrate on the task ahead, I could not shake what Huritt and his folks were planning for Hanna. I had to restrain myself each time I felt the urge to go over to their house and rip them apart. I would deal with them in due time. I did not need any kind of training to kill an animal; I do it all the time. I've killed lions and all sorts of big cats, so a wolf stands no chance with me. I will get them one at a time, even if it means wiping out the whole tribe. I will do whatever it takes to keep Hanna safe.

Nicholas, Henry, and Thomas had been around for almost two weeks and still there had been no sign of these other vampires. I was beginning to wonder if I would have to go into this battle alone. Soon enough my guests would get tired of warming their food in the microwave and start craving to feed from the host itself. I had become fond of the three of them. Being with them made me loathe the fact that I am lonely. Living alone since the death of my mother has become a little tasking, and it would be nice to have someone to share the burden of my existence with.

I could pack up, go, and join Mason, but I could not see myself leaving Hanna behind. If I had never met her, it would have been easy for me to join him. But now that she is in my life, I would rather be with her until she is no more in this world. The thought of living in a world where she doesn't exist scared me, and I knew when that time came, however soon or far, I would end my life and be at peace.

The two weeks passed, and Hanna and her parents returned from their holiday. She called me several times while she was away, but I refused to take her calls, because I didn't want to alert others of her existence. I switched off my phone and even dropped a letter for her through their letterbox. The letter told her that I travelled for a while and would be in touch with her as soon as I came back. I wrote the letter so she wouldn't come looking for me while I still have my visitors in my house.

I resumed my duty to protect Hanna once they came home from New York and lied to the others by telling them that I was going hunting each night. It was all right, because they believed me and laughed at the idea of feeding on a squirrel. Hearing the sound of Hanna's voice, especially the first night after she came back, made me so happy it felt like my insides would burst.

By the end of the third week, the vampires I was preparing to battle had not shown up, and Thomas, Henry, and Nicholas had to go. A part of me wished they could stay longer so I could finally bury the fear of Hanna dying at the hands of vampires. The other part of me couldn't stand to be away from her any longer. I needed to see her as though my life depended on it. I saw Thomas, Nicholas, and Henry off. I was no longer able to feed them anyway, because all the blood I bought from the hospital was finished, and they had to leave before people started to go missing.

The day after they left, I went to see Hanna, stopping at the jeweller on the way to pick up a gift I had bought her and had engraved to show her how much I had missed not being with her. I bought her a bracelet, expensive, but not too showy so as not to invoke any curiosity from her parents about how I could afford such a gift.

I wanted to surprise her, so I didn't call her to tell her that I was coming. When I got to her house, I pressed the bell. I was restless and excited at the thought of seeing Hanna. Joan opened the door and seemed pleased to see me.

"Good evening, Mrs Greene," I said, bowing my head a little.

"Ah, it's you," Joan said. "Hanna, you have a visitor. You won't believe who it is," she called out. "Come on in," she said. "Hanna won't be too pleased if I don't let you cross the threshold." I heard Hanna running down the stairs as I stood in the hallway, excited at the prospect of seeing her again. I took a deep breath to calm myself.

"Who is it, Mum?" she called as she ran down.

"Come see for yourself," Joan replied. It did not take ten seconds for her to appear, but that moment felt like forever before she showed her face. She looked surprised and very happy to see me. Her face was as bright as the sun, literally glowing white. It didn't seem like her parents could see the glow that I saw, but that didn't matter to me. It warmed my cold body to see her that happy to see me.

*Sebastian*

She ran over to where I stood and stopped inches from me. "I didn't think I would see you again," she said breathlessly.

"Why not?" I asked.

"I thought that maybe—that maybe I finally—"

"You finally freaked me out?" I cut in. She smiled, and I wanted so much to hold her and bury my hands in her beautiful hair. It pained me that I could not.

"I missed you so much it hurt, and then you switched off your phone," she said.

I reached out and touched her hair slightly. "I'm sorry. I was busy, but you were always on my mind," I said.

She smiled and bit her lips. "I'm okay now that you're here," she said.

I smiled, and in that moment, my dead heart seemed to beat back to life as it raced inside of me, but only for a second. "I brought you a gift," I said.

"Oh, thank you, but you shouldn't have."

"Why not?" I asked.

She smiled and replied. "Your presence here alone is enough for me. You don't know how happy I am to see you."

"Oh, Hanna, I know exactly how you feel. I was miserable all the time you were gone. I missed looking at you and hearing you talk."

I watched as her face flushed. "Looking at me? What is there to look at?" she asked.

"Everything, Hanna. Everything about you is special to me, and I missed every bit of you." She looked away from me for a moment. "I got this for you, and I would love it if you would take it," I said, holding out the gift. She took it from me and said thank you, but I noticed she did not open it.

"Are you two going to stand there all day?" Joan called.

183

Hanna giggled and I smiled. "I'm sorry. Come on, let's go and sit," she said, and I followed her to the living room where both Joan and Joseph were sitting.

I exchanged pleasantries with Joseph and sat down opposite him. After about a minute or so, they both excused themselves and went upstairs, leaving Hanna and me alone. She tried to offer me a drink, which I politely declined, before coming to sit next to me. She started to ask me where I had travelled to, and I just found a way of diverting the question back to her. I didn't want to continue lying to her, so instead, I got her to talk about her time in New York. She didn't appear to have enjoyed herself as much as I would have liked, and it appeared that was due to me not picking up my calls.

"You haven't opened the gift I gave you," I said.

She looked at it, examined it a minute, and then placed it on the coffee table. "I will later," she said. I did not want to push her, so I didn't bother her about opening it again, although I would love to be here when she finds out what it is that I gave her. I wanted to see her reaction to the words I had engraved on the back of it, but I suppose I will have to wait until she is ready to open it.

We were both quiet for a while, and then she asked. "Why are you sitting so far from me? I know you are a gentleman and all that, but I would love it if we could touch sometimes. I don't mean like that—I mean, I just would like to be able to lean on your shoulder, if you would allow me, or maybe even get a hug sometimes."

I didn't know what to say to that. I knew this was going to come sooner or later, but try as I may, I didn't know how to handle it. What should I tell her? Should I say *no its impossible* or just let her do as she bids and maybe then I could explain to her what I am and hope she doesn't run away? I thought it through and then reluctantly decided it was time to leave. I got up from the chair, without thinking. "I have to go now," I said, walking towards the door.

"Why? Did I say or do something wrong?" she asked, confused and pained at my sudden decision to leave. I turned around and saw her muddled expression, and it annoyed me that I was troubling her, but I knew that I couldn't do what she was asking.

"No, Hanna. You didn't do anything wrong, but I have to go home, I have to attend to something immediately," I lied.

"Can I come?" she asked and jumped to her feet immediately. "I promise I won't be in your way. I just want to spend time with you, please," she pleaded.

I did not like that I was making her beg to be with me. I had wanted to say "No" before, but I couldn't anymore. "What about your parents? Won't they mind?" I questioned.

"No, silly. I will just tell them we are going out for a while and that you will drop me off before midnight. You will, wouldn't you?" she asked, biting her lower lip again.

I smiled. "No. I will let you walk home." I teased.

Before I knew it, she had run upstairs and back and we went to my car. I started it up and then she said, "Wait! I forgot something." She got out of the car, ran back to the house, came back with the gift I had given her, and then we drove to my home.

# Chapter 18

When we got inside my house, we sat in the living room—she on the big sofa and I on the chair, as we did the last time.

"What did you want to do?" she asked.

I looked around for something to say, but in the end I decided to tell her the truth. "Nothing really. I just wanted to come home."

"Ah, is it because of what I said?" she asked. I looked away and thought of something to say again to change the conversation, but nothing came to mind, so I remained silent.

"It is isn't it?" she probed further, but I continued to ignore the question. She got up from the sofa and came to where I was sitting. It made me nervous, because I didn't know what she was going to do.

She knelt down in front of me, looked me straight in the eyes, and said, "I know you are hiding something from me, and it bothers you. But I don't care, because I love being with you." She continued to look directly into my eyes, and I couldn't break my gaze from hers even if I had wanted to. It was as if she had transfixed me. Then she raised her right hand to my face and gently stroked it with her hands. She must have felt my cold hard skin, but she didn't react to it. Something else was happening to me at the same time: My body felt warm all over as she touched me.

I closed my eyes and enjoyed the warmth in my body as well as her touch, and then she said, "Don't close your eyes. I love looking at them. They are gorgeous, and you—you are beautiful. The other day when we were in your kitchen, I couldn't admit it, because you consume me, being with you, being this close to you, everything about you consumes me: your jaw, your chin, your eyes, they drown me. When you smile at me, each time you look at me, I freeze, my heart stops just because you glanced at me." I was breathing so fast each time she stroked my face and I felt my body melting. We'd never been this close before, and I didn't know what to do. I could hear her heart pacing faster as her breathing increased.

"You are different, and I know that. I have known from the first time I clamped eyes on you. I don't know what you are, but your secret is safe with me." I could feel her fingers on my eyelid as she caressed my face. I was speechless and weak before her.

"I have never met anyone as mysterious, yet absolutely breathtaking," she continued. I opened my eyes like she asked. I was still in disbelief as she continued to mould her hands over my face, like it was an art work, but my eyes were fixed on hers as hers were on mine.

"Is this why you wear gloves all the time?" she asked. I nodded. I knew she was talking about my body temperature. "You don't have to wear them with me. I don't mind that you are a little cold." She reached for my hands and took off the gloves, one at a time. I sat there like a rock, dazed at what was happening. I looked at her questioningly, and she answered me, as if she read my mind. "Like I told you before, I trust you. I don't know why, but I do. I feel very safe with you, and I want you to trust me, too. So you are different. I am, too," she said and smiled to reassure me. I gathered the courage to touch her face, which I had been longing to do for a long time, and then I got up and gently pulled her up so that we were standing and facing each other.

"Does it not worry you that my body is as hard as a rock and ice cold?" I asked.

"If that's part of who you are, then it doesn't matter to me," she replied.

"My body will never be as warm as yours or become any softer. It's always going to be this cold and hard. Do you still want to be with me?" I asked, and she nodded. "But why, when you can do better with someone else?" I asked.

"I don't want anyone else," she replied.

"Why me then?" I asked.

"Isn't it obvious? Can't you tell?" she said.

"Tell me? I want to hear you say it," I said.

"Because—because I love you. I have fallen in love with you, Sebastian. I love being with you. The way I feel about you I have never felt before, and it feels right, even though I know we haven't known each other long enough. When I am not with you, all I can think about is you. Your eyes, your scent, your hair, your smile, your gentleness, your face is all I see. I miss you when I am not with you, and nothing makes sense to me at all until I am with you. I think about touching you, holding you, being in your arms. And I know this may be too quick for you. I don't even know if you feel the same way, but I am a girl in love for the first time, and I can't keep lying to myself that I just want to be friends. I want to mean more than a friend to you."

She spoke with so much passion and warmth and roused all the feelings inside of me. I knew she liked me, but I wasn't prepared for this. I tried to control myself, but I was breathing so fast that something in me felt like exploding, and I tried to keep it together.

I must admit that I had secretly longed to hear her say these things to me, and I was overjoyed that she felt this way about me. I knew how hard it must be for her to say these things to me, but as overjoyed as I was, I found myself suddenly speechless. I didn't think it was right for me to take advantage, given the history. A part of me still felt that I have no right to feel for her like I do. To want her in my life so much that it kills me to think otherwise. But having her say that she loves me and wants me in her life has broken that part of me that feels like I don't deserve her. I couldn't find any words to tell her how much she means to me and how much I want her in my life. Instead, I gently took her face in my hands. I knew what I wanted to do so desperately, but as much I desired it, I couldn't. I felt wrong loving her this way. Slowly, I caressed her face with my hands as gently as I could.

"I'm sorry, Hanna. I want you to know that it kills me to say this, but this isn't right, not for you. I am not right for you. You deserve better," I choked out, appalled at myself with what had just come out of my mouth.

"No, no, Sebastian, don't. Don't say that, not now. Not when I can see that you want this as well. It's not just me who feels this way. I know you do, too. I can tell by the way you look at me, each time you look at me. Please don't tell me I deserve better. I know what I want and it's you I want. Please don't make me beg you to love me because I will."

"Hanna, don't, don't do that." I turned away from her. I couldn't bear to watch her hurt.

"I would, if that is what you want me to do, except you don't feel the same way. Maybe I have this wrong. I thought that maybe you—you wanted this as well. Look me in the eye and tell me you don't want this as much as I do. Only tell me the truth, nothing but the truth, Sebastian, and I will not bother you again. I will leave right now."

How could I look her in the eye and lie and tell her I didn't feel the same way when it's all I want. When I know I can't survive without her in my life. I tried to tell her the truth, but I couldn't get my mouth to open. Suddenly, she bolted for the door in tears, but before she could get there, I was in front of her. Gently I wiped the tears from her face and pulled her close.

"Don't go, Hanna. I'm sorry I made you cry. I don't want you to go." Then I raised her face up to mine and slowly but softly kissed her lips. My eyes closed shut as a range of indescribable feeling rushed through me.

I pulled away from her. Her eyes were closed and her cheeks flushed. I suddenly felt human again, as if she had ignited something in me that melted away all the hard ice in me. I guided her to the big sofa and we both sat for a while. She rested her head on my chest, while I gently held her in place. I still could not believe what had just happened between us, or the fact that she said she was in love with me. I wanted to kiss her again. My lips were still burning from that first kiss. To think this was my first ever experience of intimacy, and it was with her. I knew she was very fond of me, but I never thought she could fall in love with me. Now I knew that after tonight, I was sealed to her forever.

"You haven't opened the gift I gave you." I reminded her. She smiled and reached for it on the sofa. I sat up to face her, and watched as she opened it.

"It's very beautiful," she said, admiring it. She seemed happy with it, but I wanted her to see what was engraved on the back of it. "It looks expensive as well," she said, and I shrugged.

"I tried not to get something too expensive—not that you don't deserve the world. I just didn't want your parents to question how I could afford it," I said, rushing my words still buzzed from the kiss.

She smiled and said, "It's perfect, S. I love it."

"Turn it over. I want you to read what it says," I said.

She turned it over and read it out loud, "To Hanna, my reason for existence. Yours forever, S." Tears were streaming down her cheeks by now. I wiped them away with my hand, but she kept crying.

"This was not what I expected when I bought this gift. If buying you gifts makes you cry, I guess I better not repeat it," I teased.

She laughed and then said, "All this while, I have lain awake at night worrying that you probably don't have any feelings for me like I do for you. I thought you just liked being my friend, seeing that you are always so distant, and then you give me this."

"I gave you this because what it says is true. I know it hasn't been very long since you met me, but if you ever forget me, or decide to move on with your life, those words will always remain true. I'm sorry I didn't tell you earlier. I just didn't think I deserved you, but I have loved you from the moment I first saw you, and I wanted this gift to remind you that you mean the world to me every time you wear it. That way, even when I am not with you physically, you will know that you are always on my mind."

"Sebastian, you talk about me forgetting you, when I am hoping that you don't forget me or get bored and move on. If that ever happens, I don't think I would know how to begin to live again?"

I pulled her closer to me so that our faces were just inches apart. "To forget you would actually mean that I had stopped existing," I said and watched as her face blushed again. I couldn't resist kissing her again, this time a little longer than before. I pulled away reluctantly and held her gently in my arms, and we both sat there quietly.

"Thank you, S," she said.

"What for?" I asked.

"For loving me back."

I chuckled with contentment. If only she knew who should really be grateful. "You're welcome," I said.

Soon it was time to take her home, because I knew I still had to stand guard at her house. I wished she could stay here with me all night, because that way I would be able to protect her better, but her parents would worry. "I have to take you home now," I said.

"Do I have to go? Can't I stay here instead?" she asked jokingly.

"You could, but your parents will worry if I don't bring you home on time," I said.

"But I want to stay, S. Let me stay. I will think of something to tell them."

I turned her towards me. "Believe me, Hanna, I wish you could, but not tonight. I live here all by myself and there is always going to be room for you with me, but if I don't take you home, I will lose the trust your parents have in me. Don't worry, we will soon be together again," I said.

"Okay, when you put it like that, you make a lot of sense. You won't disappear again, will you? Promise?" she asked.

"I promise not to disappear," I said.

She leaned forward to kiss me and I returned the gesture, our lips met, and my body felt like it was alive and warm as we kissed. I moved my lips around hers gently, but urgently, as if I couldn't get enough of her. The feelings in me rose up to my chest. It felt like a cloud rotating in circular motions and spreading sensations down my body. I felt my dead heart pounding. The feeling raged and tingled all over. Then suddenly, I felt the cloud in my chest combust into tiny flames circulating through my entire body and setting me on fire inside. I had never felt more alive in all of my existence. If I didn't have to take her home, I would kiss her all night long.

I found the strength to break off the kiss, even though I didn't want to. Taking her home on time was very important to me. I still could not comprehend what had just happened to me while we kissed, and I longed to do it again. We got in the car, and I drove her home. All through the drive, my head was spinning. I played the whole evening again and again in my head. I was ecstatic. I wanted to scream, but I kept my calm and kept it together. I got out, opened the passenger door for Hanna, and escorted her to the front door. "Goodnight, Hanna," I said, fighting the urge to kiss her again

"Goodnight, S," she said in return. I kissed her on the forehead and returned to my car and waited until she was inside before driving away.

I was on cloud nine. It felt like a dream. Now it was formal between us that we loved each other. I wished there were no vampires coming over to her house for reasons unknown to me, or wolves wanting to use her for sacrifice. The best way to avoid this would be to take her away from all of this, take her somewhere far where we could be together and I could protect her without worrying that someone was going to get to her.

I should just take her away. She wants to be with me, and I wish I didn't have to consider Joan and Joseph. If they really knew who I was, that I had brought her into their lives, that I was responsible for all their happiness, and that I could take it back now. But I wasn't going to pay them back with misery after all they had done for her. It would be really cruel of me to indicate to Hanna that Joan and Joseph may not be her natural parents when they had done us both a big favour. That alone might open up a can of worms that I want shut forever. I had to live with the guilt of killing her natural mother within seconds without thought that she belonged to someone or that someone may need her, and that was very monstrous of me. Every time I think of Hanna, I hope and pray that she never finds out how I really met her. If that happened, I may as well end this torturous life, because the only thing that makes sense to me right now is her presence in my life.

As I kept watch over her house that night, my mind kept replaying the time we spent together, lingering on each touch that warmed my dead heart and literally broke through my ice-cold body. I found it hard to concentrate with her being so close. I was tempted to go inside her room and watch her sleep. Her windows were open, but I decided against it. It would not be gentlemanly to invade her privacy. To divert myself from the temptation I was facing, I started to think of ways I could punish Huritt and his family to teach them a lesson. I hadn't investigated the situation further. The passion that was clouding my thinking was not helping, either, but, if anything, it reminded me that I can't show mercy when it comes to punishing them.

From what I understand, Huritt is a little remorseful, but that does not mean he gets compassion from me, because he gave his word to bring Hanna to slaughter. He has to be punished along with the rest of his family. More than ever, I wished I were a day-walker, because the amount of time I had to accomplish things each day was getting shorter and shorter with each compiling problem. To find out the details of their plan, I decided that kidnapping Huritt was the best option. When I do, he can fill me in with the information I need about his tribe and why they want Hanna. I intend to get all the details I need from him and then I will dispose of him.

I drove back home before dawn and went to sleep. I needed to conserve my energy for the things I planned to do. When I woke up, I rang Hanna to let her know that I would be coming around her place later. Then I went straight to the wolf castle to try and put my plans into action. I didn't want to alert the others. I just wanted Huritt alone for now, which was sure to put a spanner in the works for them. I waited around for him for a couple of hours, but never saw him. After about three hours and still not seeing him, I figured he probably wasn't home, so I postponed the kidnapping. Hanna was waiting, and I didn't want to make her worry.

I cheered up as soon as I saw her face. Her parents had gone out to the pub, leaving her alone by herself. She looked fine and equally excited to see me. She threw herself at me, and I had to quickly catch her before she landed on the ground. I carried her to the living room and placed her on the sofa. She was in pain—she had hurt her nose when she threw herself at me. I was upset that I didn't stop her on time, and the day wasn't going as planned. She covered her face with both hands, so I wouldn't see her in pain. But that didn't help, because it pointed to the fact that I was too careless and capable of harming her, deliberately or not. This was all my fault. I got so carried away yesterday that I forgot to tell her there were certain things we couldn't do.

'I'm sorry," I said, trying to see if she damaged her nose.

"It's okay," she replied slowly, still covering her nose with both of her hands.

"I should have warned you—that we can't really do that. Er—not that we can't hug, but we have to be really careful," I said. She was quiet and her eyes were closed, as if she was thinking, but I could hear her taking deep breaths in succession. Nervous, because she was quiet, and her face looked like she was really in pain, I said, "I'm so very sorry, Hanna. I don't know what I can say to make you—" I tried to apologise, but she just got up and faced me as if nothing had happened.

"I told you that I'm okay. I'm fine. You don't need to keep apologising," she said with a smile, but not like the ones I was used to seeing on her face. She seemed all right now. I took a closer look at her face, and it was perfect, like nothing had happened.

"I didn't realise you could heal *this* fast," I said.

"Yes, when I want to, I can control how quickly I want the pain gone. It's a good thing, because, like that day at the music centre, I had to leave the cut alone, or people would get suspicious," she said, which just reminded me that I had actually caused her bodily harm twice. I looked away from her guiltily.

"What's wrong now?" She asked.

"Just now, when you closed your eyes, was it because you were in so much pain? And please tell me the truth, don't try to make me feel better."

"Okay, I'll tell you the truth and you have to believe me. Yes, I was in pain, but only for a short while. I closed my eyes, because I was trying to make my body heal fast. I didn't want you to see me with an upturned nose, which is why I covered it with my hands." I shook my head in disapproval. "I'm not lying, S. The pain didn't last as long as you think."

"That's not what I am annoyed about. I mean, I've just battered your body for the second time, and all you care about is my reaction to an upturned nose. Do you really think me that shallow to think you would be any less beautiful upturned nose or not? The fact remains that I caused you pain, however long or short it may have lasted. It's my fault," I tried to explain to her.

"It's not your fault, S. I mean, I should have had more sense. Yesterday I touched you and felt that your body was harder than most. I shouldn't have just thrown myself at you. I was being childish and should have been more careful. Just to put your mind at rest, you didn't batter my body. That word is a little harsh, don't you think? It was an accident, both then and now." She was taking the blame for what was not her fault, and I did not like it.

"Listen, Hanna, you have every right to be childish and to throw yourself at the person you love. I don't want you to blame yourself. I should have known better, and I am sorry I didn't warn you. You know, yesterday your accepting that I am different made me so happy that I didn't think to tell you there were things we couldn't do together. It's not like we can do most things you will do with a normal boyfriend. I am responsible for you now as your boyfriend, and I should take responsibility for my actions. I promise you, I will be very careful and treat you better than I have been doing. I never want you to get hurt around me again."

"Boyfriend! Who says you're my boyfriend?" She looked at me doubtfully.

Shocked and confused by what she just stated, I said, "Sorry, but I thought after yesterday that we—er—I'm sorry if I got it all wrong. I just thought yesterday meant we were—"

"Look at your face! Of course, that's what you are. I was only joking."

I took a deep breath. "If you don't like the word boyfriend, tell me. Isn't that what it's called these days?"

"These days?" she repeated. "You sound like you're not a teenager yourself. I don't know, the *boyfriend* word just sounds very casual, but I guess it's still in the early days, right."

"No, you're right. It's very casual and cheap. You mean more to me than a girlfriend. I mean, we both said we wanted to be more than friends."

"So what are we then?" she asked.

"Hanna, there is no right word to describe what you mean to me, so let's not—what's the word—er, label it."

"Okay, I'm not going to argue with you, because we are wasting precious time talking about what we shouldn't be talking about. Just so you know, I don't want a normal boyfriend. I'm not normal myself. I just want you, so don't think I am missing out, because I'm not. You know before, you came to town, no one did it for me, and then I saw you that day. You were so worried about what happened, and all I wanted to do was find a way to let you know that I would be fine. That was it, S. I saw your face, and it kind of embedded itself in me, and I just knew in my heart that you were the one I wanted. I was pulled to you right away. I couldn't get you out of my mind. And all those times we met at the art and music centre were the happiest I had ever been, because I was with you. You were my friend, only I wanted more. I must be a very good actress, because each day I saw you, I wanted more of you. So please stop worrying about things you need not bother with. I'm going to bump into you accidentally sometimes. You can't hate yourself for it each time. That's why I can heal. You are my ice, and I am your fire. We fit. Don't you see that I'm not as fragile as you think?"

I pulled her to me carefully. "When you put it like that, it makes all the sense in the world. Still, I don't enjoy seeing you hurt, but I'm not here to argue. I missed you," I said, as I combed my hands through her hair.

"Not as much as I missed you," she said, and we both chuckled. "My parents will soon be back."

"Hmm," I replied.

"They always sit here, so we can go to your place, if you like, or we could go up to my room, but I don't think my dad will be comfortable with that idea."

"So what do you want to do?" I asked.

"Let's go back to your place. I can stay as long as I like without having to worry about my parents," she replied.

"I like that idea, only problem is—I will have to bring you back before midnight. I don't want to upset your parents."

"If you say so. Sometimes, you act like such an old man, it's unbelievable, S. That's my father's job not yours. Let's go quickly before they come. I'll leave them a note so they don't have to worry."

"Okay." I nodded and went outside to wait in the car while she left a note for her parents.

# Chapter 19

As we drove to my house, I started to weigh the possibility of finding a way to tell her what I was. If we were going to be spending time together as we were, she needed to know about my ways and how I feed. I didn't like that I was still keeping the truth from her. I knew I couldn't tell her the whole truth, but I had to find a way to just point her in the right direction and hopefully she would come up with the right answer and still, hopefully, want to be with me.

"S, it's my birthday soon, you know. I'll be eighteen, can you believe it?" she said, all smiles. It reminded me that time wasn't on my side. I needed to carry out my plan on the wolf tribe quickly. If I had my way, they would all be dead before she turned eighteen. I was a little worried, but I made sure she couldn't tell my mind was preoccupied.

"Wow, do you want to celebrate it?"

"No, I don't, but my mum, on the other hand, wants a big party. She's gone crazy with planning. I don't get it. I already had a big party for my sixteenth—which I didn't enjoy—and I'm not looking forward to another crazy event. I don't like being the centre of attention."

"Well, you can't blame her. Eighteen's a big number, and you're an only child. Most teenagers your age will be buzzing at the opportunity to have a big bash."

"It's not like I don't like parties or that I don't want to celebrate, it's just—I don't have many friends. My mother is just going to fill it with loads of people I don't really know. What's wrong with a small gathering with my closest friends and family, nice and simple?"

"I get what you mean. But you're very friendly and easy to get along with. How come you don't have a lot of friends?"

"Sebastian, I'm not normal. What if something happens in front of other kids? I know I am careful, but you can never be too careful, right? That's why I only have two friends—Huritt and Emily. Oh, and you. Seriously, I just wish she would listen to what I want for once."

"Then don't have a big party. You must always do what feels right to you."

"I want to please Mum, because I know she loves throwing parties, and it's something for her to do to while away time. Since she doesn't work, she keeps busy planning parties. She loves it. I don't know what to do, but I am dreading it, I tell you."

"Tell her exactly what you've just told me. She's your mother and loves you. I don't think she'll ever put herself before you," I said to put her mind at rest.

"You really don't know her, not when it comes to parties. I'm sure as we speak she's already drawing up her guest list," she said, rolling her eyes.

I chuckled. I found it funny when she did that. "Well, then, just let your hair down and enjoy turning eighteen. I'll be there to keep you company if you invite me."

"As if! Left to me, I would prefer to be somewhere alone with you." She placed her head on my chest, and we were both quiet for a while. I felt at peace.

Then she said, "S, I know I shouldn't really pry, but if you don't mind, what happened to you? I mean, physically—the hard body, and all. I just want to know you more. Were you born like this? Or is it something that happened to you over time?" She raised her head up slightly to look at me.

I was quiet. This was the moment I had been waiting for, only I had never practised the answer in my head. I considered my response for a while before speaking. I knew only two things could happen, but I really hoped it wouldn't be the one I had been dreading.

"No, I wasn't born like this. I was infected by something when I turned eighteen. I don't know if it's a curse or a gift, but it changed me and I have been like this ever since. That's why I can't eat the kind of food you do as my body can't process it."

She looked troubled and puzzled, and then she asked, "So this must have happened not too long ago. I mean, you're still eighteen, right?"

The conversation was beginning to head in the direction I was dreading. I didn't think I was prepared to let her know the real truth about me. "I don't mean to be rude, Hanna, but it's kind of a touchy subject for me, and I don't exactly like to remember how it happened." I was quiet, but I could tell she was expecting me to say something more. "It's given me some abilities, though. Not as cool as yours, but I am not complaining."

"Really?" she questioned.

I could see in her eye that she was eager to know what they were. "Yes, I can heal fast. I am generally fast physically. I am very strong and can fly, not like a superman, but it's something," I said.

"Gosh, don't undersell yourself. The things you can do are incredible," she said in amazement.

"Not like yours, though. I mean, I can't control the way my body heals, and I can't wake the dead. Your abilities are beyond incredible."

She got up to face me as though she just had an epiphany. "You know what we could do, S?" she asked breathlessly and eagerly.

"What?" I asked.

"We could become superheroes! You know, like the *Incredibles*. You can fly, and you're strong and fast, and I can bring people back to life. We could help families who think they've lost a loved one. Who knows, maybe there's more to my ability. We can both discover ourselves together. Now that I have you, I'm not scared anymore. We would always have each other's backs, and I would never judge you for who you are or love you any less than I do now."

I was amazed at how enthusiastic she was about becoming heroes and helping people, but I knew for a fact that I was the opposite of what she was describing. I was the monster heroes like her save humans from, and, although she might not judge me, if she knew the real me, I would risk losing her.

"You are very kind to think of me in that light. You have a very generous soul."

"Thanks, and so do you. Anyway, what do you think, S?" she asked.

"I don't know, Hanna. I mean, I may have these abilities, but don't confuse me for a hero. I am far from it."

"Oh, S, don't say that. Do you think I would be with you if I thought there was a bad bone in you? You are the kindest, sweetest, and most respectful person I have ever known. You are a wonderful and beautiful person. I know it. I feel it every time I am with you. Forget the cold and hard exterior. You are good on the inside, and that's what counts. That's why I love you."

I smiled and almost believed what she said about me being good, but I can never forget all the people I murdered and sent to an early grave after my mother's life was taken away. I killed a lot of innocents, and I regret that now. My quest for revenge gave birth to a blind, monstrous rage that was fuelled by blood, greed, and power. I couldn't sit there and let her rain praises on me that I didn't deserve.

"Hanna, I appreciate that you think I'm this good person, but I've done many things that I'm ashamed to even think about. Although at the time I thought they were the right things to do, I know better now. I was pushed to the wall. I was vulnerable and did some terrible things that I can never take back. So when you talk about me being this wonderful creature, it only reminds me that I'm really the opposite of your beliefs and undeserving of you." I got up from her side. I didn't even know why I was saying all of this to her. A moment ago, I was sure I wasn't going to say anything at all. I heard her take a deep breath, but she did not try to come and meet me.

We were both quiet for a while, and then she said, "Okay, do you want to tell me what's eating you? I mean, what is it that you did that's so bad that you can't forgive yourself? Tell me. I want to know. Wait! Don't tell me if you really think it will affect us. But, then again, I don't think you're capable of anything that bad. The past is the past, and it's not good looking back. I really think we should focus on the future, S. I really don't want to know, but if you want to talk about it, I promise I will never judge you."

"Hmm, it's really nice to know that you won't judge me, but don't worry about it. Like you said, the past is the past, and what's done is done. I was just being foolish. Forget that I said anything," I said, realizing I had been stupid earlier. I wasn't going to confide in her about murdering loads of innocent people, including her mother.

She narrowed her eyes, as she looked at me. "Really, S? You sure you don't want to get it off your chest?"

"I'm all right. Like I said, I was just being stupid. You know, foolish talk. Let's focus on the future and forget I ever said anything." I came back to sit next to her and hoped she would forget and move on to a lighter subject.

"S, I don't know. I think we should talk. I know I said we should focus on the future, but I get this feeling that whatever it is that is eating you up will always have this dark cloud over us. So just tell me because now, I'll always wonder what went wrong in your past. And if you're hiding something from me, you will never be completely free with me."

"You're really not going to let this go are you?" I tried to joke, but could tell she was not having it. "Okay, Hanna. This is it. It's not that I don't want you to know. I mean, a part of me wants you to know, and another part of me, if I am really honest, would rather you didn't know, because I fear you might change your mind about being with me. It's nothing pretty, and I'm forbidden. I can't tell humans about it."

"What do you mean by *humans*? Wait! Are you saying you are not human?"

This was it. There was no backing out now. I could either tell her the truth or I could continue lying to her. She was looking at me and I could tell that if I lied to her right now, she would know. At this point, I was tired of all the lies. I knew I could never be completely honest, but it was time I pointed her in the right direction. So I took a deep breath and gathered my thoughts before speaking. "I used to be human. I was until I turned eighteen. So, no, I am not human, Hanna. Not anymore." I watched her face to read her reaction, to see if she was afraid of me, but I couldn't read her expression. Her face was still, not giving anything away.

"If you are not human, then what are you?"

"I want to tell you, Hanna, but I can't—I can't say the word."

She looked down for a while. "What happened to you when you were eighteen? What made you change?"

"I was bitten by—by—someone." I could not bring myself to say *my mother*. I did not want Hanna running out of here.

"Bitten? And that changed you?"

"Yes," I said, still waiting for her to put the pieces together. She was thinking. She must have read about my kind in a book or seen it in a movie.

"So, you told me that you are a vegetarian. What kind of food do you really eat?" she asked. I kept quiet, and she looked at me as if she knew what I was not saying.

"This can't be true. I mean, I have read about this and watched films about it, but people always say it's a myth. You can't really be one, can you?" she asked rhetorically. It felt like she was debating with herself whether or not to believe it. "You are not feeding on humans are you?" she asked.

"Not anymore. There was a time, a short period, when I did, but not anymore." She was quiet so I thought I better explain myself better. "When I was changed, I didn't touch human blood for a very long time. I had never hurt a human for many years, which is a rarity amongst our kind. Believe me, I'm not trying to justify myself, but I had my reasons. Someone very important to me was taken from me suddenly, and it forced my hand. I couldn't control my anger. I—I wanted revenge for the life they took. I allowed a darkness to take over me, and it turned me into something I will forever be ashamed of. I tried to stop, but I had no control over my will. Then, something incredible happened to me and—and it turned me in the right direction and made me who I am today. I had a reason to live again, to be hopeful about life, and I changed. I fought the cravings, and I haven't hurt anyone since then." I couldn't tell her she was the reason for the new me. It would only lead to difficult questions.

"So how long ago did this happen?" she asked,

"Almost eighteen years ago."

"Eighteen years!" she repeated. I tried to reach for her, but she moved away.

"I mean, I am just going to be eighteen, which must mean you've been eighteen for a very long time. I know, I promised not to freak out, and you were very graceful when I told you about me, but this wasn't what I expected. It's a lot to take in. Er—don't you guys—er—how do I say this? Er—I am aware that you people live a very long time. Sorry, I'm talking all weird, and I've lost my line of thought. Okay, tell me this—how long have you been eighteen?"

I was quiet. I can't say I didn't expect her to react like this. I knew it, and I told her anyway. It's not so much her reaction that bothered me, it's because I could tell she was going to run. In my head, I could already hear her saying it, telling me this was all a mistake. With every word that came out of her mouth, I could see her slipping away.

I started to wonder how I was going to cope with her out of my life. It didn't seem fair to be so loved and then rejected, but I always knew this was going to happen. I should have continued lying, or I should have stayed away from her and loved her from afar, because I knew the hurt and hole that would remain after she's run off will never heal.

"Hanna, I am not dangerous anymore. You will never have to fear for your life with me. What I did then I am not proud of. I've lived for over a hundred years without hurting a human. Believe me, it's never going to happen again," I said dying for her to say *it's okay*, that she understands and still wants to be with me.

"Wow! You are over a hundred years old? I still don't believe this. This—what you are is supposed to be in the imagination of people. You are supposed to be a myth—people make up these stories, this fiction, yet here you are." She sounded like she was talking to herself. I noticed she had avoided the saying the word *vampire*. She walked across the room to avoid being close to me I thought.

"So where does this leave us? I need to know what you are thinking."

"It's okay. I mean—I don't know what you want me to say. When I said I was never going to judge you, I meant it but—I don't know now. I am not judging you, but I never thought I would be in love with someone who has killed a human, let alone be in love with what I think you are. I'm really trying not to be this person looking at you like you are someone else now, but if I am honest, I can't see past the part where innocent people died. I know you must have had your reason, and maybe after I've heard it, I'll be able to see the Sebastian I love, but right now I—I need some time to process the whole situation," she said, but I could tell from the look in her eye that whatever we had going, was over already. To think that just yesterday we were telling each other how much we loved each other, and today it's all over.

"Hanna, I know it's difficult for you to see past what I just told you. I almost didn't tell you, because I feared this very reaction, but I'm glad I did, because now you know the real me. Not that it matters anymore to you how I feel about you, and it shouldn't because, as much as I want you in my life, I also want you to be happy. I want you to live your life free of guilt. I want all the happiness in the world for you because I love you. I have never loved any one like I love you and I never will. Don't worry about it, because it's my cross to bear. If you decide to leave because of what I did in my past, it will be a great blow to me, the worst thing that could ever happen to me, but, then again, I say I deserve it—and more—for my past. You don't have to worry. Don't be afraid. You can go. Go and live your life. Find someone else. Be happy, and I promise I will go. You will never see me again. It will be as though you only imagined me." She stood still and looked at me with tears rolling down her cheeks, and it pained me. I wanted to go to her, but knew she didn't want me near her.

"Who was it? Who did you throw it all away for? You must have loved that person, too, yet you tell me you've never loved anyone like you love me. You've been around for almost two centuries, and you want me to believe there were no other women. Why tell me lies to make me feel that I'm special, different from the rest of them?" she asked fiercely.

"Listen, I am not lying to you. You *are* the only one, and you *are* special and different. Yes, I killed humans for someone who was dear to me, and it's haunted me ever since, but I—I cared about her because she was my mother and when they killed her, they killed my humanity. I lived a horrible life when she died as a human, and then she found me again only to be killed. She was taken from me once again, and I was all alone. I didn't know how to exist without her. She made me. She taught me not to hurt humans, how to survive without the need for human blood, and they paid her back by staking her heart and setting her on fire. What hurt me most was that she didn't even fight back. So I had to fight for her. I had to take the lives of everyone who partook in her brutal murder. After I had done that, I started to lust for human blood, which was different. It was addictive, it was refreshing, and I couldn't control my greed, but I found salvation, and I changed."

"Just take me home now," she said, looking away from me. It hurt to see that she couldn't wait to get away from me, but I didn't blame her.

"You can't even look at me anymore. If I could take it all back, I would, but I can't. I—I'm not that person anymore. I've changed. You said you could see something kind and wonderful in me. You've always said that. Is that all gone now? Am I just a monster to you now?" I asked, standing in her way so she could hear me out. I knew she could go tonight and never want to see me again.

"I'm not judging you. I understand, in a way, why you did what you did, but I have to leave now. Not because I suddenly don't love you. I do. I love you, and it's terrifying for me how much I still do, even after all you've said, so much so that I want to almost say it doesn't matter that you've killed humans. What kind of a person does that make me? What kind of a human would I be? I wish I had never asked you, but I pushed you into telling me. I wanted you to unburden yourself, and now I'm burdened with the guilt of loving you. I have never loved before, nor has anyone ever loved me like you do. I know you've changed, but I can't—I can't tell you what you want to hear. Not now. I need time to think."

I looked at her. Enough had been said already. There was no need for anything else to be said. "Okay." I nodded. "I won't keep you here any longer than you want to be."

# Chapter 20

I always knew we were never going to work. It had been a dream and should have remained so. I had been too deluded by my feelings to let reality sink in. She walks the light, and I walk the night. Surely we were too different. She is the angel, and I am the demon. I led the way, opened the car door, and she entered. I made up my mind not to talk about it anymore. The best way to deal with the pain I was feeling, was to think of the battles ahead of me instead. I will hold on to that and keep busy. I will plan strategies and make sure I see them through. I will keep Hanna safe, even if it costs me my life. The journey home was a little awkward, because neither of us said anything to the other.

When we arrived at her house, I got out of the car and opened the door for her. Without a word, she got out and ran straight to the front door. It felt like she was running away from me. I closed my eyes as I tried to fight the pain that gripped me, and then I knew she wasn't coming back. I suddenly felt dizzy and took a very deep breath to steady myself. When I opened my eyes, to my surprise, there she was standing in front of me. I didn't know what to say. I didn't even hear her walk back. I wondered how long I had been standing there. She was looking at me, and I didn't know if I should be glad or not. I was dreading what I already knew she was going to say. Perhaps she was too scared to tell me at my house, because she thought I might hurt her and waited until we got to her house.

I braced myself for the news. She said, "I know you are hurting right now, but so am I. Believe me the last thing I wanted was to do this to you. I couldn't tell you this earlier, because I owed it to both of us to do what was right. Just now when I walked through the door, it occurred to me that I may never see you again if I let you go, and I knew then that I would regret it for the rest of my life. My heart is too fragile when it comes to you. You got to me somehow. You said earlier that I should be happy and find someone, but how can I do that when my heart has chosen you? I can't tell you it doesn't matter what happened in the past. It's not up to me to vindicate you, but I can tell you it matters what we do with our future. I belong with you, and I'm sorry I turned out to be so judgmental. If I were in your shoes, I probably would have done the same thing to those who killed my mother. I do not need any more time to think about it. I've made my decision. I want you in my life, however long or short I live, as long as I can spend them loving you and you loving me."

I didn't know what to say. Just when I thought I had lost her, she comes back and says all is well. "I don't know what to say. I thought I had lost you."

"If you had, I wouldn't be standing here longing to kiss you."

"Thank you. I—I can't thank you enough for—" before I could finish thanking her for giving me a chance, I felt her lips on mine, and I wrapped my arms around her. Dazed, I could not believe how my luck had changed. We pulled away from each other, and she smiled at me. I was still dazed.

"Did you think I was going to let someone else into your arms? I'll see you tomorrow. Good night." I smiled back. She didn't really understand that she alone belonged in my arms. I drove away feeling blissful, light, and happy. It felt great having everything in the open, except for the part about my killing her mother. She need never know, and I was going to make sure of it.

The next full moon was fast approaching, and I needed to go hunting and be well prepared for the fight ahead. I planned on killing them all before the full moon. After my usual nightshift at her house, I went home to rest. When I woke up, I went in search of food—nothing big, just enough to keep the hunger away and make me strong enough to take down the tribe.

Now that Hanna knew about me, she wouldn't find it a shock when I told her what her friend Huritt has been up to. But I decided to spare her feelings on that one and deal with the situation alone. I couldn't tell her for three reasons: First, because she had known him too long to believe he was capable of wanting to do her harm, and I had to start looking for ways to prove it to her. There was no time to waste. Every minute I let him and his tribe breathe, they plot to end her life.

Second, if by any chance she believes there is a possibility the person she thought was her close friend was not normal and that his friendship was a lie, it would hurt her deeply. Not counting me, she only has two friends, and one is traitor.

The third reason is that I intend to kill them all, and there is no debating that. She most definitely would have a problem with the way I plan to resolve this situation, but I couldn't let them live and forever be looking over my shoulder.

Before I went hunting, I rang Hanna and told her I was taking her out on a proper date later that evening, not like the disastrous one we'd had before. I wanted to celebrate our new beginning, and I also wanted to do something nice with her before initiating my plans for Huritt.

I got out a new shirt, a pair of jeans, and shoes and laid them on my bed to wear when I came back. I called a restaurant to make a reservation and even booked us tickets for the movies for after she'd been fed. I was going to make every effort to ensure that she had a nice time.

# Chapter 21

## Hanna Greene

I knew it wasn't right being with him after what he did in the past, but that was the past and now is now. It doesn't mean I forgive what he did. It's not for me to decide what his punishment should be, but I am willing to look beyond who he was then. Moreover, I have no idea how to live without him. Each time I look at him, I see someone desperately trying to be better. As long as he is trying, I will always be on his side. How could I break his heart when my own heart was already broken at the thought of never seeing him again?

So it's no secret that I was over the moon when he called to take me on a date this evening. I asked my dad for money for a new outfit and went shopping, because I wanted to look beautiful for him. I bought a lovely, flowery dress that hung to just a little above the knee. I stopped by the salon and got my hair washed. Sebastian always looks stunning without trying—and that's him dressed down—which makes me wonder what he is going to look like tonight.

He said he would pick me up at seven, but I was ready to go an hour before then. I probably shouldn't always be in a rush to be with him, but I don't see the point in wasting precious time that we could be spending together fondling with make ups. I sat in the living room with my parents, trying hard to tune out my mother who was nagging me about me being ready too quickly. "Darling, you shouldn't always be the one waiting for him. He's a man and will take you for granted."

"You don't know him like I do, Mum."

"I don't have to. All men are the same. They like it when we keep them guessing. You jump when you see him, and it's adorable, but, like I said, boys will be boys. He could see that as a weakness and hurt you."

"You really don't know him, Mum. He would never hurt me. He loves me, and I love him. There is no need for games between us. I'm mature enough to know what I want."

"I don't want you to play games. I just don't want you to be too desperate for his attention."

"Leave her alone, Joan. She's young, and she likes him. It's her life, so let her live it," Dad intervened.

"I am only giving my daughter some motherly advice. We need to be together on this. Since she met him, she seems to have forgotten that she has other friends, and there is also the issue of her upcoming party. I need her here more so we can discuss what we need to do."

"Mum, you don't need me for that. I am sure you have it all covered." I kept looking at the time every five minutes, and it felt like it was crawling.

"You know you can keep looking at that clock all you want, but it's not going to go any faster than it already is. What time did he say he would pick you up anyway?" dad asked.

"Um—seven," I said. I watched as mum shook her head.

"You see what I was saying?" Mum added.

"Let her be. You were crazy about me once," Dad said, and Mum rolled her eyes at him.

"What would it take for you to tell her the truth? You spoil her, and one day soon enough, you'll both admit I am right."

I blocked Mum out my head. I wasn't going to let her put a downer on my day. I wished for once that Sebastian would come early. I was tired of my mum's nagging, and I couldn't wait to be out of the house. At this point, I felt like going to my room to wait. I looked at the time again and still had forty-five minutes of waiting to do. I was about to leave for my room when the doorbell rang.

I bet he couldn't wait, either. I gave my mum the look that said *I told you so* and then got up to go let him in. I rushed to the door. My mother tried to stop me from opening the door myself. She asked me to wait and allow her bring him in instead, but I didn't want him to come inside and be grilled by my mum so I refused. I know she sees my behaviour with Sebastian as desperate, but she doesn't understand how I feel about him. She doesn't understand that I am constantly pulled to him. It's more than love between us. It sometimes feels like we need each other to survive, and one without the other is useless. That's how I feel when I am not with him—useless and insignificant, but when we are together, I feel untouchable. There was no need to try to make her understand this, because she would never know what it feels like to love him like I do.

I opened the door and, to my surprise, it was not him. There was a girl standing there. She smiled sweetly at me, and the first thing that struck me was how beautiful she was. She was brunet, and her long, black hair fell down her back to her waist. She smelt good too, not like anything I had ever come across. She looked like she was about my age. If she were any older it wouldn't have been more than a year or two.

"Hello," I said, disappointed the wrong person was at the door, but still managing to crack a smile. She had probably lost her way and needed pointing in the right direction.

"Hi," she responded.

"Can I help you?" I asked.

"Yes, actually. Er—are you by any chance, Hanna?" she asked. I wondered what she wanted from me.

My parents were probably starting to worry about me, because my father hollered out, "Hey, Hanna, is that Sebastian at the door? Get him inside, honey. I need to have a word before you kids take off."

"No, it's not Sebastian, Mr Greene. I'm just a friend from the music centre," the girl yelled back to him. Before I could tell Dad that I didn't know her, he invited her into the house.

"Come on in then. Hanna, don't just leave your friend outside. It's freezing out there." She immediately forced her way past me, our bodies touching, and I nearly fell on my back. I sensed something from her as we touched, which made me uncomfortable, and I wished that my dad had not invited her in.

"Excuse me, you can't just storm your way inside my house," I said to her. She just looked at me as though I did not matter and went straight to the living room where my parents were. Quickly I went after her. "Dad, why did you ask her to come in? Do you know her? She just charged in."

My dad shook his head. "No, I don't, honey. I thought she said you were friends." My dad looked confused. "Joan, do you know this girl?" he asked my mother.

"I can't say I have seen her before. Honey, have we met before? How can we help you?" My mother asked her sweetly. She just looked from one of us to the other as we tried to find out what she was doing here and who she was. Then she turned her attention to me.

"So you are the Hanna I have been hearing so much about?" she asked, smiling.

"What?" I replied.

She walked towards me and started circling me. "I see you're all dressed up to go out. Do you know where you're headed then?" she asked. I looked at my parents who were now beginning to get as irritated with this stranger as I was.

"Look, lady, we don't know who you are and we don't want trouble. If you need help, tell us and we will do our best to help. If not, do us a favour and leave before I call the police. I only asked you in because I thought you were my daughter's friend," my father said to her. She stopped and looked at my parents and busted out in laughter. Her laughter must have irritated my mother, because she immediately picked up the phone to dial the police and before we knew it, the phone was out of her hands. The girl moved so fast that, before I could blink, she was at my mum's side and back to where I was standing with the phone in her hand.

"I know you are all wondering why I am here? You want to know who I am and I will tell you, but in my own time. Just so we are clear, don't try and do anything stupid or I might just skip the part where I tell you who I am and just get down to why I am here. And you don't want to know why I am here—not yet anyway." She seemed to be enjoying the effect of her words on us.

"I can see you're all shaking in your boots, and you should be, because trouble has found you today," she said and laughed aloud, wickedly. I wished Sebastian would hurry up and come. I looked at my parents who both looked scared. My father was doing his best to hide it, but I could tell he was scared for us. I looked at my wrist to check the time but I wasn't wearing my watch. I had on the bracelet Sebastian had given me, which reminded me not to worry too much, because he would soon be here. When my body had touched that girl's before, I felt her strength. I knew then that she was like Sebastian, but I also felt something iffy and dark from her, so there was no telling what she had come here for. I was afraid for us now. I feared more for my parents if Sebastian didn't get here soon.

Then she looked at me again, and I could feel the anger and hatred in her eyes as she directed them at me. "So it's you—you this fragile little thing. You are the reason he doesn't care about me. I always knew there had to be somebody. Now I know. What he sees in you is beyond me," she said, looking me over like I was trash.

"You know, flowers bloom and they look so pretty, so delicate, so full of life, but it's only for a season, a very short while. You get attracted to them because of all the colours and fragrance that exudes from them; you pick them up because they invite you; you want to look after them because you know they won't be around for long. Then you take them home, put them in a vase, and water them, but no matter how much you care for them, they start to lose hold of life and begin to shrink and whither. And there is nothing you can do to make them all perfect again, so you throw them out and then pick up another bunch and cherish them for a little while before throwing them in the trash where they belong. It's harsh, but that's life, and that's all you are to him—a worthless, trashy, pretty, little flower. You are just an ordinary girl, living an ordinary life, with less than ordinary parents, in a terrible town, yet he chooses you over me?"

"Who are you? What do you want from me?" I asked, trying to look as bold as I could muster.

"Oh, you are one brave little human, I see. Ah, I'm glad I haven't terrified you too much to think you're allowed to speak. What did he tell you to make you feel so brave?" She started her wicked laughter again. "Listen, I have known him and loved him for a very long time, and I am not about to let a little flimsy human like you take him away from me. I'm sure you were just mistaken, because if you knew he loved me, you wouldn't have messed with what we have. But I'm not going to leave without punishing your behaviour anyway. What you did hurt me. You can't begin to imagine how much it hurts to know the person I love has been with you all this time. So I will do you a favour today and end this misery of a life you think you have."

Then she looked over at my parents. "They also get punished because of you, and it will all be on you. What did he tell you? That he loves you? How can he love you when you do not belong in our world? Couldn't you have found yourself a worthless human like yourself, marry him, and live the picket-fence life. You humans: you always want what you can't have. So he sulks over you and watches over you every night like a loved-up puppet. He belongs with me. His love belongs to me. You have nothing to offer him, do you hear me? Nothing but heartbreak. If I don' kill you today, you're just going to die some other day and leave him broken hearted, and I don't want that for him, because I love him. I have loved him for over a century, and I will love him for all of eternity. Are you so deluded you can't see that you don't belong with him? Do you know how many years he's lived and how many more he will live while you rot, like the rest of your human race?"

She smiled sarcastically, knowing my parents were shocked to hear what she had just revealed. She turned to them and said, "Your daughter is besotted with a vampire, and you approved of him, didn't you?" She looked from them to me to gauge my reaction. My parents looked at me in confusion. *Sebastian where are you,* I kept thinking. I was afraid for my parents, who looked so shocked by this revelation. I could see the disappointment on my father's face, and it pained me, because it was too late for me to explain things to them.

"Oh, don't look to her for answers. If you're confused, ask me, and I will fill you in on the details. It's true, I've known him, your sweet-looking Sebastian, for almost two centuries, and I have loved him since the day I saw him. So, you must understand my anger when I learnt that he is in love with this trashy, plain, measly mortal. It's pretty pathetic you would agree," she said, enjoying every minute of her performance. My parents were so frightened, especially my mother, and I just wished Sebastian were here already.

"Stop. Please stop. That's enough! You're frightening them," I said.

She looked from me to them, and smiled. "Well, they have every right to be frightened, because they are going to die—and so are you. I love the look of you humans when you know the game is over. I particularly enjoy the fear on your faces. You all secretly wish something would happen to save you, but the truth is that no one is coming. Not even Sebastian, because by the time he arrives here, you will all be dead. I can promise you that." My mother was shaking and beginning to cry. "Oh don't be upset. You were all going to die someday anyway. I'm just helping to speed things up. Tell me, Hanna. Humour me a little. What did you first fall in love with? His beauty? I bet it was. Even I, as beautiful as

I am, I can't resist getting lost in his eyes. What else? His charm? His kind nature? Hmm, I could read you a long list of why he's so ideal. The only problem is that he is mine and not yours, and you have to pay the price of meddling where you don't belong."

I knew she had made up her mind about me, but I thought perhaps I could beg her to spare my parents' life. "Please don't—don't do this. I never knew about you. He never said anything about you. I will do anything you say, just don't hurt my parents. Please, I beg you. I will give him up. I will never see him again, I promise you."

"Oh, won't that be nice? Let's say I believe you're not lying to me just to save their skin," she said, pointing to my parents. "Let's say, for argument's sake, that I take your word for it. The only problem with that is, he won't give you up as long as you're alive. Our kind, once we find a pet, sometimes it's hard to let go. He will never be able to love me like I want him to. So you see, it will not do me any good to keep you alive. There is only one solution, and there is no way around it. You have to die. As for these ones," she said pointing to my parents again, "they are just victims of circumstances. Oh well, since they are here—the more the merrier."

"No, please. Take me. Take me. I am the one you want. Leave them out of this. You could do something and make them forget you were ever here. I know you can. Please, I beg you," I pleaded with her. My dad moved towards me, and with one fast move, she dropped him to the ground.

"I wouldn't try that if I were you. Believe me you're no match for me." Then she turned to me. "And why would I do that, spare their lives for your sake? Who are you? I don't owe you any favours, and you're not special. I bet now you wish you'd never met him. Look at what he's done to you.

Oh, don't worry. I am not going to get my hands dirty. I have my friends for that. I know after today, Sebastian's going to come looking for answers, and I'll be telling the truth when I tell him I didn't kill you. Then I'll offer him comfort. I'll be there for him while he mourns your death, and before he knows it, he'll stop missing you. He'll realize where he should have been all along. He will love me like I've always wanted him to. But you, you will be a distant memory, forgotten like every insignificant human who meddles in our world."

She smiled wickedly, and then turned to my father. "You get up. I have three friends waiting outside eager to come in, and they are very thirsty. Invite them in!" I watched as my father got to his feet, went to the door, and invited the other three into our house. I looked at my mother, who was so terrified. I couldn't meet her eyes, knowing I was responsible for bringing this evil to our door. And then three handsome-looking boys in their teens came inside the house. One had my father in his grasp and flung him towards my mother.

"My dear friends, welcome. I have a feast for you. One for each of you. I wish I could join in, but Sebastian will soon be here, and I want him to know how close he was to saving her. Drain them!" She snarled.

The three watched as she disappeared into the hallway. My mother and father were holding each other, and all I could do was cry, because I had brought this upon them. I looked at them and mouthed an apology.

"I am so sorry. I love you." I closed my eyes and thought of Sebastian. As sad as it may seem, I still loved him very much and wanted his face to be the last I saw before I died. I took off the bracelet he gave me and held it in my hands and prayed for a miracle. I heard the other two boys introduce themselves to my petrified parents, meanly toying with them.

"Hello, my name is Anton and this is Zacchary. We would like for you to know our names before we feast. I will take the man, Zack, you can have the other one." He laughed and then Anton and Zack charged at my parents. I closed my eyes and heard their screams as their lives were being snatched away.

The other two were busy with my parents, when the third walked over to me and said, "Hey, my name is Hector. Listen, I will make this as quick and painless as I can. I wish I didn't have to do this. I am sorry." And before I knew it, he had dug his fangs into me. I felt my life slowly slip away. I held the bracelet tighter and quickly scrambled in my brain to find Sebastian's face, until it was so blurry and nothing made sense anymore.

# Chapter 22

## Sebastian Francis

I got back home from the hunt and quickly hit the shower. It took me longer for some reason to pin down a meal. I was already running late, and I wanted the day to be perfect. I got out of the shower and dabbed on a good aftershave to ensure I didn't smell of the woods and blood. Then I got into the clothes I had laid out earlier. It was important that I look my best. I stood in front of the mirror and carefully brushed my hair back away from my face, and then I took one last look and knew I was ready to woo her.

 I jogged down the stairs in high spirits, picked up the car keys on the table in the hallway, and went straight to the car. It takes about fifteen minutes to drive to Hanna's, and I was already ten minutes late. I was supposed to be at her place at seven. It wasn't a good way to start, and I hoped she would forgive me. I put on the radio, and a woman was singing. I thought about changing the station, but the song wasn't bad, so I let it be. I rolled down the window to let air in. I was nervous and I was late, and for some odd reason I was panicking inside. I tried to stay calm. I couldn't quite understand why I suddenly had this unnerving feeling inside, like I was about to ruin everything by being late.

As I drove, the air coming through became very windy. I could smell the misty air. The heavens were about to open up. Nothing was going as I had planned, but I was determined to make the night as special as possible. As I got closer to Hanna's home, the fearfulness increased. Something wasn't right. I stepped on the gas. Then suddenly, I felt weak to my knees, like I had life knocked out of me. I knew it now: She was in trouble, and I was still too far away. I prayed I wouldn't get there too late. I banged my fist repeatedly on the steering wheel in anger. If this was what I imagined, it would be too late by the time I got to her.

I throttled down fully and still I wasn't driving fast enough. I could feel the tears clouding my eyes as I made the turn into their drive. When I pulled in, the air and their scents greeted my nostrils together with the smell of blood. The exact ones I had been dreading. I noticed the front door partly open. It was obvious what had happened, but I was hoping for a miracle. It was quiet. I couldn't hear or feel the presence of any living human. I sat in the car and stared at the door. I pictured Hanna running out to meet with me. Tears started to trickle down my face, and I imagined her face glowing, smiling, and happy—her shiny, blonde hair swaying as she walked and her deep, blue eyes glistening with happiness. Then a heavy downpour interrupted my thoughts and brought me back to the nightmare I was about to face.

I took a deep breath to steady myself before stepping out of the car. Still unsure of what was awaiting me inside and hoping this was all in my head, I summoned the courage to go inside. The smell of blood was heavier the closer I got. I walked into the house cautiously. I was not in any hurry to confirm what I knew to be true. I stepped into the living room and was immediately greeted by Joan's body. The room was a horror show with blood splattered everywhere. Just opposite Joan sat Joseph. No one should leave this world in the way they had. Joan was naked, and her neck was twisted so that she was facing backwards. Chucks of her flesh littered the floor. Joseph's eyes were open looking in her direction. He wasn't as mutilated as Joan. He must have been forced to watch as they murdered his wife. On closer inspection, I noticed his neck was not positioned right, and to my horror, I watched as his head fell to the ground. I sank to my feet, afraid of what must have become of Hanna. If her parents went through this, then what did they do to her? She is clearly the reason they came, it must be because of her abilities.

I could not bring myself to look for her. I could not turn around out of fear of what I might see. Why her? Who did she wrong? This was all my fault. The moment I came into their lives, they were marked for death. I could feel my body shutting down as I tried to face the unthinkable. I turned around to look for her and found her. She looked peaceful. She lay on her back with both her hands resting on her chest. She was very pale; all the colour had left her, but there was not a single bloodstain on her body. You would think she was asleep, but I knew better. My throat felt constricted at the sight of her, my eyes bulged, and I felt like I was choking. I wanted to throw up, and my knees gave way. I found myself on the floor. I reached out my hands and called out her name, slowly at first and then repeatedly, dragging myself towards her until I was by her side. She looked like she could hear me, but she wasn't answering. How could she be dead and I still be here? Why was I late? What had I been thinking? Who would do this to me? To her? To Joan and Joseph? Every part of me was clenching and raging with vengeance. I wanted to run out and find those responsible, to avenge her, yet I couldn't leave. I couldn't leave for fear of never seeing her again.

I curled up beside her. A massive hole had been dug in me, and the pain was vast. It gripped my chest. I thought I was going to pass out in pain. I had never felt so much despair in all of my existence. I took her lifeless body in my arms and held her close. She was still warm. I finally let out a loud cry. Her body slumped across my arm and her right hand dangled to the floor. I pulled her back to me. I could not believe I had let this happen. All those nights I watched over her were for nothing. I wasn't there when she actually needed me. She barely lived. She was not even eighteen yet and now she is gone.

If I had never killed her mother, if I had never come back, if I had never planned this stupid date, if I had never gone to bloody hunt, she would still be here. "I am sorry, Hanna." I whispered into her ears. "I'm so sorry, my love. I am so sorry I failed you. I failed you from the beginning. I wanted to protect you so much. I forgot to protect you from myself. But I promise you, I will make it right. I will do what's right by you. I will join you soon. I don't deserve to live in this world if you're no longer in it. I want to avenge you, but what good will it do me if you're still gone?" I thought of her ability to wake the dead, and for once I wished I had the ability just for the day to bring her back.

I sat there holding her for a while. I just could not bring myself to take my eyes off her. I never wanted to forget what she looked like. She was pale, but beautiful still. I reluctantly pulled myself up and looked at the time. It was ten at night. I picked up her body and sniffed in a familiar scent. It'd been lingering since I came, but I couldn't think. It cannot be, I told myself. But I knew very well whom the scent belonged to. It's impossible. She doesn't even know Hanna. Why would she come here? I pushed the thoughts of Isobel out of my mind. She could not have been involved, I convinced myself. She is like a sister to me, and she loves me. She would never hurt me like this. I took Hanna's body with me. It was still raining heavily. I laid Hanna gently on the back seat, drove to a pay phone, and anonymously alerted the police.

When I got home, I lay Hanna's body on the same sofa she sat on when she visited and wiped the rain off her face. Still in shock, she did not look dead to me. I sat next to her and stared at her face. I began to pray inwardly, hoping for a miracle. I knew God wouldn't listen to me, not after all the evil I had done, but it didn't stop me from crying to Him.

I traced my fingers along her face. I longed to hear her voice again. I would give my life in return for hers. I didn't like seeing her motionless and lifeless like this. I knew it now. I was doomed for a life of pain. Even as a human I had lived most of my life tormented. A fresh wave of pain surged through me. I took Hanna's hands in mine and wept bitterly. I was angry and vengeful, but I was not going to do anything about it, because it wouldn't change what had happened. Nothing mattered now. Nothing made sense. Not even her killers mattered now that she was gone. I couldn't continue living. I was just an empty shell now; a vessel with no purpose—a wasted space on the planet. I was not important to anyone, and nobody else mattered. So I decided it was time I stopped existing. I would rather die by her side than go on a blood quest and die miles away from her.

I moved the sofa to the window where I knew the sun would shine at its highest. I pulled the curtains aside and opened the windows to allow the sun to stream in. I stood with my back to the window so her body was facing me.

As the early morning sun began to rise, I started to feel my body sizzling. I was happy. I was looking forward to the end and eventually finding peace. I shut my eyes and thought of nothing but her. The heat from the sun was alarmingly painful, but it was nothing compared to the loss of her. I thought the process was going to be fast, but it wasn't. I felt my body burning, my skin darkened, but I was still here. I let out a loud cry in frustration.

# Chapter 23

## Hanna Greene

He cautiously walked over to me. I trembled as he got closer. I knew what was going to happen, but I tried not to think of it. I held on tightly to the bracelet Sebastian gave me, and my mind went to him. I was still hoping he would barge in any minute and put a stop to this nightmare. He was closer now. We were just inches apart. He closed his eyes as he inhaled, his nose almost touching my hair. I tried to look brave. Across the room I saw the other two vampires messing with my parents. I wished I had the power to make it all stop. One of the others held my father down, while the third ordered my mother to take her clothes off. I shut my eyes. This really couldn't be happening. I was dreaming, and I needed to wake up immediately. "Wake up," I murmured to myself.

 He heard me and looked over at my parents. He said, "Don't open your eyes. I wish for your sake that this were truly a dream. I am sorry this is happening to you." He gently pulled my hair from my shoulders to my back. "Don't worry, I won't make it hurt. Not like what those two are doing." He took my hands, forcing me to let go of the bracelet. He held my hands for a few seconds before letting them go. My eyes remained shut, and I could hear my parents screaming in pain.

"Why are they torturing them?" I asked him.

He was quiet a moment, and then he spoke, "They are who they are." Then he came even closer, his lips to my ears, and he whispered, "I want you to know that I wish I didn't have to do this." Then I felt a sudden sting and lost all feeling in my body. I could still hear my mother's cries of agony. I tried to think of Sebastian, but I couldn't make out his face. I was dying. I felt his hand on my body as he laid me flat on my back. I was fighting hopelessly to cling to life. *What did he do to me?* I wondered. My eyes were wide open, and I could still see his silhouette as he knelt beside me. He placed his hands on my eyes and shut them. "I am sorry," he said.

"What have you done?" one of the other two shouted. "Why did you waste a good dinner?"

"Haven't you had your fill yet? She is mine, and I can do whatever I like with her."

"Is she dead?" I heard the other one shouting.

"Don't concern yourself with her, Zacchary. You still have the man alive. Why don't you two do what we came here for before Sebastian comes?"

I heard Zacchary laugh callously. "If he comes, I say we kill him."

"We can't kill him. Not yet anyway. I made a deal with Isobel, and as long as she is on our side, we leave him be. Hector, why didn't you drain her? You fought to have her and then you wasted her blood. Zacchary, see if she is truly dead," Anton said.

"I don't want you near her," Hector said sternly, and I wondered why he was so protective. None of it mattered to me. I was dying anyway, and I had stopped hearing my mother's cries so I assumed she was dead. I wonder why I could still hear what they were saying. I tried to move, but couldn't. I was no longer in control of my body.

"Move aside, Hector. I want to be sure she is dead," Anton ordered.

"She is dead," Hector replied.

"If that's so, let me see for myself."

"You doubt my words, Anton?"

They were quiet for a while, and then Anton spoke, "No I don't. It's just that I can't understand why you've decided to waste a perfectly good dinner. Besides, Isobel wanted her to suffer, and you've done just the opposite."

"She wanted her dead, and she is dead. What does it matter how?"

"Okay, Hector, if you're sure she is dead," Anton said.

"I'll take a look," Zacchary volunteered.

"Don't come any closer," Hector threatened.

"Leave it alone, Zacchary," Anton warned.

"Besides, we still have the man to feast on. Let's get started and get out of here as soon as possible," Anton ordered. My father was going to die soon, and I tried to think about him and Mum. I tried to remember them happy, but everything I knew rapidly started to vanish, as I finally started to lose my hold on life. I could hardly hear them any longer, and then suddenly everything went quiet.

I awoke, and everything was still quiet, like the whole world had gone to sleep or suddenly stopped existing. Without moving, I looked around me, but nothing seemed familiar. A soft breeze caressed my face. I shut my eyes and I took in the lovely scent wrapping itself around me. I heard leaves rustling against each other. I opened my eyes and sat up. My eyes widened in astonishment: I was surrounded by trees, beautiful in all their glory, big and as tall as the heavens.

They stood like soldiers, one next to the other, shoulder to shoulder, an army of some kind guarding and protecting each other. All of a sudden, I was afraid. I got up and looked around. I had never seen a place as beautiful, yet unnerving. I began to wonder how I got here. Was I dreaming? I couldn't remember anything. As I walked around, I felt my feet sink into sand, it felt different somehow. I kept walking, not daring to look up. I felt as though I was being watched. A stronger breeze blew past me and nudged the trees to one side creating a path.

Quickly I walked through the path and came upon water stretching all around me as far as the eye could see: a shimmering, sparkling, peaceful sea. I was on an island and it seemed no one had discovered it yet. There was no way it would still lie empty with all the beauty it exuded if anyone else had been here. I stood in front of the water for what seemed like an eternity, not thinking, just taking in the beauty. I tried very hard to recall how I had got here, and it seemed I had no memory at all.

A cold breeze blew across the sea, disturbing the peace, and the water bellowed in response. I was startled, and then I suddenly felt cold. I turned around and all the trees were frozen. Then my eyes caught something sparkling. I walked around the trees and came upon a magnificent, sparkling ice mountain, gushing with water that looked crystalized and gleamed as though made of tiny pieces of diamonds. It flowed into the sea, making the whole surface shimmer. I walked towards the water and dipped my hands and, to my surprise, it felt glossy and warm to the touch. I took my hands out and they sparkled with tiny elements from the water. I didn't understand why the water was warm when it was coming from ice. Nothing made sense to me; nothing was as it should be.

As I walked around in amazement, my feet sank deeper into the sand. I bent down and took a handful of the sand, which felt like dust to the touch, only it wasn't. And it wasn't sand, either. It looked like gold to me. A seaside filled with gold dust. It was unbelievable how beautiful everything seemed, but still I had no idea how I came here or what I was doing here.

I heard a voice say, "Welcome home, Astraia." I heard it throughout the island echoing over and over and wondered where it was coming from. The wind blew at me in all directions. I could barely open my eyes as the dusty gold sand stormed the whole island like a fog. Everything moved in time with the wind, as if in response to the voice. I noticed the ice on the trees had suddenly disappeared. My eyes formed narrow slits to enable me see better in all the chaos. From the corner of my eye, I saw the wind twirling around, twisting the sands in circles, and the water beginning to form big, high waves. I ran towards the trees, which swished and rustled against each other, as if whispering to one another.

"Who are you? Where are you?" I shouted. I was afraid. "Why can't I see you?" I cried out, and then everything settled. The dusty fog disappeared, the wind circled all around me, and then in a moment it was gone and everything was quiet and peaceful again.

Frustrated, I began to yell again, "Who are you and where am I? Why won't you come out and talk to me?" Then I saw a shadow in the shape of a man appear beneath the trees. I stared at it, unable to move. I wasn't sure if I was ready to meet whatever was behind those trees. I looked up, and a figure of a man appeared from within the trees. He stood with his hands wide open gesturing for me to come. I looked on in shock. He took a step forward and stopped. His hands beckoned for me. Slowly, I found the use of my feet and took a few steps towards him before stopping. He walked the rest of the way and stopped about two feet from me. He smiled and dropped his arms. Somehow, when he smiled, my fear evaporated. I had never seen anything as beautiful as the image before me. He was white like a statue, his hair was long, and he was covered in a white robe. I took a step back. His feet were bare. I stared in disbelief.

"Don't be afraid," he said.

"Who are you, and what am I doing here?" I asked again.

"Astraia, you have come too early." I looked behind me to see if there was someone else he was addressing.

"Who are you talking to? Who is Astraia?" I questioned.

"You are. Welcome home, my beautiful daughter. I am your father." His voice resonated throughout out the island. I reached for my ears to cover them as he spoke. "Don't be afraid," he said.

"My what?" I replied, confused. He smiled and walked towards me, closing the gap between us.

"You look just as beautiful as your mother. Come with me, Astraia. I have so much to tell you, but so little time in which to do it. Your mind is full of questions, and your memory is gone. I would love to give you all the answers you require. Walk with me, please."

"Why do you keep calling me Astraia?" I asked.

He stopped and looked at me. "What would you have me call you?"

I thought about it, and for some reason I couldn't recall my own name. "I—I don't remember."

He didn't say anything. He started to walk towards the water and I followed. His movements were swift and graceful and left me wondering how he could so easily move his stone-like body.

"I named you Astraia, Goddess of justice, when you were conceived, that was the last time I saw your mother."

"My mother? I have a mother? Where is she? Is she here, too? Why can't I see her?"

He stopped and looked at me. "She is not here, and, no, before you ask, she isn't anything like me. She was human, a very gifted human," he said and continued walking towards the water.

"Was? You said *was*. Why did you refer to her in the past tense?" He didn't say anything. "Are you not going to tell me? What gift did she have? What happened to her?" I asked impatiently.

"Be patient, Astraia. In due time you will find out for yourself. You still have a lot to do. You are going to go back soon, even though I would rather you stay here with me, but you are part of that world. You have powers in you beyond your knowledge. You may have noticed a few already, but they are nothing compared to what you can do."

Then he stopped and looked at me. He reached his hands for mine and took them in his. "To be all that you are, you must first believe in who you are. It's faith. It's confidence. You must be assured in yourself and understand your ability. Once you believe, everything will come easily to you. You will only have to think about what you want and it will happen." Then he let go of my hands. "Of course, the fact that you are partly human means there are limitations to what you can do." He sounded sad, like that was a disadvantage in a way. It was all too much for me to take in. If I had my memory, maybe what he was talking about would make sense to me. I felt lost. He looked at me with concern. "Don't worry. I understand you don't remember who you are. That's so it doesn't confuse your mind. Your memory will come to you soon enough, but you must remember that this is who you really are."

"You haven't yet told me who you are." I said.

"But I already did, Astraia. I am your father."

"Okay, let me rephrase the question. *What* are you? I mean. If I am your daughter, what am I? And how come you have all these powers, met with my mother, who was apparently a human, to conceive me, yet I am only just seeing you. Why should I believe any of the things you're saying? Is there any truth to it all?" He took a deep breath, closed his eyes and exhaled, and the trees began to whirl. "Why do you always do that?" I asked, referring to the swishing trees.

"I am sorry. I am too used to being by myself. I forget you are not used to all of this."

"Well, okay. You've not answered my question. What am I?"

He looked up. "It's almost time for you to go, but I shall try to answer some of your questions before then. Come with me," he said, as he walked closer to the water. I was beginning to get very impatient, especially because he said we had very little time before I had to leave.

"You are not God, are you?" I asked.

He laughed out loud. "Even you can't be that silly to think I could be He, the Greatest One. do you think that, with all the glory and power and awesomeness the Most Gracious possesses, He would be restricted to this desolate place?"

"Hmm, so, if you are not He, then who are you? *What* are you? And what was all that about—the frozen trees, the sandy storm?"

"I am sorry. I was nervous and excited at the same time. I didn't really expect you here this soon. I was, and still am, one of His devoted archangels. I did as I was told for billions of years until I fell from His grace."

"What did you do?"

"I fell in love with a human. I fell in love with your mother." He looked at me and then turned and gazed at the sea as though he were trying to remember something. I waited for him to continue, but he was quiet.

"Well, go on. There must be more to the story."

He blinked. "I was sent to look after your mother, to protect her and help her. She was misunderstood by others because of her gift, and she hated herself even more for it. My job was to help her understand and accept who she was, but I failed."

"How, please explain."

"I got too close. She got to me. I knew it from the moment I saw her. I knew she was my test. I should have been stronger. I kept telling myself that I could handle it. I have been around for billions of years and thought myself untouchable, but each time I saw her cry, each time she suffered, I suffered. I was different, and I knew I should have walked away and let another take my place, but I couldn't. I didn't have the power in me to stay away. She took me over, her beauty, her vulnerability." He stopped to observe my reaction, but I said nothing.

"I wanted to help her in more ways that I should. I fell in love with her and rendered myself powerless before her. I was warned to stay away, but a part of me knew she was my test and the other part had fallen so deep in love that it was impossible to breathe without her." He was quiet again, and I let him be while taking it all in. Then he continued, "I began to appear before her in the form of a man. She needed a friend, and I was there. We started to court as a man would a woman, and each day I spent with her, I fell more and more for her." He turned and looked at me. He gracefully lifted his hand and tucked my hair behind my ear. "Then one day I threw caution into the wind and lay with her and you were conceived. I failed her, I failed myself, and I failed His Holiness. I lost my place, I lost my position—"

"What happened next?"

"I was called to answer for what I had done. I never saw her again after that night."

"So, I am the daughter of a fallen angel?" I asked, and he looked away.

"This place is my punishment, my prison if you will. He has been merciful unto me. What I did was terrible, and I should have been condemned into everlasting darkness. I was given the option to return as a human, to be with her, but I didn't take the opportunity. Not because I didn't want to be with her, but because I have served Him since Creation. I had fought evil, and helped guide humans and keep them safe for so long. I didn't know how to be anything else, nor did I want to be anything other than what I was created to be. I declined, and I was exiled here. I cannot leave. If I ever return to live within the humans, that will be the death of me, and I shall cease to exist."

"Well, this doesn't look like punishment to me. It's such a beautiful place."

"Your humanity clouds your mind and your eyes. You see what you want to see. You see this as beautiful, while I consider it hell. It doesn't always look like this. When you've lived as long as I have, you understand why you should never consider this place a luxury." He walked away, and I quickly followed. There was still so much I wanted to ask him.

"And my mother? What happened after you lay with her?"

"I don't know. On the day you were born, I felt it. I felt a part of me in your world. Your spirit, although half human, called for me each time you cried, but I couldn't come. You don't know what it felt like to know you needed me and there was nothing I could do to help. You are here because you died too soon. Your spirit sought me, because I am your source. Even as a human, you had more of me in you. It's okay that the part that made you human has now died. You will now be stronger. You will encounter many enemies, all seeking to have a piece of your power, but each battle you conquer will make you stronger, untouchable."

It was all a lot to take in. I couldn't believe I was conceived under such circumstances. "Earlier you said my mother had abilities. What did you mean?"

"She had so many gifts. She was powerful. The humans called her a witch. She could tell the future, especially dark, terrible things. Of course, she could also tell about good things, but she wasn't channelling the right energy. The energy that surrounded her determined what she saw. People didn't understand her, not even her family. They brought the wrong energy, and all she saw in their futures was doom. Nobody wanted to be around the bearer of bad news. Of course, she could have turned it around, but she didn't understand her gifts. If she were to have been happy and positive, her premonitions would have balanced out so she could see the good things that would happen to people as well as the bad. I wanted to help her. I wanted to make her happy. I loved her, and she was suffering. I wanted her to know that I understood her, that I cared. I tried so hard to fight it and remain as her guardian, but I couldn't stand watching her in all that pain. She was very beautiful, but no man wanted her. They feared her. A few men tried to be with her and left when things took a bad turn in their lives. She blamed herself for their misfortunes. I wanted to help her. I wanted her to see that it was not her fault.

"In the short time we spent together, she was happy, and so was I. she started to see good things in people's futures, and they all welcomed her back. Humans, so shallow, so fickle, so changeable, like bees to honey, they swarmed her. But I didn't mind about them. She was happy, and I was joyful. I knew there would be consequences for what I had done, but it was worth it, making her happy, turning her life around. When she conceived you, the pregnancy didn't take long like most humans births. Unfortunately, I was no longer with her. She gave birth to you within half the time it would have normally taken a human to carry a child. The humans didn't understand how she could conceive and give birth in such a short period of time. They planned to kill the two of you. I felt her fear always, and then, suddenly, I stopped sensing her."

"What happened to me?"

"You will find out for yourself and decide on your own what to do with what you find out. I have said too much already."

"Will I be able to tell the future like my mother?"

"Your mother's gift was nothing compared to what you are capable of, and as much as I loved her, she was too weak to handle her gift. But you, Astraia, you are strong. You don't know it yet, but you will be as soon as you need to be." I was quiet for a moment.

"When the wind was all over me, was that you? How come I couldn't see you, if I am like you?" I asked.

"Yes, that was me. I didn't know how to appear before you. I was not expecting to see you so soon. You took me by surprise. I always knew I would see you, but not this soon. You have not even lived up to eighteen years and already your human life has been snatched. But I am not surprised. I have been around too long to know how desperately wicked the creatures that live in your world are."

I took a deep breath. "Why haven't your powers been taken from you?"

"I don't know. I always wondered about that myself, but I guess since I can't leave, its useless either way. Nothing is impossible, Astraia, when you believe. You will see the truth for yourself. If you ever are in doubt, take a moment and think about what you need to do and the answer will come to you. Never think with your heart, most times you will make the wrong decisions, use your head always."

Just then, I felt a pain in my heart, like I had lost something very precious to me. I held my chest, like someone had just poked a sword in me. My father took one look at me and said, "You're holding on to someone. It will make you feel pain, hurt, and love like humans do. But you can learn to control it all if you want. If you don't want to feel like they do, you can block it all out, but it comes with a price."

"Someone! Who?"

"Don't worry. You will remember soon enough, not that I approve."

"But why do I feel like this? Why am I desperately in pain?"

He looked at me, his face sad, and said, "It's time for you to go."

"You said I can stop myself from hurting. Tell me how?"

"The price you pay is love, my dear."

"I don't understand?"

"You must free yourself. Cut all ties completely by breaking the bond of love you have. When you do this, you will be free of all that worldly pain and become even stronger to fight evil. The minute you do that, you will not remember who he is any longer. You will no longer have any worldly feelings for him, but he will. If he were human, his memories would be wiped out so he could live again."

"And if I don't leave him?"

"It's your choice, Astraia. I should warn you—he is your weakness. If you should ever have carnal knowledge of him, you will lose all of your powers and return to humanity."

"Just so I understand—without him I am strong and untouchable and with him I am weak and human? What happens to him if I chose power over him?"

"He will remember. He will continue to love. He will constantly want you, but he will mean nothing to you. Astraia, you've already met this person. I know, because I feel your emotions. You were happy, you are in love. I don't approve, but I cannot meddle. You must follow your path. There is a purpose to everything the Most Gracious allows. There is a purpose to your life. You are alive because He grants you life. In the past, children born of angels were destroyed. You were destined to be born, with or without me. I failed my test, but you were destined. Everything that has and will happen to you was ordained. All this I have told you, you must say to no one, not even the one you love."

"What will happen if tell him?"

"I don't know. It's not in my hands. I have said too much already, Astraia."

I suddenly felt a stabbing pain in my chest and my heart began to race. I looked up at my father and wondered if he was he reason for the pain I was feeling. "Father, my heart! It bleeds with pain! Please makes it stop!"

"You have to go now. It's time. You've got things to do."

As he spoke, I started to hear a familiar voice in pain. Faintly at first and then it increased in volume and at once I recognised the voice. It all came back to me. I closed my eyes and could see him in pain, and I knew I had to be with him immediately. "He needs me, Father. I must go to him at once."

"I know, Astraia, and you must leave, but be very careful."

"Okay, I will be careful." He cupped my face with both hands, sparingly touching my skin. We both knew we might never see each other again. Then he flicked his finger, and I found myself back in my world.

# Chapter 24

## Sebastian Francis

Any minute now, and I will be truly free. I was overcome by the heat of the sun and ready to let it consume me. Then suddenly a soothing, cool breeze gushed through me, and I was no longer in pain. I was free at last. It wrapped itself around me and lifted me up with a force. I felt like I was walking on air. Who knew dying could feel so good? I tried to open my eyes. There was a bright, almost blinding, light directed at me, and it covered my entire body. Just as I was lifted up, I was back on my feet again. I remembered Hanna. I wondered if she experienced the same sensation. I tried opening my eyes properly to see where I was. The light was too bright for me, but I recognised my surroundings. I felt my eyes forming narrow slits so I could see through them. I could just about make out the shapes in the room, and then my eyes found the sofa on which I placed Hanna, and it was empty.

    It didn't make sense to me. She was there before I ended my life. Not moving from where I stood, I turned and looked around the living room in bewilderment. Then my eyes caught a shape behind all the light. I wasn't sure what it was. I tried to move closer, but there was a force in the light making it impossible for me to move. The power of the force kept me at bay, and then it started to decrease so I could move, but I chose to remain where I was. I was unsure of what was in the room with me. As the force lessened, the light dwindled, and the shape became more defined. To my utmost surprise, it was Hanna.

I looked in disbelief. I never thought I would see her again, not even in my afterlife. "Hanna?" I questioned in shock, and she smiled. "It's you! I never would have thought this possible!" Her eyes looked sympathetic. "I never thought I would see you gain. You—came for me?" I asked.

"I've been with you the whole time. I never left you," she replied.

"I'm happy. I never thought this possible, and here we are! Even death can't keep us apart," I said.

She smiled. "I am here now, S."

"Come closer. Why are you so far away? Why are you standing over there?"

"I am keeping you safe, S."

"I don't understand. Keeping me safe? From what? I don't need saving any longer. I am free now. We are both free. I died, you know. I couldn't exist without you. I am truly dead now."

"Oh, Sebastian, but you're not. I came back just in time."

"What are you talking about? Why are you standing there?"

"I am shielding you from the sun."

"You don't have to. It's too late for me. I passed already, that's why I can see you, your spirit. We can be together now."

"Stop saying that, S. You're not dead. I came here in time to stop you."

"No, Hanna. I don't want to live. I can't survive without you. Don't condemn me to a life of agony. Let me go. Let me join you," I begged.

Her face was sad, and then she spoke, "And how am I supposed to live without you, if I let you go, Sebastian." What was she talking about. She must know by now that this is her spirit talking. How can she not know that she died; that her life has been brutally cut short. How am I going to explain it to her without hurting her all over again?

"Don't you remember what happened to you? You—you died Hanna. That's why you must let me do this, and maybe we can be together again. Please let me do this. I am not going to—I cannot live without you," I pleaded.

She smiled, and her eyes started to glow like fire, and all the light that covered me rolled into a ball. She muttered something to herself that I couldn't quite catch. Then as though she commanded the ball of light, it moved towards her forming strings of fire. Then, like a bolt of lightning, she shoved it straight into my chest. I dropped to my knees at once, with an indescribable pain taking hold of me. I could feel my body on fire and every hard dead cell was ignited. My body opened up as the fire moved through it. I rolled into a ball and tried my hardest to endure the piercing pain coursing through me. My body began to tingle like an electric charge buzzing to life. And then, just as suddenly, the pain subsided. I took a deep breath in relief, and then she walked towards me.

"What did you do?" I asked,

"Don't worry about it. It's for your protection. You'll see soon enough."

"Protection? I don't need protection. I failed you. You have to let me go."

"But why do you want to die so badly," she asked.

"Hanna, I don't know how to say this. You died, and I wasn't there for you. You are no longer here. This isn't you.

Don't you see? That is why I have to do this. Let me end this. I'm no use without you."

She came closer and held me. "I'm here. Can't you see? Feel me. I'm not dead, my love."

I touched her eagerly in disbelief. My hands moved to her face. "Is this true? Are you really here? How can this be?" I looked at her, still touching her with uncertainty. She could see my doubt and confusion. She nodded and held my face to help relieve my doubt. Her warmness surged through me, and I broke down in happiness. "I prayed that I would see you again. I prayed to God, even though I knew I didn't deserve His attention. I didn't think He would listen, not to me. You are really here." I held her very close out of fear of losing her again. "Will you give me another chance? I failed you, I know, but I promise from now on, I will never let you out of my sight."

"There is no second chance to give, Sebastian. You never lost me, and you didn't fail me, love. It wasn't you who hurt me. You could never hurt me that way. I am here now, and I feel so much stronger. I can protect both of us now. Do you have any idea how terrified I was when I saw that you had almost killed yourself?" She wrapped her arms around me, and I felt at home.

"What happened to you? You died, Hanna! I saw you. How is this possible? Were you turned? That can't be it, can it? What happened to you?" I said with mixed emotions—happy more than anything, but confused.

"Oh, Sebastian, I don't know. You know, if I could spare you all that hurt, I would. What happened to me, as sad as it was, needed to happen. I think I needed to be where I was. It didn't feel like death to me. It was like being in a dream. I had no control over any of it. I found myself somewhere, a place like no other. I couldn't describe it to you even if I wanted. None of that matters now. I am here with you, and I know who I am now. I feel very strong and confident, and I know I can keep us both safe."

"So all the while I thought I had lost you, you were just asleep? I touched you, love. You were gone, no pulse, no breath, you died."

"I thought so, too. I felt my spirit leave my body. Saying it out loud sounds strange, but I'm not dead. You know, I never thought I would see you again, either, but here we are. I'm connected to you somehow. I heard you and felt your pain, and I started to remember everything. I knew I had to get back to you. I knew I had to let you know that I was fine before you did something stupid. I was almost too late. By the time I opened my eyes, you were about to burst into flames. I didn't know what to do, but I knew I couldn't lose you, and instantly I felt this light surge out of me. I projected it towards you to cover you from the sun. I can't believe you would have killed yourself. Don't you think that was stupid wanting to kill yourself?"

"Now that you're here, yes, I admit that it was a stupid thing to do, but before then, it was the only way to stop hurting. I thought I had lost you. I died all over again when I saw you lying there lifeless. I lost my will to live, to fight. I didn't think I deserved to continue living, not without you."

"I'm glad I found you on time. I don't think I would have been able to bear it."

I still didn't understand, although I had just witnessed it. If she was saying what I thought she was, that would mean that she can't die. But how is that possible? "You were standing over there, and I was covered in this blinding light, and then there was this fire that you jostled into me, and it consumed me, then the wind rushed through my whole body and cooled me and calmed me almost immediately as it touched me. How did you do all that?" I asked. I needed to know more.

"I told you, I am stronger now. You were in pain, and I panicked. I had to make sure you were safe. I wasn't going to take any chances," she replied.

I pulled away from her so I could see her face. "You did all that? You were controlling the light and you can't die? What are you, my love? Are you a witch? But if you can't die, you can't be a witch, except if you put a spell on yourself to keep you alive. Tell me what you are? The place you went, where is it? Can you remember? What is it you found?"

She smiled and got up from beside me. "I'm not a witch. I don't know any spells. All I know is that I have a better understanding of who I am. We are both here together, S, and that is all that matters to me. It's a miracle, a blessing that I am not dead. I still don't know how it's going to be—whether I will age like the rest of the humans or if, because I survived this, I remain as I am. Nothing is clear to me yet. Let's just start again. Let's enjoy this second chance we have. Isn't that enough? Do you mind that I can't tell you what I am?" she asked.

"Do I mind? Hanna, I died a thousand deaths when I thought that you were dead. You don't know what it felt like living this horrible life even one second without you. My whole world fell apart when I thought you were gone. Now that you're here, nothing else matters. Forgive my intrusion. It's wrong of me to pressure you. In time, if you ever feel the need to share it with me, you know I will always be right here. I promise I am never going to fail you again. I would die before I let anyone harm you ever again."

She smiled. "And I promise to do my best to keep you safe as well. Not even the sun will hurt you again," she said. Just then I realised the curtains were still open, and the sun was at its highest, but I was not roasting. I looked at her. So why was I not in flames? She was not blocking the sun, and I could feel it on my body just like any human could. I looked at her again. "What is happening? Did you do this?" I asked confused.

"It can't harm you anymore. There is light in you now. When you doubted whether I was alive or dead, I thought I had better make sure you do not try this again. You are not a slave to the sun anymore." I wasn't sure I had heard her clearly. Did she know what she had done to me and what that power meant to me and every one of my kind. I got up and walked slowly towards the sun stream. I waited for my body to heat up, but nothing happened. "How—how is this—possible? That fire you shoved into me, all that pain I was feeling, is this—what you were doing? How did you know it would work? How long is this going to last for? What made you so sure it would work?" I asked. I bathed my whole body in the glory of the sun, still waiting for the trick to wear off. For almost two hundred years, I have been afraid of the sun and, just like that, now I can bask in it like any other human.

She came to meet me, looked in my eyes, and said, "I believed, Sebastian. I believed I could do it. I'm stronger than I was. Now that I've found myself, nothing is impossible, especially when it comes to you."

And without words, we held each other closely. I took her face in mine, and we kissed like it was our first time ever. "I love you eternally, Hanna. You have no idea what you've done to me." She was quiet and did not say anything. I could feel it all over me. It felt almost like she wanted me to feel how she felt about me.

We stood there together for a while and then she pulled away quickly. "What's wrong?" I asked her.

"My parents! I can't believe I forgot about them! You must take me home quickly. I have to save them," she said, running towards the front door. "Why are you still standing there? Let's go!" she shouted impatiently.

"I'm sorry, Hanna."

"Don't be sorry. It's not your fault. Let's just go now!"

"Ha—Hanna, you can't save them. They're gone," I said.

She laughed. "What are you talking about? I can save them. Don't you remember? I told you I can bring back the dead."

"I know. I remember, but I didn't know you would come back, so I called the police to come your house when I found your parents. They must have taken their bodies by now. I'm sorry. You can't save them anymore. It's been on the news. Everyone knows they are dead now."

She stood on one spot considering what to do, and I bled for her. I knew she must be remembering the horror she had witnessed, and the terrible things that were done to them. Tears began to flow down her cheeks. "I have to help them, S. How can I have these abilities and not be able to help them? I cannot—I cannot just accept that they are—gone. I have to bring them back. They are dead because of me. I have to bring them back."

I knew how painful it was to lose someone you love. I have been through it enough times already. I also knew she couldn't bring them back. Their bodies must be in an examination room by now, and they have been dead for more than twelve hours now. I went over to her and held her. She crumbled on the floor and wept. "I'm sorry, love. It's not your fault. You can't blame yourself. I am to blame. I failed you, and I failed them. They died because of me, and I'm so sorry, Hanna," I tried to console her. She wept.

It saddened me to see her so bereaved. I couldn't imagine what she must have seen them go through. I know how I had found their bodies, but to have witnessed it happening to someone you love must have been a nightmare. Now that she was here, I could avenge their deaths and hers, too. I was going to get to the bottom of this if it was the last thing I did.

# Chapter 25

For days later, Hanna remained inconsolable. Unable to sleep, she relived the nightmare of her parents' death each time she closed her eyes. I felt helpless. There was nothing I could do to make her better. She had to grieve, and I had to give her the time and space she needed. In the meantime, I preoccupied myself with plans of vengeance. With the ability to walk in the sun, I was at an advantage. I could go out and seek information on how to successfully carry out my revenge. It was implausible what had happened to me. It still felt like a dream, having lived under shadows for years on end, waiting forever for each day to almost draw to a close before stepping out, and now I could just go anywhere I wanted without any fear. Some days, I would forget and sit around waiting until sunset before venturing out. I guess old habits die hard. Some days, I just simply stayed put out of fear that whatever she had done was going to wear off and I would burst into flames.

I tried not to think about it and concentrated on my revenge, but to do that right, I needed Hanna to tell me all she remembered. But I couldn't ask her without making her relive the whole horror again. The full moon was in two days, which meant I had to deal with Huritt and his tribe before she turned eighteen. No one knew where she was, and since the police hadn't found her body, she had been declared missing. Pictures of her face have been plastered on the telly and in newspapers, and the police are searching everywhere. They believe she has been abducted by whoever committed the double homicide, which meant that wolf-boy and his tribe were still hopeful she was alive so they could be the ones to kill her. I had been careful not to let her see anything from the telly or papers. I didn't want her upset any more than she already was. I had to speed things up and stop Huritt before the full moon. I also toyed with the idea of letting her go to the police, so she could get closure and bid a proper goodbye to her parents. However, getting closure would only put her in more danger. The vampires would know that she was not dead and come back to do it properly, and the wolves would know where to look for her, which would take away the element of surprise I had planned for them. I planned to kill them all before the full moon.

I know I made a terrible and selfish judgment leaving Hanna all those years ago. If I had stayed, I would have been able to quench all this fire before anything had become life threatening to her.

There were so many things to do in so little time. First, I had to feed, after which I planned to hunt down that boy Huritt and torture him to get every bit of information about the tribe and their plans for Hanna. The problem I had was where to take him now that Hanna stays with me. I was out of options, and the only way around it was to tell Hanna what I know and what I planned to do to him.

I sat by her bed and watched as she slept. She looked at peace. I was filled with mixed emotions—relieved to see her alive and with me, but also angered because she was not yet safe, and I would do anything in my power to ensure that no harm ever comes to her. The way I saw it, every single creature that poses a threat to her life, even if it's just in thought, had to die.

I kissed her gently on the forehead, not wanting to wake her, and decided against telling her anything about Huritt. I would find a way to do it all without involving her. Since her birthday is soon, she shouldn't have to worry about her life, not if I could do something about it. I got up from beside her and was about to leave the room when she said, "Hey."

Her voice sounded faint and cracked, but I heard her clearly, and I automatically returned to her side. "Hey," I said back with a smile. She tried a smile, too, but it wasn't up to par, and I could tell she was trying hard to sound fine. "Sorry I woke you up. Go back to sleep, darling," I said, brushing her hair with my hand.

"It's okay. I should get up. I've been out of it for too long." I smiled and continued to touch her hair. "What's wrong?" she asked.

"Er—it's nothing. I just wanted to see how you were. I know you may not want to hear this now, but tomorrow you turn eighteen. I think we should do something together to celebrate."

"Hmm, I forgot. I don't know if that's a good idea. I just can't."

"I know. I'm sorry I brought it up. It's just that you've been so down that I wanted to try and cheer you up," I said, still very concerned about how she was coping.

"There is something else on your mind, S. I can tell," she said probingly. I was quiet. I didn't want to involve her anymore. "Tell me, S. Don't worry. I can handle it. There is nothing I can't deal with now. The worst has already happened," she said.

I looked at her, worried that if I told her what I had planned to do to her friend she might not like it. "Go back to sleep, love. I just have a few things to take care of. I'll be back soon."

She held my hand. "Tell me, S. It's okay. I'll be fine. Remember, whatever it is you're doing or plan to do, we have to do together. It's you and me now. You never know when I can be of help." She pleaded with me and there was no way I could keep it from her now, not with her desperate to know what I was up to. I cleared my throat before speaking and told her what I heard Huritt and his family discussing about her. Since she had wanted to know, I also told her what I was also planning to do to them.

She was quiet for a while. There was not a word, just silence. I waited patiently for her to speak, but in my mind, I had already decided that no matter what she decided I was still going to carry through with my plans. They all had to die. I couldn't spend my life continuously looking over my shoulder and being burdened with worry. I studied her face to try to guess what her thoughts would be, but she gave nothing away.

"How do you want to do it? I mean, how do you plan to get him?" she asked.

"I don't know yet. I mean, I don't know if he can change at will or only during the full moon, but I don't want to leave anything to chance, so as soon as I can get him alone, I will knock him out and bring him here," I said, and she nodded.

"There is another way you know," she said. "An easier way to handle this," she continued.

I was surprised that she was going along with it, no questions asked. "So you don't mind then?" I asked.

"If what you say is true, and I know you have no reason to lie, then it's my life or his, and I plan on staying alive, but

*Sebastian*

I want to be the one to punish him, so let me do it." I was surprised, to say the least. I had always thought it would take a lot to make her see it my way. I knew she was not the same Hanna. The look in her eyes said it all, as though he had never mattered to her.

"So what's your plan then?" I asked.

She got up and began to pace. "There are three things we can do to get him here: one, I could call him and tell him I am in fear for my life and he should meet me somewhere, anywhere, but not this place, in case he informs his family and they come along for the ride. Happy that he's made contact, he will not be foolish to jeopardize his only opportunity to take me back to them willingly. That's where you come in. I will distract him, and you will knock him out. Two, I could offer him a drink with drugs enough to knock him out. And three, if I'm sure he's by himself, I can bring him here with me. I know he'll follow, because he won't suspect anything, and we both know he can't leave when he gets here. So what do you think?"

I was quiet for a moment considering her plan. It sounded simple enough, but what if there was someone else with him? What do we do with that person? Kill him or take him hostage? "Okay, Hanna, we'll do it your way. Hopefully, he'll come alone, and I can find out what he knows before going out for the others." We smiled at each other, knowing it was the right thing to do. To have her on board meant a lot to me. But, then again, I didn't like her like this. I mean, concocting plans is not the Hanna I knew, but then, life happens and people change, including Hanna. Now she is more spirited and stronger, and I guess I kind of like that, too.

We went out to my house in Froxfield in Hampshire to get things to hold down Huritt just in case he could change at will. I've been told that a single silver-bullet to the heart is enough to do the trick, and I have the right weapon for the job, but I didn't intend for him to die such an easy death. I also knew I could rip him apart with my hands, but I didn't want to show such qualities in the presence of Hanna. We sat everything up together before she called him to meet up. Before she made the call, I wanted to be sure she was ready for this.

"Hanna, you know you don't have to do this with me. I can handle it by myself. I know you feel betrayed, but I don't want you to get involved in any of this." I tried persuading her to stay out of it.

"But I am already involved," she said. "It's me they want. I know you can do this on your own, but since they want me, let me show them what I am capable of. I will love to see the look on their faces. We are doing this together, S, whether you like it or not." She sounded certain she wanted to do this, and I knew there was no changing her mind, so I let her make the call. It was short and sweet, and she acted like she was in danger, but she emphasised that he meet her alone in the woodland, and we quickly went to the meeting point before he could get there.

It wasn't long after we arrived that I heard the rustling of leaves and then his stench greeted my nose. I stayed far off to the side so he couldn't see me or detect my presence, but near enough to hear and see everything. He had this happy smile glued to his face, and I felt like beating it out of him. I looked at Hanna, who also had the same happy smile on. I wasn't sure what to think. Was she really happy to see him, or was she still pretending like we had planned? I knew she liked him a lot, but I guess I would have to wait and see what she decided to do with him. He wrapped his arms around her and she let him cuddle her. My stomach turned, but I couldn't take my eyes off them, even though I didn't like what I was seeing.

"Thank goodness you're here," she said. "I didn't know who to call. I am scared, Huritt." She looked up at him from underneath his arms.

He held her face as he spoke to her, like he really cared for her, and it made my blood boil. "Don't worry, Hanna. You have nothing to fear. You're safe now. I was so worried about you. I feared the worst had happened to you. Thank God you're all right. Listen, Hanna, you don't have to be by yourself. You can come and stay with us. I'm sure my parents won't mind. In fact, they will be very glad to see you. They have been so worried. Trust me on this one, okay? I will take care of you so no one will harm you." He tried to sound as sincere as he could, but we both knew why his parents were glad she was alive.

"Okay, but I have to go get something. You will come with me, won't you?"

"What thing? he asked. "You won't need anything, I promise you. I have sisters, too, remember. I'm sure they can get you anything you want."

"Oh, Huritt, I know, but what I am going to get is important. I need to go back for it. It's a family heirloom. It won't take long, and then we can go back to your house," she replied.

He sighed and threw his hands in the air. I was glad she was sticking to the plan. "Okay, if it's that important to you, then we should go and get it." He sounded frustrated that she didn't oblige him, which infuriated me further. She just told him she was scared for her life, and this dog is still ready to take her to her death.

I watched as they headed for my house. Her plan seemed to have worked perfectly. I remained where I was for a little while, just to see if there was anyone hanging about that I missed earlier on. Satisfied that he had come alone, I left for the house. I knew that after tonight, if they didn't see him they would start to look for him. He must have informed them that he was going to meet her before he came, and they were probably getting ready for the big night. Good thing we were ahead of them and could punish them all.

When they got in the house, he immediately started to act funny. I chose to remain outside for a while, peering in through the window and watching him with her. I wanted to allow Hanna to do it her way. If that didn't work, then I would have to resolve it the only way I knew how.

"Hanna," Huritt said, "get what you came for and let's go. Whose house is this any way?" He asked.

"It's a friend's. He's out of town," she replied. I could hear him sniffing about.

"Don't tell me it's that guy's from the music centre, the one you hang around with these days?" he asked.

"Yes it is. He's my—boyfriend. How did you know we are in his house?"

"Your boyfriend? All this time I have known you and you chose him? He's only been here five minutes and he is your boyfriend? What, am I not good enough for you?"

"What are you talking about? You know you mean a lot to me, but he's different. He's more than just a boyfriend to me. What can I say it—it just happened. He came and everything changed. I changed. I'm different when I'm with him. I care about you, too, but in a different way. You are—you are like a brother to me. Plus, you never said you liked me like that."

"I didn't think it was necessary, Hanna. I showed you in many ways how I felt about you. Don't act stupid, like you never clued up that I wanted us to be more than friends. And you know what? Don't give me the *I'm like your brother* nonsense, either. Why did you call me then when you have him to curl up to?" He started to sound very irritated.

"He's out of town. I called you because I thought we were friends, and I wanted you to know that I'm fine. If I were capable of feeling anything for you other than friendship, don't you think I would have done so by now," she replied. I considered going inside. I didn't want Hanna in any kind of harm, just in case he can change at will. I didn't trust these dogs when they're angry.

He was quiet for a while and then he said, "I don't like it here. Let's go. Take what you came for and let's get out of here now," he said angrily.

"You never answered my question. I asked you how you knew this was his house?" Hanna questioned again.

"I guessed, that's all."

"Really? Just like that? Are you sure it was only a guess?"

"What do you mean by that? Get your stuff and let's go." His tone got more and more aggressive.

"Well, if you're going to be like that, I don't want to come with you anymore. You can leave now. I'm not going anywhere with you acting like that."

"C'mon, Hanna You called me, because you were scared. You can trust me more than him. I mean, we've known each other longer than you've been with him. Come home with me now, Hanna. Please, let's get of here before he returns," he begged. His frustration had turned into pleas.

"Why are you in such a hurry to take me with you? I'm no longer comfortable with you and your stupid jerk behaviour.

I'm staying here. You can go now, Huritt." I knew she was testing how much he would try to convince her to come with him. He started to sniff around more as I approached the door.

"Is he around? That—that jackass you're seeing? You lied! He's not out of town. He's around isn't he?" he asked, still sniffing around.

"What does it matter to you if he's around or not? Why do you care? I told you, you can go. I don't need you anymore," she snapped.

"Where is he then?" he yelled.

"On his way home, I expect. Go before he gets here," she replied.

"You think I'm scared of him? It's you I'm worried about. He can't touch me. Hanna, you are coming with me now. It's not safe for you to be around him."

"Like I said, I'm all right now. You can go. Just so you know, I feel safer with him than I feel with you right now. Leave before I change my mind."

He laughed sarcastically. "What would you do if I don't leave? Report me to your boyfriend?" He grabbed her.

I quickly opened the door to yank him off her, but, to my surprise, my help was not needed. Huritt was on the floor curled up like a dog in labour. I looked from him to her, her eyes were on him, and I could tell his pain was as a result of the look she was giving him. After a while she stopped. He got up and tried to run, but she gave him that crippling look again, and he was once more on his knees. Then she said. "Listen, do *not* underestimate me. I will stop, if you don't try to run again. Each time you try to run, you will leave me no choice but to subject you to this pain. Believe me, I don't want to, but I will if you make me. Now I am going to stop, and I want you to get up, sit on that chair, and answer all my questions as truthfully as you can. No lies, Huritt! I will know, so don't bother trying. Now sit."

I was amazed at what was happening. She didn't even need my help. I looked at him and enjoyed the surprise on his face. I guess they all expected her powers to come after she turned eighteen. I was equally surprised that she could do that, but I guess I should expect anything from her now, and nothing should surprise me anymore.

## Chapter 26

"What are you doing to me?" he screamed. "Why are you doing this to me, Hanna?" he shouted again. She sat in front of him while I kept watch of the situation. It's not as if my help was needed, though. She was handling things just fine. I guess when she said we could do things much simpler, she really knew what she was talking about, and I have to say I was amazed at how much stronger she was. I still couldn't get over all these things she was able to do since coming back to life. She meant it when she said she was much stronger. She is not that sweet little Hanna any more.

I looked down at Huritt and saw his veins popping out. He must be in great pain, but I didn't pity him. I was actually getting bored of his pretence of innocence, and I was happy Hanna wasn't buying his lies, either.

"Huritt, I don't like doing this to you, but, believe me, if you don't start talking, there are far worse things I can do to you, and I wouldn't even break a sweat," she said.

"Go to hell, bitch! Go for it! Give me your best shot. You won't get a word out of me. I'll die first before I tell you anything," he spat out.

"Well, if that is how you want things to play, then you leave me with no choice." She got up and began to walk to the door.

"Where are you going, you freak," he groaned.

"Ha, now that's not nice. You shouldn't start calling other's names. You know what they say about people who live in glass houses? It doesn't really suit you, Huritt, this *bad assness*. To think all along I thought you were my friend. I mean, just now you were having a go at me for not loving you the way you wanted me to, and all this while you were just using me, plotting behind my back? I actually thought I meant something to you. I trusted you, Huritt. I loved you as a friend, and that's what hurts the most, because to you, I was just this thing you were keeping happy so that when the time came, you can hand me over to make your life easier." She really looked sad as she spoke to him. She waited for him to say something, but he said nothing. "Just know this—you've done this and you've left me no choice." She began walking away.

"Where are you going?" he wailed.

"Where else? To your house, of course. Don't worry, they won't see me coming, but by the time I finish with your sisters, you will wish you spoke with me earlier." She reached for the door.

"Wait! Please, wait! Leave my sisters out of this, I beg you," he pleaded.

"Why? Oh, I forgot, they're very precious to you aren't they? I'm sorry, but you've left me no choice."

"Please, Hanna. Leave them out of this, please. Wait, don't go. Tell me, who told you these lies? I would never hurt you, and you know that. I've known you—for how long? Why would I want to harm you? You know me better than anyone. I would never harm you. I love you. God, I love you, Hanna, and I was never going to do it. At first, I was going to do anything necessary to be normal again. I just wanted this thing gone, and then I got to know you. I didn't count on falling in love with you. Please, Hanna, you have to believe me," he cried. If I didn't know any better, I might fall for his act, but I knew what I had heard and hoped Hanna didn't believe he was never going to do it. What even annoyed me more is the love card he was playing. He doesn't have a clue what love is, but I guess he's going to try anything to get himself out of this mess.

"So it's true then? There *is* a plot on my life. Why should I believe you weren't going to hurt me? Why should I even believe anything that comes out of your mouth? You had all this time to tell me the truth, to let me know I wasn't safe, that my life was in danger, but you kept mum. I could have helped you, and we could have figured a way out of this mess together as friends. But you choose differently, you choose to do this, Huritt, you chose tomorrow, my eighteenth birthday. God, Huritt, how would you have carried out your part? Ask me round to collect presents? Pretend you had a surprise in store for me somewhere? What did you expect was going to happen? That I would just hand myself over for your ritual? A week ago it would have been easy for you, but now things have changed. Funny how these things work out. It's been tragic for me, but there is a greater good, I suppose, when these things happen, as I am sure you know by now. So tell me again why I should believe you, why I shouldn't do to you what you planned for me? And don't tell me it's because you love me. If you really did love me, you would never have gone along with any of it. Tell me the truth. You were going to stand back and allow your parents to use me for ritual weren't you?" she asked, looking down at him in disgust.

"I don't know, Hanna, but I would have figured something out. They never said you were going to die. They just—just said that your blood would help remove this curse.

What would you have done in my shoes? I'm stuck either way, Hanna."

"If I were in your shoes, I would have confided in you, and I would have found a way so that your life wasn't in danger. I would have tried something, anything, but I would never have handed you over to die. So what were you going to do? Seeing that you say you love me, just hand me over and bleed me out to appease your curse?"

"I—I was going to stay close, and as soon as they got what they needed, I was going to drive you to a hospital. I don't want you dead, you must believe me, but I don't want to—" he quieted.

"You don't want what? Speak up, it's too late to start keeping secrets."

"I'm not supposed to say, not to someone who's not our kind, and not in *his* presence."

"I'm sorry, but you have no choice. You have to tell me why my blood is needed, why the need for a ritual, and *he's* not going anywhere, either, so start talking." She went over and sat in front of him, while I hovered behind her, wondering if he would talk or call her bluff.

"If I could, I would, but I can't, and please don't make me, because no matter what you do to me, I am forbidden to say anything to someone who's not in the tribe," he pleaded.

She turned around to look at me, to see if I believed what he had just said. I shrugged in response.

"Then, in that case, riddle me this. Why do you have to wait until tomorrow at the full moon to draw my blood? Why not now? What difference will it make? You can tell me that, can't you?"

He was quiet for a while and then he spoke, choosing his words carefully. "Without the full moon, the blood we draw from you could reverse our curse, but it wouldn't last. The full moon seals the curse forever for us, with or without your blood, but we are hoping with your blood," he said, studying her carefully. I wondered if any of this revelation bothered her at all. I mean, it's a bit much to be listening to what some animals intend to do with you.

She was quiet for a while, probably thinking what her next step would be. So I decided to take this time to ask the question that's been on my mind. "Tell me, I am curious, why, Hanna? Who pointed you in her direction? How did you know she was what you needed to reverse your curse?" I asked, not moving from where I was standing. I didn't want to get too close in case he gave me the wrong answer, and I angrily did something irrational, like rip off his head. I was sure Hanna wouldn't want that, so I kept my distance, until she wanted his head off his neck.

He looked at me with loathing, and then laughed out loud. "If you think I am talking to you, think again. You don't fool me, I know what you are. And don't think for one minute that I can't take you on," he spat.

For one, I hated the way he was dirtying my house with his dog saliva, but I chose to ignore it and asked the question again. "Okay, listen, I'm going to ask you again, and I beg you to answer. I hate getting angry. It brings out the worst in me and makes me do things I am not particularly proud of, and the last thing I want to do is rip you apart in front of a lady. Now, it's a good thing you know who you're dealing with, so we both know where we stand, because if you don't talk, I will take it personally, and I might just make it my mission in life to kill every last one of your little tribe until I get the answers I need. It's your choice. So, now I'm going to ask you again, and please don't give me a reason to do what I have been longing to do all day, how did you and the rest of your tribe know that Hanna is special?" I looked at Hanna to let her know I needed to handle things from here, and she nodded in response.

"Go screw yourself, idiot! You aren't getting a thing from—" Before he could finish, I was at his side, and, to my amazement, he had transformed into a wolf. So they *can* change at will, not only at full moon. That's nice to know. Before he could open his jaw, I smashed him into the wall, and quickly went over to dig my fist into him, but he was also fast and pounced and landed on the opposite side of the room, crouching to attack. I had anticipated that move and waited for his leap and leapt up and met him mid-air, held him by the neck, and brought him straight back to the ground, smashing his head into the floor. I could feel my fangs as I dug them into his arm to start biting out chunks of him.

"Enough, Sebastian!" Hanna yelled. Enough, don't do that!" But I was so angry and I wanted to rip him apart. "Sebastian, stop! We aren't animals, stop." I took one look at him to make sure his gaze was centred on me.

"You are no match for me," I said and loosened my grip on him. I got to my feet, but he was on his feet immediately, ready to pounce again. But before I could beat the life out of him, Hanna was already at work on him. She gave him that look, and he was quivering and whimpering on the floor. I wished she had just let me deal with him myself and teach him a lesson, but I didn't want to argue in front of a dog, so I let it go and kept my distance from the animal. I could taste his blood in my mouth and it tasted awful. I went to the kitchen to wash the stench out of my mouth. I still wanted an answer to my question. Either she gets it out of him or I'll have to do it my way. I waited in the kitchen until I was a little more composed before going back to where they were. I don't want to get angry in front of Hanna and am actually annoyed with myself for letting myself get like that in her presence. By the time I got back, he was calm and she left him alone.

I watched as he changed back into his human form, still in pain, but naked, so Hanna had to look away. But before he could do anything funny, I was at his side to hold him down in case he wanted a fight again. There is one thing I am certain of: Never turn your back on a wild animal, not to mention an angry wolf.

"He ripped his clothes," Hanna said, "we have to get him some of your clothes to wear, S."

I was quiet. I didn't want this animal near my clothes, let alone wear them. "Well, Hanna, he chose to appear this way. He should have thought about that before turning into a dog," I said, staring at him.

"I don't want your clothes, you blood-sucking dead head," he snarled at me.

"We are on the same page, dog," I replied.

"Enough already," snapped Hanna. "I don't care what he wants, just get him covered up."

"What's the hurry, Hanna?" Huritt said smugly. "Why do you want me covered up so badly? Don't tell me I turn you on. You want some of this? Just say so. I will even do you in his presence."

I punched him in the mouth and broke his jaw for being so rude. "You will not—make such inappropriate remarks about Hanna. Not in my presence, not in my house, not ever, do you understand."

He started to laugh rudely, wiping his awful smelling blood off his mouth. "You don't know what you are dealing with, the two of you. They know I'm gone, and they're going to come and find me very soon. Don't worry. They know exactly where to look. We made it our business to know where our enemy sleeps, and we happen to know you are on your own. I may be no match for you two, but you have no idea what you'll be facing soon enough," he said and cackled.

I looked at Hanna. We both knew we had a battle on our hands. If what he was saying was true, there was no telling how many of them have conveyed at his house for the breaking of the curse tomorrow. "I am going to take him to the basement and lock him up there. You wait here," I said to Hanna.

I picked him up and dropped him at the bottom of the stairs and then locked the door with a padlock. There was no getting out for him until after we were done with his tribe. I returned to the sitting room where a worried looking Hanna was waiting for me.

"I can't believe what just happened here. I truly loved him. We were good friends. I wanted so much for this not to be true. I guess we're at war now." She looked really betrayed and upset. It had come to this between them, not that I had any sympathy for him. "What are we going to do, Sebastian? I don't know if I can handle so many of them at once. I've never tried this before, and I don't want you out there fighting them by yourself."

I went over and gave her a cuddle. "Don't worry about me, Hanna. I'll be fine. You shouldn't be worrying about me like that. Let me do the worrying. Listen, if what he said is true, then they have probably figured out that he may be here, and they'll be coming for him and you. I don't know how you did that crippling thing just now, but you did it. Just believe in yourself, and you'll be able to hold off as many of them as you can, while I deal with the remaining. You're stronger now, you said so yourself. You're not that fragile little girl anymore. Don't worry, we can take them. I promise you."

"Okay."

"I have to go somewhere quickly. It's weird to tell you this since we've never discussed my diet, but I have to feed so I can have enough strength for what's ahead."

"So what are you going to feed on, you said you don't do humans," she interrogated.

I chuckled. "No, I don't do humans any more. Don't worry, you stay here. I'll be back very soon. I'm not going far."

"Let me come with you," Hanna said.

"No, Hanna. Stay here. I'm just going to the farmhouse to feed. I'll back in ten minutes at the latest."

"Okay, but hurry back."

Before she knew it, I was out the door. In a way, I was glad it was so late in the evening. I sneaked in to the farm and fed on a few animals. I didn't kill any of them. I just fed on as many as necessary to boost my strength. After I had my fill, I started running back home. I had a feeling they were going to arrive sooner than we expected.

I was hit by the stench of those fowl dogs the closer I got to the house. I guess Huritt wasn't lying. I went a little closer to the house, trying not to alert them of my presence. By the looks of things, there were at least twenty, maybe more, of them. My mind immediately went to Hanna. I should be with her now. I should have foreseen this situation and fed before this. It was a stupid move to leave my feeding until this late. I wondered how she was feeling in there by herself. How I was going to get inside without their knowledge puzzled me.

I knew I had to take them on by myself, like I had planned originally. If push came to shove, I could take on four of them at once. They were all still in their human form, and I felt it unjust to attack them without it feeling like murder.

Then all of a sudden, Huritt let out a big howl from inside, and I saw them starting to change, one by one. I didn't wait. I grabbed the first one and broke his neck before he even had the chance to change. I must have killed at least seven when they started coming towards me. It looked as though there were about fifteen of them still left, and I knew I couldn't take them all by myself, but I also needed to know that Hanna was okay. So I leapt from their midst to the top of the roof, and about five or six of them followed. I held the first one by the throat and ripped his head off. The next two who followed weren't so lucky, either. If only they weren't so fast, but thank goodness, I had just fed, because once I got hold of them, they were like rubber in my hands. Four or five of them at a time I could handle, but they were beginning to dig at me in larger numbers, digging their jaws into me. I took one of them, held him by the neck with both hands, and waved him round, using him to fend off the others. I jumped to the ground so I would have more room to fight them and to give me a view of what was coming so I could anticipate what to do next.

I was still worried about Hanna. All the while I'd been fighting, I hadn't heard any movement from inside. And as often as I tried to get into the house, they gave me no leeway. They piled on me as I desperately tried to fight them off. I yanked two of them away from my legs, and punched one who was pulling on my hands. It wasn't about killing them anymore; it was about defending myself, because there were now about eleven of them attacking me at the same time.

Suddenly, I felt a strong wind blowing from behind me and could see the wolves being pulled away from me, one at a time, as the air sucked them up and forced them away. I looked up and saw Hanna, her hands stretched to her sides, like she was pulling them apart. I watched as the force of the wind blew them meters away from me. I sighed in relief—I was glad for the help, but mostly glad because Hanna was all right. Now we could battle on.

Then I saw two wolves leaping to attack from behind her and I quickly went to them. I got hold of the first one and ripped his jaw open and kicked him into the air. The second one I smashed into the tree and quickly went to ring his neck before he had the chance to get up. I looked behind me and saw that Hanna was still holding the remaining at bay with some kind of force. I was going to pick them off one at a time and finish it, but she looked at me and shook her head. Then she looked at them and said, "I am going to let you go and forget this ever happened on one condition. I want you to change back to your human forms. I only want the Denali's. If you are still alive, I want you here now, and the rest of you can go. If you don't do as I say, I will let Sebastian finish you off, one at a time, or I could just incinerate you all together to save time." Incinerate? That was a new one for me, but I guess with Hanna, it's always going to be something new.

I looked at her. It seemed they were calling her bluff. She glanced in my direction and nodded, and I knew she was going to teach one of them a lesson. Then I could feel all that wind starting to gather up and begin to twist around. I moved back. I didn't know where she was going with this or even if she was in control of it. The wind suddenly gained more power, twisting and making a loud noise, almost like a small tornado, and I watched as she directed all that in one of the wolf's direction. Then suddenly, a ball of fire broke out from within the twisting wind and wrapped itself around the wolf. I heard him howl in pain and, within a matter of seconds, it was consumed. I looked at the others still in their animal forms, whining and howling. A few of them leapt towards us and, with one swing of her hand, Hanna sent them reeling back to the ground, whimpering.

I watched as the wolves began to change, one at a time, to their human form. Three women and five men remained, including Huritt's parents, who stepped aside. Huritt's dad was very hairy—his body hair covered most of his skin. He had freakish-looking, long, greyish-black hair that fell to his shoulders, and his face looked like it could do with some shaving. The mother, on the other hand, was well groomed, for her age. I looked away, but kept my eyes on the rest of the pack. "Now the rest of you, get your dead and get out of here. Don't leave any one behind and don't try anything funny. I might just change my mind and let you all die here. The two of you," she said to Huritt's parents, "come closer. We are going to have a little chat, after which we will decide what to do with you." They all scattered about, gathering the remains of their comrades, while I kept watch.

It's a good thing Hanna asked them to take their dead with them, which I wouldn't have thought of doing. Not that we would be staying after tonight. We may not have the police at our doorsteps, but I knew those she had let go were going to reinforce before the full moon tomorrow and come looking for us. As much as I would love to kill them, I didn't actually want to keep bathing in their stench.

I dragged the two remaining dogs inside. I knew why she wanted to interrogate them, and I needed answers, too.

# Chapter 27

We waited until the survivors left with their dead. At first they waited around, refusing to leave without the remaining two. Then Huritt's father, who seemed to be the leader, instructed them to leave. Before they left, I warned them not to come back or try anything funny if they wanted their leader and his family alive.

They all glared at me in anger before reluctantly leaving. I wondered what effect they thought their actions had on me. There were more than twenty when they arrived and only five are leaving, yet they had the audacity to glare at me. I scoffed in disgust at their pathetic attempt at a fight. One thing I will accord them is their loyalty to each other. My kind can never be loyal to each other, not in such a large group. We could never accept one leader; it's mostly every man for himself. The only thing that keeps us in check is the fact that the older we get, the stronger we become, which helps to keep the newborns in control.

"Take a seat. As you know, we have your son, so I wouldn't try anything if I were you. Moreover, I am tired of being mean today, so let's all be civilized. I will ask you a simple question and all you have to do is answer truthfully and promptly. And if you do that, maybe I will let you go, but I must emphasize the fact that we haven't got all day. Okay, here we go. Why me? And how many other tribes out there know about me?" They were both quiet. I don't think they understood that we had the upper hand here, and honestly, if not for the answers we needed from them, I probably wouldn't be holding my cool, but it was imperative that we find out about the other tribes so we would know what we were up against.

"Seriously, guys. I've been through enough already, and I don't have time for silly pretences. We all know why you are here. I need to know if there are others out there looking for me."

Huritt's dad looked at me, repulsion written across his face. You'd think we'd been warring against each other for centuries. "I am not talking to you! Not in front of this blood sucker," he shouted. I smiled and thought, *I don't very much like your type, either, but I will watch my temper for Hanna's sake.*

"Well, don't hold your breath," Hanna said, "because he's going nowhere. You are in his house after all, but I'm sure you know that already. Have some respect please. You should be thankful he hasn't ripped you apart by now. If I were you, I wouldn't give us a reason to be mean, and I'm sure, as you know by now, I am a whole different person," she pointed out to him. He looked down and glanced over at his wife. They knew there would be no getting out of this one; not for them.

Huritt's mother looked up at Hanna, and I could see her expression had changed, softened more. Before she spoke, I kind of knew how she was going to stir the conversation. "What hold does he have over you, Hanna? This can't be you talking. You are not this person. You are kind and sweet and gentle. I am sure he's compelled you to be this way. You do know that vampires have the power to control people's minds. We didn't come here to hurt you. We heard what happened to your parents. Believe me, that was not an animal attack. It was probably him," she said, tossing her head towards me, "who killed them for food, or perhaps for sport. We came here to make sure you were okay, Hanna. We came for you, Hanna, to rescue you from him. You wouldn't believe how relieved we were when Huritt said you called him. This is one big misunderstanding, darling. We came in numbers, because we thought he took you hostage. We are on your side. He is the enemy, not us. We came here to rescue you, darling. It's what your parents would have wanted." Huritt's mother sounded very convincing. Any fool would have believed her lies, any fool who didn't know better. I looked at Hanna she looked at me.

"Don't look at him for answers, darling. He is the problem not us. He is the cancer between us. Come home with us, Hanna. We will take care of you. We've known you for a long time now. Do you really think that after all these years we would hurt you? You are our Hanna. You know you can trust us." She continued her act. Well, I have got to give it to her though, she would have made one hell of an actress had she ventured along that route, but we knew the real truth so therein lies the problem.

"You must wonder why I have been mean to you, when all you want to do is take me home with you, right? So you can take care of me?" Hanna asked.

They both looked at each other, and as if they read each other's mind they spoke at once. "We don't understand it, Hanna. Er—you speak," Huritt's mother said, gesturing to her husband.

"Um—Hanna, like Pat said, we have not come here to hurt you. We just wanted to make sure you are all right. You are like a daughter to us. You know that don't you. It doesn't have to be this way. If you can't trust us, then who else can you trust? Let's put all this misunderstanding behind us. Get Huritt, and the four of us can just leave now. I tell you, Sebastian will be no match for the four of us. I know we are not your parents, and we're not trying to be, but to us you are family. What happened down at your house was a terrible tragedy, and this place is the last place you should be, let alone be around his kind. Join us, and we can take him down together." He spoke as though I was not standing there.

"*Ha ha*, very funny. You do know I'm standing right here, don't you? I mean, if you're planning to kill me, it's really daft that you're planning it in front of me, and with my girlfriend," I said, fighting the urge not to laugh out loud. They must really think she is that dumb and stupid to buy the garbage they were spouting out.

"Well, even if I went to acting school, I don't think I would ever be as good as you two," Hanna said, and then she began to applaud. "Your offer is so good. You almost had me jumping out of my seat. So tell me, if I decide to go with you, what happens next? I mean, am I going to live with you forever so that we can play happy family or do you have other plans for me? You know you can tell me what I am to expect, since we are practically like family. I can trust you guys, right?" Hanna asked.

They looked at each other and nodded eagerly. "Of course, you can trust us. Why shouldn't you? You're like a daughter to us," Pat responded.

"Well, I'm having trouble believing that. Let's see, for starters I never knew you could change into animals. I mean, living with your kind, I would have to fear for my life always, and we all know animals are unpredictable. You can never tell when they will go for the kill, especially wild ones like wolves," Hanna said, getting up from her seat and walking towards me.

"What are you talking about? We know we are not normal, but we can't help what we are. We were born this way, but we wouldn't hurt you, not on purpose. And you must know by now that it's not the kind of thing you can tell anyone," Huritt's father defended.

This was beginning to irritate me, and I could tell that Hanna, too, was becoming irritated by their lies. She took a deep breath before talking. "Well, you can both drop the caring act now. I've got to give it to you two though, you are great actors. A couple of weeks ago, I would have bought your lies. Back when I didn't know who I was, but I bet you guys knew about me all this while. I would have fallen for every lie that came out of your mouths. And you two and your son would have led me to my death. Tell me that is not true? I can't wait to hear you tell another lie. Anyway, let me cut to the chase. I want to know what would happen to you and your tribe if I'm not included in your ritual when the full moon rises tomorrow." They both looked surprised, like they had no idea what she was talking about. "Oh, not again, don't—don't do that, I know. I know about your little sick plans, so don't act like you have no clue what I am talking about." They were both quiet but they looked rattled. "Listen, you can tell me straight up, or I could force it out of you two. Either way, you're going to talk. So what's it going to be?"

"It's complicated. We are not allowed to say," Huritt's father said.

"Now were getting somewhere, and I'm glad we are finally on the same page. I don't care how complicated it is, you will tell me what I need to know." They both looked down with no response. "If that's how you want to be, you've really left me with no choice but to do this." She looked at Pat and before long, I saw her drop to the floor in pain.

"What—what are you doing to her? Leave her alone, please! If I could, I would tell you!" He begged while his wife screamed in agony, but it was just the beginning. The next thing I knew, I started to smell hair burning, and I wasn't surprised to see that it was coming from Pat's hair somehow. Without burning her up, she fried her hair and left her head bald.

"Okay—okay stop! I will tell you what you want to know! Just stop please! Stop hurting her! I will tell you everything," he cried, running to his wife to hold her. For a second there, I almost pitied him, but I couldn't forget that they had brought this upon themselves.

Hanna stopped to give them time to gather their thoughts. Huritt's father looked at me, then at Hanna, and then at his wife, who was now curled in his arms. He placed his jaw on her now patchy scalp and tightened his hold on her. I looked at Hanna to try and guess how she was feeling, her face was like steel. I could tell she wasn't falling for them acting like the victims.

He looked up from his wife and then began to speak. "About eighteen years ago, blood appeared on the moon during a full moon. The whole moon turned red. Our people, our ancestors, believed that when this act of God happens, that God has finally decided to answer our prayers. The blood on the moon signified the birth of the extraordinary child who would take our curse away. It meant we'd been forgiven of whatever sin that had brought this curse on us. But we didn't know where to look. We sent people everywhere, but the earth is one big place. There was no point in a cure that we couldn't find, so after a couple of years we gave up and began accepting our fate all over again. But as fate would have it, as if planned by God himself, you were delivered into our hands when we weren't even looking. When—when you were little, maybe two, my little sister worked for your parents as your babysitter. One day, she said she was ironing and left the iron to go get something in the kitchen. Before she came back, you had pulled the iron cable down and the iron fell on you and burnt you badly. She called an ambulance immediately. But you were in so much pain that she decided to rush you to the hospital herself instead. So she left you for a minute or so to get her car keys and some other stuff. Anyway, before she came back, your body had healed and you were playing like nothing had happened. It was as if nothing had even happened to you. She couldn't believe what she had just witnessed. When she told me about it, I asked her to keep an eye on you and not to tell your parents what she had seen. We had to be sure you were the one, but everything fit, the age, your ability—"

"So I could heal, what was the big deal?" Hanna interjected.

"Well, you are special. No human child can do what you could. We didn't know what you were, but we knew you couldn't be completely human. The only way to break this curse, according to our ancestors and the oracle, is by sacrificing the blood of a special child. Once in a life-time a special child, like you, a child who doesn't belong here in this world, will be born, and only by sacrificing her blood will our curse be removed forever and we can be normal again—all of us. All of our children will be free of this curse. Every child we have is soiled. Our boys turn at thirteen, the girls when they turn eighteen. I never believed that such a child would ever exist, not to mention in my lifetime, but there you were. It was as if the answer to our prayers had just dropped into our laps, and we had to take it. As the head of our tribe, I had to decide what we were going to do with you. We had a meeting, and some of us wanted you kidnapped and raise you as one of our own until it was time, but my wife and I couldn't do it. We didn't want the emotional ties that would come with raising you. It would have made things too difficult. Well, now it's difficult because we got to know you, but this isn't just about us. So I made the decision to keep you under my watch. My sister kept an eye on you until your mother fired her because she was being too possessive of you. We sent others from the tribe to apply for the same position, and one of us was picked again, so we were aware of every development and could control the situation if need be. When your parents moved down here, we had to move, too. You can't blame us. You don't know what it feels like to be like this. My daughters don't know about this yet, because they are only sixteen and fifteen, but if we don't break this curse they will soon be like us, and I don't want that for them. I can't have them going through life like this, not being able to have boyfriends because of this plague on us. So I figured, why tell them since you were going to turn eighteen before they did. It's nothing personal, but a lot of lives and generations depend on the outcome of tomorrow. In the past, we accepted our fate, but that was because we had no way of breaking the curse and we could live as what we are, human and wolf, but since your birth, after the full moon tomorrow, we won't have that choice anymore. You can't blame us for trying."

"Hmm, so all my life you had someone watching me. I thought your son was my friend, but he was just another pair of eyes. To think I loved you people. My parents held you in high esteem, if only they knew the kind of people you really are. I guess now they will never know. I came to your house, ate at your table, laughed with you. You dined with my parents, we came to all of your Christmas parties, exchanged gifts, and all this time I was just your ticket out."

"I'm sorry, Hanna. We didn't like the idea, either. We always knew it was going to be hard, especially as our families became close, but it is what it is. We have children, and we want a better life for them. Our descendants will be free to live in the true human form. You would do the same if you were in our shoes." He tried to defend their action.

"No I wouldn't. You don't know me, so don't put me in your shoes. You took my kindness and gentleness for weakness. You would rather cut my life short for the sake of yours and your children. You knew if you had children they would inherit this curse, so why did you have them? Don't you think it was selfish of you?"

"We didn't want children! Who in their right mind would want to pass this on to their child, but it's an inevitable circle. When we are in our human form, we take care not to conceive, but when we are in—in the other form we mate. We have no control over it. It doesn't matter how careful we are or what we do in the human form, we end up with a child. I know you know we can change anytime, but on full moons, we have to change even though we don't want to. After we had Huritt, we decided it was better not to be together on full moons so we didn't end up with another child, but sometimes, life just throws us together, and that's how we ended up with Suzan and Hilda."

I understood what it felt like to be cursed. I felt like that for half of my existence, but I since stopped seeing it as a curse and have accepted what I am. They have lived generations with this ability. It's what makes them different. They have to accept the ups and downs of what they are.

"You still haven't told me what will happen after tomorrow's full moon, since I won't be taking part in your ritual?"

"That I can't say. Please don't make me. It's not like I don't want to tell you, but there is a penalty if I talk about it to someone outside the tribe," Huritt's dad said.

"You don't have a choice. You've come this far now. Why keep it a secret? Just tell us. Whatever is going to happen is still going to happen anyway, because there is no chance in hell that Hanna will be part of your ritual. The odds are really not in your favour here," I said, looking at Pat, who was still clearly in agony. Huritt's dad looked at his wife who nodded at him in approval. He then jerked his head back and took a long deep breath before letting it all out. I held my breath for a minute or so to stop myself from gasping as the stench as his breath filled the whole room.

"Well, seeing that you've left me no choice, I will tell you. I will take the consequences. It's no less than I deserve. You were precious to your parents, Hanna. They loved you very much. Your father once asked me if I would consider taking you in should anything ever happen to him and Joan. And you can imagine how horrible I felt when he asked me to be your guardian. I knew I would never be able to do it, but I lied and promised him he could rely on us. You must understand that this is difficult for us all. I'm sorry it has to come to this between us. But before I say anything else, I want you to know that my son, Huritt, didn't want to do this. He loves you. He loved you even before he knew he was plagued with the curse. It hasn't been easy for him to have to spy on you. We made him, so please forgive him. We made him do it. He didn't care what the consequences were for him, but this isn't just about him alone. There was no getting out of the situation for him. We came tonight because a part of me thought he foolishly ran away with you when he didn't show up like we expected." He stopped talking briefly to catch his breath. I looked at Hanna to see if the talk about Huritt had softened her, but her face was blank. I couldn't tell what she was feeling. Then he began to talk again.

"If we can't stop the curse by tomorrow's full moon, then the curse is sealed forever. When we turn tomorrow we can never change back to our human forms, but we will have all our human memories. It will be as if we are trapped in the body of an animal. But because I told you this, as you're not part of the tribe, when I turn tomorrow I will have no memory of who I am. I will not remember my family or the tribe. They will mean nothing to me. I will still be human inside, but it will be as if they never existed." I looked over at Hanna whose eyes were now filled with tears. I could tell she felt guilty that we had pushed him to tell us, but I felt no pity for him, at least he got to live, which was still a reward in my view.

"When you say *sacrifice*, what will you—what would you have done to me? I need to know," she asked. I looked at her because I didn't think she should be asking that kind of question.

"Hanna, I don't think you should—" I tried to say, but she cut in.

"No, I want to know. Tell me what you would have done to me," she asked again.

"We would have drained every drop of blood in you. There is no other way around it. I'm sorry. It's the only way to lift the curse. We were going to—cut you and let your blood pour out so we could all have a drink before the full moon. And when the moon was full it should turn red to signify your death, just as when you were born. Then we would turn for the last time together as a tribe. Every tribe wanting to lift the curse will be present. The alphas of each pack in each tribe would jointly tear your remains into pieces, each of us keeping a piece of you so that you can never be put together again, even in death. That way, we and all generations to come would be free of the curse forever. Any blood left after we changed back to our human forms we would keep for our children who have not yet transformed for the first time, up to four generations, to properly cleanse us of the curse. If ever all of your pieces were put together again before the cleansing was complete the curse would return and seal itself on us permanently. That's everything you need to know and, Hanna, I don't know if it matters anymore, but I am sorry for everything." He looked relived, but pained. Then he dropped to his knees and gathered his wife in his arms. I looked away from them to Hanna. I didn't care what they were going through, not after hearing what they had in store for Hanna.

Everyone was quiet for a while. Hanna looked shocked. I held her shoulder to reassure her. It must be tough to hear all the evil they had planned. It's a good thing it's all now a fantasy in their head.

"Did you just make that up? How sick are you to want to do that to her, to anyone for that matter," I asked, disgusted, even as a vampire.

"I'm sorry, I am not making it up. It's the only way the ritual will work. It's been passed down from generation to generation. We have been looking for a cure to this—

sickness—if you like, for centuries. Our ancestors believed the oracle about your birth, we just didn't know when it would happen. So this information has been passed down from one generation to another. So, yes, it's all true. I'm not making it up. Your birth triggered the seal. If you weren't born, we would exist as both human and wolf, but since your existence, the eighteen-year countdown began. You asked me, and I am telling you what would have happened, but there is nothing to fear since it's not going to happen anymore. I am sorry I ever even considered doing it, and hearing myself say it makes me realise how cruel the ritual is."

"I'm sorry, too. I'm sorry your lives have turned out like this, but I am not to blame for your curse. If there was anything I could do to help, I would have, but I am not going to trade my life for yours or for your children's. I am entitled to live my life and be happy, even though it comes at a price to you all. I had other plans for you before, but I have changed my mind. I will let the three of you go. The curse is enough punishment for you I think. There is one thing I can do though if it happens like you say. I can help you forget when you turn for the last time tomorrow, so you don't feel trapped. I can take your human memories away if you want. That way when you turn for the last time, your life as humans will be gone as well. You would have no burden, no pain, and no memory."

"What about my daughters? They don't know what we are. What is going to happen to them?" he asked.

"Well, I suggest you go home and tell them the truth so they know what to expect. It's about time, don't you think. I will try my best to see that they are fine, and when they eventually turn I will bring them to you wherever you are so you can live together as a family if you want, although I doubt it will matter at all," she said, and I wasn't happy that she wanted to help, but that's Hanna. She is good.

"Thank you. I don't know what to say. We've all wronged you so much, but still you show mercy, but I will have to decline. Our memories are all we have left. If you take them, then we are no good. We'll take our chances, but thanks for the offer." You could hear the defeat in his voice. I couldn't stand to be around them anymore. I was annoyed that they were playing the victims. They wanted pity, but I had none for them. I left and went to get their son from the basement. I had planned on cutting off one of his limbs before releasing him into the wild, but seeing as Hanna is in the forgiving mood, I guess I have to do the same. I pushed him towards his family and stayed back to give Hanna space with him. I watched as he joined his parents, and they held him in relief. Huritt peered up from under his parents embrace to look at Hanna, but I noticed that she turned away quickly to avoid any conversation with him.

"Okay, now that you're all together, I want you to go. Please make sure that I never see you again. I will ensure that your daughters join you when it's their time. And one more thing, you have to leave town today, before the full moon. When it's time for your daughters to join you, I will find you and bring them to you. Now get out."

"Hanna I—" Huritt tried to say something to her, but she cut him off.

"Go on, get out," she said firmly. He looked away disappointed, and, together with his father, he helped his mother up and they made their way out.

Hanna ran upstairs immediately. It had all been too much for her, and I couldn't wait for us to leave this town and this whole situation behind and start afresh. We could start by having a birthday celebration for two tomorrow. I sat down, relieved at the outcome of today's events. "One battle down, one more to go," I muttered to myself.

## Chapter 28

I waited an hour before going upstairs to Hanna's room. She was lying on her back on the bed, eyes staring at the ceiling. I sat at the end of the bed and wondered what was going through her mind. I didn't know if and how to broach the subject of leaving town for good.

I placed her feet on me and gently gave them a squeeze. She looked at me from the corner of her eyes, and then looked away. I wished I knew what was going through her mind just then, but I wasn't going to push it. We sat quietly for a while and my mind drifted to my next battle. I knew it wouldn't be as easy as this one, and I might not come back from it, but then it had to be done. I had to be sure Hanna would be safe, even if it means I die.

"Hey," she said. I looked at her, my mind still working out how I could keep her from days like today. I squeezed her feet in response. She sat up, and I let go of her feet to allow her room to move. "Let's get out of here," she said.

"What?" I was surprised.

"Let's go and leave this crazy town behind us. This past week has been tough, hasn't it? Who knew so much drama could take place in such a short space of time. I don't like it here anymore. There is nothing for me here. This place—I mean this town—is ghost to me now. My parents are gone and my childhood friend is a wolf and a traitor. All I have left is you. You are the only one in this world I can trust, the only one who truly matters." She was trying not to cry, but I could hear it in her voice. I tried to say something, but she continued before I could form any words. "I know we've only been together a short while, but when I'm with you I get the feeling I've known you all my life. I don't know why. Sometimes, I see your face in my past, like we've met before, but I can't connect it. I don't understand it. I close my eyes and see you in my past being kind to me. Am I dreaming it, or I am just wishing we've been together longer. It doesn't matter the length of time in between. What matters to me is that I know that I can trust you, and I feel deep down that I belong with you. Sebastian, it's important that we are truthful with each other from now on. So you will tell me if there is any truth in these visions of my past that I keep having or if it's all just in my head?" she asked.

Her question caught me off guard. One minute, she was telling me I was the one person in the world she could rely on, and the next, she is asking me to tell her a truth that could destroy us for good. I stared at her with the answer to her question on the tip of my tongue. How do I tell her she is right? How do I tell her the truth without revealing how I came to be in possession of her? As much as I was dying inside to tell the truth, I couldn't risk the price I would pay if she ever knew the whole truth, so I lied.

"It's possible, that I may have met you when you were young. I am not sure of it, though, but it's very possible," I said, regretting every lie that was coming out of my mouth. In my mind I knew one day she might find out the truth, although I pray that such a day never comes. If I were not responsible for her natural mother's death, then I might have been able to explain to her why I had kept her in the dark, but now it was too late to visit old stories. She looked at me funny, like she knew I was holding something back, but she didn't say anything, and I was glad she did not, or I wouldn't know what to do. We were both quiet for a little while. She lay back on the bed, and I joined her. I held her hands and stared into space, praying she wouldn't ask me any more questions about the past. Then she spoke again.

"We definitely need to leave and make new memories, S. Let's leave now, tonight. We can go anywhere as long as it's not here," she said pleadingly.

"Are you sure that is what you want?" I asked, and she nodded. "What about your parents' burial? It's in three day. Are you sure you don't want to wait around for it?" I asked. She was quiet for a while and then she spoke.

"They will understand why I have to leave. I know I should be there but the police—I can't do it. I can't. They will ask too many questions. Where have I been, why I didn't come forward earlier. I don't want to be part of all that stress, and I don't want to be here surrounded by all these bad memories."

"Then it's done. We leave tonight. Pack up a few things that you need and we are out of here." That was what I came up to suggest to her anyway.

"Really?" she asked and sat up.

"Sure," I responded, a little shocked that she didn't already know that I would do anything for her. She jumped on me, and I carefully rolled her off so she wouldn't hurt herself and gently pinned her down with my arms guarding her torso.

"Thank you, S. it means a lot to me," she said looking happily in my eyes, as she put her arms around my neck and pulled me towards her.

"Don't do that," I said.

"What?" She looked concerned.

"Sorry, I meant to say, don't say that. Never thank me for anything I do for you. I am the one grateful to have you in my life. I am not worthy of your love, yet you give it to me. Let me make you happy. Let me help keep you safe. Let's make new memories together. From now on, no more sadness. Anything you want, just ask, and I will do it, on one condition only," I said.

"And what would that be?" she asked eagerly.

"That you never thank me for anything I do for you."

"That is going to be hard to do. There must be a way I can thank you without ever thanking you. Tell me what to do," she said.

I brushed her hair back with my hands and admired her beauty. I took a deep breath before answering her. "You take my breath away each time I look at you. You are all the thanks I need. Your being in my life has changed everything for me. So as long as you remain in my life, I have all the thanks I need. Just be who you are, Hanna," I said and she smiled.

"You know, you are unbelievable, Sebastian. You do this to me each time. You have a way of making me feel like the most precious person in the world, and I get scared that one day I will stop being important to you. Promise me, S, promise me that as long as life continues you will always remain in my life."

"As long as you will have me, Hanna, I will always be with you. And I promise I will never stop loving you, nor will I ever go back on my word. Now, I know you may not feel like celebrating, but you only turn eighteen once. Let's go to Paris and celebrate being alive."

She smiled and said, "I should feel bad about celebrating, but you know what? I don't mind that at all, so let's get moving."

While she packed a few essentials, I went around the house to ensure that all the windows and back doors were locked. I went to my room and picked up my getaway bag. She was already waiting downstairs with a packed bag. We both took one last look at the house and got in the car. I knew we wouldn't be returning to the house anymore.

At the airport, I bought first-class tickets to France. I have a beautiful house in the village of Pezenas, Languedoc Roussillon, in the south of France. My mother and I lived there whenever we stayed in France. I have not been back there since our last stay when she was alive, but now it seemed like a good time to move on, and I was sure Hanna would love it there. Before heading to Pezenas, I checked us into the Four Seasons in Paris. We would stay there for a week before moving on. I didn't want Hanna too stressed out with a long journey.

Hanna loved the service at the Four Seasons, and I was glad. The expression on her face was all the satisfaction I needed. She immediately hit the shower, while I ordered her breakfast. By the time she was through, breakfast had already been delivered by room service. I excused myself while she got changed and returned as soon as I was sure she was decent. She looked tired. I placed her breakfast on her lap and went and had a shower myself to wash the stench of the dogs off me. I deliberately stayed longer so she could finish her meal before I got out. By the time I returned, she had barely touched her food, and she was slumped on the sofa asleep.

I picked her up and laid her on the bed, being careful not to wake her, and then I pulled the cover over her. Her hair was spread over the pillow and she looked like a goddess. It felt wrong to watch her sleep, but I couldn't take my eyes off her. Her beauty possessed me. I felt so contented and pleased just watching her all night.

## Chapter 29

Hanna slept through the day and didn't wake until two in the morning. So much for the birthday celebration, but I refused to wake her. She was clearly exhausted. I got room service to deliver some food, just in case she woke up hungry. I was glad I had, because she descended on the food as soon as she woke up.

Because I was now a day walker, thanks to Hanna, I was able to leave the room to arrange places for us to visit together. As soon as she finished eating, she fell asleep again. She tried to stay up, but I could tell she was out of it, so I encouraged her to get more sleep. She needed the rest so she could have strength for all the sightseeing I had planned for the week. Moping around the room with nothing to do, I felt a little exhausted, too, so I lay on the sofa and caught up on some much deserved sleep. By the time I opened my eyes, Hanna was standing over me already dressed.

"Hi," I said. She smiled and sat next to me. I held her hand. "You look great."

"Thanks. I am sorry I woke you up. I didn't mean to."

"No. it's all right, what's the time?" I asked.

"It's four in the afternoon. I was just going to head out to the restaurant downstairs to get some food in me. I was waiting for you, but you looked very tired so I thought I would go on my own."

"Wow it's four already? I guess I'm still not used to being awake in the daytime. Why don't you get room service to bring something up for you?"

"I want to go out. It's day two and the day is almost over and I have been sleeping mostly. I'm sorry about yesterday, the birthday thing, I wanted to stay awake so much, but even I can't cheat nature."

"It's all right. You have all the time in the world to make it up to me," I replied.

"I just need some fresh air. I'll be back before you know it," she said.

"Let me come with you. I'll just have a quick shower and be dressed in no time."

"No, don't worry. I'm sure you have plans for us tonight. If you don't, I will be very disappointed. Stay and go over your plans. You never made it on time for our first date, so you really need to impress me tonight," she said, and I chuckled.

"Don't worry, I'll do my best. Hurry back, okay? I'll be waiting." She bent over and planted a kiss on my lips before leaving.

After my nap, I hit the shower and then got dressed. I looked at the time. Hanna had been gone for a while, and I tried not to panic. *She is fine*, I told myself to calm my nerves. I sat by the grand piano in the suite and ran my fingers through the keys. "I should have gone with her," I muttered to myself. "She is fine, of course she is fine," I reassured myself. Then I heard footsteps and inhaled her scent and then the door opened.

"Sorry, I took so long," she said as she closed the door behind her.

"It's okay. Did you have a nice time?" I was relieved to have her back.

"It was okay. I wish I had waited for you, though."

"Why, what happened?" I stopped playing at once.

"Oh, it's nothing serious. The food was good, but there was this man who kept staring at me when he thought I wasn't looking. He just gave me the creeps," she said, taking off her heels and throwing each one into the corner of the room.

I turned around to face her. "What did he look like?" I asked, annoyed with myself for not going with her. This was supposed to be a fun get-away and already we may have another crisis.

"It's okay. I don't think he's dangerous or anything like that. He just made me uncomfortable, and I kind of wished you were there, that's all. Perhaps I was taking everything too seriously. I need to relax and not think that everyone is after me."

"You're right, it's probably nothing. Perhaps he was just attracted to you. I mean, who in their right mind wouldn't be? You're gorgeous. I can't believe I let you go out by yourself in Paris, the city of romance. I must be out of my mind," I said, moving toward her and taking her gently in my arms. I planted a kiss on her lips, and whirling her around in my arms. "I have to warn you though, I am taking this dating thing very seriously from now on. No more leaving without me. I need to impress you. I want to share everything with you. Remember this is all new to me, too."

"Don't worry, I didn't like not being with you, either, and I'm ready to be doted on. Didn't anyone tell you? I am a little high maintenance."

"Then it's a good thing, because I have everything thing in place to meet all your needs."

"What would I do without you?"

"Or me without you? I am all yours this evening. Just tell me when you're ready to start off?"

"Well, then, there is no time like the present. Let's get going before the day draws to a close," she replied.

"You read my mind exactly." I went over and picked up her shoes that she had flung across the room earlier and helped her slip them on.

We took a twenty-minute drive to Le Marias district, where we took a nice stroll through the beautiful historic square. All the while I kept checking to see if she liked it, and she seemed to be enjoying every minute of it. I booked us on a dinner cruise along the Seine River in a *bateau Mouche*, but found it a little difficult tearing her away from Le Marias. When she finally had enough, we took a taxi down the foot of the Eiffel tower to catch the cruise up the Seine River. I had a window seat reserved for us, just so she wouldn't miss any of the beautiful city lights. She had a bite of dinner with music playing in the background.

I enjoyed watching her face light up all through the night, and I was very delighted that I was responsible for making her happy. She was drunk on the city, and I was drunk on her beauty. She danced and jumped until she was too exhausted to stay awake. By the time the cruise was over, she was fast asleep in my arms, so I carried her up to our suite and once again laid her on the bed.

The following day after breakfast, we went to the Paris department stores to shop for clothes for her, and then I took her to Avenue Montaigne to do some more shopping. I watched as she tried on different outfits. She looked breathtaking in each of them. I could see that she was enjoying every minute of it, and so was I. It was a whole new experience for me doing this with her. She wanted me to choose, but I liked them all on her, so we ended up buying the whole lot.

When we got back, we were both too exhausted to go out, so we decided on a night in. I wanted us to watch a new movie, but she insisted we watch an old movie called *An affair to Remember*. I had seen that movie with my mother a number of times, but I would gladly see it again with Hanna. She sat with her head nestled on my shoulders, and before I knew it, fifteen minutes into the movie, she was already asleep. I couldn't laugh out loud for fear of waking her up. To think she argued so much to have her choice of movie, only to nod off fifteen minutes into it. Like I always do, I carried her to bed, before returning to the couch to see the movie to the end. I wasn't entirely sure why I watched it to the end, but turning it off because she was sleeping felt like I was going back on my word. When it finished, I lay on the sofa and rested myself.

The next morning, Hanna went downstairs by herself for her breakfast and then came back and had another nap. It looked like all we did was sleep. The week wasn't turning out how I planned, and I was going to salvage it. While she slept, I occupied myself with the keyboard. When she woke up, she had her bath and then I took her for a walk in the Luxembourg Garden. Later we went for a tour of the Eiffel Tower. We then stopped at Ducasse's Restaurant for lunch before going to watch the sunset from Port des Arts. We ended the day with dinner at the Dame du Canton.

The following day, we were out again, shopped some more, and kissed in parks and crowded shopping malls like no one else existed but the two of us. We were having the time of our lives, and I felt alive, I felt free. We were making new memories together, plus the freedom of walking in the sun without fearing for my life was the icing on the cake.

Soon the week had come to an end, and we had one more night. We went back for a cruise up the Seine River because she had loved it so much and wouldn't stop talking about it. She was looking out the window enjoying the night when suddenly she turned around and said. "S, do you remember the other day when I went for lunch by myself?"

"Mm-hmm," I responded.

"Well, it's just—you know that man I told you about who was staring at me that day? He's here with us again. And I've seen him two other times since that day. It seems like he is following us or something."

"Why didn't you say something before, Hanna? You've seen him twice and you kept quiet about such a thing? When and where did you see him last?"

"At the mall, I think. But he's here now, at the table adjacent to ours. He's pretending to be enjoying the cruise, but I think he's only here because of me. The first time I thought it was just a coincidence, so I didn't think I should bother you with it, but now—he has been spying on me all night. I can feel his eyes on me," she whispered to me. I was annoyed that she hadn't mentioned this earlier. After what we had gone through in England, she needed to understand that there are no coincidences in our world. I looked around us. The place was packed with people enjoying their romantic evening. I needed to get the man on his own and find out who and what he was. If he was truly spying on us, then he should follow us as soon as we were off the boat, and he did. I got Hanna to the room and went back to find the man. He sat in the lobby with a newspaper in his hands to cover his face. I sat down opposite him and cleared my throat to get his attention. He peered up from above the paper, took one look at me, got up, and ran out of the lobby into the street. He hailed down a taxi, but I tapped his shoulder before he could get in. He spun around and looked at me in shock, as if he had never seen my face before. I poked my head in the taxi, dropped a few notes on the passenger's seat, and asked the driver to leave.

"How can I help you? What do you think you're doing? Hey wait," he shouted in a French accent at the back of the departing taxi.

"Calm down," I said, but he kept yelling.

"What do you want?" I dragged him away from the street into a side alley.

"Why are you following us?" I asked.

He was shaking. He looked confused by my question. "Look, stop pretending like you don't understand me. Why have you been tailing her? What do you want? Who sent you?"

He shook his head nervously from side to side. If I didn't know any better I would believe it was all a coincidence. So instead of shouting, I decided to try another approach. "Listen, I'm not going to harm you, so don't be afraid. I am going to ask you a few questions. I don't want to hurt you, okay, unless you give me a cause to do so. Do you understand?" He nodded. "Look at me." I had to compel him, as his heart was racing, and I could hear blood pumping through his body. He was fearful, and that assured me he knew who or what I was. "Why are you scared of me?" I asked.

"Because I've met someone who is just like you and he hurt me. He has my wife and son. Please don't hurt me." I took a minute to take this in. It meant he was on a vampire errand.

"I told you, you have nothing to fear from me. Why are you following us?" I asked.

"I was told to follow her around."

"Is it the same person who has your wife and son?" I asked.

"Yes. Please, please don't hurt me—I was just doing it to protect my family."

"What's this person's name?"

"I don't know. Honestly, I don't. I don't even remember anything about him, apart from the fact that I am supposed to follow her and that he has my family."

"Describe him to me, can you" I asked him impatiently.

"I honestly don't know, I—I don't remember what he looks like. Please believe me. I don't remember." I believed him. It was just too soon after England. We didn't even get to complete a week and now we had to go to war again.

"Okay, calm down. I believe you. Get out of here now. Go before I change my mind." I stood behind and watched as he scrambled off. I waited until he had gone far enough before following him. I spotted him as he entered a dark alley. I moved closer but stayed back far enough so my presence was not detected. He was talking to someone.

"I followed her again today like you asked. She is back at the hotel. She is alone now."

"Hmm," I heard the other person respond, but I didn't need to hear the person speak. I could smell him, and I immediately knew what I was dealing with.

"Can I have my family back now, please. I did as you said. I spoke to no one about you."

"You failed. I asked you to do one simple thing to save your family and you couldn't even carry that out."

"I'm sorry. I tried my best. You must believe me. I tried. Please give me back my family."

"You led him here, you fool. You did not only fail, you also led him here. You just killed your family."

"I am sorry! Please don't hurt them! Don't hurt my family! Please, I beg of you!"

Then I heard a loud cry from the man and a tumble. I didn't need to be there to figure out what had happened. I rushed over to see the man, but I was too late, his neck had been snapped. I didn't bother following his killer, it had to be one of the three vampires from Hanna's house, and the scent belonged to one of them. But I didn't understand. They had left her for dead and if they were back, they must know that she didn't die. I rushed back to the hotel and dashed into the room to deliver the bad news, and to my astonishment, Hanna was already packed. It was as if she knew what I was going to say. "You're packed already. I was just going to tell you we have to leave tonight."

"I know. I felt your energy. You were worried and concerned for me. I knew then whatever you found was not good news, so I packed up our stuff."

"My energy—what—how do you mean?"

"S, now is not the time, I will explain later," she said, and she was right, but there was something else that worried her.

"What's the matter, Hanna?" She picked up her shoes from the floor and sat on the bed to wear them.

"Nothing, I was just getting used to a little normalcy. I mean, it's barely a week and already we have to fight again."

"I promise you, Hanna, it's not always going to be like this. We will find a way out of this mess."

She smiled weakly and sighed. "So what's the story this time? Who was that guy? And who is after us this time?"

"I will tell you on the way, love. We have to leave now, I'm sorry."

"I'm not going until you tell me who I am supposed to be running from."

"I'm not sure, but we are being monitored by one or more vampires." I gave her time to sink in the information.

"Do you know which ones this time around? If they're the same ones from before, they must know I didn't die then."

"I'm not sure, but if it's them, then they must know and that's why they're out here."

She took a deep breath, got up on her feet, picked up her handbag from the chair at the foot of the bed, and began to walk towards the door. "Well, then, let them come. We are going to give them a hell of a fight."

"First, we have to figure out how to defeat them."

"I know. What about the man from the cruise? Is he one, too?"

"No, he's dead. He was compelled to follow you, and his family should follow him soon, if they are not already dead. They were held captive by his killer."

"Who killed him?"

"I didn't see his face, but I'm sure now, it's definitely one of the ones that attacked you."

I picked up her bags of clothes and followed behind her. When she got to the door, she turned towards me and said, "Sebastian, we can't run all our lives. This time around, when they come, they won't believe what's hit them."

I didn't say anything. Left to me, I wouldn't want her involved, but I knew there was no telling her to sit this one out. She has to avenge her parents. I hired a car and we drove to my house in the south of France, all the while checking that we were not being followed. As I drove, I began to think of various ways the fight could go down. I didn't know if her powers could cripple a vampire like the wolves, but then I guess we could test it out on me. Unfortunately, I had spent a week without feeding, and I was beginning to crave blood very much. I tried to subdue my hunger until we safety got to the house and then I quickly went hunting.

The house had been prepared for our arrival by my caretaker, Gilou, and, as instructed by me, he has stocked the house with various kinds of human food. I had known the caretaker's family for years. Before Gilou, it was his father who looked after all my properties in France. After his father's death, Gilou took over and has been working for me for over fifty years. His daughter will take over when he dies. They know about us, and have kept our secret. In reward, they are handsomely taken care of, but they don't do it for money. Vampires need a handful of humans who know our secret to help make our existence a little easier.

Before I left to hunt, I thanked Gilou for his help and went inside with Hanna. Gilou had offered to help take Hanna's things inside, but I politely declined. He was too old now to do any heavy lifting. I carried her bags upstairs and settled her in the best room in the house. I put my stuff in the room next to hers. Gilou brought her breakfast upstairs, I sat with Hanna and watched as she picked around her food. She looked exhausted. We had driven all night, and I knew her mind must be working on overdrive. She curled up in her bed and slept. I left to hunt almost immediately after she slept. I hated being around her when I was hungry, plus we had a battle looming, and I didn't want to be caught off guard

It took me almost half the day before getting back to the house. Upon entering the house, I sensed the presence of the vampire from the night before, and I got scared. I ran to Hanna, and, to my astonishment, she was still there sleeping.

I went over to her. She shifted her body and lay on her tummy. She seemed fine. I ran into all the rooms upstairs to ensure he was no longer around before going downstairs to lock all the doors and windows.

It wasn't looking good. They knew where we were, even though I was careful. Coming here while I was out and leaving her to sleep was a message. I was annoyed. We hadn't even practised. We didn't know how we were going to win this battle, and already they were letting me know they could find us anytime.

I went back to her room and lay next to her, being careful not to wake her. "How long have you been here?" she asked sleepily.

"Not long," I replied.

"What's the time, S?" Hanna asked, poking her head up, looking around for a clock. I smiled at her, while at the same time wishing we didn't have trouble looking for us.

"It's just a little past six."

She immediately sat up. "Don't tell me I've slept that long." I nodded, trying to keep the worry out of my face. "What's wrong?" she asked. I thought about telling her that there was a vampire stalking us, but I decided against it, because she deserved a night off from this circus we seemed to be on.

"Nothing at all, just worried because you've been asleep all day."

"Hmm, why do I feel like you are hiding something? You've got on that face you wear when you're trying so desperately to keep something from me. Sebastian, this isn't just your battle. It's you and me against the world."

I caressed her cheek with the back of my hand. "I know, love, and believe me I don't want to keep anything from you.

Okay, I didn't want to bother you with this—not now anyway, but as much as I want to protect you from it all, you deserve to know. I'm worried about your safety. We've been followed, and it's not safe here anymore. I know we've just arrived, but we need to go, and we need to go now."

She looked annoyed and irritated. "Are you saying they've been here?" she asked. I could see the annoyance on her face.

"Yes, exactly. Someone's been here. It's one of the three brothers. I'm sorry, my love, but I think we'd better leave. We're at a disadvantage; they know where we are. I promise you I will find us a place where we can't be found." I tried to persuade her, and she buried her head on her knees. I moved closer to her and lightly held her shoulders to comfort her. I didn't know what else to say to make her feel better.

Then she looked up. "I'm not running away anymore, Sebastian. I don't want to put you in harm's way, but we have to stand up to them."

"It's you I'm thinking of, Hanna, not me. I know you have these abilities, but you haven't really tested it on vampires. We don't know if it's only the three of them looking for us or if they have reinforcements. If they know of your abilities, like those dogs did, I'm sure they won't be alone. Hanna, I can't bear to lose you again."

"But we can't keep running. Once we start, we'll always be looking over our shoulders, and I don't want that life, S." She was right. We needed to fight them now, even if it ended badly.

"Okay, we'll stay and deal with this once and for all, but we have to work out a plan. Also, you have to practice with me to see if your power works on vampires and generally get a feel of how much damage we can deliver when they come." She looked reluctant. "Trust me, Hanna. It's the only way. I trust you with my life, and I know you can do this without actually killing me. Plus, it's the only way to know for sure."

"I just don't want to hurt you."

"Don't worry about it. I'll be fine. You need to do this, and don't hold back. Remember, these vampires are old. We get our chance and we take it"

"Okay, if you say so. But before we do this, I need to ask you something?"

"What is it?"

"Do you promise to tell me the truth?"

I was suddenly concerned now, because she looked very serious. "I always tell you the truth."

"Okay then. Before me, was there a woman you loved, a vampire lover from your past? I'm sorry, I know this is a silly question to ask and the timing is all wrong, but this has been bothering me, and I need an answer for peace's sake. I mean, you've lived for almost two hundred years, of course you must have had a lover."

I gently held her hands until she stopped talking. "Hanna, I have lived many years, but in all of those years, I loved no one until I met you. You are the only one I have loved, and I'm still in love with, and that is never going to change." I looked at her, concerned, wondering why the sudden question about my past. I panicked inside. I already suspected why she was interested in my past relationship, but I hoped I was wrong.

"The night my parents were killed, there was a girl, tall and beautiful, with long dark hair. She said I stole you from her. She had my parents killed for sport. Sometimes, I can't help thinking that if I had not met you, if I had not fallen in love with you, they would still be alive. If you weren't lovers, then why was she so bitter and vicious? She said killing me left you free to return to her. Who is she to you, S?"

I was enraged and sad at the same time. This situation had only one ending: Isobel's death or mine. Even if I chose to forgive her, I knew she would never stop plotting to kill Hanna. "Isobel," I said beneath my breath. My fists clenched and my jaws tightened when I mentioned her name.

"So you know her, then?" she asked.

"Yes I do. She's my sister—er—she's like a sister to me, nothing more, but—she has feelings for me. She says she loves me. She's maintained her claim of love for me for centuries. But I don't want—er—I don't love her the way she wants me to. I love her as a sister and nothing more. I'm so sorry. This was entirely my fault. I did my best to keep you away from her. I knew she'd be jealous if she ever found out about you, but never in a million years did I think she'd deliberately do something that would hurt me this much. So she did the killings, did she?"

"No, it wasn't her. She didn't do the killing. She brought three other vampires with her. I'll never forget their names. One was called Anton, the other was Zacchary, and the one who—who attacked me was called —"

"Hector," I said before she could finish. I felt sick and weak at the same time. It was impossible to believe that she would actually do such a thing and not once think I would find out that she was behind such evil. She had just made an enemy of me when she dared to kill Hanna.

"What are you thinking, S?"

"I'm thinking we had better start practicing now, Hanna. There's no time to waste. Practise on me. Somebody knows you're alive, and it could be her or one of those three or all four of them. If they decide to come together, we have to be able to weaken them long enough to kill them all."

"What about your sister? You don't mind if we kill her, too?"

"She stopped being my sister the moment she conceived the idea to have you killed."

"Well, then, if that's the case, let's get started."

## Chapter 30

We stood facing each other in the living room. "Are you sure you're ready for this?" Hanna asked.

"Just do it," I replied.

"Okay," she said, looking nervous.

"Don't be nervous, just do it. Forget it's me standing in front of you and just take yourself back to that horrible day. What would you have done if you had the power to save your parents."

She took a deep breath and her face changed. I could see the anger and vengeance in her, and I knew at that moment that whatever was coming was not going to be good. Before I knew it, I was off the ground and thrown hard into the wall. I leapt up almost immediately, but before I could get to her, I was bounced off the wall again. "You're going to have to do better than that," I shouted. I needed her to get angrier and stop worrying about hurting me. I sprung at her, and she stopped me mid-air, smashing my head to the ground. I could feel my bones cracking, but I knew that wasn't enough to stop one vampire, let alone four. "Is that all you've got," I snarled. I was up on my feet and at her side straightaway. "Stop thinking about what you are going to do, and just do it! Vampires are fast and very strong! You've got to be better and faster! You've got to show them who the boss is! Do what you did to the wolves, but be ten times more aggressive!" I shouted to get her angry.

She looked at me and her eyes turned red like fire, and I felt a force push me away from her with such power that I couldn't resist her. My body curled up in pain, and I felt the air around me burning up. I was helpless, trapped in midair, and in excruciating pain. Then I began to choke. I tried looking up to get her to stop. I was drying up, and I couldn't find her. My body started to sizzle as though any minute I would burst into flames. And then from behind me, I heard her say, "You have to give me more credit, S. I am capable of much more."

I felt a rush of ice flow through me as I dropped to the ground. I lay there for a while not daring to move. My energy seemed to have been sucked out of me. "Well, that was impressive. Remind me next time to never underestimate you," I said breathlessly. "So why didn't you do the crippling thing? You know, the one you did with the wolves. That should put another spin on things."

"This one?" she asked, and I was once more in agonizing pain. My spine felt shattered and my bones pierced me horribly. I was crushed and in despair. I wanted her to stop, but I couldn't even find the strength to talk. I held on to my body trying desperately to stop myself from dying from the torment that consumed me. I had never felt so incapacitated and powerless. Now I understood what it was the wolves went through at her hands. She finally stopped.

"So what do you think? Do you think we will be ready when they come to pay us a visit?" I couldn't speak. Although she had stopped, my body was still in shock, and I had to slowly build up my strength again. I felt so vulnerable. "Are you all right? I've hurt you, haven't I? I'm sorry, I didn't mean to. I just got carried away." She rushed to my side.

"I'm all right. I just like it here on the floor," I said weakly. I didn't want her to feel guilty.

"You're lying, S. I can always tell when you're lying."

I tried to smile to reassure her. "Yes I am. I never want to go through that again. The good thing is that we know it works on vampires as well. They won't know what's hit them."

"I'm just glad we don't have to practice on you anymore," she joked, offering her hand to me to help me get up, but I pulled her down to me and moved her beneath me.

"You didn't have to make it hurt for that long," I whispered in her ear.

"Remember, you asked for it. I didn't want you to be disappointed," she replied.

"Well, now, you know you have to pay, don't you?"

"In what ways do you suggest I pay you back?"

"You will have to wait and see."

I moved my lips over hers and gently kissed her only for a second.

"Is that all you've got?" she asked, her eyes tempting me as she spoke, and it aroused me.

I shook my head before responding. "No love, I'm going to render you powerless by kissing you slowly and passionately until you begin to melt under my power, and I will stop only if you beg me to," I said.

She chuckled. "Show me what you've got then," she responded, and for a moment we stared into each other's eyes. I was lost in hers for a while before slowly moving in to kiss her again a second at a time. We let our passion build, our bodies moving closer to each other. My body began to ache for her. I felt her body tighten against mine as she held me even closer. The more we kissed, the more I yearned for her, and the more reckless I was beginning to feel. I wanted to melt into her. I had never felt like this before, and I wanted more of her than I should. I grabbed her thighs and pressed them against mine. In my head, I knew I shouldn't be doing this. I closed my eyes and tried to find the strength to keep me from wanting to go further. I trembled all over as I tried hard not to submit to my desires. I knew I had to stop. We had never discussed doing anything further, and, although she wasn't complaining, I didn't want her consenting to anything that she might later regret. I finally found a little strength and immediately stopped kissing her and rolled over onto my back.

I got up and helped her to her feet, immediately excusing myself from her presence. I went outside for a walk to cool down. I couldn't stay around her, not with the way she made me feel.

***

## Hanna Greene

I knew I couldn't sleep with him. The warnings my father had given me were still very fresh on my mind. I thought I would be able to control the situation, but I find myself weak to my knees each time he touches me. I cannot resist him. I enjoy kissing him, and I wanted more just now. How can something that feels so right be bad for me? How is it that people always want what they can't have? In my case, I have him yet I can't have him the way I dream of being with him night after night.

Most girls my age already lost their virginity two or three years down the line, and I will forever keep mine if I want to remain powerful. This was torture. I knew the only way I could do this was to stay away from Sebastian, like my father had said. Being so close to him was a constant threat to me. But no one can pry me away from him. He is my life, the very air I breathe. To give him up would mean to give up living. Then how do I keep him in my life and also keep my powers when the instant he touches me I melt. I am ashamed to say that if he had wanted to go further just now, I would have submitted to his will.

The right thing to do would be to tell him about it, but my father made it clear that that was not an option. No one must know about my weakness, not even him. He has been committed to me so far, but I worry that, over time, he will want from me what I can't give. Would he still be by my side then, or would he find comfort somewhere else. I made my way to the kitchen to fix myself a meal. I needed to stop thinking, and eating usually helped. I opened the fridge and brought out two slices of bread, buttered them, and then added a dollop of strawberry-vanilla jam. I had barely taken two bites when I heard something move behind me. I spun round and there he was.

That face! How can I ever forget the face that drained the life out of me. For a moment, I froze in shock and, then like a jolt to my brain, I remembered what I had to do. He tried to say something, but I didn't give him time to speak. I threw him across the room, and before I could blink he was on his feet heading straight for me. I stopped him mid-air and forced him backwards. It took more strength from me than I envisaged. Frustrated, I gathered the furniture around him into a cluster and hauled the cluster towards him, forcing him to land on his back.

"Hanna—"

He said my name, and it angered me that he thought he had a right to speak to me, let alone say my name. I moved towards him, but he was already on his feet. In a flash he had dashed across me. I turned around to face him, and he had his hands up in surrender.

"Please, Hanna. I just want to talk. I'm not here to harm you."

"What makes you think you can hurt me?" I asked and raised him up and held him in place with my gaze. I thought about setting him on fire, but that would be too easy for him. Without taking my eyes of him, I pulled everything around me—furniture, carpeting, curtains, mirrors, and paintings from the wall, flowers in their vases—and threw them at him one at a time. I needed to show him I was in charge. At first, I threw them at him one after the other and then I hurled them at him all at once. My mind raced back to that night I saw the terror on my mother's face and the fear in my father's eyes, and my anger grew. I dropped the items in the room on the ground and started to heat him up. He held his neck as he choked. He had turned grey, and I knew any minute now, if I didn't stop, he might die, and I still needed answers from him. I dropped him to the ground and held him in place with pain.

"Hanna, please stop. I knew you weren't going to die."

I stopped immediately. "What did you say?" I asked. How could he have known about me?

"Please let me breathe, and I will explain. Please, I didn't come here to harm you," he mumbled.

"I don't believe you."

"Obviously, if I had wanted you dead, you would have died earlier today when you were sleeping," he said.

"If you truly know about me, then you know you can't kill me." In my anger, I increased his pain.

"Listen, please. If I die, then you won't know who is truly after you."

"Who? Isobel? That's no secret."

"No, not Isobel. She doesn't know you're alive. Please stop and let me explain. Please. I know I did you wrong, but I had to make it look that way. If you remember, I was kind to you, I fought my brothers so they wouldn't dismember your body." He spoke softly. I had drained him of his energy. Still angered, my mind went back to that night, and I heard him fighting his brothers to leave me alone. Then I didn't understand. I remember thinking I was dying and wondered why he was protecting my body. Reluctantly, I let him loose and dropped him to the ground. I gave him some time to regain a little strength before speaking to him. "I remember you were kind, but that doesn't change things. You still killed me."

"I had to, you had to die." I looked at him, and he raised his hands in protest. "Please, let me explain." I nodded. "I knew about you. I knew about you even before your birth."

"Seems that the case these days. Everyone seems to have been expecting my birth," I said sarcastically.

He looked surprised, but continued. "I have been keeping an eye on you from afar to protect you, as a favour for a friend."

A friend? What friend?"

"I can't say now, but in time, you will find out yourself."

"Sorry, that is not going to cut it."

"Listen, Hanna, you had to die to get rid of the human inside you holding you back. I just helped, that's all. When Isobel came to us and asked for our help, I knew I had to do it. I fought off my brothers so I could have you to myself."

"Why?"

"Because they don't know about you. We don't share everything"

"What do you know about me?"

"I told you, a friend asked me to keep an eye out for you."

"And you can't tell me who this friend is and why the hell I matter to whomever this person is."

"You matter a lot to this person."

"Enough of this nonsense. I don't believe you. You have one second to tell me why I should let you live." I cranked up the heat and the gut-wrenching pain.

"Your mother," he blurted out.

"What?"

"Your birth mother begged me to look out for you."

I must admit, that took me aback a bit, but he could be lying and making things up, so I didn't kill him. "You're lying!"

"No, I'm not. Please believe me."

"Prove it."

"How? I know you don't remember her."

"Prove you're not lying to me or God help me—"

"Okay! She had a gift. I don't know if you know this, but she had a gift. She could tell the future. She saw your future. She knew she wouldn't be in it, so she came to me and asked me to promise to watch over you."

I knew now he wasn't lying. The revelation shook me. "How did you know her?"

"I met her through a friend, a witch I once knew."

"Tell me everything you know. I want to know everything you know about her. Is she alive? Where does she live?"

"Slow down. I don't know if she is still alive. I haven't seen her since your birth, the day she made me promise that I would keep you safe."

"Yeah, I heard that part before. Perhaps you should have mentioned to her that you would snuff out my life in the process, too."

"Listen, I know you don't have any reason to believe me, but what I have told you is true. She knew you would get into trouble and asked me to make sure I killed you myself. I didn't understand then, but now I do. She was very sure killing you would solve your problems."

"But you weren't sure, and you did it anyway? What if I hadn't come back to life?"

"Her premonitions have never been wrong. I came back after your boyfriend found your body. He was in pieces, and so was I. I thought you would have woken up by then, but you hadn't. For the first time I thought your mother had gotten it wrong. I followed your boyfriend back to his house. It was torture, because I could feel his pain. Although you met your death through me, I had known you since your birth. And believe me, I wish we had met under different circumstances. But it's okay. Now I can see that you can take care of yourself, you don't need me, you don't need anybody, and you definitely don't need that guy you call your boyfriend. I know he loves you, and you love him, but there's more to his story than he's letting on."

"Hey, let's say I believe you for a second, don't go believing you can tell me who I need in my life."

"Okay, I'm sorry."

"So is this why you came here? Or is there something else I need to know?"

"No, I came to you because I need a favour."

"What do you want?"

"Since I drank your blood, something changed in me."

"Enlighten me?"

"I felt human again in ways you can't possibly understand. In the past, I could block all the guilt away, switch it off, but ever since that night the face of everyone I've killed has haunted me. I feel their anguish and the pain they went through. Yours mostly. I thought with time, things would return to normal, but they haven't."

"So what do you want from me? A hug or someone to tell you all those lives you took amount to nothing?"

"I haven't been the same since that night. Your face haunts me, but that is the pleasant part, it's the other faces I can't bear to see. Why am I being tormented? I know it would be difficult, but I need you to give me a chance to do better. Please make it all go away." He paced about fidgeting as he spoke.

"You still haven't told me how you found us?"

"I followed you from England. I had to, not only because I needed your help, but in a way I was glad that you were alive."

"What if I refuse? It's not my place to forgive you for the lives you've snatched. What if I ask that you leave now and never bother me again? What then, would you honour it?"

"It wouldn't come to me as a shock. I see killing as humans see breathing. It's a natural instinct for our survival. We can't all be like your boyfriend."

Hanna laughed out loud. "Well, thanks for being honest and not lying to me. But there is more. I can feel it from you."

"Yes, that's true. There's another favour I need from you."

"Favour is a word used amongst friends, and we both know you are not a friend, even though you are painting yourself a different picture. You and your brothers are monsters, however you dissect it, and that's how it will always come down with me"

"Hmm, still, I consider myself an ally, and I know in this world and the situation in which you will soon find yourself—since I now know that you are able to make us vampires into day walkers—you will need me on your side, however powerful you are."

"So, if I understand you correctly, you want me to make you a day walker? Whatever gave you that idea?"

"Your boyfriend is living proof."

"Are you out of your mind? What makes you think after all that's happened that I would put a monster like you on the streets during the day so you can do even more harm? I don't think so."

"I knew you would say that, but I also know you would do anything to avenge your parents' death. So, what if I'm willing to make a deal with you—your forgiveness and the ability to walk in the sun for the lives of my two brothers?"

"I will get them eventually. You'll have to offer more for me to even consider it."

"Well, I thought you might say that. Your forgiveness, my brothers' lives, and the promise to help find out what happened to your birth mother. Think about it carefully before you make up your mind. Your boyfriend is on his way, and I have to go now. He is out for blood, and I didn't come here for that. I will see you later." Before I could blink, he had disappeared. He had just put me in a tight corner and made me wonder about my birth mother. Everything he said about her was true. He probably knew her and he's the only one apart from my father who seems to have met her.

## Chapter 31

"Hanna, go up to the room quickly, there is someone here," I said, as I rushed into the house, annoyed with myself for taking such a long walk. I looked around and saw everything in a pile, windows smashed, mirrors and vases broken, and curtains torn. I couldn't believe I went away for such a long time and left her alone to battle on her own. I ran to her side at once remorseful for having left her by herself. "What happened here, Hanna? Are you all right? I'm sorry I left you all alone. I'm so sorry, love. What happened? Someone is still around, I can taste it in my mouth." She was quiet and didn't say anything or express much, and she looked like she was deep in thought. I looked around once more and wondered what took place here. She looked fine, unruffled, not a hair out of place. I didn't know if I should sit with her or if I should run and find the intruder. I looked from her to the mess all over the place and waited for to tell me what happened. It must have been tough for her, I concluded, and I wasn't here when she needed me. I failed her again. I promised I wouldn't, but I did.

She looked at me very concerned. "Don't worry about it, S. I already dealt with it."

"What do you mean you already dealt with it? What happened? Did you kill him?" I asked amazed, at what went down. *I had been gone only for half an hour*, I thought to myself.

"No, I did no such thing."

"I still don't understand? Why not? Did he get away? If you didn't kill him then what happened? Was it one of the three who attacked you?"

"Yes, it was. The very one who took my life."

I stood with my mouth opened, confused. Why would she spare his life, and what did he even want with her? I brushed my hair back with both of my hands "You seriously let him go? Hanna—why? I mean, if you are so sure he was the one. Did he overpower you?"

"No, it's nothing like that. He came to talk—that's all."

"Talk? What the hell? You two talked, after what went down the last time you saw him? And you listened? I'm I hearing you right? What did he want from you anyway?"

"He wanted my forgiveness." If this was meant to be a joke, she was taking it too far already. I couldn't even entertain the idea that she listened to that monster.

"Forgiveness? You're kidding, right? You know he's only going to come back. You can't listen to his lies, let alone believe them. He would say anything to you now that he knows he can't harm you. He has to die. When next he comes we have to kill him. They all have to die!"

"I know, S. I know what he deserves, yet I can't bring myself to do it to him. That doesn't mean we won't kill the other two, but him? I don't know what it is, but I can't kill him. I believe his story and his reasons and everything else he said. I don't know why, but I do."

I half laughed. Is she out of her mind? What's happened to her? Just now we were target practicing, and the next she is letting her killer off the hook. "You what? How is that even possible?"

She gently held my face. "I know you don't understand, but he was kind to me, and what he did to me, he had to do. If he hadn't then someone else would have done it and made me suffer. He told me things, things that made me believe him. I don't know, Sebastian, but I can't kill him, not if he's telling the truth. I want to spare his life. Allow me to, S."

None of what she was saying made any sense to me, but it's what she wants, so for now I will let it go until I am somehow able to prove her wrong and make her see there is no good sitting beneath that monster. "Was that all he wanted then?"

"He knows I am different. He knows about my powers, and he knows that I made you a day walker. He wants the same thing."

"What?"

"Yes, he wants me to make him into a day walker."

I walked away from her for a moment. In my mind, I knew she wouldn't do that, but I had to ask. I mean can you blame me? One minute, we're planning to kill them and the next she is starting a friendship with him. "So, you're not planning to make him one, are you?"

"Of course not! How could you even think that?"

"I don't know. You're the one who is best friends with him all of a sudden."

"S, trust me. I have my reasons."

"I don't know, Hanna. If you say so, I guess I just have to go along with it."

"Don't worry, I'll be fine."

"I know. I know what you are capable of, but I love you, Hanna, more than life itself, and I know what it feels like not to have you in this world. I never want to go through that again. I trust you, and I trust you to make the right decision. Remember, I am always here, and if that's what you want as much as it kills me, I will go along with it."

"Thank you, S. Listen to me, I know these vampires are older than you are, and as much as I know you want revenge, I also don't want you dead. If anything happens to you, believe me, I will take my life. You are everything to me. You are my heart. You are my love. Sebastian, I need you to do me a very big favour."

I took a deep breath, I could tell what she wanted to ask, but I hoped I was wrong. "You know I will do anything for you, but don't ask me not to do what I think you are about to ask me."

"I don't want you to fight for me. It's my battle, and I don't want you involved."

"No, Hanna, you can't take that away from me. Please, don't ask me to give this up. When they attacked you, they attacked me. It was my fault. Isobel came after you and brought those monsters into your world because of me. Please, let me do this. I know you've suffered, and I feel all your pain. They took away your family, but you're my family. You loved them and I loved them because you did. Isobel knew she couldn't have me, long before I met you she knew this. She did this to punish me. She wanted me to suffer your loss. Since she can't have me, she didn't want me to have you. What she did is unforgivable. She crossed the line and there is no coming back from it. As much as it's your fight, Hanna, it's my fight too and we would not be fighting alone. I have friends that you don't know about."

"What friends are you taking about?"

"I have a very powerful friend. He's like family to me. He will help. I just don't want him to know about you. I don't want any vampire to know about you. They will all want to walk the day at any cost."

"I will deal with them, S. I'm not afraid of any of them."

I took a deep breath and went to her. She didn't understand what I was trying to prevent here. I sat her down on the sofa. "I know you aren't afraid of them and you shouldn't be. I don't want you involved, not because I think they can harm you, but once they know of what you can do, we'll have to watch our backs for the rest of our lives. The rumour will spread worldwide, and it'll always be one fight after another for us. That's not how I want us to spend our time together, and that's why Hector has to die. If he doesn't, he'll continue to come after us until we either kill him or give him what he wants. And if we do give him what he wants, it won't take long for other vampires to know he can walk the day and start finding the source. You are my life, Hanna. I'm not going to dangle you like a carrot. Please let me fight this battle for us."

She was quiet. She looked at me cautiously and then got up and went into the kitchen and came back later with a cup of tea. "Well, I never thought of it like that. These friends you talk about, are you sure they will help?" I nodded. She looked pained, and I knew how much it meant to her to avenge her parents' deaths, but I didn't want to take chances in case someone escaped and spread the news of what she was capable of. "Okay, S. You can do it on your own, but leave Hector out of it."

"But—why?"

"I don't know. I just want him alive."

I got up and started tidying up the room, dumping the broken vases in the bin, and picking up broken furniture from the floor. "You have to have a valid reason to not want him dead, Hanna, otherwise he goes down with the rest of his brothers."

"He said something. He mentioned something to me, and I would like to know more. If you kill him, I won't have anything to go on."

"Are you going to tell me what is so important that you are willing to let your killer walk?"

"He knew my mother."

"Is that it? And he helped kill her, too, didn't he?"

"No, Sebastian, you don't understand. I have to explain something to you about my real birth mother." Pieces of broken mirror in my hand immediately dropped to the ground the moment she mentioned her birth mother. "Are you okay, S?"

"Er—yes, I'm fine—I—I was a little clumsy."

"You? Clumsy? Are you sure you're fine?"

I was quiet for a second, my mind racing. I knew it was time she learnt the truth about me, and I was terrified, but I also knew I couldn't go on lying to her. She was staring at me, concern written all over her face. I had to snap out of it. I *will* tell her, but this wasn't the right time. "Er—I don't understand what you mean by real birth mother. Isn't Joan your mother?"

"That's what I want to talk to you about—"

"And you're just going to take the word of a killer as gospel, Hanna? I thought you knew better than that?"

"No, S, am not just going by what he said. Something happened to me when I died. I met my—"

I couldn't let her finish, knowing I would be pretending it was news to me. "Darling, I'm sorry, but I'm not as taken by his story as you are. Forgive me, love, but I'd rather concentrate on the battle ahead. Let's talk about this later. If there is any truth to it, we will soon find out together."

She sighed in frustration. "Okay, S, have it your way, but whatever you do, I want Hector alive." She left and went upstairs. I waited 'til I could hear her in her room before sitting down to process what had just happened.

I debated whether to go to her room and tell her the truth. I got up and walked towards the stairs, but I couldn't find the strength to climb up. I paced back and forth, confused about how to proceed. Somehow I knew that if I told her the truth, she would never forgive me. I had witnessed how she felt about Huritt's betrayal and I just couldn't bring myself to telling her, not now at least.

To take my mind off it, I made a call to Mason Benedict about needing help again, and, as usual, he obliged me.

# Chapter 32

Since I would soon be receiving visitors, I didn't want Hanna here anymore, so I went to her to explain that we had to leave. "I have other houses in France, and I already called Gilou to prepare one. We should leave now. Plus, I'm not comfortable with Hector knowing where to find us. It's only a matter of time before every other vampire starts to visit."

"I don't want to go, S. We just got here, and I am not running again. And what makes you think Hector wouldn't track us down anyway? They will just keep finding us."

"I know, but we don't have a choice. How do we know he hasn't told his other brothers about your location or that you're not dead?"

"I like it here. I have accepted that I won't get involved with the fight. Please just give me this. I can't keep running each time there's a threat. I'm not afraid, S. They're the ones who should be afraid. Meet with your friends elsewhere. You can go back to England. I'll be here when you get back."

I sighed. She was stubborn, but she was partly right about not running away. But I wanted to get her away from Hector. I didn't know what he knew, but I wasn't ready to take that gamble. I knew that if it came down to it she could fight her own battles, so I wasn't scared for her life, not anymore. That made it easier for me to accept her decision to stay. "Okay, Hanna. I'll stand by your decision, but listen, I don't want us to spend the rest of our lives fighting off one vampire after another. We have to choose our battles wisely. I say Hector and his brothers should die. You want him alive, so he stays alive, but I know this will come back and haunt us. He is not to be trusted, Hanna. I guess if you are sure this is what you want—"

"I am, S. I'll be fine."

I went downstairs and she followed. "I have to go away for two weeks. It could be less, I don't know."

"Where will you go?"

"It has to be England. I'll tell Mason to send the guys there. I also need to brush up on my fighting skills. Hopefully, these guys will help me out."

"I know I said I would let you do this by yourself—"

"Hanna, you need to let me do this. It was my fault, and I thought we'd been through this."

"Yes, and if you let me finish, you would actually hear what I was about to say."

"Okay, I'm sorry."

"I was thinking that I could get the location of the other two vampires from Hector in exchange for what he wants, and you can figure out the girl's location for yourself."

"Why would he give you his brothers' location? Are you seriously thinking of making him a day walker, Hanna? I can't even believe we are having this conversation."

"Listen, don't get angry. You need to know where the other two are. You can't find them on your own. I know he'll give them up if I make him a day walker—"

"Can you hear yourself? Am I actually listening to this? Don't worry, I'll find them! You don't need to do that. Those three never leave each other. They stick together, no matter what, and that is why I don't trust Hector. Once he gets what he wants, there is no limit to the damage he could evoke. They must know he's here, and that means they're up to something. Please, Hanna, don't do this. I can't imagine what makes you think he's any good. For goodness' sake, he attacked you! Listen, those three are inseparable. It's as if they are in tune with each other. Hector is subtle, but equally as dangerous. Do you know how many humans you will put at risk if you make him a day walker? He may look innocent and beautiful, but believe me, he is not. He's a killer. He lives on human blood and has for over five hundred years and will continue to do so. What is it about him that you like so much? I'm beginning to think that there is more to this."

"He would be a day walker for a while, but it wouldn't be forever. Trust me, S, I know what I'm doing."

"How do you mean?"

"The light I put in you is part of me, which is what enables you to walk in the sun. I can call it back easily if I chose to do so."

I paused. "You mean I could be out one day enjoying the sun and, depending on your mood, you could decide to barbeque me?"

"Sebastian, I would never do anything to hurt you, believe me. I love you, and you are my life. Why would you even think that I could do such a thing to you?"

"I don't know. Hector—you seem to have taken a liking to him, and anyone can be replaced."

"Are you jealous of him? How could you be? He killed me. You think I would choose him over you—"

"I'm sorry. I don't know what came over me. It's just that I don't want to lose you, not to anyone, you have no idea how much you mean to me, Hanna."

"And you should know how much you mean to me by now. Look, all I'm saying is that I give him the ability to walk in the sun in exchange for the location of his brothers. I can always take it back whenever I want if I think he's going to abuse it, because no matter where he is, as long as he has a part of me in him, I will always know what he's up to."

"So when I go to England you will be able to know my every move?"

"If I chose to, but you know I will. You're going to fight vampires who are stronger and more vicious than you. I will be paying attention, Sebastian."

"I'll be okay, I promise you. I'll be back before you know it. Listen, Hanna, if you're sure you know what you're doing, go for it, but I want to be there when you make this deal with Hector." She smiled happily. I wish I could say the same about myself. Sometimes, I don't even know why I bother trying to talk her out of things, because I always seem to just do what she wants every time.

To stop myself from overthinking things, even though I knew I was right about Hector, I went to my piano and began to run my fingers along the keyboard. I shut my eyes and pictured myself as a child sitting behind the piano like I used to do when my mother was alive and still a human. She loved to hear me play for her. I could see her sitting there facing me and listening to me play. I started to play the song I had composed for my mother after she passed. I wasn't happy inside, and it showed in my choice of songs.

I heard Hanna move closer to me as I played, but my eyes remained closed. "I didn't know you were this good with the keyboard, S," Hanna said. My eyes remained shut. I was trying to stop myself from feeling like the world was going to crash down on me any second. The inevitable end was near, and I could feel it. "All those times at the music centre, I thought I was keeping you from learning, but you—you're a maestro."

"I've been playing for a very long time, darling," I responded, trying to keep my feelings beneath.

"Wow, and I thought I was good. You're incredible."

"Hmm, thank you."

"What is this song you're playing? It sounds old."

"I used to play this for my mother. She taught me how to play, but I improved over the years."

"Oh, I get it now. It's a sad song. Why are you playing it like the world is about to end? It's not meant to be sad—nothing this beautiful is meant to be sad."

I stopped playing at once. "You're right, it is sad. I don't know what came over me." I smiled and got up.

"What happened just now, S? You seemed fine just now until you started playing."

"It's nothing. I'm all right. It's that song. I shouldn't have played that song."

"Then play something else, please."

I felt bad that I had inflicted my feelings on her. I went back and started to play a different song—one that I had composed for Hanna all those years that I had stayed away. I had always wanted to play it to her. The timing was right. I knew I may never get another chance. I glanced at her, and, by her expression, I could tell that she liked this one. I could feel her eyes on me, but I avoided looking at her. I was concentrating on getting the song right instead. When I eventually looked up after I had tapped the last key, she was tearful. I was confused. I thought she had liked this one. "Was this also sad?"

"No, S. It wasn't sad. It was stunning, and it moved me to tears. Did you compose this, because I have never heard anything like this until now?"

"I wrote this for you the day I met you, but it's still not finished yet."

"For me? I didn't know you wrote this for me. Thank you it's—it's a very beautiful song. I feel like the luckiest girl alive, S. I don't think it needs any more work, its perfect. The other song is beautiful, as well. It's just that you played it with so much sadness. Have you always played it that way?"

"For years. I was a sad little boy when she first died as a human, and then I lost her again. I didn't know how to play anything that was not sad, until I met you."

"And the one you composed for me has so much depth. It's hard to believe you just composed it."

"It—it took me a while as well. It came naturally to me. The song is the interpretation of how you make me feel." I knew right then that I had to tell her the truth, no matter what the consequences were. "Hanna, there are things you don't know about that I haven't told you, because I know the moment you learn about them, it will be the end of us. Things I want to tell you, but I don't have the courage to, only because I don't want to lose you."

"I don't understand, S. It's me. Remember, it's you and me against the world. We shouldn't have secrets. Anyway, it's not like you killed someone. I know you, S, and I trust you with my life. If I'm willing to forgive Hector, what makes you think I can stay mad at you whatever you think you've done? You are the good one, S. I know that."

"Hanna, you don't understand. I don't think you will be eager to forgive once you hear what I have to say. But I'm going to tell you anyway. You're right, there should be no secrets between us, no matter how bad it is. I will tell you everything after I come back from England."

She went quiet, and at the same time, I sensed we weren't alone anymore, and I could tell who the august visitor was.

"I hope I'm not interrupting you by any chance."

"I see you think you can just wander in here anytime you choose. Make yourself at home, why don't you? What do you think you are doing here?" I charged at him.

"I'm not here to fight. Your girlfriend knows why I'm here, that is if she hasn't already filled you in."

"Get out of my house at once."

"I think we both know I will do no such thing."

"Then I will fight you."

"I have no interest in such things, trust me. I have done a lot of fighting in my life time and I will be glad if we do not end up in one."

"You picked the wrong house then"

"I am only here to make a deal with you."

"And we already know what you want in return. We are not interested."

"Believe me, you will be once you've heard what I have to say."

"There can be nothing so mouth-watering that will make me ever think you deserve what you want." I know I promised Hanna I would go along with this, but seeing him just infuriated me.

"I know how you must feel, but you and I know I did her a favour. You hate me because I took her life, but here she is with you, stronger, more confident, and untouchable. I'm not upset that you hate me. I could do worse in your shoes. I know what it is to have loved and lost, and I can't take back the pain I must have caused you, however brief it was, but we have to move forward"

"Did you just say you know what love is? How can you? You are nothing but a killer, that's all you are."

"That may be so, but I was once in love, centuries ago, and in my quest to try and control the monster I have now become, I took her life myself. I was hungry, and she became nothing but food to me. I tried to fight it, but her blood clouded my mind. It was all I could think of, so I thought if I only took a bite, if I only drank a little, she would be fine. But once I sank into her, I couldn't stop and didn't stop until she was white and lifeless. I don't know how you do it. How you can be with Hanna day and night without once seeking her blood."

"Do you really think I care what you think?"

"No, of course not. You are who you are and I am me. You tried protecting her and failed. I helped her become stronger."

"Can you two stop talking as though I'm not in this very same room with you?" Hanna asked. I backed away from Hector, but my eyes remained on his. "What do you have to trade that you think is enough for me to make you a day walker?" Hanna asked.

"My loyalty, amongst other things. I will give you my brothers' location, but I will never fight against them. What you do with what I tell you is left up to you."

"Is that all you've got? It's not enough. We can find them on my own," I responded.

"That's not all. I will help you take down, Isobel. I have never been a fan of hers, and I know you can't take her down by yourself, because Margret will fight for her. As much as she loves you, her daughter will always come first," Hector added.

"Don't worry about me," I said. "I have that covered. I don't need your help. If that's all you've got, I'm afraid we can't do business." I looked over at Hanna and knew she wasn't liking how I was handling this, but I didn't trust him. If he can betray his brothers, who he's known for over five hundred years, then who are we to him?

"Why won't you let me help you? I have more experience, and I'm a better fighter. I'm older, so naturally I'm stronger, and I know more about the vampire world than you can ever imagine. You're young, Sebastian, and I know you feel you can take on the world, but don't fool yourself. These are vicious vampires, I know because I have been in several battles with them. I can help. Let me help."

"I don't trust you. If you're willing to give up your brothers so easily, what's to say you're not just lying to us? How do I know I'm not just walking into a trap with you?"

"Because I want to start afresh. All the killing and violence has to stop," Hector said.

"Did you think about that before you killed your informer the other day? You took his family, his wife, and child. Did you kill them, too?"

"I had to kill him. He was not only working for me, but Zacchary got to him first. He was spying on me for him. If I had let him live, he would have told Zacchary that your girlfriend is alive. Is that what you want? I think not."

"Why would Zacchary be spying on you?"

"Since I didn't kill Hanna the way he expected me to, he has been suspicious of me. I need a fresh start. I want all the violence behind me. I want to change, and I know I can."

"I don't believe a word of what you are saying. Do you believe him?" I asked Hanna.

"I don't know. Some things are true. I'm just not sure."

"I don't think so, Hector. You almost had me, but you're a monster. If you couldn't resist killing the woman you loved, what hope does the rest of the world have? I will pity any young girl whose path you cross. You can't become a day walker. We both know you can't stay away from human blood, so don't pretend like you can."

"Yes, I know that, and I'm not going to lie and tell you I can, because I can't. It's all I've known, but I won't kill anymore. I'll only take what I need. I'm telling the truth. Help me to start all over."

"Your reasons are good, but not good enough," Hanna said.

"Okay, I will tell you about your mother—everything I know about her. And if that's not enough, I have more chips to bargain with. There's something no one but me knows about someone you consider to be family. If everything I say is true, then you must promise me that you will make me a day walker."

"If we find out that everything you have told us is true, and it all comes down to what you haven't yet told us, and when Sebastian comes back from England, if he thinks what you have to say is worth making you a day walker, then I promise I will make you one," Hanna said. He chuckled and nodded, and for a moment, I wished that I could just wipe that smug look off his face.

We sat down and he gave me the address of where his brothers would be in the next two weeks and then he left.

# Chapter 33

I left for England the next day, after much persuasion to take Hanna somewhere else just for the two weeks that I would be away, but she stubbornly insisted on remaining in the house, so I gave in.

I didn't return to my house in Grosmont. Instead, I went back to Hampshire in Froxfield where I called Mason Benedict again and awaited the arrival of the three vampires he sent to help me: Henry, Nicholas, and Thomas.

I made sure to stock enough blood to keep them away from the streets. Immediately upon their arrival, we started brushing up on my fighting skills. For three days, I battled with them in groups of two. I was focused, and I trained hard. At the end of the third day, Thomas told me that Mason had given them instructions not to include me in the fight. It annoyed me that Mason thought he could control my life. Thomas insisted that I was only allowed to go with them, but not to participate. That was the only condition in which they were to offer their help to me. So I refused their help and asked them to leave. Since they were no longer needed, I didn't see the need for them to continue to hang out in my house. However, they hit me with another of Mason's instructions. If I did not accept the terms, they had been directed not to let me leave the house. "Well, tell Mason I appreciate that he cares, but I don't need his help anymore, and he doesn't get to decide what I do," I told Thomas.

"I know how you must feel, but he has his reasons. I know we've been training for a while, but you can't face those two alone. On your own, you will be no match for either of them. Let us handle this," he said, putting his hand on my shoulder.

"Why would you want to risk your lives if they are so dangerous? This is my battle. It's personal to me, and no one, not even Mason will tell me how to handle it."

"Listen, it's not just your battle. Those three have encroached on so many territories that we were going to come for them eventually. I had a run-in with them two hundred years ago, but they got away. They have more enemies than you know. Let us handle this."

"I need to be part of this. It's important to me that I be a part of this. You must understand that, Thomas."

"I am sorry, but Mason made it clear that he doesn't want you involved. He must really like you. What do you care, as long as they are dead?"

"What's this got to do with Mason? Why is he so keen that I don't go along, anyway? I knew it was a mistake to call him. I shouldn't have asked for his help. This is my fight and has nothing to do with him. It's my life, and it's my choice to risk it."

"He sees you as a son, Sebastian. I'm sure you know of their reputation, which is no news to any vampire young or old. Those three have begun to form an army, getting other vampires to form some kind of alliance. They've managed to recruit a few strong vampires on their side and they have to be stopped now before it gets out of hand."

"I don't understand. Why form an army? What war are they waging? Who are they planning to fight?" I looked at each of their faces.

"What don't you understand?" Nicholas Snapped. "Everyone knows that Mason leads and controls the vampire population—all of South and North America, Asia, Europe, the Middle East, and Africa. He knows everyone and everything and keeps things in order so they don't spiral out of control. Those three cockroaches think they can change things, expose us all with their greed and viciousness. They want to take over. At first we didn't care, but they are getting stronger in number, and we have to take them down now."

"Okay, I understand how you feel. But I need to be part of it. You can't stop me. What are you going to do stay here and babysit me while those bastards get away? Look, I know you always do what Mason tells you, but I don't, because he doesn't own me. I called you, and only I have their location. That has to count for something. Please. Mason doesn't have to know, guys. This is personal to me. I have to do this."

"If we let you fight and something happens to you, we might as well be dead. You are good and fast. I've watched you train. You learn very quickly, but those three are stronger. If they get you by any chance, you will be dead, and Mason doesn't want anything to happen to you. We've been doing this all our lives, and it's all we know. Let us handle this for all of us," Henry said.

"So why come here at all? Why didn't you guys just go straight to them?"

"Because they know we're after them. They have lookouts everywhere who give us away each time we come close to catching them. Even our best trackers find it hard to pin them down, but you got your intel from Hector, and that's the best we can get. I hope you haven't made a deal with Hector, because as soon as we are done with his brothers he will be next."

"No, you can't touch him. I made a deal with him, I don't like him much, but I always keep my word. I'll have to have a word with Mason myself if that's what it will take."

"You do what you have to do, but all we know is that we have to eliminate him too. If Mason sends word to spare his life, then we would let him live. You know where we can find him?"

"No, I don't," I lied. Well, not exactly, as I don't know where he resides.

"Be careful. Mason hates it when he is lied to," Henry said.

"Like I said, I don't know where you can find him," I said, looking him straight in the eye. I remember Hector saying something about telling me something about someone I considered family. Now I think it has something to do with Mason Benedict. It can't be Isobel—that bridge has been burnt. Something does not set right with me about Mason, which is why I've avoided him in the past. I wonder what Hector will reveal to me.

"Okay, then do you agree to let us do the fighting alone?" Thomas asked. I nodded reluctantly. It was clear they wouldn't involve me, no matter what I said. It made me wonder about the kind of power Mason had over them. I had to pretend to agree, but when we get to them, it will be a different story. "Okay, then, where are they?"

"San Pietro in Sardinia, Italy."

"Hmm. Okay. Then we take the next flight out this evening and stay at the nearest hotel. By tomorrow evening, they won't know what's hit them. We'll take down Anton and Zacchary and anyone who's with them."

"Wait. You said anyone who's with them. Will you at least give them a choice to change sides?"

"No. They made their choice when they sided with them. Do you have a problem with that?" Nicholas asked. They all looked at me to see if I was down with their decision.

My mind went to Isobel. There was no getting out of this now. If I don't kill her they will, and they were right, she had made her choice already. "No, I don't," I finally said.

"One more thing, in Italy we have to feed from the source itself. Don't worry, we won't be taking lives. Mason gave strict instructions not to do such things in your presence. You must mean a lot to him, because I have never seen him care so much about another vampire," Thomas said. I nodded it's not like I can actually control what they do outside of this town. They've spent centuries surviving on just human blood. "What about you? Have you fed? Since we arrived, I haven't seen you feed on anything. How do you survive without real blood?"

"Animal blood is real enough for me. I fed five days ago, actually. My body is trained to control the cravings. I was hoping to go hunting tonight, but since we have to travel as soon as possible, I guess I'll have to wait 'til we get back."

"What do you mean? You haven't had anything for the past five days and you can function?" Nicholas asked in shock.

"How is that even possible?" Henry asked.

"I don't know. I guess it's mind over body. I control the blood—it doesn't control me."

"I don't think I could survive without feeding at least once or twice a day," Henry joked. "No disrespect, but that animal blood thing is not for me. It reeks. How you can stomach the stench. It's disgusting. We're never going to have a shortage of humans to feed on, thankfully. They're constantly breeding, and our future is safe. I respect you, though. Your endurance, strength, and self-control are commendable. So many have tried what you're doing and failed with significant consequences," Thomas added.

"Well, thank you, Thomas. I do my best, which is all I can do," I said.

My mind began to wonder. I wasn't sure if Hector was trying to set me up or if he really had changed. If only Hanna weren't so stubborn, she would be somewhere that I consider safe. All this could be one big trap to get rid of me. Anton and Zacchary probably had been in France with Hector all along, and what better way to gain power over Mason than for all three of them to become day walkers, then they could attack him and take over?

I was troubled and confused. I needed to decide to either continue with the quest or abandon it and go back to Hanna. I couldn't share what I was thinking with anyone. It didn't matter what decision I reached, it wouldn't impact on them anyway—after all, they've been instructed not to let me fight. I finally made the decision to go after Anton and Zachary. If Hector wasn't lying, this might be my only chance, and I didn't want to miss it.

By the evening, we had taken the next available flight to Italy. We stayed in a hotel and continued our journey after the sun had gone down. I was careful not to let on that I was now a day walker. When it was safe for them to go out, they each went out to feed while I waited for them.

On their return, we took a ferry from Sant'Antocio to San Pietro Island. By the time we arrived at San Pietro, it was quite dark, so we set about our business. Henry began tracking them down. Strangely, as we moved around the island, I couldn't sense a single human. It felt like the place had been evacuated.

I didn't feel too well. Something felt wrong. I was on edge. I knew I shouldn't have trusted that worm. We all knew by now that this was a setup. Everywhere was quiet, except for the sound of the water hitting the banks and a bird chirping away. Then from the corner of my eyes, I saw a body rising from beneath the water. On closer inspection, I recognised the form—Isobel. She started towards me, walking casually; her hair wet and her transparent white tunic clinging to her body showing her breasts in detail. Upon seeing her, I saw red. I was going to go for her when Thomas held me back.

"They knew—they knew we were coming. I think this is a set up." Thomas confirmed what we had all been thinking.

"Let me talk to her. I know her."

"Okay, but be careful."

"I know." I nodded and moved towards her. "What are you doing here, Isobel?" I asked.

She Smiled and said, "The last time I checked, I still lived in Italy. You're the one who needs to explain yourself. I can see you have bodyguards now. I take it this isn't just a visit."

"You gave me no choice, Isobel. How you, of all people, could hurt me like that is mind boggling. You were like my sister. You knew killing Hanna would make me suffer yet you still did it. You don't know the meaning of the word love. I loved you the best I could. Wasn't that enough?"

"Enough! Seeing you once a decade and hoping you'd changed your mind? I must admit I've been a bad girl, Sebastian. Are you here to punish me? Don't you understand? I had to do what I did. For us. I love you. I have loved you from the moment I first saw you, but all you've ever done is thrown it back in my face. You chose her over me, and she a mere human. That scrawny, fragile, piece of human trash! She had to go, my love. Don't you see? She was clouding your mind. I tried, Sebastian, to see things your way, but I didn't *choose* to love you. It just happened, and you can't have it easy, either. You have to understand that I did what I had to do. You would have done the same in my shoes."

"No, I wouldn't. I wouldn't stand in the way of your happiness. I would never stoop that low. You've spoiled things between you and me. What we had was fine, but you had to push until you made an enemy out of me. You show no remorse, Isobel, and I cannot forgive you for that."

"You talk as though you can take me on. You forget that I have three centuries on you. Let's not fight. I hurt you. It was selfish of me, but I will do it again if it means that you will realise I am still here. You said you loved me as a sister, but I'm not your sister. You've never given me a chance to show you, to help you love me back. Surely I'm not as bad as you make me out to be. There must be something worth redeeming."

"That's just it, Isobel. I don't see anything in you worth loving. I've always been repelled by the darkness in you, which is why I could never bring myself to love you like you want. You are evil."

"Evil! You deluded fool—it's a way of life for every vampire. The humans need air to stay alive, and we need their blood. It's the cycle of life. Everyone has to fall in line. Do you consider your humans evil when they kill to put meat on their table? You see how deluded you are, my love? It's what we do, and it's who we are. I see there is no convincing you, so we should settle this once and for all. I would rather see you dead than see you love another."

"It's settled then. Now we both know where we stand. Then by all means, let's begin."

Suddenly, out of nowhere, we were surrounded by about six other vampires. I looked around, but there was no sign of Anton and Zacchary. I knew there was no way I would be sitting around watching the others fight, not when we were outnumbered. I looked at Thomas from the corner of my eye, and he gave me a nod. "Be careful," he said. I nodded, making sure I never lost sight of Isobel.

"So now you do their dirty work for them, too?" I asked Isobel.

"It's a new age. We all have to get with the wind of change. Let's get this over with."

She leapt at me, and I quickly evaded her. I looked around quickly to see what was happening, and the other three had two opponents each. We knew we were going to be fighting. It's a pity Anton and Zacchary were not here as well. I thought of Hanna and knew she could sense me, too, armed with the thought of seeing her again. I went at Isobel with all I had. Isobel meant business. She came at me from every angle. I knew I wasn't strong enough to take her down, but the trick was to never let her get hold of me. I wriggled and dodged each attempt she made to hit me, and then I slammed my fist into her jaw. She lost her balance and staggered backwards, and I took advantage and followed quickly with a kick that sent her flying. I followed after her and landed a punch in her stomach mid-air. She crashed to the ground and instantly did a backflip and came at me again, looking fiercer now. I tried to dodge her hold, but she got me by my neck and brought me to the ground. I landed on my back, with Isobel on top of me, and she pumped her right fist into my face and held me down with her other hand. This was what I had been trained to avoid. I tried to shift her off of me, but she felt heavy and way too strong. Things were not going according to plan, and I knew I had to distract her somehow. "You're fighting a losing battle, Isobel," I choked out.

"It's too bad you won't be around to see how it ends," she said. "It could have been different."

"I would rather be dead than be with you."

"And here I was just thinking about sparing your life."

"Don't bother, because I am not dying today, you are!" I held her right fist before it landed on my face again and kicked her into the air. I went after her immediately and brought her to the ground, switching positions. I returned the favour and began pumping my fists into her face. I couldn't stand looking at her. All the anger I've had since that night I found Hanna, Joseph, and Joan's body flowed through my body into my fist. Then I heard her whisper my name. "Sebastian." I stopped hitting her for about a second, and she kicked me in the groin and sent me flying. I landed in a tree and, before I knew it, she was on top of me. "Say hello to your mother for me," she said. I knew that whatever she did now was going to be final. I reached for a branch and thrust it into her belly until it came out her back. "You know Margret will never forgive you. She will hunt you down until you're dead," she cried out in pain.

"That may be so, but she might change her mind when I tell her what you've been up to." I quickly pulled the branch out from her belly and thrust it into her again. I knew that was not enough to kill her, but I just couldn't will myself to do it. As much as I hated what she did, I realised I didn't want her dead. "Give me a reason not to kill you please, Isobel. I don't want to do this."

She cackled in pain. "Do it, Sebastian. Don't waste this chance, because as long as I'm alive, I will not rest until you are dead."

"Why? It doesn't have to end here for you. You don't have to die today. If you promise to stay out of my way, I will spare you for Margret's sake. But remember this, if you come after me again, I won't be so forgiving." I pulled out the branch and threw it to the ground. I couldn't bring myself to kill her, even though I knew it was a stupid decision to make. I pushed her to the side and walked away. I knew she was going to come after me, but I hoped she didn't. I looked up and saw Nicholas run past me. Before I turned around, he had severed her head from her body, and I watched her fall to the ground holding the same branch I had just thrown away.

"You killed her!" I yelled at him in shock.

"She was going to kill you," he said in his defence.

"You could have stopped her instead! I didn't want her dead!"

"That's the kind of thinking that will get you killed! She had to die, and you know it! Besides, if anything happens to you, we're good as dead." I knew what he said was true, but looking at her headless body made me sad. I knew Margret would never forgive me for this, even if I told her what happened. I had just made another enemy I really didn't need.

"Don't just stand there! You wanted to fight! Let's go help Thomas and Henry kill the remaining three!" I nodded and followed him. There was no time for mopping about. I joined forces with Henry who had one vampire left, and together we ripped him apart. Nicholas took one off Thomas, and while they battled, Henry and I began gathering the bodies of the dead vampires. I avoided Isobel's body. I couldn't bring myself to look at her. Henry noticed my reluctance to touch her and dragged her body over to the pile. We finished just in time to witness Thomas dissect his opponent with his hands. Henry clapped to commend his efforts. I went over and dragged the body to the pile.

The last of the seven panicked and tried to run. She flew high, aiming for the trees. Nicholas went after her, but somehow Henry got to her first, knocking her straight down. She started to plead for her life. I looked away, knowing they were not going to let her go. I heard a struggle and then a snap. She was dead. Together they dragged her, each holding a hand. Nicholas wasn't happy that Henry had come to help.

"I didn't need your help. I would have caught her," Nicholas moaned.

"I know, but it was fun. Did you see her face when she knew she wasn't getting out of this one?" Henry said. I tuned them out. Thomas was scouting around to ensure we left no evidence of our presence here. I found myself looking at Isobel's body. Any minute now it will be engulfed in fire, and I will never see her again.

"Set fire to it," Nicholas told Henry.

"Wait! Don't forget this!" Thomas threw Isobel's severed head into the pile. I looked away as Henry finally set them all on fire.

"Hey, you did well today," Nicholas said to me. I nodded in response. "Look, don't feel bad. She was bitter and is better off dead. That bitch would have killed you." I winced. I knew he was right, but I couldn't celebrate her death. "Hector set you up. You have to tell us where we can find him. Whatever he's been telling you, he was lying," Thomas said as we walked around the island. We had to ensure that Anton and Zacchary were not hiding away somewhere. "Well, they definitely are not here. Hector sent you here to die. He will be surprised when he sees you next. What I don't understand is that if he really wanted you dead, why didn't he kill you himself? He's older and stronger. Why send you here? What kind of deal did you make with him?" Thomas asked. I looked at him but said nothing. They were right, but I couldn't tell them anything. Killing me himself would mean Hector could never get Hanna to give him what he's always wanted, so he sent me on a wide goose chase, hoping I would die here.

I knew he couldn't be trusted, and I had been right. If only Hanna would have listened. I guess now she'll see him for who he really is. I needed to go back to France without alarming these guys. I had to convince them I would kill Hector myself. "I know how this looks, but what if he didn't set us up and they somehow found out that he had betrayed them? I made a deal with him. I can't go back on my word. If he's been lying to me, trust me, I will kill him myself."

"How do you plan on doing that? I had to kill that bitch before she killed you. I know you think you can do this, but you don't have what it takes, because you are not a killer. You are controlled by humanity. Your emotions are still tied to your human choices. This is war, and to survive you have to switch that off," Nicholas snapped at me.

"I'm a lot stronger than you think," I said. "If I say to you I will kill him, then that's what I will do. Trust me, I can handle him. If he's played me, then I should have the chance to repay him in kind," I protested.

"I'm sorry, but we can't do that. We can't let him get away, not now. Mason wants him dead, and he will be disappointed if he finds out that you refused to cooperate with us after all the ways he has helped you."

"So, let's say I give you Hector. What about Anton and Zacchary? We don't have a clue where they are, but Hector can lead me to them. Let me do this, I beg of you. Just give me a few days to sort things out."

"Okay, listen, we will give you one day to do what you have to do, but we will come with you—"

"How's that going to help?" I cut in.

"You interrupted me," Nicholas barked. "We will come along with you to whichever country or town he is in, but we will stay back. We won't make our presence known. Do whatever you have to do. If you do it right, we get the three of them. If not, I still want Hector," Thomas said. I nodded in response.

This was going to be dicey. Hanna wants Hector alive, I want him dead, and Mason and his goons want him dead. I hope Hanna changes her mind quickly. After I tell her what he did, I know she'll understand why he has to die. "That sounds good enough."

"Okay, let's get out of here before dawn."

## Chapter 34

We went back to the hotel, and then took the next available flight to France. I was famished and drained. We said our goodbyes at the airport. They checked into a hotel nearby, and I went to hunt before returning home.

The door was unlocked when I got home, and I rushed inside, but there was no sign of Hanna anywhere. Fear gripped me. I looked around for notes and wondered if she had gotten bored and went shopping. I noticed the house was tidy, which meant there had been no fighting, but I was still worried so I went to her room for the second time. It was then that I noticed her things were gone. The first thing that came to my mind was Hector and his brothers. They probably found a way to get to her, and perhaps the three of them where too much for her to handle at one time. I ran downstairs in desperation. How would I begin searching for her? I knew she shouldn't have stayed alone. I should have dug my heel in. She's in trouble and I don't have a clue where to look for her. I have no idea how to find that bastard, Hector. In annoyance, I repeatedly slammed my fist into the dining table, smashing it up in the process.

"I see you made it back in one piece," Hanna said from behind me. I spun round and saw her face. Words cannot describe how relived I was.

"Oh, Hanna! You are all right! I went crazy! I—I thought something had happened to you." I moved towards her and tried to cuddle her, but she stepped away. "I'm sorry. I know I stayed away longer than I was supposed to, but I had to go hunting. Where were you? Where did you go?"

She looked upset, and I wasn't sure if it was the fact that I was away a day longer than I was supposed to be, but something was wrong, and I couldn't tell what it was. Her facial expression and body language were cold, like the way she had been with Huritt. I knew this was more than me coming back late.

"Are you all right? I looked in your room, and your things are gone. What happened? Talk to me, love," I said, ignoring the fact that she didn't answer the question about where she had been.

"I'm okay. In fact, I've never been better."

"Then why do you look sad? If I'm right, I'd say you don't look happy to see me. What's wrong, love?"

She laughed coldly. "Everything, Sebastian. Everything is wrong."

"What happened? It's Hector isn't it? He set me up. Everything he's told us was a lie. There is this big thing they are planning. I will tell you all about it later. Did he come here? Were they here, Hanna? He lied about giving up his brothers."

I tried to touch her, but she moved away again. Now I knew her behaviour had something to do with me. I stepped away from her to give her some room. "What's wrong, love? What did I do? Why are you so cold to me?" I asked, confused.

"Did you really think I would never find out, Sebastian?"

"What are you talking about?"

"Don't play dumb with me. You've taken me for a fool for too long, but not anymore."

"I'm confused. I don't know what you're talking about, love." I said, worried in my heart. I knew this couldn't be about what I was afraid it might be, because no one else knows about it except me, so it has to be something else that I don't know about.

"You know, the crazy thing is, I always knew I had met you before, but I just couldn't put it together. Each time I asked you, you found a way to convince me I was wrong, but I wasn't was I? You knew me before the day that I thought we met for the first time. Tell me, I am wrong again? C'mon, spin another lie," she said, looking me in the eye.

I knew this day would come, but I didn't think it would be like this. I had wanted to tell her, hell I should have told her before I left. What do I do now? How do I stop this disaster from crashing down on me? "Where is this all coming from, Hanna?"

"Don't call me by my name! Just answer the question!"

I sat down for a brief moment, and my head began to spin. I didn't know where to start, what to tell her, and what to omit. I didn't want to tell her any more lies, but the truth was too heavy to say. I looked up at her. "You're right. That was not the first time I had met you."

"So it's true then? How long have you known me?"

"I've known you since you were a baby," I answered.

She looked like she was going to pass out. "What? How—how can that be, Sebastian? You knew me since I was a baby? How—I mean what—what do you mean by that?"

"I found you in a bag, and I took you home with me, but I couldn't raise you, as much as I wished I could do the job. You were perfect, but you were also human, and I knew I had to find you a place where you would be safe and loved. So I found Joan and Joseph. They had just lost their child, and

I felt they would be perfect for you. I dropped you at their front door, rang the bell, and watched as they took you into their lives. I kept going back until I was certain they were keeping you. To ensure you had a good start in life, I gave them money annually. I didn't want you or them to lack for anything." She was quiet. "Say something, please."

"I'm in shock. I really don't want to believe what I'm hearing right now. You said you found me in a bag? Was I abandoned? I was abandoned?" I took a deep breath. I knew after I answered this question, everything would change.

"Hanna, why don't we do this later. This is clearly upsetting you, darling. Can we do this later?"

"Do not *darling* me, Sebastian. You will give me answers to my questions or I will force them out of you. Now tell me the truth. Was I abandoned?"

"No—you—you weren't abandoned, you—you were with—er—your birth mother. She hid you in the bag. I don't know why. And she was taking you somewhere."

"Go on, what happened?"

"Please, Hanna, you have to understand, I was in a dark place, I was angry about my mother's death, and I was still vengeful and implacable. At the time, I wanted every human I came in contact with to pay for taking my mother away from me. I wasn't myself. I wasn't who my mother had raised me to be. I killed your mother. I killed her, Hanna, but I didn't know she had a baby with her. Not until after she was dead. Then I heard you cry. I opened the bag, and there you were. You were incredible. You were perfect and you took my breath away. I knew then what my purpose in life was. My job was to protect you, to love you. And I have done so since then. I am so sorry, Hanna. I wish I hadn't done it. Believe me, my love. It hurts me every day that I took her from you, that I killed her and robbed you of the chance to be raised by your mother. I hate myself for taking her life, but I hate myself the most because I had to lie to you every day, knowing what I had done. But I love you, and you know that without you, my life is meaningless, so I couldn't tell you, because I knew I would lose you."

Her eyes clouded with tears, her breathing increased, and her heart began to beat fast. "Nothing is real in my life, because you took my mother from me. Then you set up this fake life where everyone I thought I loved was only after what they could get. Huritt, my parents, the money. You took away my life and replaced it. And you lied to me every day that I saw you, pretending we had just met. You watched as I threw myself on you, proclaiming my love for you. You controlled everything from the start. You made me trust you, and you wanted me to believe that you were the only one who would never fail me. I introduced you to my parents, even shared the knowledge that they may not be my parents, and you knew all along, but kept quiet. You fooled me into loving you. I feel sick."

"I am sorry, Hanna."

"Tell me one thing, though. Did my parents know where the money was coming from?"

"No, they didn't. They could never trace it to me. I couldn't give you what I took from you, so I had to ensure you didn't lack for anything. Joan and Joseph loved you like their own."

"Do you know how it feels to have lived a lie? A life where all the friends you think you have, turn out to be traitors? A life where my boyfriend happens to have known me all my life and my parents were there because I was bringing in the money? I was just a cash cow to them."

"That's not true, Hanna! They loved you, and you know they did!"

"Why didn't you kill me? I was a baby. Why did you not kill me after you killed my mother?"

"I couldn't," I said, looking away from her. "I couldn't kill you. If I had sensed your presence, I wouldn't have killed her."

"Why couldn't you do it? I was just a baby. Surely, I couldn't fight you."

"I loved you from the moment I set eyes upon you, and I still do."

"You are sick. I feel sick to my bones. You make me sick, and you disgust me. How can you talk about love? I was a baby. I guess your plan worked then? You planned to groom me until I was ripe enough for the plucking?"

"No! It wasn't like that, believe me. I loved you, but not in the same way I love you now. You must understand that if I could take it all back, I would. I'm not sorry I met you or that I've known you all of your life. You helped make me better. It's because of you that I am who I am today. I stopped killing. Having you in my life gave me the will to change. You empowered me, and I was able to fight my demons. You did this, and I wanted to be better all because of you. I loved you. I still do love you, Hanna. There is no word that I can use to describe what you mean to me, how much joy you've brought me. You're the most important person in my life. You're the reason I'm alive. Please, Hanna, forgive me. I know I can't atone, but surely you see the reason I kept you in the dark. I meant you no harm, my love."

"You're wrong. You've harmed me in all sorts of ways, and you've fooled me into loving you. Each day you pretended like you were just getting to know me, when you've known me all my life. You made me think you were the one person on earth whom I could trust, when indeed you are the enemy."

"Stop, Hanna! Don't say these things. How could I ever be the enemy when I would freely give my life for you? I know that I lied to you, but I never counted on falling in love with you. I fought it so many times. I tried to stay away from you, but the more I fought it, the more I felt pulled towards you. You know that I would never deliberately harm you. Believe me, I wish I could do it over again. I wish now that I had summoned the courage to tell you the truth earlier. I had planned on telling you. Remember I told you I had something important to tell you, and you said you would forgive me for anything?"

"Yes, I was foolish to promise you that. I thought I was in love with you, but I can't be. It's been one big lie all along. I have loved this illusion of you, but I see you now for what you are. Nothing that I felt for you was real. It can't be, because you don't exist to me anymore."

"Don't—please don't say that—you know I love you! I *am* real, and you are real. Let's start all over again. Let's wipe the slate clean and start again," I begged.

"You—you disgust me! I hate you! I hate that I met you! I hate that I ever cared for you or even thought about you. I hate every moment that I spent with you. You are a revolting, deceitful liar. I don't ever want to see you again!"

"You don't mean that, Hanna. You're angry I know, but don't say such terrible things. Let me give you some time, some space to think things through. Please, Hanna, do that for me. We've shared a lot. We've been through a lot together. You can't just throw it all away. You can't tell me I don't mean anything to you now. Please, my love, do not do this. You are my life. I need you in my life."

"But I don't need you. I don't want you in my life."

"What happened? What changed while I was away?"

"Hector told me that it was you who can't be trusted. But as usual, I defended you, because that's what you do when you think you love someone. But then it came to me. I went to bed and had trouble sleeping. I kept seeing your face in my past—like a vision. I was five again and there you were in my room. I travelled back in time and witnessed it myself. Hector wasn't lying, was he? Because I saw you there. I always knew that I had seen you before. Don't look surprised! At least Hector didn't pretend to be something he isn't." I got up and walked towards her. "Don't move any closer, Sebastian."

"Please tell me what to do to make things better and I will do it. I don't want to lose you. Whatever it takes, I will do. Please, Hanna."

"Anything?" she asked. I nodded pleadingly. "Stay away from me," she said through gritted teeth.

"Hanna, Hanna—Please don't do this. You love me. It's me. You're angry, you're mad at me, and I deserve your anger. I'm not a monster. You know who and what I am. Don't destroy what we have. You still love me, deep down you do. You just can't switch it off just like that."

"Watch me as I walk away from you. Whatever I felt for you repulses me now, and you are wrong. I *can* switch it off just like that. From this day forward, Sebastian Francis, you mean nothing to me. You do not exist in my world. You are nothing to me."

I couldn't believe what had just happened—what is still happening. I let out a laugh in disbelief. "Kill me instead, Hanna. Do it now, I beg you."

She laughed callously. "Death would be too easy for you," she said and began to walk out the door. I ran towards her, and she waved her hand and sent me to the ground. I immediately got up and ran towards her again, and she threw me back into the wall and forced me to stay put in pain. I looked up at her, forcing myself to get up through the pain. Her eyes were clouded with tears, but she fought it, as she wanted me to feel the pain she was feeling. "Don't follow me, Sebastian. I want nothing to do with you. I am going to live my life like I should have without you in it." She walked outside the house. I got up and ran outside to meet her. I looked up, and the sun was at its brightest. She could do it now. She could take away whatever she did to make me a day walker, and I wouldn't run away. "Kill me, Hanna. Please do it. Take the light you put in me and let the sun do the rest. Please, if you are going to leave me, at least give me the chance to end my own life."

"Like I said, death would be too easy for you. Goodbye, Sebastian."

"Where will you go?" She didn't answer. I sank to my knees and watched her walk away until she disappeared from my view and my whole world collapsed around me.

I looked up, and it felt like the sun had fallen out of the sky and everywhere and everything was now covered in darkness. Nothing mattered anymore. I got up and went inside, hollow and empty inside. I sat down and contemplated what to do next, but nothing seemed to matter anymore. I thought about Thomas, Henry, and Nicholas and laughed out loud. They would be expecting me to bring Hector's location to them, but what they didn't know is that I didn't care anymore about anything. She was the reason I was fighting, and now that she was gone, there was no reason to fight, no reason to hate, love, or live anymore.

## The End

Lightning Source UK Ltd.
Milton Keynes UK
UKOW04f0912160215

246348UK00001B/49/P